THEY ALL FALL DOWN

To Ron & Karen
Thank you and
Many Blessings
Sharon House

THEY ALL FALL DOWN

SHARON HOUSE

TATE PUBLISHING & *Enterprises*

Published by Tate Publishing & Enterprises, LLC
127 E. Trade Center Terrace | Mustang, Oklahoma 73064 USA
1.888.361.9473 | www.tatepublishing.com

Tate Publishing is committed to excellence in the publishing industry. The company reflects the philosophy established by the founders, based on Psalms 68:11,
"The Lord gave the word and great was the company of those who published it."

Cover design by Leah LeFlore
Interior design by Jacob Crissup

Published in the United States of America

ISBN: 978-1-60247-538-0
07.08.01

Ecclesiastes, 3:1, 8: [1]*To every thing there is a season, and a time to every purpose under the heaven:* [8]*A time to love, a time to hate; a time of war, a time of peace.* (NRSV)

I thank you, *Lord,* for the gift of friends that help in so many ways. Thank you for Jon, *Lord,* my best friend and confidant throughout these many years. Thank you for Wanda, Tammy, Gerry and Laurie, who lent their expertise. A special thank you, *Lord,* for Dawn, a friend who believes in dreams.

CHAPTER 1

When the ad appeared in the fall of 1938, Jane thought it was a mistake:

Wanted RN w/tropical medicine training
Reply P.O. Box 231, New York, NY

The ad appeared again the next day, and she sent a copy of her resume, credentials, and transcript that same afternoon. *There isn't anything to hold me here now,* Jane thought as the grievous loss once more cast a shroud over her soul. *Not with Jim gone.*

Tears began to spill onto the open newspaper lying on the small kitchen table where they had shared so many dreams together. Jim's face was etched in her memory with his deep-set hazel eyes and thick sandy blonde hair. Her hands ran unconsciously over her arms when she thought about how he had held her to him.

I'll never see that warm smile again or how it made his eyes crinkle. I'll never hear that wonderful laugh that started somewhere deep within him and came out in such a rich, resonate sound, she thought. "Jim, why did you have to die when our life together was just beginning?" she whispered through the lonely tears that fell unheeded.

Jane thought back to the night they celebrated the news that Jim would be under Dr. Burdict for his surgical residency at the University of Michigan. A sad smile briefly touched her lips, as she recalled the plans they made over the celebratory bottle of wine for the bright tomorrows that lay before them.

"You know my time at home with you will be limited, Jane, especially with a surgical residency under Dr. Burdick. He is the best around. But he demands a lot from his residents," Jim had said. "I hope you won't feel like I'm neglecting you."

"Of course I won't feel neglected, silly. I am a floor nurse. I see how hard the residents work all the time. Besides, it's only a year or two of residency, and then you can go into practice. You know, golf every Wednesday," Jane had responded with a smile, before brushing his cheek with a kiss. Jane caught her breath, as she recalled how her heart had fluttered when Jim drew her closer, before gently lifting her chin to kiss her.

"Why not take a class this semester to fill some of the time," Jim suggested, as they celebrated. "I know—tropical medicine. You never know. When some bizarre fever case comes in, it could be tropical."

"Right," Jane laughed. "We have so many malaria cases that require quinine in Michigan. The snow brings it on."

Jim's residency began the first week of July 1937, with long hours and more studying. Jane decided to take Jim's suggestion to enroll in a fall semester class, after the first weeks of long evenings spent alone, to fill her free time. The only opening available a week before classes began was in the RN tropical medicine course. Jane laughed at the registration desk, remembering Jim's joke, and signed up. Jim said, "It will broaden your horizons," when she told him.

Jim was right; the class had filled the endless lonely days and nights, but not the way he intended. A call from the emergency room to the nurse's floor supervisor was common enough. Over half their patients came to them that way when an unexpected accident happened or an illness got out of hand. "I understand, doctor. Yes sir, I will take care of it," Nancy, the charge nurse was saying.

Jane heard Nancy's responses but didn't think much about it, having heard the same one-sided conversation many times before. *Must be a new patient,* she thought. *Looks like Donna's going to get a bed ready—normal procedure.*

Jane turned her attention back to the chart she was updating when Nancy approached. "Jane, I'm so very sorry. That was Dr. Merritt from emergency. Jim has been in an accident. They're taking him to the operating room now. Dr. Burdict is going to personally handle the surgery."

At first it didn't penetrate. *Jim hurt…he can't be…he was fine just a few hours ago. I talked to him. He kissed me goodbye,* Jane thought incoherently.

Nancy was talking again. "Jane, are you all right? Did you hear me?"

"Yes…yes…thank you…I must go up to surgery. I have to…Nancy, will he be okay?" Jane shakily asked, as tears began to cloud her vision.

Nancy briefly spoke with the other ward nurses and the charge nurse at the adjoining ward, before going to sit with Jane in the waiting room outside surgery. It was 1937, and great advances had taken place since Nancy first became a nurse nearly twenty-five years before, but the extent of injury Dr. Merritt had indicated didn't sound good. Even Dr. Burdict couldn't perform miracles.

Dr. Burdict worked quickly, trying to repair the horrendous damage that had been inflicted on what was only a short time ago the healthy body of a promising resident, as he muttered incoherently behind the surgical mask. Jim's heart rate was slowing, and his blood pressure dropping, as the surgical team fought the ticking clock for the chance to save the ebbing life beneath Will Burdict's scalpel. The fight against death's cold finality lasted nearly an hour, before he finally had to admit defeat. "Call it," he wearily instructed the attending second year resident. He turned back a moment at the doorway and sadly shook his head before leaving the operating room to bring the unwelcome news to the young nurse in the surgical waiting room.

Dr. Burdict looked tired and beaten when he brought the news that Jim had not survived the surgery. "The damage to his internal organs was too extensive," he told her. "His body gave out after a hard struggle for life. I'm very sorry. Jim was going to be a good doctor," he consoled before leaving her alone in the empty void that death had brought. They had been married one year, two months, and four days.

It's not supposed to be this way, Jane's mind screamed. "We're supposed to grow old together, have a family, be grandparents. He can't be dead. I was just with him this morning. He kissed me goodbye," she stammered in stunned disbelief, before her mind began to absorb the awful truth that he was gone forever. The first tears of grief became great racking sobs when she thought about the endless empty future of shattered unfulfilled dreams without him.

Jim's parents looked so fragile after their pastor broke the news to them about the death that devastated their world. Jim's father met Jane at the depot when she got off the train that carried Jim's body to his hometown. He told her Jim's mother just couldn't bear to come and see the hearse that would take his coffin away. Jane briefly remembered the joyful reunions that had taken place on this same platform. Then she saw the hearse and Jim's coffin being carefully unloaded from the baggage car.

"Come along, child," Jim's dad quietly said, swallowing the growing lump in his throat and putting a protective arm around her. "Let's get you to the house."

The three days leading up to Jim's funeral were an appalling nightmare.

Jane thought she would soon wake from the horrible dream to find him lying next to her peacefully sleeping. She didn't really hear the words of comfort the pastor tried to give her the day of his funeral. She only saw the closed pall-covered coffin that was the end of their life together.

The last moments at the cemetery seemed surreal. Jane brushed away the long shimmering wind-blown chestnut hair, which Jim had called her angel's mane, that clung to her tear stained face when Pastor Jenkins gave the final reading. He blessed Jim's grave with holy water before friends and relatives said *The Lord's Prayer,* and it was over. Jane laid a single yellow rose on Jim's casket and turned away to walk alone through those assembled to pay their final respects. *I'll always be alone now,* she sadly thought.

Jim's parents told her to stay with them as long as she wanted, but she couldn't bear to stay and told them she thought it would be best to go back to work at the hospital. She couldn't tell them it was too painful to be there with them, where every corner within the small Victorian house brought vivid memories of Jim. She only saw the empty chair at the dinner table and struggled to be strong.

Jane finished the tropical medicine course with high marks and signed up for the advanced one the next term. The apartment was empty without Jim there. Everything was empty without Jim. Leisure time was the enemy now and not the luxury it had been when he was with her.

Jane finished the second course in the spring term of 1938 thinking, *What now?* And then the ad had appeared. *Maybe Jim was right about broadening my horizons.* At least it would be away from the loneliness of Ann Arbor and the haunting memories too painful to bear.

Jane had half forgotten about the ad when a letter postmarked New York City arrived.

> Dear Mrs. Green:
>
> I was pleased to receive your resume and am interested in speaking with you further. Please contact me through the New York address to arrange a time to meet. I plan to be in the United States during the month of July and will be coming to Ann Arbor to see an old friend at the University of Michigan.
>
> Sincerely,
>
> Dr. Martin Jamison, MD.

Jane replied she was available nearly any time other than her work hours. A time was arranged during the third week of July to meet at the university's hospital.

Dr. Jamison was a medium build fairly slender man with slightly graying brown hair and intelligent gray eyes who appeared to be in his early fifties. She believed he might be rather stiff when she discovered he was English, but instead Jane found him to be kind and personable.

"Now then," Dr. Jamison began. "It says Mrs. on your resume, but no comment is made about the status of the marriage."

Swallowing hard Jane replied, "I'm a widow. Jim was killed in an accident. He was a doctor."

"Oh, I'm very sorry." Martin Jamison saw the hurt, haunted look before Jane lowered her eyes. He felt a stab of compassion for the young woman he saw trying to maintain her composure in the midst of her pain. He remembered Will Burdict talking about a surgical resident who died on the table the previous year. Will told him it was a terrible waste, even worse than during the war, saying it was a drunk driver left without a scratch, while a promising young doctor was cut down who left a young widow behind. Dr. Jamison thought to himself it was a terrible waste and tragedy in more ways than one.

"Would you be willing to leave the country for at least two, possibly three years?" he asked.

"There isn't anything to hold me here," Jane answered simply. "Yes, I could do that. I would need to give proper notice at the hospital and make the necessary preparations here."

"I understand. By the way, do you have a current passport?"

Jane shook her head, "No, I just never thought about it. Where is the hospital?"

Dr. Jamison smiled when he answered, "Malaya."

"Where exactly is that, Doctor?" Jane asked a little diffidently.

"Near Singapore. A small village named Helen's Landing about 120 miles north on the Malayan Peninsula."

"Well," Jane sighed, "at least I've heard of Singapore. Does this mean you really want me?"

Martin Jamison rubbed his nose with his forefinger, a habit he had when thinking. "Yes, young lady, I believe I do," he thoughtfully replied. "Yes indeed."

Jane and Dr. Jamison traveled by train to San Francisco where they boarded a ship bound for Melbourne, Australia. Arrangements were made to ship a new x-ray machine to the hospital from Melbourne before they sailed to Singapore in the late fall of 1938. Their arrival at Helen's Landing on the western coast of the Malayan Peninsula came just before Christmas.

It was very different to have the Christmas of 1938 in the tropics with no snow or pine trees to decorate than any previous Christmas celebrated in Michigan. It was difficult for Jane that first time away from the familiar, but at least it was away from all the memories. It was 1940 now and more than two years had passed since Jim's death on that awful fall day in 1937, but the painful loss was never very distant. *You can't run away from yourself,* Jane thought. *You can't just leave and expect to forget.*

She had heard from Jim's parents again this past Christmas and felt sorrow and compassion for them in their grief and loneliness. They had written encouraging her to return to Ann Arbor in their Christmas letter, saying they feared for her safety with Britain declaring war on Germany in September of 1939. Jane reassured them she was completely safe at Helen's Landing. She didn't tell them the thought of returning to Ann Arbor and the painful memories of Jim's loss was more than she could bear.

The most positive thing Jane could say since coming to Malaya was that Dr. Jamison had become a friend, almost like a father, and someone she respected. She found herself telling him about Jim and their courtship and short marriage during the time she had been in Malaya. He listened, not interrupting when Jane hesitated, waiting for her to continue at her own pace. He knew from her work records and transcripts that Jane was a good nurse and had not been disappointed. Martin Jamison had never seemed to find the time to start a family, but Jane was changing that, stirring his paternal instinct, as he grew to know her better and witnessed her quiet sorrow. He felt a father's sentiment to protect her and give her the time she needed to grieve and heal.

Jane briefly thought about the changes to her life since arriving in Malaya. She had formed a small number of friendships at Helen's Landing, and she and her roommate, Sally, would soon be taking a much-needed break to visit Singapore. But the joy wasn't there like it had been when Jim was with her. She wondered if a time would ever come when joy would return.

Jane briefly checked her watch and shook herself out of her musing. It was time to make rounds. She smiled as she approached the first patient's bed, hoping to lift his spirits.

CHAPTER 2

The brochure said the Raffles Hotel was named for Sir Stamford Raffles, founder of Singpura, *The Lion City.* The hotel was considered one of the most famous in the world. It was a place of transit for world leaders and business rendezvous because of its rich history as a geographic crossroads between the East and the West. The world famous *Singapore Gin Sling* was created by one of the barmen in the hotel's *Long Bar* and frequently served in the hotel's *Cad's Alley.* It was at this famous hotel with its rich historic past that Jane found herself with her friend, Sally, in late February 1940.

"Jane," Sally called from the veranda of the hotel's second floor promenade. "Come and look at this wonderful view."

"It is wonderful," Jane agreed, somewhat awed by the vastness of the city and large outlying harbor. "Singapore, the Pearl of the Orient," she quoted from the hotel's brochure.

Jane and Sally had decided to indulge themselves by staying at the famous Raffles Hotel to experience first hand the luxuries only a privileged few took for granted. They lingered on the hotel's long outdoor veranda, while their travel bags were whisked to their room by one of the numerous native Malayan bellhops under the supervision of a British born bellhop captain.

A second bellhop escorted the two young women from the elevator to their room, waiting for his expected gratuity and asking about any last minute request before handing over their room key. The sitting room was exquisite with its silk wall hangings and plush red velvet wing chairs that sat invitingly around a marble topped table. A crystal vase of freshly picked flowers from the vast hotel gardens graced the table center.

"Let's go exploring tonight, Jane. I want to see some of the night life we keep hearing about," Sally enthusiastically suggested. "We can wear our evening dresses and high heels. No starched cuffs and nurses shoes for us tonight," she quipped lightly, while fingering her long formal gown. "I love to wear this beautiful soft yellow and experience the feel of satin. I think the silver shoes set it off just right."

"It looked very nice on you at the Christmas party," Jane agreed. She had brought her emerald green satin gown with the sequined bodice that made her eyes shine and matching tapestry slippers, when Sally insisted they would have a need for formal attire in the city.

The last time Jane had dressed up was to celebrate Jim's graduation from medical school. *Why did you have to die?* her heart cried out. She had consented to an occasional social gathering, but it wasn't like being with Jim. The hollow ache subsided after a moment, and Jane turned to her unpacking.

Jane and Sally were seated at a table near the center of the large hotel dining room that evening which was filled with people from around the world dressed in their native land's formal wear. The oval table was flawlessly set with linen tablecloth and napkins, boasting delicately patterned sterling silverware formally placed beside the elegant hand painted china bearing the hotel's crest. Crystal glassware, awaiting a patron's whim to receive a liquid delight, complimented the table's impeccable appearance.

"I feel like we're on display," Jane whispered, leaning toward Sally after the maître-de left.

"I know. But at least we passed the first test."

Jane wrinkled her brow questioning with her eyes.

"We didn't trip coming in," Sally quipped.

Jane laughed with her friend at the remark, appreciating Sally's wonderful sense of humor. Sally's large blue eyes sparkled when she laughed and heightened the color in the soft milky skin of her small round face framed in shoulder length auburn hair. She was from a small town in England and had studied nursing in London. Sally came to Malaya shortly after Jane, as she had explained, "To see some of this world before I settle down." The two young women were drawn to each other when they first met and soon became friends and roommates. Sally could draw Jane out of herself and make her laugh. She also had a kind heart. When a patient was suffering, Sally tried to help.

The feeling of unease evaporated by the time their meal was served that lived up to the hotel's flawless reputation, and conversation flowed freely. They made plans for the rest of the evening and some sight seeing the next day.

The two friends talked a little about the hospital gossip and the rumor a new doctor was supposed to be joining Dr. Jamison. The conversation turned to the day's headlines about Japan's increasing aggression in China, when they overheard a nearby table discussing the situation.

"The British announced today the Yangtze River Boat Flotilla is being reduced from thirteen to three," the tall thin man with the bushy white eyebrows at the next table told his dinner companion.

"Yes, I heard earlier today about the Flotilla's reduction," the rather round man, boasting a heavy salt and pepper mustache, responded. "The Admiralty certainly didn't hold firm this time."

"What can you expect with Chamberlain as PM?" the thin man asked in disgust. "He's just trying to appease Japan's desires because of the treaties we made with them after The Great War. Still, can't see what business it is of the Japs if we want to put boats in China. After all, Hong Kong is Britain's possession, and we have a right to protect what's ours. Mark my word, Britain will regret caving in to the Japs."

"Well, the Yangtze is a ways off from Hong Kong. But I do agree, our river boats are none of the Japs' business."

Turning her attention back to Jane, Sally whispered, "What I want to know is, where the Yangtze River is? And what does it have to do with England?"

"I've no idea," Jane responded to her friend's question. "I understand too that Japan wants a new Most Favored Nation Treaty with the United States when the current one expires. My father-in-law sends me the Sunday *Times* once a month. His last letter said the papers at home were saying the U.S. wants Japan to stop fighting in China before a new treaty would be considered. I think we should stay out of Japan and China's affairs. I mean, what can we do anyway?"

Sally nodded agreement. "I don't know, but tonight we have fun."

The hotel manager recommended the entertainment in the hotel's Cad's Alley as, "Safe for white ladies who are unattended." Jane still had trouble understanding the strict caste system between the varying ethnic races in Malaya. The layers of socio-economic differences transcended even the segregation of the Negro in the United States. It seemed there were different places to go depending on whether one was Caucasian, Malayan, or Chinese, as well as your perceived station in life. She didn't have any idea where a person went if he was biracial, which was frowned on even more.

Jane and Sally entered the famous Cad's Alley and ordered a *Singapore Gin Sling*. They watched a little enviously of the people dancing to the latest tunes. Jane said it was almost like hearing the big bands in the United States that played at the big name nightclubs. The two friends were somewhat startled a short time later, when an unnoticed man's deep voice spoke next to them.

"I say, would you consider us rude if we asked you to dance? My friend and

I are harmless I assure you." A tall young man was standing beside Sally, his gray eyes dancing with humor, dressed in what appeared to be a uniform. His friend, standing an inch or two shorter and wearing the same dress whites, stood red faced with embarrassment behind him.

"I've never been asked quite like this. I'm usually introduced first," Sally coolly replied, trying to subdue laughter bubbling just beneath the surface.

"Well, that can be remedied," the young man said, with an engaging smile that made his eyes sparkle. "My name is John Hartman, and my friend here is Peter Romans."

Sally giggled slightly before responding to the easy manner that this John Hartman used in response to her attempt at decorum. "A pleasure I'm sure, Mr. Hartman. I accept your invitation to dance."

"Might I be so bold as to ask your name?"

"Sally Vilmont."

"A pleasure, Sally Vilmont. Shall we?" Sally happily took John's arm and went to the dance floor.

Jane noticed that Peter was still standing red faced before her. She took pity on him and invited him to sit down. "I believe your friend has made an impression on my friend. By the way, my name is Jane—Jane Green."

"A pleasure to meet you, Jane Green. You're not British are you? Perhaps from Australia or Canada?"

"No, America."

"An American! What brings you to Singapore?" Peter asked a little startled, before turning red once again. "I'm sorry, I'm being rude. I guess I'm a bit nervous. I don't normally come to places like this, but John talked me into it. A last fling before burying ourselves in the jungle, so to speak."

Jane thought Peter was a little shy, when she noticed his face was still somewhat red with embarrassment after he finished speaking. He wasn't bad looking though with his fair skin and reddish blond hair. A strong jaw line helped to set off the deep shaded blue eyes that looked at the world with wonder, as if not quite believing what they saw.

"Sally and I aren't usually at places like this either. We're usually in nurses' uniforms carrying pills and thermometers at a small hospital on the Malayan coastline."

"That's interesting. I'm going to Malaya in a few days. Tell me, is it as civilized as I keep hearing?"

"I find it very peaceful. The town is small, and the people are friendly. I like it."

Peter knew that there was more when he looked into the dark green eyes that seemed to be holding something back, but thought better of asking. He had never just walked up to a strange girl and engaged in conversation, but John had talked him into coming along to get away from the boat for a few hours. Peter gave in, and now this American was in front of him. She was rather pretty, but looked a little sad. He wondered why. "Would you like to dance?" he asked a little awkwardly. "I'm not very good, but I'll try to stay off your toes."

"All right, I'll take a chance. Thank you very much."

In the days that followed, Jane and Sally explored the city and outlying areas of the island state, touring museums and formal public gardens. One day they window shopped the long boulevards that were bursting with exclusive shops where the selections seemed endless.

"This has been an absolute ball. No bedpans or smell of antiseptic and really good shops to boot. I'm telling you, Jane, they should move the hospital to Singapore," Sally said with a broad smile, tossing back her thick auburn hair.

"They already have one here!"

"Well, two would give people a choice," Sally gaily quipped, when they entered the hotel lobby in the late afternoon. "How about an evening drive by the harbor to see all the ships?"

"You just hope to run into...What was his name? Oh yes, John Hartman. You're hoping to run into him tonight."

"Now what's wrong with that? He is rather good looking with those gray eyes and that tanned face. Besides, he was a perfect gentleman. And we don't want to spend our last evening in Singapore sitting in our hotel room do we?"

"No, I'm just teasing you," Jane relented. "The harbor would be interesting to see."

What Jane didn't say, and did not want to admit to herself, was the idea of seeing Peter Romans felt a little exciting to her, but it seemed just the thought was being unfaithful to Jim's memory. Jane knew Jim wouldn't want her to be alone, but this felt wrong somehow, as if she was a schoolgirl instead of a grown woman and a widow at that. Besides, she loved Jim and missed him terribly.

Awe washed over the two friends that soon turned to humbleness when they reached the large harbor. Endless stars greeted them across the night sky, reflecting like liquid glass off the water's flat surface. The moon rose shortly after their arrival and cast a soft light across the quayside, accenting the potential of unleashed power, as it bathed the powerful looking ships in its pale glow.

"I never believed anything could be so beautiful, yet reveal such a sense of impending menace at the same time," Sally reverently whispered.

"I know. It seems...it seems no one would ever dream of going to war after seeing any of this." Jane thought a moment more and looked at her friend. "I don't understand man's need to have such power...to...I don't know how to say it."

Sally somberly nodded her head in agreement. "I know what you mean. I don't know either. We better start back to the hotel. It's an early day tomorrow."

"Yes," Jane sighed, turning away from the scene.

"After hearing about the war in Eastern Europe and England declaring war on Germany last fall, I can find no humor tonight," Sally quietly said, letting her eyes linger a moment longer.

Jane recognized Sally's changing mood and sensed some of her despair. Sally's family was in England and closer to the threat from Germany. Malaya and Singapore seemed far removed along with the islands, rich in their natural resources, dotting the South China and Java Seas.

While Jane and Sally looked at the harbor from a distance, the Officer of the Deck (OOD) saluted Peter and John when they returned aboard the gunboat that would take them to their final destination. The ship was due to leave port at 0700 to cruise the western Malayan coast with its sisters, stopping at small settlements and towns along the way. *They're really civilians, not officers,* the OOD thought. *The Navy is getting too many of the "Wavy Navy" with their wavy sleeve stripes. At least the wavy stripes let us know they are only temporary. We'll see how these interlopers do when the real fighting starts.*

"Well, Peter, didn't I tell you we would have a fling before being buried in the jungle?" John asked.

"I have to admit it was a fun time. Although, I thought I'd keel over last week when you just walked up to those two girls. I didn't know what to say. At least they won't ever see us again. They probably think we're mashers or something."

John laughed and told his friend not to worry so much. "After all we just danced with them. Women don't mind just dancing with them. The one you were with, what's her name? Jane? What's her story? She seemed a little different."

Peter reflected a moment, seeing Jane's eyes again and the note of something unsaid. "I don't know really, but she is an American."

"Oh, well, I mean an American, that explains the difference," John said off-handedly, putting the matter aside.

"I suppose," Peter hesitatingly agreed, but wondered if there was something more. He could vividly recall the hint of sadness in those emerald green eyes he had found so enticing.

CHAPTER 3

Dr. Jamison finished writing on the chart and turned to Jane. "Make sure she takes the medication and try to keep her comfortable. These postoperative infections are difficult sometimes. Helen, you do what Nurse Green tells you now. All right?"

Helen Burns nodded and tried to smile a little, but it didn't reach her eyes. "You know, he is a great man," Helen told Jane after Dr. Jamison left. "He saved my Andy." Jane smiled and said he was a very good doctor, and then suggested that Helen rest a little before lunch was served.

Jane saw Dr. Jamison emerge from the ward doorway when she left Helen's private room, and went to ask about her patient's state of mind. "Is Mrs. Burns all right? She's said something two or three times now about you saving her Andy."

"Helen Burns was one of my first patients nearly twenty years ago," Dr. Jamison responded, smiling at the distant memory. "Her son, Andy, was sick, and she brought him into the hospital when it was just a small building with two rooms. It turned out he had appendicitis. The operation was a simple procedure, but another boy died the year before because there was no hospital. Helen has supported the hospital and promoted my ego ever since. She and Ralph Burns were two of the first settlers here. The village is named after Helen."

"I see. I thought she might be delirious from the fever. What became of Andy?"

"He left Malaya about fifteen years ago to join the Navy. I believe he's an officer. And Jane, will you take a few of your off hours and spend them with Helen? She's a special friend."

"I'd be glad to. She reminds me of my Aunt Lois who raised me after my parents died. She even looks a little like her, slim and fairly tall, with wavy hair and bright intelligent eyes. My aunt in many ways was ahead of her time. I get the impression Mrs. Burns is like her in that respect."

"That's a fair description of Helen, Jane. She's a unique individual and a driving force in our little part of the world. She and her husband, Ralph, became friends when I first came to Malaya. Since Ralph's death, Helen has worked hard for what she has today."

Helen and Ralph Burns agreed with Martin Jamison about the people of Malaya needing and deserving good medical care and supported his efforts over the years. When Martin Jamison came in answer to the ad placed in a medical journal for a doctor to move to Helen's Landing, Ralph had said Martin *was the goods.*

Helen had spent the summer of 1939 in England promoting the family's coffee export business and raising funds for the hospital. By late August it became apparent that diplomacy had failed between England and Germany, and war was imminent. Helen flew out of Liverpool in early September to Australia to firm up business ties and see old friends before returning to Helen's Landing in early 1940. The gall bladder attack shortly after her arrival home landed her in the hospital.

"Good afternoon, Mrs. Burns. How are you today? Did you take your noon medicine okay?" Jane cheerfully asked her patient a few days after her talk with Martin Jamison. She was checking the chart and noticed marked improvement in Helen Burns' condition over the past twenty-four hours. Jane glanced at the bedside stand and noticed an unopened envelope. "I believe you have a letter here, Mrs. Burns. Would you like me to open it?"

Helen recognized her son's handwriting, when Jane handed over the letter. "Why, Andy is coming to visit," she said a bit surprised. "He says here his ship is going to be in Singapore, and he'll have leave to come home to Malaya," she happily continued. "I must tell Martin about this. He'll be pleased to see him."

"That's really wonderful, Mrs. Burns," Jane said, smiling at her patient's enthusiasm. "How soon will it be?"

"It doesn't say," Helen answered, scanning the pages again. "He just says, 'I'll see you in a few weeks.' I wonder when this was mailed."

Jane picked up the envelope and looked for the postmark. "Last week Tuesday."

"Well, it shouldn't be long. And me still here and not home to get things ready for him. I guess I had best get down to the business of getting better so I will be," Helen stated with returning spirit.

Jane smiled and noticed the spark in her patient's eyes. *Yes,* she thought, *this has been like a tonic for her. I hope she has a long happy visit with her Andy.*

Andrew Jacob Burns was a full lieutenant, and the First Officer, sometimes referred to in the lower ranks as "Jimmy-the-One," aboard His Majesty's Ship, *Mariah.* She was a Tribal Class destroyer with a complement of 145 men at her current wartime status. Built in the early 1930s, she was one of few in that class with a captain's sea cabin on the bridge. She had four 4.7-inch guns, one 3-inch antiaircraft gun, six 20-millimeters, four 21-inch torpedo tubes, and two depth charge throwers. The *Mariah* had reached an average speed on her initial sea trials of 36.7 knots and had a radius of 6,000 miles at a speed of 15 knots. She was a thing of beauty with her sleek lines and a weapon to be respected when brought to bear.

At the moment Andy Burns was Officer of the Watch in the early morning hours just before dawn. He had learned over the years how to flex his tall lanky body to keep his muscles limber. His bright blue-gray eyes, set in the long wind burned face, were trained to notice any discrepancies on the water or aboard the ship and to take instant corrective action. He smiled to himself thinking about the final destination, Singapore, a wonderful and exciting city. He had not been there for several years. As a boy he remembered visiting Singapore with his parents who owned a small coffee plantation on the Malayan Peninsula.

Andy resolutely turned his thoughts back to the ship. After reviewing the chart, he went to the voice pipe. "Course to steer is one seven zero," he ordered.

"Aye sir," the helmsman replied. "Course to steer is one seven zero. My course is now one seven zero, sir."

"Very well, carry on," Andy responded to the routine exchange.

"Cocoa sir?" the young messmate asked.

"Yes thank you, it is welcome at this hour."

Andy leaned over the screen sipping his cocoa to check the deck watchmen. The *Mariah* would be docking in Melbourne, Australia, to take on fuel and supplies. She would then join a small convoy transporting the initial personnel and supplies to increase defenses at Singapore and on the Malayan Peninsula.

The "Old Man" Captain Troy Edmon would be on deck soon sitting in his chair. He filled the captain's chair with his large forty-two-year-old frame. He often stretched his legs out in front of him and crossed his arms across his chest, letting his clean-shaven chin rest upon it while his dark brown eyes scanned the bridge, missing nothing.

Andy and Captain Edmon had been together since the spring before the war broke out and England joined in the melee. He and Troy Edmon had a serious talk when the announcement came that England would go to war.

"Number One," Troy Edmon said to Andy, "from now on it will get harder not easier. If we are called on, and we will be, we need to be ready. You have a responsibility to keep the ship and men prepared to meet any call. If I'm killed or wounded, you need to be ready to take command and bring the ship and her crew home."

Andy often thought back to that first day of war and what Edmon had said to him. It brought home the enormous responsibility to the ship and her crew that rested with him. Troy Edmon was a young midshipman at the end of the last war and saw some of the action. Andy knew Edmon was a reasonable man. He expected a disciplined ship, but he also was fair in his judgment. Andy had learned a lot serving with him. The *Mariah* had not yet been tested in battle, but Edmon assured his first officer the time would come soon enough.

"Captain on the bridge," the bridge rating announced, as Troy Edmon strode confidently onto the bridge and reviewed the chart and log for the previous watch. He crossed to the front of the bridge in a few short steps, with his long stride, and raised his glasses to scan the horizon. The *Mariah* was to join with two other ships at 0800 before sailing into Melbourne's harbor.

"There seems to have been some activity in the English Channel last night. The Admiralty has signaled all ships to watch for mines. A couple of freighters were damaged and one sunk." Edmon said in a clipped voice, while still scanning the sea. He turned to Andy, "Number One, at 0730 I want the duty section to man their battle stations with extra lookouts," he ordered.

"Sir, do you really think the Germans are this far east?"

"Probably not. But there is always the possibility."

"Yes sir. I'll see to it."

Andy had turned to leave the bridge when Edmon added, "And Burns, remember to never assume anything where the enemy is concerned. You don't get second chances like you do in the war games—ever."

Andy thought about what he had just heard. It would be a good drill. But could the enemy come this far so soon? They were more apt to see Japanese vessels as they approached the area leading to Singapore. China and Japan were at war, and Britain wanted the Japanese to end the conflict, but Japan and Britain were allies in the last war and still tied by tenuous treaties. *No,* he thought, *Germany wouldn't be this far east, not with the Japanese Navy here.*

The *Mariah* was quiet with most of her crew on a day's leave after she docked in Melbourne's busy harbor the previous evening, following an uneventful voyage. Edmon had drilled right up to the time the ship entered the harbor. His dark brown eyes took in everything around him as he watched *Mariah*'s crew practice the skills of war and tested his own ability to bring the ship and her crew safely home from battle. Andy was relaxing in the wardroom scanning some of the newspaper headlines from the past few weeks.

> February 7, 1940—Japanese government announces considering abrogation of 1922 Nine-Power Naval Pact.
> The Hague, Netherlands, announces plans to build three battle cruisers and modernize the harbor at Surabaya, Java for defense of Netherlands East Indies (NEI).

Rummaging through a few more papers he spotted:

> February 13, 1940—Japan announces abrogation of Arbitration Treaty with the Netherlands.

"What cha readin' there, Andrew, me boy?" Lieutenant Quentin Patterson, MD asked, sitting down next to him.

"Hi, Doc. Just catching up on my current events. Tell me, Doc, do you think the press is overreacting? I mean these headlines are pretty grim."

"Andy, I learned a long time ago not to put much stock in headlines and politicians. It's a toss up which one will blow things out of proportion and give the public less than an accurate account."

"You're very cynical and probably right," Andy responded with a grin. "I believe the gin pennant is up. May I buy you a drink?"

"Don't mind if I do, me boy, don't mind if I do."

Quentin Patterson joined the Navy when England announced she was going to war and talked the Admiralty into letting him go to sea, even though he was approaching late middle age. The *Mariah* was his first assignment. He barely passed the height requirement, and his glasses were accepted for shipboard duty only because he was a doctor and not expected to stand a watch where near perfect vision was required. His five-foot eight-inch frame carried a little more weight than in his younger days, but Quentin Patterson could command like any ship's captain in the operating room. He was a temporary officer (some said temporary gentleman) for the duration. Captain Edmon was satisfied with him, and Andy found him to be a good officer, even if he was a bit unorthodox. They were becoming good friends. "To ships and sailors and ports of call," Doc declared, raising his glass in salute.

The passage to Singapore was uneventful, except when one ship in the convoy spotted what they thought was a periscope. A few tense moments passed before the sighting was found to be some friendly dolphins. Their fins made a fine spray as they cut through the water, shadowing the ships most of the day. On March 1, 1940, the *Mariah* dropped anchor in Singapore Harbor with the first convoy bringing Australian reinforcement troops and supplies to increase defenses at Singapore and throughout the Malayan Peninsula.

CHAPTER 4

When they disembarked the gunboat at Helen's Landing, a replica to the villages that dotted Britain's coastline greeted John Hartman and Peter Romans in the midst of tropical flowers and Malayan jungle foliage that breathed English tradition. John and Peter were placed on reserve status with the understanding they would study under Dr. Martin Jamison, who had answered an early call when the growing population sought a doctor willing to spend his career with them. He was considered a leader in the field of tropical medicine and often consulted when dealing with any accident or illness that occurred in the tropics of Malaysia. The two young men didn't know what the connection might be between this hospital and the Navy. They just knew the Navy worked in mysterious and unpredictable ways.

"Excuse me, nurse, would you direct me to Dr. Jamison's office please?" John asked. Jane raised her eyes and hesitated a moment before answering, when she thought she recognized the man standing at the nurse's station. She decided after he walked away that she could not possibly know him.

"Why are you looking so funny?" Sally asked, when she returned from the ward. "You look like you've seen a ghost."

"I just thought I recognized someone. But I must be mistaken. How did it go with Mr. Tibbitts today?"

"Don't ask," Sally groaned. "He just grumps at me no matter how cheerful I am. He probably thinks I'm empty headed because I'm a woman." Jane smiled and told her friend it was a hazard of being a nurse.

"Who's that coming from Dr. Jamison's office? Holy cow! I don't believe it," Sally suddenly exclaimed.

"Don't believe what?" Jane asked.

"I'm sure it is...it's John Hartman...the fellow from Singapore. Is he one of the new doctors we've been hearing about? Jane, do I look okay?"

"You look fine. I never would have thought he was a doctor when we were in Singapore. I wonder if he'll remember."

"Oh, Jane, I hope so. He was so much fun. I really liked him."

"Jane, Sally, I would like to introduce Dr. John Hartman. He's on temporary loan from His Majesty's Navy along with Dr. Peter Romans," Dr. Jamison said, when the two men reached the nurses' station.

"I've already met these lovely ladies a few weeks ago in Singapore, Dr. Jamison. I never forget beautiful women," John remarked, smiling at the two friends.

"Really, I had nearly forgotten," Sally placidly replied. "It's nice to see you again, doctor. Will you be here long?"

"The foreseeable future at least. Peter and I have come to work under Dr. Jamison and study tropical medicine," John explained, before turning to shake Dr. Jamison's hand. "Thank you for the tour, sir. Peter wanted to come here first as well, but we decided it would be best to have him secure our quarters for us. We'll be ready for rounds with you this evening as you suggested. We have very little to unpack to settle in. Ladies."

Sally waited until everyone was out of hearing range to speak. "I thought my legs would give out my knees were knocking so badly."

"I didn't notice," Jane said. "You sounded very cool and calm."

"I hope so. I wouldn't want John to think I was too interested too soon." Jane looked at her friend, hoping she wouldn't get in over her head.

The rest of the day Jane's thoughts kept turning to Peter Romans. *So, he's a doctor.* She wondered what Jim would have thought of him. "Jim, why did you have to be killed and leave me alone?" she whispered aloud. "I still miss you. I don't know if I'll ever stop missing you."

That evening Jane went to the small-enclosed garden behind the bungalow she and Sally shared. She liked to sit in solitude to pray and think there when something troubled her. Tonight her thoughts were in turmoil, thinking about Peter and feeling as if she was betraying Jim.

Andy Burns arrived at his boyhood home two days after the *Mariah* made port. He had hitched a ride with a group of engineers going north to build battle reinforcements that had sailed with the first of many convoys slated to come to Malaya, as the British government sought to increase its military presence in the outer reaches of the Empire.

Andy strolled through the village looking in shop windows and remembering boyhood haunts. He remembered as a young boy watching the Malayan workers laboriously grinding the cobblestones used to tame the muddy pathway that led from the harbor into the main street of the town. He noticed many new faces and more businesses and houses had sprung up since he last visited.

He rounded a corner of the northern most road where the hospital stood on its own grounds at the village edge overlooking the sea. He had come to see his long time mentor Dr. Martin Jamison and to learn first hand about his mother's health. She had dismissed her recent surgery and its aftermath as nothing. Andy wanted to be sure Helen was recovering the way she should.

"Good morning, is Dr. Jamison in by any chance?" he asked a passing nurse.

Sally turned to find a man in Naval uniform standing in front of her. "Is the Navy thinking of becoming an infantry force?" she lightly asked.

"What? Oh, my uniform. No, just temporary shore patrol. Why do you ask?"

"You're the third man in two weeks to turn up at this hospital in a Naval uniform asking for Dr. Jamison."

"I see. Is he in?"

"I'll have to check. Whom shall I say is inquiring?" Sally asked with a touch of coolness.

"Burns, Andrew Burns. And, you are?"

"Nurse…Nurse Sally. I'll be back to let you know. Why don't you have a seat across the hall in the waiting room?"

"Thank you, Nurse Sally," Andy answered, grinning at her. "I'll do just that."

Sally went down the hall and peeked into Dr. Jamison's office. "Doctor, there's an Andrew Burns in the corridor waiting room asking for you."

"Andy Burns! Bless my soul!" Dr. Jamison responded with a smile coming to his face. "I haven't seen him in several years. Tell him I'll be out in a few minutes, would you, Sally?"

Sally wondered just who Andy Burns was. Dr. Jamison appeared almost excited at seeing him. "He'll be with you in a few minutes," she said, putting her head in the door. Turning a little, Andy thanked her and returned to his thoughts. He was looking out the window at the broad expanse of lawn and garden leading down to the sea that had been created since his last visit. It looked like a very restful place to recover, perhaps to contemplate after the body had been ravaged by illness, with lawn chairs and tables scattered around a large shaded patio. He hoped it would remain as it was, peaceful and quiet, and untouched by war.

Martin Jamison stood in the doorway for a moment contemplating the man whose back was to him. If Jane Green seemed to stir feelings in him as a daughter, Andy Burns seemed almost a son. He had never revealed sending a few letters when Andy applied to Dartmouth or that he followed Andy's career with interest and knew his rank and its importance. Taking a breath and putting a smile on his face, Dr. Jamison entered the room. "Andy, let me get a look at you, son. You've grown into a man. I want to hear about everything since I last saw you."

Andy shook the offered hand and smiled warmly, as he took in the changes age had brought to the man greeting him so enthusiastically. "Dr. Jamison, it's good to see you, sir. The hospital has grown since I was here last."

"Well, we did add just a couple things while you were away. When did you get here?"

"Yesterday afternoon. Ma said she wanted me to herself for one evening, or I would have come then."

"Helen must be beside herself having you home for a while. How long do you have?"

"I have to be back on the 20th. We sail again on or about the 25th. With the war showing signs of escalating in the North Atlantic, I expect we'll be sent somewhere near there." Andy answered, before turning to more personal concerns. "I really wanted to ask you about Ma. Is she recovered from her recent surgery? She says she is, but Ma never complains. Dad used to say, 'Helen, you'll never die. You won't slow down long enough to drop.' I'm inclined to agree with him."

Dr. Jamison rubbed his nose a moment before he answered. "I believe she is healing from the initial surgery, Andy."

"And?" Andy prompted.

"I believe if she does like I tell her and doesn't try to rush her recovery, she will be all right. She had some postoperative infection and a fever, but I think she is recovering. I know you want a definite answer, but I can't give you one. Medicine isn't an exact science." Dr. Jamison saw the concern on Andy's face and continued. "I can tell you this, Helen has a strong will and that counts for a great deal."

"Thank you for telling me. I'll try to get her to slow down some while I'm here. Now for my official errand, which is to invite you and some of the staff to the house for dinner next Friday evening. Ma's exact words were, 'Don't let Martin put you off.' She wants a real party. I told her it would be too much for her, but she pointed out the houseboys and a couple of daygirls would do it all. I couldn't think of any argument to that."

"It will probably raise her spirits a great deal. I think a few of the staff would enjoy coming. I have a couple of your Navy doctors here. Maybe I'll bring them along to see what a plantation is like. All they talk about is the ships they've been on and some of the women they've seen since joining the

Navy. They need to feel some firm ground under their feet. Tell Helen I would be delighted, but she has to take a nap in the afternoon."

"I'll tell her. She won't like it, but I'll tell her."

"Didn't say she had to like it," Dr. Jamison replied with a grin.

The two men went on a tour of the hospital and grounds, with Dr. Jamison pointing out the changes over the years and reminiscing about the past. As they were returning to the office, Sally was coming out of the ward with a half-empty dinner tray and collided with Andy.

"Bother!" she muttered under her breath.

"I'm sorry," Andy apologized. "Let me help you...Nurse Sally, isn't it?"

"Yes, I'll need to get a mop." The catastrophe was quickly cleared away before Sally departed, saying, "Thank you."

"My pleasure...Nurse Sally," Andy grinned, his eyes dancing with amusement.

Martin Jamison took everything in without a word. He saw the humor in Andy's eyes and thought he saw a little more than humor, interest perhaps.

"I should let you get back to your patients, sir. Thank you for showing me everything. I hope we can get together while I'm here and have a long talk," Andy said, after watching Sally retreat down the hallway.

"I would like that, Andy," Dr. Jamison smiled, shaking Andy's hand. "And tell Helen we'll be there Friday next."

Sally convinced Jane that they should accept Dr. Jamison's invitation to join him at his friend's dinner party. "Just think, Jane, an evening out. It will be fun," she had pointed out. Jane consented then, and the two young women were at their door when Dr. Jamison came to drive them to the Burns' residence. Jane was surprised when she got into the car and saw Peter and John there also. "Dr. Jamison thought we should meet some of the local people," John remarked after the car door was closed. "I must say that a meal away from our own cooking is well worth going to."

Dr. Jamison drove the dinner party guests up the winding road that led to the top of the bluff overlooking the hospital. A palm shaded gravel drive offered glimpses of the pale yellow two story stucco house built similar to an L-shaped long house with an extended roof over the veranda that wound around the structure, offering shade to the interior during the hot humid daylight hours. Tall fan-like travelers' palms growing across the expanse of the lush green lawn gave the house a sense of privacy from the rest of the property. The war was a distant event that seemed to be outside the realm of this peaceful existence.

A houseboy led the party into a comfortable sitting room decorated in soft blue and green pastels with bold cushions in contrasting colors accenting the comfortable sofas and chairs. A baby grand piano sat facing into the room at one corner with dozens of framed pictures scattered across it, which appeared to reflect the family history over the years in Malaya. A gentle breeze barely stirred the lace curtains, adding to the room's feeling of serenity. Jane found the room inviting and started to feel more at ease.

Andy Burns' eyes sparkled with pleasure in the rugged features of his face that reflected the many hours he stood watch on the open bridge when he greeted the guests. "Dr. Jamison, it was good of you to come. Ma will be out in a few minutes. She wanted to make a last minute check with the kitchen. By the way she did take the nap, under protest."

"Thank you, Andy," Dr. Jamison said, chuckling at the comment. "By the way I noticed your dad's boat out this week. Did you get a chance to get some fishing in?"

"Oh, no. I had some repairs made to the hull while I've been here. She's back in the boathouse until I get a chance to take her out. I've arranged for old Mr. Refner to keep her in good order."

"Refner's a good man. Well now, let me introduce everyone. John Hartman and Peter Romans are on loan from your Navy for a while."

"Gentlemen, a pleasure," Andy acknowledged, shaking their hands. "I take it you are both doctors."

"Yes," Peter answered, "John and I came to work under Dr. Jamison. This is a lovely view by the way," indicating the array of colorful flowers lining the bluff that dropped to the sea's deepening shades of blue, as the night overtook the day's bright light.

"Yes...yes...it is. Dad always said when you've finished working on the land all day that you needed a distraction," Andy agreed with a momentary distant look, before turning to Jane and Sally. "And these lovely ladies are...why...it's Nurse Sally. Hello," Andy grinned, while his eyes danced with mischief.

"This is Sally Vilmont and Jane Green. Both nursed your mother when she was with us," Dr. Jamison said.

Genuine warmth came into Andy's voice when he took each of their hands in turn. "Ladies, I am most grateful to you both. Ma said she had wonderful care. It is a pleasure to make your acquaintance."

The men rose from their seats when Helen Burns appeared at the doorway. "Sit down, sit down and be comfortable," she said. "Martin, you look in need of a home cooked meal."

"Helen, you say that every time I come. I expect it's because no one has better fare than you."

"I believe you know Sally Vilmont and Jane Green, Mother," Andy said.

"Why yes, it's nice to see you both outside a hospital."

"Thank you for having us, Mrs. Burns, this is a beautiful home," Jane said.

"You're welcome my dear, but call me Helen."

"All right...Helen."

"It is nice to see you again and looking more fit," Sally said with a quiet smile.

"Ma, this is John Hartman and Peter Romans. They're both doctors on loan from the Navy," Andy introduced next.

John rose, bringing Helen's hand to his lips, "It is a great pleasure to make your acquaintance, Mrs. Burns. And many thanks for rescuing us from our own cooking."

Helen laughed, "I believe you are a bit of a Romeo, Dr. Hartman."

"Please, call me John."

"Very well, John."

Blushing slightly, Peter thanked his hostess for inviting him. Jane noticed the momentary discomfort and Peter's heightened color when he spoke. *He is shy,* she thought. *Maybe that's why he hasn't said much to me. John is more flamboyant and at ease. Sally's been out with him a couple times already. She said they had fun together.*

Dinner was announced, and the party adjourned to the dining room where a beautifully set mahogany table sat on an inlaid teakwood floor. A large china closet with beveled glass doors and a sideboard holding inviting dessert crépes completed the furnishings. An overhead fan slowly circulated the cooler night air drifting in from the double set of screened French doors where the two outer walls met.

The dinner was very good and the conversation stimulating after the initial awkwardness of new acquaintances began to wear away. The discussion eventually took a natural turn to the war in Europe.

"I don't see Hitler going into France with the Maginôt Line at his western border," Peter commented.

"You're probably right. But he could pretty easily go east into Russia," John replied. "I don't see Germany coming this far from Europe. They wouldn't have any allies."

"Yes, but Germany signed that non-aggression pact last year with Russia dividing Poland in the process," Dr. Jamison reminded them. "Of course, that could have been a ploy to keep Stalin at bay."

"That's an interesting theory, Dr. Jamison," Andy said. "I've also read a little about the Japanese grumblings regarding the 1922 Naval Pact. I gather they're unhappy with its restraints."

"You don't seriously consider Japan a threat do you?" John asked.

"No, not really. It's just some observations from recent headlines. No, Japan was our ally in the last war and, if history is correct, a pretty good one. Germany may find her war a lonely one with no one to back her."

"Do you think the United States will come in?" Peter asked.

"The United States wants to keep out of it I'm sure," Jane blurted out before anyone could comment. "President Roosevelt is trying to use diplomacy, yes, but go to war, no. I don't believe we will. The letters I receive from home say people there don't believe the United States should fight another war in Europe."

"That's right, you're from America," John remarked with interest. "So, you don't think they'll be in this one? It seems though that the American people would want to aid in bringing peace. The Treaty of Versailles was primarily influenced by America's President Wilson when it was drafted at the end of The Great War."

"That's true, John. But The League of Nations was a significant part of the treaty that the United States never joined. Their Congress defeated the proposals to be part of that body after Woodrow Wilson was out of office," Peter interjected.

"And that was the beginning of the end, and now we have another war," Andy pointed out.

"Gentlemen," Helen interrupted, "Enough of this war talk. Martin, will the Social be on again the end of May?"

"I believe so, Helen," Dr. Jamison said, and then turned to John and Peter to explain. "Every year we have an event at the hospital to raise funds for equipment and other expenses. Two years ago Helen organized a variety show and a dinner dance that was quite successful. I'm anticipating even greater success this year with the increased staff, motivating larger donations and participation by the community." Dr. Jamison turned back to Helen, "Now that you've settled back down with us, I'm hoping to call on your expertise. What do you say?"

"I think something can be arranged, Martin."

Two more hours passed in lively conversation about the local gossip of the day. The monthly church potlucks were reviewed with a discerned agreement that Mrs. Pridget's chocolate cakes were to die for, and Mrs. Crump's most recent attempt was definitely too much improvisation and not enough of the recipe. The time to depart came all too soon.

"Helen, this has been a wonderful respite," Dr. Jamison said at the evening's conclusion. "But it is time for us to return to our duties. If we stay too much longer, you'll have to sweep us out with a broom."

"You're always anxious to get back to the hospital, Martin. You need to follow your own advice and relax, as you tell your patients to do," Helen responded with animated spirit.

"Thank you, Mrs. Burns, I mean, Helen, for a lovely evening and a delicious meal," Sally offered her hostess, preparing to leave.

"Yes, thank you very much," Jane echoed with genuine sincerity.

"You're welcome. Perhaps we can plan to see each other again."

John and Peter shook Andy's hand and thanked their hostess for the enjoyable evening, stating it had been a delicious meal with interesting conversation.

Helen was pleased with the outcome of the evening, graciously accepting her guests compliments. She had also noticed that Jane and Sally were bright energetic young women who were an asset to their small community. John and Peter were similar to Andy in many ways. Both showed an astute understanding of world events and concern about the present conflict escalating in Europe.

CHAPTER 5

The last Monday in March 1940, at 0700 local time, the *Mariah* began her return journey to England, into the Atlantic's war tainted waters. Andy had spent his time since returning from Helen's Landing seeing to the ship's unending needs. Fresh water and food stores, fuel, ammunition, toilet paper, soap...the list was endless. The first officer's duties intermingled with a series of drills Edmon began before the ship sailed. "It's best to keep our edge," Edmon had commented to his second in command.

A few days before sailing Andy and Quentin Patterson toured the city's nightlife and witnessed first hand the unchanged societal interactions. The strict separation of the Caucasian British landowners was enforced with a callous disregard to any outside their class who cast a shadow near their places of relaxation.

"Andy me boy, I don't believe the folks here believe there is a war on," Dr. Patterson observed.

"Doc, in Singapore life takes a different turn. After all, Europe, and Germany's threat, is half way around the world."

"For now at least. I wonder how Singapore would react if the Germans had a mind to sail into the harbor?" Doc asked, with a glimmer in his eyes.

"Probably ask for their antecedents before letting them into their clubs," Andy responded, showing a lighthearted grin.

Mariah dropped her anchor in Alexandria, Egypt, following an uneventful voyage. She had traveled the Indian Ocean and Persian Gulf before entering the Suez Canal and transferring into the Mediterranean Sea, where she met the beginnings of a convoy on the first leg of its journey to England. The rich oil deposits in Iran and Iraq were producing the much-needed fuel that ran the machinery used to power a modern day war. A tanker transported the fuel through the Persian Gulf and Suez Canal, where freighters containing food and raw materials met them near Alexandria to join the precarious voyage to the home island in the northern reaches of the Atlantic. A hungry society patiently waited at the journey's end to meet the many simple needs of everyday life, buying another month of time to defy the odds against them.

"Number One, we sail at 1800 hours today," Edmon informed Andy, when new orders arrived one day after their arrival at Alexandria. "We've been assigned convoy duty back to England. All liberty is canceled."

"I only gave leave inside the perimeter, sir. I thought it best, since we didn't know how long we might be here."

"Good, I want us to be on our toes. The crew for the most part has never fired a war shot. As soon as we're outside the port, I want you to begin regular drilling on gunnery and fire control," Edmon ordered.

"Boy, *Jimmy-the-One* is fairly aside 'imself," Bert *Mariah's* expert gunner drawled.

"Whad-da-yer mean. 'e's been follerin' what the ole man tells 'im is all," Bert's buddy Ernie retorted.

"Bet we're goin' sub 'untin'," Bert ventured.

"Yer daft," Ernie growled. "Ain't never been no such thing as that."

"Well, we could be first ya knows," Bert countered.

"Ya best keep them idears ta yerself. They cum get ya and put ya in the loony bin," Ernie cautioned.

"Here, you men, get ta yer stations. We're a leavin' soon and yer a dallyin' around like old ladies at market," Tim Parker gruffly ordered, watching to insure the grumbling friends from the ranks, and *Mariah's* two best gunners, obeyed the orders given.

Tim Parker had joined the Navy at the impressionable age of fourteen and was at sea by the age of eighteen. He had slowly worked his way up through the ranks over the years to the current rank of Warrant Officer. Captain Edmon took him aside when the promotion came and told him he was a valued crewmember. "The ranks will look to you for guidance and leadership from now on Warrant Officer Parker," Edmon finished. The icebreaker though was how the First Officer, Lieutenant Burns, had treated him—making Tim part of the wardroom—and the others had followed.

Tim had found his niche by the time Dr. Patterson joined the ship. Quentin Patterson was introduced around the wardroom saying, "Just call me Doc," to everyone there.

At first Tim thought Lieutenant Patterson was just patronizing him, but he soon decided the doctor really wanted to learn about the ship. Tim taught him about bridge etiquette along with a few of the less official traditions and superstitions a sailor harbored. Dusk would often find Tim's large shadow cast over the doctor's small frame, as his heavy rough hands guided the doctor's long delicate fingers in the finer art of tying a suitable sailor's knot. For his part, Quentin Patterson appreciated the skilled knowledge imparted by this self-made man. He learned under Tim's tutelage what a "*proper sailor*" was about.

The *Maria*'s forward lookout sighted the gathering convoy outside Alexandria's busy port at sunset and she soon settled into the zigzag sailing pattern designed to confound an enemy attack at a steady ten knots. The ship rolled with an unsteady motion at the slow speed, making anything not tied down roll as well. Captain Edmon gave orders for all nonessential items to be stashed away or secured. Still, loose crockery slid to the deck smashing to pieces and forgotten tools rolled back and forth waiting for the unlucky to stumble over them. Dr. Patterson set two broken arms and stitched a number of cuts and gashes. One unlucky sailor had a badly broken leg put into traction and was told his sailing days were over for a while. The rest were mostly bruises and a few sheepish looks.

The watch changed every four hours, leaving men drained of energy and fatigued, while nerves were stretched thin waiting for the unknown. New ships joined the convoy as they traveled past the Island of Crete, bringing initial fear of an enemy attack until the recognition signal was received. The closer the convoy came to Gibraltar the greater the risk of encountering German forces.

"Char sir?" Yeoman Smidt asked. "Sir...char sir?"

"What, oh, thank you, yes," Andy absently answered.

"Another day and we pass Gibraltar," Smidt commented.

"Yes. Smidt, take a look over the port side, about ten o'clock. What do you see?"

"Just some moonlight reflecting off the water, sir," Smidt answered, looking puzzled.

Andy gripped the yeoman's arm and pointed, "Do you see that?"

"Sir? Wait a minute. Yeah, I see...what was it, sir?"

"I'm not sure, but it looked for a couple of seconds like a periscope," Andy grimly replied.

The color drained from Smidt's face before he spoke. "Sir, you don't think?"

"I don't know for sure. Keep watching," Andy ordered, turning to the voice pipe.

"Edmon here."

"Sir, we've spotted something about 3,000 yards out," Andy reported.

"What is it?" Edmon asked when he approached the screen.

"Not sure, sir," Andy replied.

"But, you think what?"

"It appeared to be a periscope. But I'm not sure now. I haven't seen anything since the initial sighting," Andy calmly responded.

"All right, keep me informed," Edmon ordered, scanning the sea again with his glasses.

"Yes sir." Andy returned to the front of the bridge and brought his glasses up once more to scan the area. "Did you see anything more, Smidt?"

"No sir."

"Very well, carry on," Andy ordered. A sense of unease gripped him, but no more sightings were reported by any of the other watch keepers.

"Hear we had a little excitement in the wee hours," Dr. Patterson said across the mess table.

"The crew thinks I'm jumpy...seeing things in the night," Andy dryly replied.

"Well, I expect we're all a little jumpy this trip. The Far East had a lot less teeth and was bloody well warmer than the damp chill that creeps into the body and depresses a man's soul here," Dr. Patterson emphasized.

Signals were sent between the escort ships, but no one had seen anything during the night. So far, the voyage was uneventful. The *Mariah* was north of Gibraltar though now, and another sun was setting.

"Captain on the bridge," the bridge rating announced.

Captain Edmon strode across the bridge shortly after midnight with his eyes darting from one place to another checking each detail. "Pilot, how far north of Gibraltar are we?"

"Forty-seven kilometers, sir, on a mean course of 2–2-0 degrees zigzagging at a speed of ten knots," the navigator replied.

"Mm, thank you, Mr. Johnson. Mr. Burns, have extra lookouts posted," Edmon ordered.

"Yes sir. Are you expecting something to happen, sir?"

"Maybe not. But better to be safe." Edmon responded unconcerned, taking his bridge chair.

Andy thought Edmon seemed tense, almost as if he were anticipating something. There had been no more sightings since what appeared to be a false alarm the previous night. A false alarm he had started.

Once again, Andy pressed the glasses to his eyes and slowly swept the sea for any irregularity. At first he thought it was a trick of the faded light, then his body tensed, as he saw the thin broomstick shape being lowered. In an instant, Edmon was beside him. "What is it?"

"I'm pretty sure I just saw a periscope about 1,500 yards ahead off the port bow, sir. It was only a few seconds."

"Signal the lead escort...use a well-shaded lamp," Edmon instantly ordered. "We may still evade it. I thought we might just see something tonight. That sighting you had last night must have been a scout. I've heard German submarines are starting to attack in pairs. We'll swing back and drop a few depth charges and see what develops."

"Bunts, signal the lead escort, 'possible submarine sighting, am going to investigate,'" Andy ordered.

Ensign Liggett, better known as Bunts because of the many signal flags he used known as bunting, looked wide eyed at the first officer. The endless training took over as Liggett's hands flashed the signal, while his heart raced, and his mind tried to grapple with the imminent danger just beneath the sea's moon bathed glassy surface. The reply came at once, "*look about and report.*"

"Bunts, you okay?" Andy asked.

"Oh, yes sir," young Liggett replied a little shakily. "Just a little excited. Never seen no submarine before."

"Neither have I, at least not at sea. Keep alert and be ready for more messages."

"Yes, sir, I will, sir."

Brilliant light suddenly radiated across the night's sky, then quickly dimmed, followed by a deep rumbling explosion that filled the air with its reverberating roll. A salvo of German torpedoes had found their mark, leaving an oil tanker burning out of control. The dying ship had been split in half by the exploding torpedoes that combined with her volatile cargo to cause a spectacular demise. She quickly slipped beneath the waves, extinguishing the intense wall of fire with a sinister hiss. A burning oil slick marked the spot where her crew would now lay in wait for the last day. Another explosion was heard and a third, leaving two more ships in the convoy damaged. One began listing heavily and suddenly slowed, when fires appeared on her decks. Men ran about like ghostly shadows in the reflection, as they fought to save their ship, and with her their lives as well.

"Turn to 0-1-2 degrees, steady, amidships," Edmon ordered. "Set charges for fifty feet. Fire!"

"*General quarters; man your battle stations,*" still echoed throughout the ship, as the first depth charges reached beneath the ocean's surface searching out the invader. Geysers of water towered toward the heavens then rained down a deluge of seawater onto the ship's decks as she re-crossed her path.

Andy appreciated now the constant drills and Edmon's demands for faster times, when he saw the results under fire. He quickly made his way toward his station that was well away from the bridge in case it was hit. The ship would not be left without a commanding officer.

Yelling above the din of explosions, Andy ordered the guns aimed at the lead boat before ordering his gunners to open fire. The loaders had the breech opened to replace the powder sack and armor piercing shell before the first rounds fell about 200 feet ahead of the lead boat. Again the guns fired and just as Andy thought it would be another miss, the lead boat turned to squeeze between two freighters, taking a direct hit below the conning tower. It might have dove, but it appeared to have been badly damaged. The second boat was nowhere in his sight.

Two ships were sunk and one damaged when it was over. Numerous casualties littered the decks of the convoy's ships with even greater numbers left behind awaiting the trumpet call for the sea to give up its dead.

Mariah's orders were to circle the area and destroy the enemy, while searching for survivors. Helping hands waited on her lower deck to pull the shivering victims up the hastily deployed nets to safety. The men stranded in the Atlantic's frigid waters felt an icy numbness penetrating their fragile bodies and knew this was their only chance. Some too weak or injured to help themselves were roughly plucked from the unforgiving sea's watery grip.

Blood soaked gauze littered the infirmary floor, where the broken and burned bodies of those who were rescued awaited the doctor's ministrations. Dr. Patterson thought few sailors would live to tell about the ships lost this night. The thought went through his mind about *man's inhumanity to man.*

Dawn saw a gleaming sea sparkling like diamonds, when the sun began to dance across the smooth glass-like surface. Andy stood the bridge watch while the *Mariah* made eighteen knots to catch up with the convoy. Captain Edmon had dismissed from general quarters about 0400, when it appeared the enemy submarines were not stalking the convoy for now. "They'll be done for now. Have to recharge their batteries," Edmon had remarked. "They might try to catch up yet today. We'll have to see. Right now we're the hunted not the hunter, so we need to be extra cautious."

CHAPTER 6

Andy rolled over on his bunk when sleep eluded him and contemplated what Edmon had said about being the hunted. *I suppose we are in a way,* he thought, *Man turning against man, each able to think, to plan, and ravage one another. It's not like the animal kingdom where it means survival. We become savage and kill to gain a political advantage or in some societies to oppress a population that does not meet the norms of those currently in power. England has certainly experienced her share of political upheaval in past centuries,* Andy reflected. *She still has not found a way to keep man's primal instincts from asserting themselves.*

Following a restless four hours off watch, Andy went in search of Dr. Patterson before reporting to the bridge. "How are the men we rescued doing, Doc?"

"For the most part they're suffering from the oil they swallowed when they were plunged into the water. The injuries are mostly from flying debris, some burn cases and a few broken bones. I do have two more serious cases. I took two bullets out of one man's chest, and he has second degree burns over a large part of the lower body. The other man has a broken pelvis, a questionable lung and second and third degree burns to the upper body and face. If the lung collapses I'll have to reinflate it, and I don't relish doing a tricky procedure at sea, especially if the Germans come along at an inconvenient moment."

Quentin Patterson often thought a doctor was like a soldier caught up in an enemy attack, except the human body was the battlefield. He looked at death as the vilest failure of his profession and fought it with every weapon at his disposal. No admiral or general engaged his tools of war more carefully.

His sword was the scalpel, and his ammunition the medicines that fought infection and disease.

Andy left Dr. Patterson to check the ship's readiness before returning to the bridge to report to Captain Edmon. "I've made the rounds of the ship. All guns are ready when the enemy returns."

"Very well. So, you believe there will be a next time," Edmon acknowledged, firmly nodding agreement. "So do I. We were fortunate to spot them before they had a chance to strike without any warning. Perhaps we upset the battle plan to some degree. Still, we lost men and ships. The men have tasted battle now and begun to understand its bitter harshness, and the challenge that is facing them."

"The crew is in good spirits. Mr. Parker reports things are '*shipshape.*'"

"Parker was a new rating when I was a midshipman aboard my first ship," Edmon reminisced. "We go back a long way. We were in battle together in the last war. He'll know the importance of preparedness. What about sick bay?" He questioned, returning to a new war's need that was never supposed to happen after The Great War ended barely twenty years before.

"Dr. Patterson reported he had two cases that are at risk. Many of the men have some burns and there are some broken bones."

"We have at least six more days before reaching port," Edmon pondered, when Andy finished reporting what Dr. Patterson had told him. "Keep me informed, Number One. I'll see Patterson myself in a bit to get a better idea of what he may be up against."

Andy and Troy Edmon were in Edmon's sea cabin conferring the following day when the general quarter's alarm sounded. The sub-lieutenant on bridge duty reported planes approaching when the two men came out onto the bridge. "Report to your station, Sub," Edmon ordered in clipped tones, as he quickly assessed the situation.

"Yes sir."

"Burns, before you go, check with Parker. Be sure he has enough runners," Edmon ordered.

Andy descended the bridge ladder and approached Tim Parker. "Have you all the runners you need, Parker?"

"Yes sir. I got four on this here side, three on the other one. If I need to, I can borrow from one side-ta-the other," Parker answered, wondering why *Jimmy-the-One* was asking. He then remembered seeing Burns with Captain Edmon. Leave it to Edmon to remember all those years ago when the gunner was out of ammunition and no runner to get more. The other ship kept firing on them until they turned to bring their starboard guns to bear. Four men were killed that day, and Edmon and Parker had never forgotten. Edmon had been in charge of the work party that cleared the torn and bloodied bodies away, a new midshipman, along with Parker, a new rating, one of the men detailed to do the grizzly job.

Andy reached his station just as the German planes started their runs. The gong sounded and *Mariah*'s guns opened fire. The 20-mm guns joined the fight, adding their staccato voice to the deeper bass of the 4.7-inchers when the planes came closer. Tracers flew from the enemy at astounding speed, leading a deadly projectile aimed at the Mariah. A rating firing the aft anti-aircraft gun screamed and clutched his abdomen as blood spread through his fingers, oozing out, and flowing down the front of his body. Andy was motionless for a moment, and then yelled for a medic before helping to ease the man onto the deck. Another gunner took the wounded man's place as soon as he was out of the seat and renewed the continual firing to keep the enemy at bay. "Let's be havin' ya now," the new gunner kept repeating.

Andy went to the forward 4.7-inch guns when the planes departed and noticed Mason Roden, a reservist sub-lieutenant, was putting up a good front to his men. His eyes were the only part of him that showed his inner fear. Andy briefly wondered if his own eyes showed fear, or if he had achieved the same blank mask Edmon wore, the battle mode it was called, that he had just witnessed a few moments ago on the bridge.

"Are things in order, Mr. Roden?" Andy asked.

"Yes sir. The men and I were just discussing that during the next round we would be sure to bring one down, as we don't want to waste His Majesty's ammunition just shooting at the sky," Mason replied with a toothy grin that went no further than his lips. Andy nodded at the attempt to appear unfettered and wagered a glass of ale that his guns would be the first to down an enemy plane. "Payment to be made upon reaching our destination," he concluded.

Mason offered his hand, "You're on, sir," taking on the challenge.

"What ya spose made *Jimmy-the-One* come down 'ere to make that there wager with Mr. Roden?" Ernie asked.

"Probably keepin' 'is mind off the next time I spect," Bert reasoned. "We bein' under Mr. Roden though should do our best ta 'elp win the wager for 'im. We don't want 'im ta look silly."

Andy checked with Parker on his way to the aft anti-aircraft station. "The runners are replacing what we used during the last sortie now, sir. I figure they'll be back, probably more of 'em than before. They were just toyin' with us then. Probably 'bout out a fuel, or they would 'ave stuck around longer," Parker concluded.

"If that was toying, I don't think I'm going to like the real thing," Andy ruefully responded.

The general quarter's alarm sounded again and Andy headed for his station. Three more men were wounded and two killed before the day ended. Looking back, Andy could vividly recall the plane the 20-mm guns hammered that crashed into the sea and the one that came so close he thought he could reach out and touch it.

Between the attacks Andy made rounds of the ship and reported readiness to Edmon. He discovered on one of his trips that he indeed owed Mr. Roden the wagered glass of ale. Roden's men had done well to win the wager for him. Andy hoped Sub-lieutenant Roden realized the significance behind the support of his crew.

Ascending the bridge ladder to report at dusk, Andy's legs felt like they had lead weights on them. He wanted to lie down anywhere and sleep for at least the next twelve hours. "Sir, the ship is battle ready," he wearily reported.

"Very well, we'll wait another fifteen minutes and then stand down. I think they're done for today. It looks like rain clouds coming our way," Edmon noted, looking skyward. "They could be useful to us now that we're in the home stretch."

"I fear this is the beginning of a long siege," Andy heard Edmon quietly say to himself, when he went to sit in his bridge chair after securing from general quarters. Andy wondered what would happen before the war ended, and how the *Mariah* would fair.

CHAPTER 7

"Well, Martin, will I live out the day?" Helen asked with her usual spirit.

"Most likely. You seem to be more or less back to normal."

Jane smiled to herself while closing the office door at the exchange. Helen appeared to be doing well and certainly had plenty of spunk.

"A letter came from Andy yesterday," Helen said. "He's back in England as far as I can tell."

"I had one too, Helen. He wrote about the crew and how England is faring, as much as he could tell me anyway. He also asked me to make sure you take care of yourself." Dr. Jamison didn't tell her Andy had sent the necessary papers along with a letter for his mother in case he was killed in action. From what Andy wrote in his letter, and reading between the lines, Martin Jamison believed the *Mariah*'s voyage to England had seen more than one attack by German forces.

"I need to talk to you about the upcoming fundraiser," Helen said, turning to local concerns.

"What do you have in mind?"

"Well, I thought maybe something like the American Vaudeville show. I hope to get Jane Green and her friend Sally Vilmont to help."

"Perhaps, but go easy with Jane. She's had a rough time," Dr. Jamison cautioned.

"Is it something I can help with, Martin, or would it be prying?"

"No, not prying really. Her husband was killed a few years ago in a senseless accident. I'm sure Jane will tell you about it when she's ready and gets to know you better. She doesn't like to let on to very many, thinks people will feel sorry for her."

"Maybe working on the fundraiser would help to draw her out a little more, get to know people better. I'll ask her and see what she says. I'll start making plans and putting committees together this week."

"Just remember to pace yourself, Helen. I don't want you to wind up back here as a patient," Dr. Jamison warned.

"Martin, I always pace myself," Helen impishly smiled, getting up to leave.

"Uh huh," came Martin Jamison's doubtful response, as Helen gave him a serene smile and walked out the door.

Jane watched Helen leave Dr. Jamison's office, before she turned a little startled to find Peter standing next to her.

"Jane, would you help me for a minute?" he asked.

"What is it?"

"Mr. Smyth has managed to tear some of his stitches. I need a stitching kit and another pair of hands to assist me," Peter explained.

"Right away, Doctor."

"Mr. Smyth, we're just going to numb this a little and patch you up here. Try to be careful from now on and wait for a nurse to help you in the future." Peter smiled as Jane began to spread the instruments out on a sterile cloth, when he noticed his patient's eyes growing larger at the sight of what he must surely believe were instruments of torture.

"Jane, that was good planning," Peter commented in the hallway afterwards.

"What do you mean?" Jane asked, looking a little confused.

"Letting Mr. Smyth see the needles and scissors used to stitch him. I'm sure he'll follow directions in the future. His eyes nearly popped out of his head," Peter answered, with a satisfied grin at the patient's reaction.

"I didn't mean to frighten him. It's just the table was handy."

"Well, it didn't do him any harm. He's been difficult right along and hindering his own recovery. Don't worry about it," Peter told her offhand.

Jane went back to the nurse's station feeling let down. She not only unintentionally caused a patient alarm, but it seemed Peter was only interested in her as a nurse. "Why the downcast look?" Sally asked.

"Oh, nothing really. Mr. Smyth had to have some stitches repaired."

"Well, maybe now he'll listen when a doctor tells him to do something. Did Dr. Jamison bawl him out?"

"No, Peter Romans stitched him. I assisted."

"I see," Sally said, raising her eyebrows, "And?"

"And what? There isn't any and. I need to go check on Mr. Smyth, be sure he's comfortable."

Sally watched her friend enter the ward, and the thought crossed her mind that it would be nice if Jane and Peter became friends. *If only Peter weren't so shy,* she thought.

Peter entered the small nurse's office a few days after the incident with Mr. Smyth while Jane was reviewing patient charts. "Have you got a minute?"

"Sure, what do you need?"

"Oh, nothing really...well...that is...I was just wondering," Peter trailed off, as his face began to flush.

"Wondering?" Jane asked, raising her eyebrows slightly.

"Just that...well...if you might be interested in having dinner with me tonight?" Peter nervously asked in a rush.

"Well, I...yes, that would be very nice. Thank you," Jane answered before she could change her mind.

Peter released the breath he realized he was holding and said he would pick her up at seven o'clock. "Don't you need to know where I live?" Jane asked. Turning red again, Peter said it would be a good idea.

Jane sat in front of the bedroom dressing table that evening contemplating Jim's picture. "You know I'll always love you. But how do I go on alone? Jim...please understand," she whispered to the unchanging image in the glassed frame. Finally, with a nod of determination, Jane turned the picture face down in the dressing table drawer.

"I borrowed a car so we could go into town. There's a little place by the harbor John recommended," Peter said.

"That sounds fine," Jane agreed a little nervously. Jane scolded herself for acting like a schoolgirl on a first date. Unable to think of anything else to say she finally asked him, "What brought you to Malaya?"

"Oh...well, the Navy really."

"Yes, I know you came here because of the Navy, but why tropical medicine?"

Peter thought a moment, trying to find the right words. "I suppose most medical students go into either general practice or surgery. That's all well and good, but a real need exists out here for good medicine. I thought about it before war was declared, but I guess I just went with the crowd."

"What does war being declared have to do with coming here?" Jane asked, wrinkling her brow in curiosity.

"You see...well, maybe you don't. I better start at the beginning. When war was declared, John and I were fresh out of our internships and joined up the next day feeling very patriotic," Peter explained. "We were sure the bombs would be falling on England any day."

"I see," Jane said, leaving the next question unasked.

"It seems there were a great many like us, and the Navy didn't quite know what to do with all of us after our basic training. Since John and I had expressed interest in tropical medicine on our enlistment papers, here we are."

"You said something about there being a need here, which there is. What made you think that?"

"There were several articles in the medical journals just prior to when I graduated. I started reading them and thought I might like to have a go at it. It sounded interesting."

"And is it?"

"Most of the time, and we're lucky to be here under Jamison, though I really don't know what, if anything, Helen's Landing has to do with the Navy. But enough about me. What about you? How did an American girl wind up in Malaya working for an English doctor?" Peter asked, looking at her for a moment.

"I answered an ad in the newspaper."

"What prompted that?"

Taking a deep breath and looking straight ahead, Jane quietly explained. "My husband was killed in an accident. I wanted to get away for a while."

An awkward silence followed Jane's unexpected statement until Peter parked the car. He turned and looked at her a moment, as she stared through the windshield. "Jane, I'm truly sorry," he softly sympathized, gently taking her hand in his. "I had no idea anything like that had happened. Do you want me to take you home?"

Jane turned her head seeing the concern on Peter's face and offered a faint smile. "Thank you, Peter, but I'm all right now. It's just…sometimes it comes back, and I feel it all over again."

"Well then, if you're sure," Peter said, smiling a little, "I guess we should give John's restaurant a try."

"I'm sure. And, Peter…well, you know, thanks," Jane said a little shakily, as she turned to face him. He looked at her a moment and nodded, gently squeezing her hand once more before releasing it and getting out of the car.

"So, how was it?" Sally asked, as soon as Jane closed the door to the bungalow they shared near the hospital.

"It was very nice. We had a really good meal and went for a walk along the harbor afterwards."

"Jane, you exasperate me!"

"What do you mean?" Jane asked, wrinkling her brow.

"You haven't told me anything!"

Jane smiled and said she was going to bed. They had to work tomorrow.

Peter asked Jane out several times after that first evening for picnics or the rare cinema. He was kind and friendly, but made no romantic advances toward her. They at least seemed to be developing a friendship.

"Have you scanned a newspaper lately? I wonder what's really going on in Norway," John said, after reading the latest edition. Peter, John, and Tom Linn, a new Malayan intern just out of medical school in Australia, were sitting in the lounge before starting rounds with Dr. Jamison.

"It appears Germany may have given a second thought to their western border," the young intern remarked. "Hitler may have thought France too formidable, considering her fortifications there. Something like Singapore with her big guns pointing toward the sea."

"We'll have to wait and see," Peter said. "It looks like we're sending troops and supplies to Norway from what I can gather in the news reports. The paper doesn't give a whole lot of information."

"Doctors," Sally said, putting her head in the door, "Dr. Jamison awaits your pleasure." Looking at the time, the three men quickly joined Martin Jamison for rounds.

"Gentleman, I'm glad you could make it," Dr. Jamison said, peering over the top of his glasses. "Well now, Mr. Smyth, I believe you're doing much better. No more trouble since Dr. Romans repaired your stitches I see. I think that maybe by Wednesday we can send you home. Remember, you'll have to follow instructions to avoid a relapse and a return to the hospital."

"I understand, Doctor. I will," Mr. Smyth assured everyone present.

I bet he will, Dr. Jamison thought with a slight smile. *Peter said his eyes nearly popped out of his head when he saw that needle.* "We'll see how you are in a day or two," he told his patient.

Rounds were nearly finished when Jane quickly came down the corridor. "Dr. Jamison, there's been a terrible accident where the army is having that new roadway put in. One of the men was sent ahead to warn us. He said several people are seriously injured."

Harry Joston had been working construction for nearly twenty years in Malaya, and as a foreman the past twelve. He didn't like working with dynamite. But the job couldn't be done without it this time. The charges were in place for the next clearing, and the men were starting to trickle back to the safe area. A sudden explosion came without warning, sending rock projectiles hurtling toward the unprotected workers. Several more explosions followed in rapid succession, leaving a swirling cloud of dust in its wake. Feeling numbed, Harry hollered for help, realizing that something had gone terribly wrong. "Please God," Harry prayed, "Please don't let us lose anyone," before he began to move the rubble away, fearing what rescuers might find.

"Peter, I want you to go down to the emergency room and set up as many cots as you can find. Tom, go with him and help there. John, set up a triage to get the most severe cases into immediate treatment. The worst ones will probably be the last to get here if they have to dig them out first," Dr. Jamison directed like a general in battle. "Sally, call in Lois and Beth early and have the nurses' aides that are here stay. We'll need the volunteer nurses for the emergency room and on the floor. I want you and Jane to go down to the emergency entrance once things are in order up here."

Everyone started leaving to make the necessary preparations, when Dr. Jamison called Jane back. "Did the man give you any idea how many? Who was he?"

"No, he wasn't sure how many," Jane replied. "I think he said his name was Johnston, or something like that. He brought two men in and said there would be a lot more."

"Not Harry Joston?"

"Yes, that's it, Harry Joston. He said, '*Tell Martin it's bad,*' and then left to help with the rescue efforts."

Dr. Jamison nodded and told Jane to go down to emergency and headed toward the operating theater. If Harry said a lot of injured, he wasn't exaggerating. Martin Jamison had known Harry for twenty years and knew him to be level headed. Just then he heard the first of the commandeered trucks arriving.

"B/P is 55 over 39, Doctor."

"Get a blood type and set up for a transfusion. He's lost a lot of blood already. We have to get him stabilized before we can operate," Peter ordered with authority, showing no signs of the shyness he experienced in social situations.

The victims had been coming in for over three hours. Dr. Jamison was already operating, and John was getting ready to scrub in. Tom Linn was stitching the less severely injured and arranging beds for those going directly to the ward from emergency. He would soon be assisting in surgery with Dr. Jamison. The first few to arrive were at the perimeter of the explosion and had suffered cuts and bruises from flying debris with mild concussions. Those coming in now were more serious. This last one might not make it.

Peter looked up to see Jane with blood smeared across her forehead and the front of her uniform, holding a cup out to him. "I thought while you waited on the blood type you could use a cup of tea."

"Thank you," Peter gratefully responded, taking the cup into his hands. He was struck again by her gentleness, when he watched her carefully washing the injured man's hands and face while quietly reassuring him. Peter thought Jane deserved so much more than life had given her so far.

Looking back, John and Peter were amazed they had worked fifteen straight hours before the last man was tucked into a bed. A continual flow of victims coming into this small oasis of medical help were punctuated with scenes of men lying in writhing pain alongside those that were deathly still. The stains of dirt and blood, on men's clothing and flesh, stood out on the white sheets where they laid in vivid accusation of the fate that had made them victims. There were thirty-three in all, but four had died. Of the twenty-nine survivors, twelve had devastating injuries.

Jane and Sally returned to their bungalow after Dr. Jamison insisted they get some rest. "That was quite a night," Sally commented, when they walked through the door.

"Yes, it was," Jane agreed, looking distracted.

"What are you thinking about?"

"Nothing really, just, you'll think I'm maudlin or something. I wondered if that's what war is like, only on a larger scale. I guess the news about Norway the past few days made me think about it."

"That was plenty big enough for me," Sally said.

"I'm sorry; I guess I'm just tired. It was thoughtless of me to bring it up with your brother in the Army and your parents living in England."

"I really don't think about it. Nothing much has happened according to the news reports. The last letter I had from home Dad said he didn't think anything significant would happen either. Besides, Wesley is in France the last I heard. Well, I'm for bed."

Yawning, Jane agreed, "Me too, after a bath to soak away the aches."

CHAPTER 8

The *Mariah* spent one day in a busy Harwich harbor to resupply at the end of her journey from Singapore, before new orders were hastily issued. Her crew joined the hodge-podge of quickly gathered ships at the end of April 1940 to meet the unforeseen need to evacuate English troops and salvaged equipment from Norway across the cold North Sea, before the German Army overran the ports.

Hitler's troops invaded Norway's southern shores without warning, catching Britain and her allies unprepared for the swift German advances. *Mariah*'s crew fought endless Luftwaffe attacks that blurred into overlapping watches, leaving the crew near exhaustion. Andy couldn't remember the last time he had slept more than two or three hours before another airborne strike brought him to his battle station.

"Planes, incoming," the lookout shouted. "Ten o'clock off the starboard bow." The harsh clang of battle stations invaded the late afternoon quiet when German planes descended like swarms of killer bees, stinging with their cannon fire, before dropping bombs that exploded at close range, sending shock waves throughout the ship. The enemy planes seemed to be concentrating on the destroyer to *Mariah*'s distant starboard. Flames suddenly appeared enveloping it in a curtain of oily black smoke.

"Cease fire," Andy ordered. "They're too far off to do any good." The stand down sounded, and Andy went around the ship. "No casualties, sir," he reported upon reaching the bridge.

"Good. Take a look to our port side—the transporter closest to us. He's all over the ocean," Edmon noted, snorting his disgust at the poor seamanship by her commander.

"Looks like the rudder could be damaged. Should we see if they need any assistance?"

"The leader is signaling him now. Can you make out what the reply is, Mr. Liggett?" Edmon asked.

"It's a little shaky, sir. I think he said, '*That was a might scary. Sorry about that.*' But I'm not sure, sir. Wait, the leader is signaling again. Wants him to take position in the rear."

"Probably afraid he'll ram someone the next time," Edmon remarked in further disapproval. "Amateurs," he uttered in disgust. "Keep an eye on them, Number One. We don't want that ship wandering off by herself. "

Lying in his bunk between watches, Andy remembered the destroyer that was on fire and the signal they could remain on station, but their captain was killed in the battle. Edmon had looked down for a moment before speaking after receiving the signal. "I knew Shaffer. He was a good man. He'll be missed." Edmon had returned to his bridge chair then, and for a long while said nothing. *If this was just the beginning, what would it be like before it was over?* Andy wondered.

"Sir, signal from the leader. Possible submarine spotted. Nothing else," the radioman reported early the next morning.

"Post extra lookouts, sound battle stations," Edmon ordered. "Number One, go to the bow and see if you can spot anything."

"Yes sir." When he reached the main deck, Andy quickly walked toward the bow of the ship where Parker was already scanning the wave tops. "Do you see anything?"

"Nothin' sir. Came up here soon as the men were closed up. Tain't seen a bloody thing."

"How's that ship doing in the rear?" Andy asked.

"The one got sent ta the end of the line with 'is tail 'tween 'is legs?"

Andy nodded.

"Well, sir, 'e's still there. Seems ta be keepin' station better. Probably afraid a bein' sent off alone if 'e messes up again."

"You're probably right, Mr. Parker."

A runner came up panting, "Sir, Captain Edmon wants ta know if ya saw somethin'."

"I'll go report to him. Keep an eye out and send someone quick if you see anything," Andy ordered before leaving Parker.

"Aye, sir."

"Nothing sighted so far," Andy reported. "I have Parker on the bows keeping a look out. By the way, the ship from yesterday is keeping station at the rear, sir."

"Parker is dependable," Edmon commented. "The captain of that ship is probably afraid of making another blunder."

"Parker said almost the same thing," Andy observed with a slight smile.

The *Mariah* arrived in Harwich after leaving the most recent convoy in Scotland two days before. They would be here a week, and Captain Edmon had granted four day passes to most of the crew. He had gone home for a few days to see his wife and children, leaving Andy in command to have necessary repairs made and stores replaced. Even Dr. Patterson had left to visit friends who lived near by.

"Morning, sir, I brought you a cup of cocoa to warm yourself," Liggett said.

"Thank you, Mid, it is welcome at this hour," Andy acknowledged. The smell of bacon drifting up from the galley made his mouth water when he anticipated the possibility of a real breakfast.

It was May 7, 1940, and the newspapers were filled with commentary about The House of Commons being in turmoil after the crushing defeat in Norway. Prime Minister Chamberlain, by all reports, had lost all political support in the House with a "no faith" vote. Andy thought this should be the time when those who governed would pull together rather than bicker over what could not be changed. If they did not learn from this, how would they be ready for the next move? And he was sure there would be another move. The question was: where would it be, and when?

"The resupply is nearly completed," Sub-lieutenant Mason Roden reported, entering the wardroom. "The rest is supposed to come tomorrow. Boy, these dockworkers sure are keen on their tea breaks and quitting time. I couldn't budge them into moving the last few crates."

"What about the repairs to the shaft?" Andy asked. During the last attack a bomb had exploded just aft of the screw, causing the shaft to bend slightly and the screw to rotate unevenly. The Admiralty in Scotland ordered the *Mariah* to Harwich to complete the necessary repairs.

"The new shaft is in place, and the screw has been inspected and declared safe. The bomb didn't seem to affect the rudders at all. I'm told the repair crew will have it back together by midmorning tomorrow," Mason reported.

"Good job, Mr. Roden. Take a seat and let me buy you a gin."

"Thank you. I will."

Mason Roden joined the Navy for the duration when England declared war against Hitler's Germany. The *Mariah* was his first assignment. Previously he served two years on a merchant ship as an officer, but Mason preferred being home more often than that life allowed. He left the Merchant Marines to complete his education before selling insurance with the prestigious Lloyd's of London. Then the war broke out.

Mason was gratified when the first officer kept his bargain and treated him to a beer at the officer's club the previous evening. Andy brought up the loyalty of the men that were under Mason and how they in a sense had won the wager, since they were actually firing the guns. Mason appreciated the point the first officer was making and told Andy he was grateful to the men and felt a sense of responsibility for them.

It was raining by the time they returned to the *Mariah,* causing the young midshipman, who was Officer of the Deck, to look rather miserable when he saw them over the side. Mason remarked that he felt a bit sorry for him. But Andy knew it served a purpose beyond the tradition it represented.

Mason found the Navy to have some odd ways about it, but the Army appeared to be worse. The soldiers evacuated out of Norway looked cold, hungry, and like they hadn't bathed since arriving when they boarded the ships taking them back to England. *At least on a ship the crew was fed fairly regularly,* he thought. *And there was something to fight back with when the planes came over.*

"I'll see the repair crew in the morning to be sure they complete the job on time," Andy said, handing Mason a gin and tonic. "The crew will be returning by sixteen hundred hours tomorrow. Be sure we don't have any missing. Parker will help you with it. Leave is then restricted to inside the perimeter."

"Yes, sir. Sir, do you think we'll be doing more fighting? I mean, won't France be too much for the Germans with all their defenses and us there too?" Mason asked.

"I expect we'll be called on again, but not for a while," Andy thoughtfully replied. He considered a moment more before continuing. "The Germans will need to reorganize after the offensive in Norway. They may try attacking France, but I don't think they'll get through so easily there. You're right about the defenses being in place. I believe they are quite formidable. In the mean time all we can do is prepare ourselves."

"What about the rest of our supplies?"

"I have every confidence you are fully capable of handling the situation," Andy smiled.

"Thank you for your vote of confidence. But these dock workers are stubborn."

"Think of it as a challenge. Something like a difficult client in the insurance business," Andy responded.

Dr. Patterson arrived with copies of the latest headlines out of *Fleet Street* the next afternoon. "What a bloody fiasco," he said in disgust, throwing the newspapers on a table. "The House is calling for the government to adjourn. Papers are full of nothing else. Not even any comment about the Army troops or the Royal Air Force, not to mention His Majesty's Navy. We might as well send open invitations asking the Germans to come and conquer us."

"I thought you didn't believe what was in the papers," Andy noted.

"Don't really, but the average good citizen takes it as gospel. It's in print, so it must be true," Dr. Patterson answered, still agitated. "Wouldn't be surprised if *Gerry* isn't keeping an eye on this one," he finished, using the most current popular buzzword that degraded the enemy's ethnicity.

"What do you mean?"

"Well, me boy, history shows a government in chaos is a government that can be defeated. We need to rally and unify."

"Signal from headquarters, sir," the radioman reported on May 10. Edmon read the message and handed it to Andy. "You know what this means don't you?"

"I think so, sir. If we don't hold them, it could be another Norway."

"That about sums it up," Edmon confirmed. "Be sure everyone is alert. I'll make the announcement to the men."

"Now hear this…now hear this," the speakers all over the ship blurted, causing men to stop for a moment and listen. "This is the Captain speaking. The Admiralty reports German forces have broken through north of the Maginôt Line, invading Holland and Belgium in the Ardennes. That is all we know at this time. The *Mariah* will soon be called on to give aid to our Allies. Keep alert, and God be with us." Men bleakly looked at each other for a moment after the speakers went silent, wondering if they could do it all over again. Others felt a cold chill, as they contemplated the future.

"It seems you were right, Doc," Andy said that evening. "Germany took advantage of our internal government crisis and attacked. Though I must say, I never expected they would try now or that they would attack in the Ardennes."

"I do hate it when my predictions come true, especially one like this."

"Sirs, Captain Edmon wants ya ta report ta 'is cabin," one of the new ratings said at the wardroom doorway.

"Thank you, Billings, carry on," Andy responded. "I believe our Rest and Rehabilitation is about to end," he commented to Dr. Patterson, as they rose from their chairs.

"Number One, Dr. Patterson," Edmon acknowledged, returning their salutes. "Please be seated. I've just received orders that we are to sail at zero hundred hours. We're to perform escort duty across the Channel and prepare to transport casualties being evacuated on the return trip. Dr. Patterson, check your medical supplies to be sure we have a sufficient amount. I don't know when we might be able to resupply at this time."

"We should be alright, but I'll do an inventory with my assistant. He can run ashore if we need anything."

"Very well, carry on then," Edmon ordered.

"Where does the ship stand, Number One?" Edmon asked, after Dr. Patterson closed the cabin door behind him.

"Repairs are complete, and we finished fueling at 1500 hours today. The stores have all been loaded and stowed away. We have about a dozen men away from the ship right now, but they should all be aboard by 1700 hours. They're all inside the perimeter," Andy reported. "Mr. Parker will send a runner, or go himself if necessary. I suspect they're together at the canteen."

"They should all be aboard on time. Have Parker check when they're due back and tell him to round up anyone sleeping it off somewhere," Edmon ordered.

"Yes, sir. Is there anything else you need?" Andy asked.

"No, carry on, Number One."

The *Mariah* sailed with little fuss on May 12, arriving at Rotterdam early the next morning. She immediately began boarding the first casualties to fall in this latest conflict.

"Enemy aircraft eleven o'clock off the port bow," a lookout shouted in the early afternoon.

"Battle stations, man your battle stations," sounded throughout the ship; causing men to feel a momentary pang of fear before their training took over.

"Commence firing," Edmon ordered. "Mr. Liggett, signal the tower we will be getting underway immediately."

The *Mariah* was the last in a line of ships moored at the end of the wharf. The crew had grumbled about the long walk to help with boarding the wounded, but it made leaving an easier task. "Mr. Roden, go aft and inform the first officer we will be getting underway," Edmon ordered.

"Aye, sir."

Bombs began falling in the harbor and onto the waterfront warehouses in increasing numbers. The eerie banshee shriek of the German Stutka planes diving out of the sun sent a chill through each sailor's soul, as blood stood still in their veins, awaiting the fatal impact. One unlucky ship was engulfed in leaping flames by a direct hit that began to spread across her decks, when another bomb fell to seal her fate.

Edmon saw the planes concentrating for a few moments on the sinking ship and grasped the small window of opportunity to get under way. "Let go spring," he quickly ordered, allowing the current to swing the ship out into the harbor. "All back one third. Ease your rudder, speed one third, steer 0–7-4."

"Course is 0–7-4, speed one third," the Quartermaster calmly responded.

"Very well, maintain speed and course," Edmon ordered, while keeping one eye on the enemy planes and the other trained on *Mariah*'s course. "Turn 50 degrees to port," he ordered at the harbor's mouth, conning the ship toward the relative safety of the open sea, when German planes once more turned their attention to the escaping destroyer.

The *Mariah* was overflowing with wounded who were lying anyplace large enough to hold a man. Edmon ordered the gangplank pulled when the attack began, or several more would be lying in the nooks and crannies around the ship's infirmary. Many of the casualties were Dutch troops who were unable to speak English.

"Sponge...clamp...quick, a bleeder, get that...there that's better. Shrapnel is all over the place in here. Enough holes in his small intestine to make a sieve." Once more Dr. Patterson ran his fingers along the internal organs, searching for anything he may have missed. "Ah, there you are, me devil, thought you could hide from me. Not this time. That should do it. Let's close him up." Quentin Patterson had been at it for several hours and scarcely noticed when the ship got under way.

When the *Mariah* sailed without warning two Dutch doctors were still aboard assisting Dr. Patterson. "We'll return you to Holland in a day or two," Edmon told them between attacks. "I'm sorry you were caught off guard, but the ship had to come first. It has been most fortunate to have you aboard with the number of wounded we have. Dr. Patterson tells me you both were very helpful to him."

"Yes, thank you captain. Our families, is there a way to notify them?" One asked in broken English.

"I'll look into it," Edmon assured them.

The *Mariah* steadily steamed toward her English home, giving those who sheltered aboard her hope of seeing another sunrise. The crew faithfully served to keep her ready to answer the call when battle stations sounded. They hoped in return she would bring them safely to shore.

CHAPTER 9

Wesley Vilmont watched the armored equipment and men retreating across the last bridge in this sector to span the Meuse River in the Dutch countryside. The slow-moving procession was hindered by constant German air raids, sending soldiers and panicked civilians to what little safety the roadside ditches offered where cherished possessions laid alongside their owners' bullet riddled bodies. God had surely forsaken this land and was meting out His punishment for their sins. No heavenly prophet waited to lift his staff at God's command to part the waters this time. And there was no whirlwind of fire to protect those fleeing the quickly advancing Swastika. This Pharaoh's troops would soon be upon them and destroy anyone in their path.

Wesley's orders were to destroy this bridge at the first sight of German armor. "Place the charges here, here, and here," he ordered, pointing to stress points along the support spans. "I'll start running the connectors. This shouldn't take long."

Wesley heard the sound of airplanes overhead but didn't see the lone fighter swooping down to strafe the crowded bridge. He did, however, feel the sudden slam against his left shoulder that threw him to the ground, and the piercing pain that quickly followed. Everything after that was a haze of brief images. He remembered being taken to an aid station before being loaded onto a truck transporting the wounded to the rear. He woke briefly, when he felt a rather painful shot being injected in what appeared to be a room where everything was tilted. It seemed a moment later like someone was observing him that wore a funny looking hat with a mask over his face, leaving only his eyes and a little of his forehead showing. Now he was in a small room that felt like it was slowly swaying back and forth.

Dr. Patterson briskly opened the cabin door to check his next patient. "I see you're awake. How do you feel?"

"A little groggy right now," Wesley weakly croaked. "Where am I?"

"Aboard the destroyer *Mariah* headed for England," Dr. Patterson cheerfully replied, holding a half-filled glass of water to Wesley's lips. "Here, drink this."

"Thanks, that's a little better," Wesley said, after the few sips of water trickled into his mouth and eased the crackling dryness in his throat. "What happened? We were setting charges, and the next thing I know I'm here."

"Well, I took a bullet out of your left shoulder that just missed shattering the shoulder bone and severing an artery. If that had happened, you probably would have bled to death. As it is, you should be fit as a fiddle in a month or two."

"I heard a plane, but I didn't see anything," Wesley slowly responded. "Guess I was lucky."

"Mm, yes. Well, I just came to check on your condition. You'll be transferred to an Army hospital when we dock. One of the men will be around to help you wash up and shave in a while. That is if *Gerry* takes a break from shooting at us."

Wesley tried to sit up after the doctor left and felt a sudden sharp pain in his left shoulder that made him gasp. He gingerly fingered the bandages before limply falling back onto the narrow bunk. He briefly wondered if the bridge had been destroyed before drifting into an exhausted dreamless sleep.

"A signal just came in, sir," the radio messenger reported, handing Edmon the flimsy message sheet.

"It seems we have a new Prime Minister, Winston Churchill," Edmon informed the bridge. "It was decided a few days ago. It seems the Admiralty is just getting around to notifying the ships at sea, as they've been busy with other more pressing matters."

"I thought Churchill wasn't in the best favor, but it appears I was wrong," Andy commented a little surprised at the news. "I had heard rumor King George wasn't overly fond of him. He did warn the government though that Hitler was a danger. But with the Conservatives out of office he was pretty much ignored."

The *Mariah* docked at 0530 in Harwich on May 14, 1940. As soon as the gangway was in place the wounded were taken to ambulances lined up along the concrete pier. By midmorning the last of the casualties were taken off the ship, along with the Dutch doctors, and transferred to England's overflowing hospitals. Once they were gone the more tedious job of loading underwater mines began.

"There you are, my pets. Just sit in there nice an' easy like," Tim Parker was saying. He and Andy were keeping a careful watch, as the loading process continued.

"We want to be sure they're well secured in the rack, but will roll off without snagging when we're ready," Andy cautioned.

"Don't you worry none, sir. The boys an' me will make sure they're done proper," Parker assured. "I don't fancy gettin' blowed to little pieces."

"Neither do I, Mr. Parker...neither do I," Andy responded with a rueful smile. "Let me know when you're satisfied."

It took another three hours before Parker was satisfied the mines were as safe as they could be. He cautioned the men not to smoke around them, stating a spark in the wrong place would cause *Mariah*'s crew to have a very bad day. "They're about as snug as they can be there, sir," he reported.

"I believe you're right, Mr. Parker," Andy agreed. "Now all we have to do is make a safe delivery."

The *Mariah* was preparing to sail again when word came the Dutch had surrendered only four days after Germany began the offensive in Western Europe. There was little the crew could do but continue the fight.

Mariah's crew anxiously watched the sky for German planes when they entered the English Channel before dusk, but it appeared the Luftwaffe was busy over France and Belgium. With her deadly cargo, it would take only one accurately placed German bomb to blow the *Mariah* and all aboard her to the hereafter. Captain Edmon had timed the departure so they would arrive in darkness to commence the operation, coming within a few miles of the Dutch coast to position the underwater mines to lie in wait of an enemy ship. The *Mariah* was off the coast of France on a heading toward Dunkirk by dawn.

The crew heard at the French pier that German armored divisions had penetrated a sixty-mile gap in the French front, which left little defense between the enemy and Paris. Anticipating the need to defend England's shores, British Fighter Command gave the order on May 20th to withhold their Spitfires from France. It didn't help the *Mariah* though. She was more vulnerable to attack without continuous British fighter cover.

"All the wounded are aboard, sir," Andy reported.

"Very well. We'll sail as soon as Mr. Roden returns with the latest dispatches," Edmon replied. The *Mariah* was once again being used as a hospital ship. Those not needed as lookouts or in other vital parts of the ship were assigned to assist Dr. Patterson.

"Gad-free! That last zig nearly bowled me over," Dr. Patterson groused. He was in the wardroom checking patients when battle stations sounded, and Emil Harris, the young rating assisting him, started to leave. "Here now, where do you think you're headed?" Dr. Patterson gruffly asked.

"Battle stations, sir. I gots-ta report."

"I need you here," Dr. Patterson ordered. "It takes two sets of hands here. They'll manage this time with one less runner."

"Where's Harris?" Parker shouted.

"'Ee's 'elpin' the doc," Bert hollered. "I 'eard the doc say 'e 'ad to stay wit 'im. Needed 'is 'elp wit ta wounded."

When the stand down sounded, Parker went in search of his absent runner. He saw Harris, wearing a blood stained surgical gown bent over an injured sailor from the last attack assisting Dr. Patterson through the dispensary window. "Give me that gauze there, Harris," Parker heard Dr. Patterson instruct his helper. Thinking it best to not disturb them at the moment, Parker backed away from the closed door.

"By gad, that was a doozy," Dr. Patterson remarked with relief. "You did well, son. I think he'll have a chance now."

"Thank you, sir."

"We sail tomorrow at 2100," Captain Edmon said at a quick briefing with Andy and Quentin Patterson the following afternoon. The *Mariah* had arrived the previous evening at Harwich with the latest group of evacuated soldiers. It seemed for now she would be doing double duty, providing protection against enemy attack and serving as a troop transporter as well. "Doctor, your resupply is due to arrive at 0700."

"Fine...fine. I want to speak with you about Emil Harris, sir."

"Harris...Harris. Oh yes, the rating that missed battle stations I hear. That, Lieutenant, is a very serious offense and punishable by court marshal, especially in a time of war," Edmon gravely stated.

"Yes...I know...I know. I needed him with the wounded and ordered him to stay. He is quite adept by the way. I'd like to get him assigned to me in the dispensary."

"I see. Doctor, I'm going to go easy this time because some of the Navy regulations are still new to you and may appear too concrete. The Navy, however, has a reason for each regulation," Edmon said conversationally.

Edmon rose from his chair and leaned across the desk, looking Dr. Patterson straight in the eye. "Don't ever interfere again with a sailor and his duties aboard my ship. Is that clear, Lieutenant?" he ordered, with an intensity that made the veins stand out on his neck and forehead.

Looking back at Edmon, Quentin Patterson knew he meant it. "Yes, sir. It is very clear." Edmon had never given him a direct order since he boarded the ship, other than to become familiar with the standing orders and to do his job. In fact, Edmon had been pretty lenient and allowed him to perform his duties as a doctor the way he saw fit.

"As for Harris, I'll see what can be done," Edmon said, under control once more, after receiving the doctor's assurance. He hoped Patterson understood the seriousness of the matter.

"Thank you, sir."

"I'm afraid the civilians are going to turn the Navy inside out," Edmon confided to his first officer after Dr. Patterson left the room. "We need them right now, but heaven help us to survive it."

"I'm sure Dr. Patterson meant no harm. He is a good doctor."

"Oh yes, I know he's good. Wouldn't have him if he weren't. Heard of a ship the other day that had to give their doctor the bum's rush. Seems he was a drunkard and not much good to them. Patterson is a good doctor. Now he needs to become a good *Navy* doctor," Edmon emphasized, before moving on to other ship's business. "What have you arranged with the men?"

"I gave four hour passes for inside the perimeter. It gives them time to let off steam, but not enough to get into trouble," Andy reported. "We topped off our fuel tanks and took on ammunition and fresh water. The fresh water supply was getting a little dicey with all the wounded we've ferried lately."

It was clear by May 26 that things were not going well for the British and her allies. It seemed nothing could stop the German offensive from rolling deeper into Allied territory. The *Mariah* was once again docked at Dunkirk and about to take part in what would become one of history's greatest feats against considerable odds. Operation Dynamo, the evacuation of 338,226 men from the northern coast of France was beginning.

"We've boarded 215 evacuees and put some wounded in the wardroom and dispensary, sir," Andy reported. "Most of the evacuees appear to be administrative types, clerks, and cooks."

"Very well," Edom acknowledged. "We sail in ten minutes."

The *Mariah* made three spine-chilling trips under constant air attack between Dunkirk and Dover in as many days. Endless lines of evacuating soldiers waited for their turn to board a ship each time the *Mariah* docked and put out her gangplank at Dunkirk's war damaged pier. The Belgium Army capitulated to Germany on May 28, 1940, and the race was on to rescue as many men as possible before the door closed for good to the European allies.

"Keep a watch out for small ships," Andy cautioned. "They're taking men right off the beaches. Hundreds of small boats manned with old men and boys have answered the government's appeal. I even saw one with a white haired woman at the wheel."

The *Mariah* was approaching Dunkirk when the pier once again came under enemy fire. Andy and Edmon watched as one destroyer was bombed and her keel settled on the harbor bottom in a matter of minutes, with her mooring ropes still tied to the pier. Another was damaged and listing to port but still underway. They could see men scrambling with fire hoses and axes to put out the fires before spreading to something more vital. Captains and ships' crews were fighting not only to stay alive, but also to keep their ships afloat to fight another day.

"We need to make this fast, Number One. Start boarding as soon as we dock," Edmon ordered. "When we've taken on our quota, we sail."

"Yes, sir," Andy acknowledged.

It took four hours, with the crew watching the sky at their battle stations, to load as many as the *Mariah* could handle. The gangplank had to be pulled to stop the unending flow of dazed and panicked soldiers that threatened to swamp them.

"Look out past the harbor, what do you see?" Edmon asked.

"A bit of haze and the sea. Wait, maybe a sea mist?" Andy hopefully asked.

"I think so. If it is, we should be able to load without the Luftwaffe interfering."

As the hours and days passed the evacuating troops were more disciplined. "These are fighting men," Edmon commented. The crew even witnessed a group of Scots marching to bagpipes calmly boarding a ship. The soldiers sat wherever they were directed, eating or drinking whatever meager rations were given them with little recognition, too exhausted and defeated to care. Some closed their eyes and began to dream, then woke in a cold sweat from the nightmares that robbed them of the rest they so desperately needed.

Twice the *Mariah* was strafed, causing casualties, but she was luckier then some. Andy saw more ships bombed and sunk and others collide, as they twisted and turned to avoid the constant enemy attacks. The *Mariah* had a near miss with a freighter being used to transport troops, when it turned suddenly trying to avoid enemy bombs. She docked in Dover with her last evacuees and a grateful crew the evening of June 3, 1940 to await the next move by the enemy. "*Would England be next?*" was the question that hung in the air.

CHAPTER 10

Britain might be at war, but life in Malaya went on as usual. Helen had recruited Jane and Sally and plans for the annual hospital benefit were well underway. This was the biggest social event of the year at Helen's Landing, and every detail must be perfect.

The three women sat at a small table on the patio outside the hospital cafeteria's French doors rechecking their lists for anything they might have missed when an aide approached holding an envelope. "Sally, a telegram just arrived for you," she said, holding out the envelope. Sally's face paled and her hands began to shake, as she tore open the sealed envelope.

"What is it?" Jane asked with concern.

"My brother, Wesley, he's been wounded," Sally gasped.

"Oh, Sally, I'm sorry. Does it say how bad it is?"

"No, just that he's in the Army hospital. Mother says here that she and Dad went to see him at the hospital near Harwich. '*Now he's at a nursing home closer to us, so we can go more often,*'" Sally quoted.

"It sounds like he must be improving if they moved him," Jane encouraged.

"I hope so. Wesley is my only brother," Sally explained, still in shock at the unexpected intrusion the war had brought to her life. "I don't know what I'd do if anything happened to him. He's got to be all right...he's just got to!" she emphatically persisted.

"Now don't you worry," Helen soothed. "We'll have Martin send a wire and find out just how he's doing."

"Do you really think he can?" Sally hopefully asked.

"I'm sure of it," Helen reassured. "You just leave it to me."

Three long days and nights passed before an answer came to the inquiry that Dr. Jamison sent to an old Army friend stationed near London. Sally tried to stay occupied to keep her mind off her concerns about Wesley and waited for the mail to come, hoping to hear more from her mother or Wesley himself. It was late afternoon on the fourth day when she saw Dr. Jamison approaching the nurse's station.

"Sally, I've received a reply to my wire. My friend reported Wesley was wounded in the shoulder by a German plane that strafed a bridge. According to all reports, he'll be fully recovered in a month or two."

"Oh, Dr. Jamison, thank you. I'm so relieved to know Wesley will be all right. It was really kind of you to go to all this trouble. Thank you," Sally concluded with a radiant smile.

"You're welcome," Dr. Jamison smiled. "I hope you'll hear from home soon. Let me know how he gets on."

"Jane...Jane, Wesley is going to be all right! Dr. Jamison just told me," Sally excitedly told her friend, when Jane returned to the nurse's station.

"That is good news."

"I'm so relieved. Now I can give my full attention to the benefit," Sally happily concluded.

"Holland is overrun," Peter quoted in disbelief from the news dispatch to those in the doctor's lounge. "According to this, they capitulated to Germany on May 14th. Why, that was nearly a week ago," he finished in astonishment.

"I've been trying to get the BBC on the wireless but haven't had much success," John responded somewhat frustrated by the lack of information being made public. "I can't tune it in very well. But what little I did pick up doesn't sound encouraging."

"I wonder if we'll be reassigned because of this," Peter questioned.

"We were sent here because of the doctor shortage in the Empire's outlying regions. So many doctors signed up in '39, the Navy must have plenty they kept closer to England," John reasoned.

"Gentleman, Dr. Jamison awaits you," Jane reminded them, peeking in the door. "Oh, by the way, don't forget you promised Helen Burns you would help finish her backdrop for the fundraiser this evening." Peter and John both groaned, when they remembered volunteering their services. "You promised her," Jane admonished.

"I know," John sighed in resignation, "I just forgot how hard it is to paint inside the lines. Never did do very well with it in grammar school."

"This will make up for your failings as a youngster," Peter laughed. "Just think of it as a repeat exam."

"Thanks for the vote of confidence there, my friend," John wryly grinned.

It was May 28th, the day of the hospital party and fundraiser. The hospital staff performing the skit had rehearsed for countless hours, and Helen seemed to work with endless energy to ensure every detail was perfect. Jane hoped Helen didn't tire herself so much that she became ill. She heard someone knocking at the door and thought it must be Peter coming to fetch her.

"Hello. I'll be right with you, Peter," Jane said, leading him into the softly lit sitting room before she noticed he was staring at her. "Is something wrong?" she asked.

"What? Oh...no...it's just you look very lovely this evening," Peter answered a little hesitantly.

"Thank you," Jane smiled. "I'll just get my wrap."

Jane and Peter arrived at the hospital grounds where round tables set for eight sat on the large patio facing the sea resembling an outdoor dinner theater. A gentle breeze floated across the water's surface onto the adjacent land, which softly stirred the low delicate orchid floral arrangements gracing the center of each carefully set table. Nothing was overlooked, right down to the individual glass salt dishes set above each china place setting on loan from households throughout the community. A stage was set to one side complete with a backdrop and curtains. Large citronella candles flickered on long poles around the perimeter that gave intimate lighting under the clear starlit sky. It was a fairytale image of luxury usually reserved for kings and princes.

"This is really something," Peter declared, looking around.

"I think it's wonderful," Jane softly agreed. "Sally and John have Tom Linn with them. Should we join them?"

"Hello you two," Sally greeted, when they approached. "Isn't this nice? Who would have believed yesterday the hospital lawn could become so elegant?"

"It is very nice," Jane agreed. "Helen has really done an outstanding job. I think we better get a table before they're gone. It looks like they're about to begin."

Helen stood at the center of the small stage waiting to welcome everyone. "Good evening everybody and welcome to our fifth annual hospital benefit. You all know Martin Jamison, our founder and director," bringing an energetic round of applause when he rose to his feet. "Would you introduce the additions to the staff, Martin?"

"Yes, thank you Helen. It is with pleasure I introduce Doctors John Hartman and Peter Romans, on loan from His Majesty's Navy, and one of our own, Doctor Thomas Linn." Another round of applause was given for the three men who stood momentarily, looking a little embarrassed by the attention.

"I don't want to give a boring speech, but I would like to thank everyone who helped with preparations for tonight's event and to the merchants who donated goods as well," Helen said. "Now, on with the show."

The skit was funny and successful. The staff had created a very good farce of life in a city hospital with blunders and outrageous props, including a needle big enough for an elephant and a rubber mallet to administer anesthesia. Surgery was done on a cafeteria table only between breakfast and lunch, with a long coffee break and gossip session held over the unconscious patient. People laughed again at the humor in it during their meal. The best Malayan cooks in the settlement prepared the dinner that was served by Malayan houseboys, also on loan from the British households throughout the region.

The small community orchestra provided music to dance by to the delight of many later in the evening. Jane danced with several acquaintances, but she liked dancing most of all with Peter. She had not enjoyed an evening this much since Jim's death. Peter walked her back to the nearby bungalow at the evening's end, and Jane asked him in for coffee.

"I'll only be a minute," Jane said from the kitchen doorway. Bringing a tray in, she set it on the small oblong coffee table and handed Peter a cup and matching saucer that bore an intricate fall leaf pattern.

"This is nice," Peter smiled, "I enjoy quiet time after a big event."

"Mm, yes, it does let you unwind a little," Jane agreed.

Peter casually looked around and noticed what was called *a woman's touch* throughout the room while he and Jane sat together in comfortable silence sipping their coffee. He felt a sense of serenity settle over him, as he contemplated the two friends that had created this peaceful place with its soft colors and delicate accessories.

"I better head back. It's getting late," Peter finally said, breaking the quiet.

Jane took his cup and saucer and put it on the tray, before she rose to see him to the door. "I had a wonderful time."

"So did I," Peter softly replied, lingering at the foyer door.

Jane looked up into Peter's eyes and felt herself being drawn to him, as he lowered his lips over hers and kissed her with tenderness. She hesitated at first, but then gave in to the strong emotion beginning to well up within her. Pulling back, he touched her cheek with his hand before kissing her once again. "I better go," he said. "I'll see you tomorrow," and he was on the other side of the door.

Jane stood by the closed door until she could no longer hear Peter's footsteps crunching on the gravel roadway. She felt a sense of happiness she had not known since Jim's death. *Is it possible that love could come a second time?* she wondered. *Jim is the only man I ever loved, and he was so different from Peter,* she thought. Still, Jane knew she had felt something.

CHAPTER 11

Belgium capitulates to Germany was the unexpected morning radio announcement out of Singapore two days after the hospital benefit. The small staff gathered in the doctor's lounge listened in stunned disbelief, as the newscaster continued to relate the startling details of the latest disaster to befall the Allied forces.

"So soon? But what about our Army's defenses?" Peter asked, startled by the unexpected statement.

"Maybe they're planning to hold a line at the French border, and then push the German Army out of Belgium and Holland," John reasoned. "Wait there's more."

"German armored divisions continue their lightening speed offensive out of the Ardennes that has already left two countries overrun. It appears Paris may now be in jeopardy, with the German Army making this unexpected move. Meanwhile, in the East, Japan continues the slow negotiation process with Britain and Holland over the East Asian Sphere in the Indonesian basin."

"This is the BBC, Singapore station, reporting."

Dr. Jamison reached over and switched off the radio when the newscast ended. "When will they learn?" he asked no one in particular.

"What do you mean, sir?" Peter asked.

"Oh, nothing really. I was just reacting to current events. Someday maybe we can all get along and end this senseless bickering."

"Germany seems to only be interested in becoming the conqueror right now," John commented. "I don't know how long we can keep them out of England if America doesn't lend us some type of aid. The way German troops are advancing, it looks like France is in jeopardy of falling as well. Belgium must have fallen the same day as the hospital benefit."

"It's only been eighteen days since Germany started her offensive on the Continent and already two countries are overrun," Peter noted. "I still can't comprehend that since April there has been no stopping them, first Norway and now this. It seems wherever they go the Nazis conquer." Peter shook his head, wondering how far Germany would go before calling a halt to its offensive drive.

Jane watched the four doctors file out of the small staff lounge and enter the first ward. Peter had made no further attempts to kiss her since the night of the benefit. She had lain in her bed afterwards and thought about the way he had looked at her. She was sure it was more than interest. Surely there was emotion, maybe even caring, in his eyes, when he had kissed her with such tenderness. They were to see each other tonight, and Jane wondered if Peter might kiss her again.

"That was a good dinner," Jane said, as she and Peter left the small Malayan eatery they often frequented with what Jane called the American diner atmosphere.

"What would you like to do now?" Peter asked.

"How about a walk by the harbor? It's really very relaxing in the early evening. The fading light reflecting off the water makes me think of sunlight shining through prisms."

The young couple strolled along the waterfront watching the reflections and quietly talking about the benefit and the troubling events taking place in Europe. Jane slipped her arm through Peter's and leaned her head against his shoulder while they walked out onto the pier. A wooden bench sat at the end, where she and Peter stopped to sit and look out at the sea still arm-in-arm to watch in silent awe at the beauty of God's creation. The setting sun suddenly caught a reflection off some distant clouds where the sea met the sky that sent a kaleidoscope of colorful twinkling light skipping across the water's gently rolling surface.

Peter turned after a while and softly stroked Jane's cheek with a gentle touch before drawing her lips to his. "Jane, I find myself thinking about you all the time. I don't want to rush you, but do you think you could care for me someday? I know that you had a terrible loss, but is there room for me to hope?"

"Jim was a wonderful man, and I loved him very much," Jane quietly answered, looking up at Peter and into the eyes of another man that showed compassion, and something more, as she began to open her soul to him. "I'll always have a place in my heart for Jim. He once said, 'Jane, life is full of surprises and doors open all the time. We shouldn't be afraid to go through them, or we might miss out on something wonderful.' I haven't forgotten those words. They helped to bring me here and to meet you, Peter. I find myself thinking about you often as well. At first I thought I was betraying Jim, but I've realized that I have to let him go. He would be the last person to say, 'live in the past.' I don't know if it's love I feel yet. I do know I care for you, and it feels right to be with you."

Peter was silent for a moment, before drawing her close to him. "I shall be content with that, for now. Jane?"

"Yes, Peter?"

"I love you."

Jane looked up into Peter's eyes again and knew he meant it when he said he loved her. She kissed him, putting her arms around his neck and felt him drawing her closer to gently caress her in his arms. Their lips parted, and then came together again, as the rising moon's reflection broke through the distant clouds to stretch out across the water near the place where they sat. With a shock, Jane realized that her body was reawakening to the stirrings she had not felt for more than three years, sending a shiver down her spine. "Are you cold?" Peter asked.

"N…no," she stammered, "I'm fine."

"I better take you home before I'm arrested for indecency," Peter said.

"Yes…all right," Jane shakily agreed, still in turmoil at the disquieting revelation she just experienced.

The days passed by in peaceful existence at Helen's Landing, as tension rose about the swift German advance across France that was closing in on Paris. The residents of Helen's Landing followed news of the narrowing pocket of Allied held territory with a growing sense of alarm that the Germans could so quickly defeat the struggling Allied forces. The final blow came when the news from Singapore radio reported what citizens heard in England for those with small ocean craft to cross the English Channel and lend aid in rescuing Allied and British troops off the coast of France.

"Jane!" Sally excitedly exclaimed. "Did you hear the news? The Navy brought over three hundred thousand men out of France! It's on all the news reports!"

"I'm so glad. I hope it's over now, the fighting I mean."

"My dad said in his last letter that he had joined the Home Guard. I just don't know. If the Germans cross the Channel, well, it could get very bad. Dad said everyone is up in arms about this. Mr. Churchill did remind everyone on the BBC that Dunkirk was a defeat."

"I see. Sally, what do you think will happen now?"

"I don't know."

Jane said nothing more, afraid of the emotions stirring within her. She felt a sense of panic that Peter would be caught up in the terrible war. "Jane, what's the matter?" Sally asked, seeing the shadow that crossed her friend's face.

"Just…Sally, do you think Peter and John will be recalled?"

"I wouldn't worry about that. They're too far away to be sent clear back to England. Jane, are you falling for Peter?"

"I don't know…I…just…I don't know."

Jane's thoughts were in turmoil the rest of the day, wondering what would happen next between her and Peter. She wondered what she would do if he were recalled by the Navy. That evening Peter found her sitting out on the hospital lawn deep in thought. "A penny for them," he said, walking up to her.

"I was just thinking about what Sally said earlier…about England," she softly answered, looking up at him. "Peter, do you think you and John will be recalled? I mean…have to go to England because of what is happening?"

Sitting next to Jane, Peter thought for a moment before answering. "I don't know, Jane. John doesn't seem to think so now. A lot of doctors joined up when we did, and most of them stayed in England. It was the outposts, places like here that needed doctors." He looked at her and smiled. "I do know I would miss you if I had to go."

"Peter, I keep thinking about you…us really. I tried to imagine what it would be like if you were called away." Jane turned toward him then and looked up into the face of a man she realized she had grown to love and feared would be taken from her. "I lost a husband once. I couldn't survive it again." Her voice began to shake and tears started to spill down her cheeks, when Jane whispered, "I've grown to love you, Peter. You can't die and leave me alone again, not again."

Peter gathered Jane into his arms and gently whispered comforting words until she quieted, resting her head against his broad reassuring shoulder. Jane realized her feelings for Peter had grown into love, and she feared his loss if he were recalled to England. They sat for some time together on the expanse of lawn before rising to walk toward her bungalow with their arms around one another, unwilling to break the contact between them.

Throughout the months of June and July, Jane and Peter reveled in their newly found happiness. Japan rumbled about the Dutch East Indies and French Indochina and tried to lure those colonies into the *East Asian Economic Sphere.* At the end of June Britain was forced to close the Burma supply line into China, which brought vital medical supplies and needed guns and ammunition to that besieged, war torn nation. Jane and Peter read about it, even heard talk about the global situation, but world events had little impact in their private pristine world.

Helen invited Martin Jamison and those who helped with the planning of the hospital benefit to a thank you dinner in late August. She wanted to do it sooner, but Martin insisted she take a restful holiday.

"Things don't look good," Dr. Jamison said, looking up from his dinner plate.

"What do you mean, Martin?" Helen asked.

"Since early July, Germany has sent planes over England to bomb factories and shipping. Now they're putting on more pressure."

"Surely the Royal Air Force is defending England. It was reported the planes were held back last May from France because this could happen," Peter said.

"I believe they're having some success," John put in. "But I don't know if it will be enough. Sally, what do you hear from home?"

"Just that everyone is preparing for an invasion. I had a letter from Wesley that his leave was cut short because of the emergency."

"Your brother's an engineer isn't he?" Jane asked. "I don't understand what he would do, unless he had to go with the infantry."

"Engineers know how to blow things up as well as build them," John answered. "I expect he's preparing some surprises if German forces attempt to land on English soil."

"Helen, have you heard from Andy? Is he all right?" Sally asked.

"Oh yes, he writes regularly. He thinks I won't be concerned about him if he does. I believe he was at Dunkirk when it happened. Still, he isn't in the Army at least. A foot soldier has a hard life."

By general consensus, the party gathered in the large sitting room that overlooked the peaceful moonlit sea to await the nine o'clock BBC broadcast. Dr. Jamison warmed up the radio's tubes a few minutes before increasing the volume when the broadcast began.

"This is the BBC reporting from London; *a London that is burning,*" the newscaster ominously began. "During the night watches, the Germans have committed an unpardonable act against humanity, as aerial bombers, with total disregard for what lay in their path, bombed the city in a spate of satanic destruction. Even with the selfless heroism that our brave pilots have shown, His Majesty's Royal Air Force was unable to prevent the terrible deed being committed. Prime Minister Churchill reports he is incensed by this fiendish act being perpetrated by Nazi aggressors against the citizens of this great nation."

The broadcast ended with the statement that Britain would fight back against the Nazi terrorists at every opportunity until freedom was restored.

Turning off the set, Helen turned to the others looking troubled. "Hitler has no conscience. I can hardly believe such an attack could be carried out."

"Helen, I think there's more to it," Dr. Jamison tried to explain, while trying in his own mind to grapple with the unprecedented viciousness the attack implied. "London is also a major port. Maybe the navigators got off course somehow." He knew that sometimes civilians became the victims by accident. But a planned attack against a civilian population by a nation's military was unconscionable.

"I can't believe it," Sally said, looking shocked. "What is the point in bombing a city?"

"I don't know, Sally. I just know the people of England will be fighting mad now. Any overtures of peace that might have existed were sacrificed tonight," Helen sadly answered.

"Jane, you're very quiet," Dr. Jamison commented.

"I just can't comprehend it all. What is the purpose of doing something so terrible? Bombing innocent people like that. I wonder if my country will be as angry as I am."

"They may be inclined to lend aid anyway," John interjected. "I've been following your *New York Times* on aiding Britain in their plight, and there seems to be a great amount of debate about it. This may swing the decision in our favor. At some point the Americans will have to make some kind of commitment."

"President Roosevelt will do what's right, I'm sure," Jane responded a little defensively.

"Enough of this," Helen interceded. "I asked you here to celebrate the success of our benefit. Martin, what is the final word?"

"We made enough to continue another year or better in operating funds, and I have an announcement. The Petersons and the Wards are contributing a new six-bed ward for maternity care. This is something we've needed for some time."

"That's wonderful, Martin!"

The friends talked for some time about the new maternity ward and how much it would mean to everyone at Helen's Landing. The evening passed quickly and it was soon time to leave the quiet serenity of Helen's home.

Jane was quiet on the short drive back to the village, feeling distracted about England's most recent trouble. The others in the car were talking about the attack on London and speculating about whether German forces would cross the Channel. Yet here, where it was peaceful and no shots had been fired, it seemed almost like a bad dream that would go away when she awoke.

CHAPTER 12

The frightening news out of England continued into early September as Germany increased the aerial attacks. The residents at Helen's Landing speculated daily what new disaster the next nine o'clock evening broadcast would bring, and whether an invasion of the home island was imminent. To the friends at the hospital it was more personal. They wondered how Andy Burns and the *Mariah* would fair against this newest threat.

"This is the BBC, Singapore Station, reporting," intoned the excited voice. "Germany has once again surpassed all human imagination of evil. Nazi bombers have mounted continuous attacks against London in an all out effort to destroy the British capitol. Angry red flames swirl into whirlwinds sucking the air out of buildings, as the progressively more powerful inferno feeds on itself and keeps London's helpless firefighters at bay. New fires are joining the already out of control blazes after each new attack, consuming everything in their path with an endless appetite. All the merchant wealth of London, including the Woolwich Arsenal and Bishopsgate Goods Yard, is being consumed by the uncontrollable inferno. This is the BBC, Singapore Station. Good night."

"I can hardly believe it," Helen said. "So much senseless killing and destruction. I wonder how Andy is fairing in all this. I wonder what he is thinking."

"I don't know Helen, but I'm sure he will be writing soon and let us know as much as he can," Martin Jamison replied, shaking his head at the viciousness of the attacks.

England watched the eerie glow emanating across London's sky and held its collective breath, waiting to see whether German troops would cross the English Channel to invade their sovereign soil. The Blitz, Germany's attempt to destroy London and force England's capitulation, had begun. The *Mariah* was docked at Harwich, where the fires in London could be seen reflecting off the horizon like the *Borealis Glow* above the North Atlantic seaway.

"It looks like the sky's on fire," Mason said in a hushed voice.

"The Germans are trying to destroy London," Andy grimly replied to Mason's shocked comment. "They'll have to answer for this one day."

"First Officer, report to Captain Edmon," came over the loud speaker, while Andy and Mason stood at the rail watching the fiery reflection with undisguised horror.

"Number One," Edmon said, closing the door to his cabin, "We've been ordered to sail to the outer harbor of London, where we are to await further communications."

"How soon do we sail, sir?"

"In thirty minutes. I trust all the ship's company is on board."

"Yes, sir, except the postman who should be returning about now."

"Very well, carry on Number One."

Saluting, Andy left Edmon's cabin and headed for the wardroom. "Gentlemen, report to your stations, we sail in less than half an hour," he ordered at the wardroom doorway.

"What...but we just got in," Dr. Patterson indignantly objected.

"It's just one more perk of His Majesty's Navy, Doc. You never know when you'll have an unexpected ocean voyage," Andy replied with a brief grin, before turning to the midshipman standing near the doorway. "Mr. Liggett, notify Mr. Parker, he's down in the engine room, then report to the bridge," he ordered in his no nonsense lieutenant's voice.

"Yes, sir," came the instant response to orders.

The officers left the wardroom knowing something was about to happen, or had already, for the *Mariah* to be ordered back to sea so quickly. *Are the Germans crossing the Channel?* men wondered with foreboding, as they reported to their stations. After clearing the harbor Edmon announced the destination to the crew.

"Cor blimey!" Ernie exclaimed. "The *Hun* must be crossin' the Channel!"

"If'n they do, Tilda an' me 'ill give 'em a taste a what fer," Bert confidently stated, patting his gun.

"'At's right, Bert. We can show 'em Germans 'oo's best at sea. 'Ey won't 'ave no tanks ta 'elp 'em on ta water," Ernie agreed.

"Those people must be terrified," Andy breathed, when he witnessed the horrific site that turned night into day when London came into view. The crew watched the unseemly wall of towering flames in silent contemplation of what was yet to come, while Edmon carefully conned the ship through the approach to London's outer harbor. *Mariah*'s anchor nervously came to rest at 0230 hours to await the next chapter to be entered into her ship's war log.

"That's right, Mr. Thompson, keep the engines on stand by. I want to be able to leave faster than we came if need be," Edmon ordered into the voice pipe. Edmon met the messenger at the ship's ladder, when new orders were swiftly delivered by a fast moving torpedo boat. Following a brief encounter in the map room he returned to the bridge still holding the hand-delivered envelope. "Mr. Roden, you have the bridge. Keep a sharp lookout. Call me if anything happens. Number One, you're with me," he briskly ordered.

The door to Edmon's sea cabin was carefully closed before he turned to speak. "We've been ordered to escort the Royal Yacht through the Channel and into the Atlantic, where the Cruiser *Orion* and three destroyers will meet us to escort her to Canada."

"Sir, is the Royal Family aboard?" Andy asked, a little breathless at the magnitude of their orders.

"I haven't been told. The man sent on the launch said to open the sealed orders in front of him," Edmon responded, indicating the envelope he still held. "When I finished reading it, he simply said, '*Go with God*,' saluted, and left immediately. We will continue with the assumption they are aboard. The Prime Minister wants to keep this as low a profile as possible. The men are only to be told when we are well out to sea. I think you understand the enormity of our responsibility."

"Yes, sir. I understand, sir. Why the *Mariah* though? Surely, there are other ships that are better armed."

"I was only told the job was ours. According to the messenger, we were available and not so conspicuous."

"Do you have any special instructions you want carried out, sir?" Andy asked.

"Until we turn over to the *Orion*, I want double the lookouts and gunners to rotate on stand-down at their stations," Edmon ordered. "I want to fire the first shot if the Germans come hunting, before they can do any harm."

"I understand, sir. I'll see to it. When do we sail?"

Edmon looked at his watch. "In forty minutes."

Andy turned back from the closed door when Edmon spoke again. "If anything happens, if I don't make it through, get them to safety at all cost," pausing a moment, he finished, "even the ship if necessary."

"They won't be lost while in our care," Andy responded with conviction. Edmon nodded slightly as their eyes met, and then ordered his first officer to carry on.

"Mr. Parker, we sail in thirty-five minutes. Have all guns manned and ready, double the lookouts, both sea and air. Make sure the men stay alert." Andy ordered. "I'll have the galley send sandwiches and cocoa around to help them stay awake."

"Yes, sir. Is there anything else you need, sir?" Parker asked.

"Not right now, maybe later. You'll understand in a few hours, carry on."

"Yes, sir."

The *Mariah* sailed down the Thames toward the English Channel to the starboard of the charge entrusted to her, leaving the fires of London in their wake. As they made the course change into the Strait of Dover, the rumble of approaching planes could be heard overhead. The guns were brought to bear, but none were fired. Edmon hoped the darkened ships wouldn't be spotted in the night's darkness and dense cloud cover of black smoke drifting out to sea from London's innumerable fires. The cover broke for a moment, showing the sky infested with bombers, like a swarm of locusts, on a direct course toward Britain's capitol.

"My God," Mason breathed, when he glimpsed the number of enemy planes through the break.

"Mr. Burns, go around the ship. Be sure all the black out dead-bolts are in place," Edmon ordered.

"Aye, sir."

Andy ordered that all porthole dead bolts be made secure before checking the lookout stations and gunners' readiness, reminding the officers in charge to keep alert. His last stop was the starboard 20-mm. "Could you see anything, Mr. Parker?"

"Not really, sir. I just pity them poor souls in London right now. They must be thinkin' the gates ah hell have opened."

"Hopefully, they've taken to the shelters. At least it would safeguard them against some of the horror."

Andy wondered momentarily if there really was any safe haven for anyone right now. He thought about the innocents who were dying, as the two nations unleashed the cruel weapons that warriors inflicted on one another. The *Mariah* was built to be a weapon as well, and she could defend those innocent lives and perhaps bring redemption one day. Their current mission, however, was a beginning toward preserving instead of destroying. He knew the men around him would be proud to be taking part when they learned about their orders.

"Are the men doing all right?" Andy asked when the thought about what was being asked of the crew crossed his mind.

"A little grumblin' 'bout standin' by at their stations, but they're buckin' up," Parker firmly answered.

"They'll understand shortly," Andy assured Tim, before returning to the bridge to report all blackout procedures were properly carried out. "I checked with Tim Parker also. He says the men are standing at ready."

"Good. We should be off Hastings soon. I'll inform the crew of our mission then," Edmon responded. His words were clipped and his body language showed his increased sense of alertness, as the *Mariah* worked her way toward the Atlantic in the darkened night.

"They'll be very honored, sir," Andy commented.

"Perhaps. I'm more concerned right now about when the sun comes up. With the constant heavy bombing of London, no fighters are available to give us an air umbrella if we need it. It's less noticeable without one, but a few fighters can chase off a German pilot determined to paint a ship's flag on his plane."

"Let's hope we have cloud cover."

"Precisely," Edmon agreed. "Pilot, are we off Hastings yet?"

"Yes sir, just passing it now, sir," the navigator answered.

"Very well."

Edmon switched the bridge microphone to speaker and thumbed the activation button. "This is the captain speaking," came over the ship's speakers, momentarily catching the crew's full attention. "The ship to our port is the Royal Yacht. We will escort her into the Atlantic, where she will meet the Cruiser *Orion* and three other destroyers. Until she is under the *Orion*'s protection, we will need to give our all to provide her a safe journey. Stay alert. That is all." Edmon replaced the microphone in its rack and went to his chair on the bridge, where he would stay until the mission was completed.

Tim Parker whistled softly at the end of the short announcement. He never dreamed the Royal Yacht's safety would fall to a single destroyer, let alone the one where he served. He cast his eye to the *Mariah*'s charge and silently paid her tribute, vowing to fight with his last breath to defend her. "You heard, men. I want extra vigilance," he ordered. "The *Hun* won't be havin' 'er."

Mason stared at Captain Edmon's back, as he returned to his stationary command chair on the bridge. *No wonder he didn't leave the bridge after clearing Margate,* he thought. *That's why the captain and first officer seemed so tense. The Royal Yacht, phew. The pressure must be unbearable. We'll get her through,* Mason resolved, setting his jaw. "We must," he said aloud.

The *Mariah* and her charge were passing the Isle of Wright by morning when the sun began to rise, announcing the dawn of a glorious day. "Rain and fog never seem to come when you want them," Edmon commented to Andy.

"Planes, eleven o'clock," a lookout suddenly yelled. Andy looked up and saw six planes in the distance forming up to attack. Men that had been relieved to catch a few hours rest scrambled to their stations with adrenaline pumping through their veins, as every muscle tensed, in response to the urgent sound of the general quarter's alarm. The officers held their breath awaiting the command to fire, knowing the privilege of the heavy responsibility they bore.

The diving German planes targeted the destroyer in their sights, dropping bombs and strafing it, before climbing back up to the sky after their shrill descent. Andy remembered the howling screech of German planes at Dunkirk designed to inflict fear in the defenders at Germany's mighty weapon descending from above. He steadied his breathing, waiting for the time to open fire and destroy these mechanical birds with their infernal screech.

Mariah's guns responded with a vicious barrage of lead streaming toward the attacking planes in unison when Edmon gave the order to commence firing, keeping a constant protective eye to the Royal Yacht. The diving German Stutkas came around to strafe both ships, dividing their number between them. Again *Mariah*'s guns fired, covering the Royal Yacht with a ceiling of deadly lead projectiles. She brought two planes down that nose dived into the sea and sent another limping away with smoke trailing from its right wing.

Andy watched the three remaining planes dip their wings to the southeast and follow their injured comrade. He shaded his eyes against the bright sunlight to search the sky for another threat to dive at them. "First Officer to the bridge," came over the loud speaker, breaking the sudden silence.

Andy climbed the bridge ladder to find chaos. Glass crunched beneath his feet where the map table had been shattered accompanied by the groans of the wounded. The navigation officer had several nasty cuts but said he would be all right. "It's Captain Edmon, sir, he's been wounded."

Dr. Patterson was leaning over Troy Edmon, telling him to take it easy. "Have to see to the ship," Edmon weakly protested.

"First I have to see to you, Captain," Dr. Patterson soothed. "Andy, tell him."

"Sir, the Royal Yacht was not harmed. We brought two enemy aircraft down and sent one back smoking," Andy reported, hoping to ease Edmon's anxiety about their mission.

"Good...good," Edmon softly whispered. "You'll have to take over, Number One. Get them there," he finished, with the last of his ebbing strength.

"Yes, sir. I will, sir." Nodding to Dr. Patterson, Andy went to the front of the bridge. He couldn't allow himself to be horrified by the terrible wounds inflicted on Troy Edmon, or the luxury of time to wonder if he was ready to take command. The time was now.

"Mr. Roden, go around the ship," he ordered. "Make sure we're ready when the enemy returns. We'll need to be on the lookout for submarines when we approach the open Atlantic."

"Yes, sir. Sir? Will Captain Edmon be all right?" Mason asked.

"I sincerely hope so, Mr. Roden...I sincerely hope so."

The *Mariah* and her royal charge continued westward past the southern entrance into the Irish Sea to where the Channel flowed into the Atlantic. They expected to rendezvous with the *Orion* at early dawn the next day well out into the Atlantic Ocean, where land-based planes were stretched to the limit of man and machine to reach.

"Mr. Liggett, signal the Royal Yacht we are entering the Atlantic. Tell her to keep a sharp lookout," Andy ordered. *Has it only been a few short hours since our departure from a burning London?* he briefly wondered. So much was now changed, and he was in command of what might be the *Mariah*'s most important mission in the war. Edmon had said, "*Get them through,*" and he intended to obey that whispered order.

The sun was low in the sky after a tense day of watching for an unpredictable enemy. Andy was sitting in Edmon's chair with a sense of occupying a commander's seat that was not rightfully his. Mason Roden had the bridge, but Andy felt, like Edmon, a need to be on the spot. He could still hear the sounds Dr. Patterson and Harris made while working on Troy Edmon before moving him to sickbay.

Dr. Patterson operated to remove two bullets from Edmon's body. One pierced a lung and caused it to collapse. The second bullet hit his abdomen and caused extensive damage to his left kidney, before grazing the liver and lodging in his spleen, which had to be removed. Doc reported Edmon had lost a large volume of blood and gave him a 50–50 chance of recovery.

Andy left the bridge long enough after Dr. Patterson reported Edmon's condition to go to sickbay and see him for a few moments. "The recognition signal is in my safe. Study it, and then destroy it," Edmon had whispered. With a great deal of effort, he raised a hand to grip Andy's shirt. "Get them through, and then get the men back to Harwich. The orders are with the recognition signal." His hand had fallen back limp from the effort, as sweat beaded across his forehead.

"I'll see to it, sir. Just rest for now. I'll let you know when we make contact," Andy assured him.

"Carry on," Edmon murmured, before closing his eyes to drift back into a troubled drug induced sleep.

The first tentative strands of morning light appeared on the eastern horizon, when a lookout spotted the outline of ships emerging out of a wispy sea fog in the western darkness. Andy ordered the guns to bear on them until they were identified; taking a position that shielded his charge. A signal lamp flashed from the swiftly closing cruiser demanding the recognition signal. "Send

H-R-H, Mr. Liggett," Andy calmly ordered. "Mr. Roden, inform Captain Edmon we have made contact."

"Aye, sir."

Within a matter of ten minutes the *Orion* and her destroyer screen encircled the Royal Yacht and laid a course due west, relieving the *Mariah* of her charge. "Bring her about," Andy ordered. "We are to return to Harwich and maintain radio silence until we reach port. Mr. Roden, return the men to regular ship's routine. You have the bridge."

"Yes, sir."

Andy descended the bridge ladder and went to Troy Edmon's cabin, where he had been moved to during the night, to report. "We've come about, sir. The Royal Yacht is now under the *Orion*'s protection." He had drawn a chair next to the cabin bunk and thought Edmon looked terribly drained and ill. He hoped his captain would survive the time it would take to return to Harwich.

Edmon gave a barely perceptible nod, before speaking just above a whisper. "They made it then."

"Yes sir, they made it," Andy replied. "I've returned the ship to normal routine. Lieutenant Roden has the bridge at present. We're following the course laid out by the Admiralty to draw attention away from our return. We should meet the inbound convoy by tomorrow evening, as the orders stated."

Again Edmon nodded with an effort. "Carry on Number One."

Andy left Edmon's cabin, softly closing the door, and sought out Dr. Patterson. "Doc, what is Captain Edmon's condition?"

"Andy, I can't give you a definite answer. He's weak from the initial injuries and loss of blood. He doesn't help himself any by insisting on remaining awake," Dr. Patterson frankly answered. "He needs to rest, be made to rest if necessary, to allow the body to heal."

"What can you do?" Andy asked.

"If he would let me, I could give him an injection of sleeping medication to make him rest and ease the pain of his injuries."

"Dr. Patterson, as First Officer I find it my duty to declare Captain Edmon unable to make competent decisions in his present condition," Andy boldly stated.

Quentin Patterson slowly nodded, before acknowledging the difficult command decision Andy had made. "I think I know what that cost you."

Andy silently returned the doctor's intent look for a moment before going to the radio room. "Are there any signals for us or the *Orion?*" he asked. According to the orders if there were no signals, the ruse had been pulled off; and the Germans were unaware the Royal Yacht was on her way to the Americas.

"No, sir, nothing for us or them since we sailed."

So, it had worked. But at what cost? Andy wondered. *Will Troy Edmon make it back to Harwich, or will I have to bury him at sea and go tell his wife that he died bravely? The cloak of command, like the cloak of manhood, is not always comfortable,* Andy thoughtfully acknowledged. *Today it was particularly heavy.*

CHAPTER 13

The *Mariah* met a convoy sailing the North Atlantic corridor out of Iceland's overworked ports at the northern turn into the Irish Sea thirty-six hours after handing off her royal charge. Ships barely seaworthy passed her rails, showing the latest scars inflicted by the increasing horrendous submarine attacks. *Mariah*'s crew silently watched those that had survived the newly born submarine *Wolf Pack,* as the battle weary merchant and escort vessels sailed past her rails, before taking position as rear escort.

Andy watched from the bridge at the journey's end when Troy Edmon was transferred to one of the many ambulances that lined the pier at Harwich. Captain Edmon's survival was a small miracle and a credit to Quentin Patterson's surgical abilities. At least he wouldn't have to face a grieving widow with the news about how her husband had bravely fought and died for his country. Andy looked across the harbor to see derricks busily dipping into the bowels of the merchant ships off-loading their meager cargo in preparation for the turn around journey. He wondered momentarily if the *Mariah* would be sent across that foreboding stretch of ocean.

Rear Admiral Benson, the Port Commander, summoned Andy to his office two days after the *Mariah* docked. "Lieutenant Burns, Admiral Benson will see you now," the female clerk informed him. Andy had not yet gotten used to having women in the Navy. He thought it was a good idea because it released men for assignment to combat duty, but it was still unnatural to him.

"Have a seat, Lieutenant. I'll just be a moment here," Benson said, returning Andy's salute.

"Thank you, sir."

Andy glanced around the office and noticed few personal items present. The battered desk appeared unusually clean for the times, with a nearly empty in-out tray at the left corner. Four small silver frames containing pictures of a woman and three young girls sat at the top right corner alongside a box of Cuban cigars that completed the visible signs of occupancy. Andy briefly wondered how the admiral had come by such an unknown luxury.

Admiral Benson looked up after several minutes, closing the file he was reviewing. "It appears you have a good record," he said, tapping the file with his index finger.

It surprised Andy to be told it was his file the admiral had been reading. "Thank you, sir."

"I talked with Troy Edmon this morning," Admiral Benson casually remarked. "He says you've been a good officer, even when you told the doctor to knock him out."

"Sir, I thought it was the only way to give him a chance. Our mission was accomplished."

"Oh, I'm not condemning your decision, Lieutenant. In my opinion it was the only choice you had," Benson told him. "I told Troy that, and he agreed with me. Said it took guts to do it too. That's why I'm recommending you for promotion to Lieutenant Commander, and to become the *Mariah*'s next commanding officer. It should be made official in a day or two when the Command Board meets."

"Captain Edmon, sir, he won't be able to return?"

"Don't you want the command, Lieutenant?" Benson roughly asked, with his head tilted slightly to one side, as his eyes bored into the face across his desk.

"No, sir, I mean, yes, sir, I do, sir. Please don't get me wrong. This has just taken me by surprise. I assumed Captain Edmon would be able to return," Andy answered a little stunned at the sudden promotion, which in normal times was still a year or two away.

"Yes, I see. I better bring you up to date then. Captain Edmon will be in the hospital for some time and a nursing home for a long recovery period afterwards. Our doctors say your Dr. Patterson did a first rate job just getting him here alive. I don't know all the technical medical terms, but I do know he was badly wounded."

"I knew it was serious. I didn't know how serious. Thank you for telling me, sir. Captain Edmon has taught me a great deal since I've been with him. I believe when he's recovered he still has much to offer."

Nodding approval of the statement, Phillip Benson eyed Andy closely for a moment. "So, Lieutenant, I take it you would accept command of the *Mariah*."

"Yes, sir, and thank you. Will the ship's company remain intact?"

"Not completely. We have new volunteer personnel coming out of training pretty quickly now. They're needed to fill those slots that have become vacant for various reasons. We need to integrate them with seasoned sailors, so it's necessary to rotate some of the regulars to accomplish this."

"I see."

Andy knew how the various vacancies had come about, at least a great many of them. He feared there would be a lot more vacancies before this war ended.

"I'm leaving your Mr. Parker and Dr. Patterson in place. Tim Parker understands the ranks, having come through them. Patterson is familiar with his present post, no sense in moving him to another ship. I've not decided on a first officer. Do you have anyone you would consider recommending?" Admiral Benson asked.

"Yes, sir, I do. Sub-lieutenant Mason Roden has been with the ship since Britain declared war on Germany. He is a reservist, but I believe he has a feel for the ship. He sailed for two years on a merchant ship before returning to Oxford to take his degree. I know personally he's cool under fire and values his men," Andy responded.

"I'll take it under advisement. You're dismissed, Lieutenant."

Standing, Andy saluted, expressing his gratitude to the admiral for a chance at command.

"Good luck, Lieutenant," Benson responded in his no nonsense manner, returning Andy's salute. He sighed after the latest lieutenant left that would receive a premature promotion and command one of His Majesty's ships. *They keep getting younger,* he thought. *Well, at least this one was regular Navy and seems to understand the grave responsibility being entrusted to him. And Edmon said he thought Burns was ready to take command. Time will tell.*

Andy's promotion to Lieutenant Commander came on September 19, 1940. He added the thin gold stripe between the two wider ones on his sleeve and the greater responsibilities that came with it to his duty roster. He read the orders to the crew assembled on the deck to take command of the *Mariah,* making it official, before summoning sub-lieutenant Roden to his cabin.

"Mr. Roden, I have here your official promotion to full lieutenant," Andy said.

At a loss for words, Mason simply said, "Thank you, sir."

"Don't thank me yet. There's a price that goes with that stripe."

"I don't understand, sir."

"I requested you as my first officer. It means bearing a heavy responsibility and having the ship ready when I need it."

"Sir…I…I don't know what to say. Thank you," Mason responded, showing obvious surprise at the unexpected statement and wondering for a moment if he was ready to meet the challenge. "You believe then that I'm ready to fulfill the duties, sir?"

Andy looked intently at the man he had requested as his first officer. He believed Mason Roden had leadership qualities that would be a genuine asset. But that decision had to lie with the newly appointed lieutenant. "The question, Lieutenant, is: Do you believe you are ready?"

Mason considered these words momentarily and saw the searching in Andy's eyes. He knew from working with this man he could do the job. "I believe I can. Yes, sir, I believe I can," he firmly stated, taking the first step on the journey toward a full command.

Andy saw the resolve on his newly appointed first officer's face and breathed a momentary sigh of relief that his instinct had been correct. "You'll find Tim Parker very helpful. I know I did. We'll be receiving new crew members and losing some of our seasoned ones. Talk with Tim about drilling. We'll also be receiving a new midshipman. Mr. Liggett will be returning to school for his next level of education," Andy explained. "When we do sail, I want the new ones as ready as they can be. Our survival will depend upon it. I'm not sure yet what will happen with the other officers. I do know our navigator is returning to Dartmouth for specialized training. Other than him and Mr. Liggett, I can't say right now."

"I understand, sir. How soon before the new men report?" Mason asked.

"Probably by the first of next week." Andy was pleased the question was asked, showing an indication his first officer would seek information to better prepare the ship and her crew.

"Sir, about Captain Edmon, will he recover?"

"I know his injuries are severe, but I believe in time he will have a full recovery."

"I see," Mason slowly said, sensing the inner strength of his new commander and a growing self-confidence from within. "I'll get with Tim Parker then," Mason said.

"Very well…carry on…Number One," Andy said in dismissal, feeling for the first time the sense of command. He knew there was no one to fall back on now to make the final decisions. He could talk a situation over with his officers, using his first officer as a sounding board, but the final decision would lie with him. *For better or worse,* Andy thought. *Just like in the marriage vows, but they also say until we are parted by death.*

"All right, ya got thirty minutes to find yer lockers and stow yer gear," Parker gruffly ordered, with a hard stare. "Yer ta report ta me on the quarter deck to begin fire drill instruction at 0730 dressed in number five workin' gear. This here is the real Navy, and I don't want no slackers. Dismissed!" He sternly concluded. The dejected group of new recruits shuffled away with their duffel bags in the sure knowledge that life, as they knew it, was forever changed.

"I see you have things well in hand, Mr. Parker," Andy commented, crossing the deck en-route to shore.

"Sir," Parker responded, saluting, "I just like to be sure the men are prepared, sir."

"I'm glad of that. Carry on, Mr. Parker."

"Yes sir."

Andy knew Tim Parker would work with the new crew members until they could do the necessary jobs of war in their sleep. Many of them were civilians three months ago and had barely learned starboard from port, let alone the skills necessary for a combat ship at war. This was not only true of the enlisted men, but the officers as well. A young untried Midshipman, who was regular Navy, joined the ship for his first tour of duty. Three sub-lieutenants and Lieutenant Brian Jones, their new navigation officer whom had previously served as an officer on civilian ships, joined the crew two days later. Andy needed to gauge Lieutenant Jones' skills before being at ease with him. Andy knew if he and Mason Roden were severely wounded or killed, Brian Jones would be third in line and have to take command, most likely in a combat situation. He said a silent prayer as he approached the Admiral's office that the crew would have time to learn before being called on to give possibly the ultimate sacrifice on this war's altar.

Andy scanned the early morning sky in anticipation of the sunrise, and then turned his attention to the waiting bridge. The previous day Admiral Benson told him they were being sent out and wished them good luck on Andy's first voyage as *Mariah*'s commander. Andy knew it would take more than luck to bring the ship and her crew safely back to England.

"Sir, the ship is ready for sea. Engines are on stand by," Mason reported. Mason had spent hours pouring over each detail needed to have the ship ready to sail. Tim Parker gave helpful comments, yet never made it appear he was advising a superior officer. Mason thought that in civilian life Tim would have gone far with this ability.

"Very well," Andy said in response to Mason's readiness report. "Let go forward, let go aft." The men on deck quickly pulled the mooring ropes onto the deck, neatly curling them away, before they became tangled in the screw, causing the ship to falter. "Let go spring, all back one third." Andy watched orders become reality, when the *Mariah* moved away from the pier, as the current swung her bow out toward the harbor. "All ahead one third, steer 1–3-0."

It was a natural instinct to bring the ship out to sea, watching the water with one eye while conning the ship with the other.

"Number One, take us to sea," Andy ordered and sat in the captain's chair, appearing to be indifferent to the routine procedures. He often wondered how Captain Edmon could look so relaxed sitting in this chair. Andy now knew he hadn't been, but Edmon was a master at not letting on.

Andy thought about his visit with Troy Edmon the previous day. "Remember to trust your first officer," Edmon had said. "If you don't, ask yourself is it him or you. Then take action. Good luck to you, Number One. And bring the ship back in one piece."

"Yes sir. Thank you, sir," Andy had responded, before saluting and leaving Edmon to watch the harbor out his hospital window.

"Steer 1–4-7," Mason ordered, penetrating Andy's thoughts about the *Mariah*'s last commander.

Good, we'll cross the wake of that freighter now, Andy thought. He held his breath when he noticed the freighter that would cross their path, wrestling with the impulse to intervene before the command to turn was given. He knew a ship's commander had to walk a very thin line to not break a man's confidence, yet not endanger the ship at the same time. Andy hoped he would be as good at it as Edmon had been.

"Sir, we are approaching the harbor limits," Mason reported.

"Very well," Andy acknowledged, rising from his chair to approach the center of the bridge and carefully scan the horizon before issuing the usual orders when entering the Channel. "Post look outs. Steer course 2–1-0."

"Turning to course 2–1-0," the quartermaster crisply responded. "My course is 2–1-0."

"Carry on," Andy ordered.

Mariah's orders said they were to turn west into the Channel and join a convoy sailing to North Africa by nightfall. The commanders and ships' officers had attended a briefing that morning with details about their upcoming cruise. The latest intelligence information was reviewed and what defensive tactics were proving to be the most effective.

The new navigating officer appeared to be accustomed to sailing into exotic ports and was unruffled by the present developments. "We sailed to Alexandria several times," he commented after the briefing. "This sounds like the places we visited along the way with a few surprises thrown in. Interesting."

"Mr. Jones," Andy had said, "You have an unusual way of putting things."

"Ships approaching off the port bow," a bridge lookout excitedly yelled, when the evening's darkness began to settle over the ocean's surface. He was frightened until he realized it was the convoy forming, but pleased he had remembered which side port was for his first combat voyage sighting.

"Commander," Mason said into the voice pipe, "Ships to port, sir."

"I'll be there," Andy answered from his sea cabin. Andy lay on the narrow bunk fully clothed, sweating out the wait for the convoy to be sighted, while Mason conducted the routine job of sailing the ship to the appropriate coordinates. Andy knew he was only steps away from the bridge, but the fact remained someone else was sailing his ship. He wondered if Edmon had lain awake on this same bunk waiting for something to happen when he had the bridge watch.

When he emerged onto the open bridge Andy walked over to the navigator's station and checked the chart. He noticed the precision the navigating officer used not only in course and speed, but depth was also noted. Andy knew that in shallow approaches it could mean the difference between safe passage and grounding, and made a mental note to take notice of his navigating officer's abilities more closely. It appeared Brian Jones might have that rare natural sense of the sea that so many sailors could only hope to learn over time.

"We just received the recognition signal, sir. Lead escort has ordered us to bring up the rear of the convoy," Mason reported when Andy approached.

"Very well," Andy said. "What speed are they making?"

"I'm sorry, sir, I should have told you, eight knots, sir."

"Very well, slow to five knots until the next to last ship passes, and then bring us back to speed slowly. We don't want to make a large bow wave, too easy to spot," Andy ordered. He had seen too many escort ships race to their assigned station and the catastrophic results, when the enemy was alerted by a fast moving ship's noise and the bow wave it created.

Ship after ship passed the *Mariah* while she patiently waited for the end of the convoy. Men and equipment were being poured into North Africa to halt the advancing Axis Army's march across the ancient desert plains and villages that had fostered dispute since before the time of Abraham. Andy knew if all of Egypt fell into German hands the Suez Canal would be lost along with the oil supplies from Iraq and Iran.

The first days on escort duty were tense for the untested crew, but more dangers lurked in the night. Andy remembered their voyage back from Singapore and the submarine attack north of Gibraltar. He appreciated Edmon's insistence on continually improving response to general quarters and drilled the men until they were honed to a razor sharp edge. Andy knew the men hated the constant call to stations "this is a drill…this is a drill" reverberating throughout the ship, but he also knew it was necessary.

Mason understood the reasoning and worked like a demon to accomplish better results. He knew the first time under fire was the hardest. A man needed to keep his wits about him when the enemy dove out of the sky with guns firing or sent torpedoes from beneath the sea's peaceful surface to destroy them. He was rewarded as the days and weeks passed with the new officers and ratings doing it right every time.

When the convoy reached the western Mediterranean near the Island of Sicily, an ear-splitting explosion penetrated the night's peaceful watch. It was followed by a searing white hot flash spiraling high into the sky, illuminating the surrounding sea like the sun. An ammunition ship had simply ceased to exist, leaving a flickering slick of burning oil that soon dissipated.

The second ammunition ship, well separated from her sister, continued the trek. Her captain cringed when he saw a ship the same as his disappear in an instant. *Will we be next?* he briefly wondered.

"It's most likely a submarine," Andy was saying, "unless they laid mines. The waterway narrows through here before opening up again. Keep a close lookout for anything unusual moving through the water. If it is a submarine, they're reloading as fast as they can to strike again."

"Yes sir," Mason responded, before heading to his battle station at the aft anti-aircraft gun.

The crew waited in nervous apprehension for something to happen, but there were no more explosions and nothing was sighted. A tense hour passed before the stand down sounded.

"Mr. Parker, could you see anything?" Mason asked on his way back to the bridge.

"No sir, just some debris left by the blast. Could be there was nothin' there to see, and someone got careless."

Mason grimaced at Parker's conclusion. The thought of someone sneaking a cigarette and a spark setting off the explosion made him shiver. He thought it would be a good idea to remind the men and officers about the no smoking lamp, as he turned toward the bridge to report.

CHAPTER 14

Jane opened the latest newspaper to reach Helen's Landing and scanned the front page with increasing dismay:

> Japanese Diplomat and Trade Mission seek greater access to raw materials, especially oil arriving at NEI.

The weekly papers out of Singapore and the local bimonthly were filled with headlines about trade missions and Japanese troops using transit routes through French Indochina, as quickly as the government released the information. The ink was still wet on one headline when the next piece of the East's diplomatic puzzle fell onto the table. The war in the Atlantic and the deserts of North Africa were relegated to the second page in deference to this latest defiance to western demands, leaving local citizens wondering if Hitler was writing the agenda for his less competent Japanese partner.

Jane read the reports and wondered if the tropical paradise had a Judas in it. Peter told her not to worry, but she couldn't help being concerned he might be called away. The news from Britain grew continually worse, and now Japan was starting to look like a threat.

"Jane, are you going to stare at that newspaper all through lunch?" Sally asked.

"What? Oh…no. I was just thinking the news isn't very encouraging."

"John has been following it pretty closely. I think he feels like he's missing out. You'd think after hearing about Wesley's experience in Holland that he wouldn't be quite so anxious about not being in England."

"Peter hasn't said much about it. I suppose he's afraid it will upset me. Sally, I know doctors are usually pretty safe, but I can't seem to shake the feeling that something terrible will happen here." Jane shivered, wondering why she felt such a strong premonition.

"What do you mean?" Sally asked.

"I don't know, just an eerie feeling. We better get back to the floor," Jane said, pushing the troublesome thought aside.

Jane and Peter entered a favorite little restaurant close to the harbor that evening. The small establishment had eight tables and a counter with twelve swivel stools, but managed to stay in business with its cozy atmosphere and limited home cooked menu. The radio quietly playing in the background faded from their senses, until a dramatic announcement caught their attention.

"This is the BBC, Singapore Station. London is burning," the announcer dramatically stated. "Continuous flights of enemy planes are dropping bombs and incendiaries on the civilian population, and all manner of commerce, in a merciless attack."

"Peter, what's happening?" Jane asked.

"I'm not sure. Could you turn the radio up a little please?" Peter asked the owner.

Jane and Peter, along with the little establishment's English born owner, stared at the radio in disbelief at the horrendous picture being depicted.

"Impenetrable walls of swirling fire leap toward the heavens, causing unbearable heat and leaving fire fighters at a loss in their courageous efforts to bring the dreadful holocaust under control. Frightened citizens are fleeing our great nation's capitol with little more than the clothes on their backs, as they rush to escape what one described as a glimpse into the unquenchable fires of hell."

"Peter, it's awful. How could one nation do that to another?" Jane asked, reflecting horror in her eyes at the description of wanton destruction being carried out across London.

"I don't know. Helen Burns was right though. Any chance of a peace accord being reached with Germany now is definitely lost."

Jane and Peter sat in silence after the broadcast ended, leaving the food on their plates untouched and walked to the harbor. It was still peaceful here, and the young couple found comfort in that after the shattering news from Britain. They knew Peter could be recalled to active duty at any moment with the escalating events that were taking place. They found it almost a relief four days later when Peter received orders to report in Singapore the following Monday. The escalating air war in Britain, coupled with the threat of invasion, led them to wonder if this was the first step toward him being sent back to England.

"I don't believe we'll be in Singapore for long. The orders John and I received say only Singapore, and state they are temporary. It could be they just want a progress report from us," Peter said. "I do know I'll miss you while I'm gone."

"I'll miss you terribly," Jane responded, looking up into Peter's wonderful blue eyes where his gentle soul looked out in its continual wonder at the world. "I know you'll be all right though. God wouldn't ask me to give you up now."

"It'll be all right, Jane. I'll write as soon as we're told what we'll be doing," Peter reassured her. "Now, let's enjoy this time together." Jane snuggled close and felt a sense of being at home, something she had not felt since Jim's death. *He has to be safe, to come back to me,* she thought.

"We've been waiting for nearly three hours," John complained on Monday morning at Naval headquarters in downtown Singapore. He and Peter were sitting in a waiting room where an uninterested clerk had placed them and left. John was beginning to think the clerk had forgotten about them. "Maybe they forgot about us."

"I doubt it. That's why I brought some reading material along. I remember when we reported at Harwich and waited several hours. It appears Singapore is no different. It's to remind us that we are mere lieutenants most likely."

"Lieutenants Romans and Hartman, the Admiral will see you now," the same clerk summoned.

"About time," John mumbled under his breath.

Entering an average sized inner office with a picture of Winston Churchill on the wall behind the desk, they saw a broad shouldered, clean-shaven, middle-aged man, who appeared to be in good physical condition, with gray starting in the dark blond hair at his temples. The well worn Navy issue office desk where he sat was littered with manila files and loose papers waiting for some form of action to be taken. The in-out box at the left corner sagged under the weight of other files waiting to be reviewed or filed away in one of the staggering number of file cabinets lined up like soldiers across the walls in the outer office. John and Peter stood at attention before the desk waiting for the Admiral to speak.

"Gentlemen, have a seat. I imagine you wonder why you were summoned here," Admiral Edwards began, with his voice filling the room, as his steel gray eyes quickly assessed the two young men. "We naturally want a report about how things are progressing at the hospital where you've been serving. Also, we hope to draw on your experience to assist the Army and Navy in a joint venture to build and supply medical outposts to be manned sometime next year."

"Does this mean we'll be staying in Singapore?" John asked.

"Probably for the next two or three weeks to do some preliminary consulting. Since the Navy will also rely to some extent on these facilities, and they will be near Naval interests in some instances, we thought it prudent to have input regarding their construction. The two of you are the only medical officers we have available with long-term experience at a small hospital in this part of the world right now," Admiral Edwards briefly explained. "I also know Dr. Jamison is considered an expert in tropical medicine and too busy to come to Singapore at this time. We believe the knowledge Jamison has passed on since you have been working under him will naturally be of value to us. I understand the tropics create additional difficulties in medical practice."

"Sir, do you know who we will be working with?" Peter asked.

"Let me see, I have it here someplace," Edwards answered, rummaging through one of the piles on his desk. "Oh yes, here it is. A Captain Wesley Vilmont," he informed them, snapping the folder shut.

"Wesley Vilmont? But he was wounded at Dunkirk!" John said in surprise.

"Do you know him?"

"We know of him. That is, if he's the same Wesley Vilmont. His sister is a nurse at the hospital," John explained. "When did he get here? If you don't mind me asking, sir."

"He isn't here yet. He and his crew arrive tomorrow afternoon by plane. The day after tomorrow there is a meeting with Army and Navy representatives to review the parameters of what will be expected. You'll be asked for input, both of you," Admiral Edwards emphasized. "That's why I wanted to see you beforehand, so you have time to formulate some general ideas."

"It would probably be a good idea for Captain Vilmont to see Dr. Jamison's facility and talk with him also," Peter quietly suggested.

"You're right, Peter," John agreed. "When it comes to laying out a hospital, Dr. Jamison's the goods. Look how well things flow, even in a crisis like that blasting disaster a few months back."

"I heard about that indirectly," Admiral Edwards remarked. "I understand there were lives saved because of the quick response time. I didn't realize you were both involved with it. That knowledge will be helpful to us. Well, the day after tomorrow report to the base conference room at 0800. Until then, you're free to go into the city if you like."

"Thank you, sir," John and Peter both responded in turn, before coming to attention and saluting.

The conference room seated twenty people around a fifteen-foot long cypress table, with rank seeming to designate how far down the table a person was seated. John and Peter, being mere lieutenants, were seated at the bottom end, feeling like a man finding himself at a black tie affair in his gardening clothes. "I've never seen so much brass in one place," John whispered to Peter, as Admiral Edwards stood to bring the meeting to order.

Eric Edward's counterpart, General Obadiah Hughes, sat stoically alongside Admiral Edwards eyeing both sides of the service-divided table, when the meeting was called to order. He wondered how long it would take to bridge the distance across the table's sleek surface to bring the two sides to some sense of agreement. The fact the meeting was at Naval headquarters was a strategic agreement with Eric Edwards to foster an open-ended conversation about the joint Army-Navy project.

"Gentlemen," Admiral Edwards began, "Welcome. I believe most of us know each other. Let me introduce Captain Wesley Vilmont from the Army Corps of Engineers, recently arrived from London, and Lieutenants Romans and Hartman, who are Navy doctors on temporary assignment here. We're here today to set the parameters needed for Captain Vilmont not only to further defenses in the north, but also for medical facilities to give immediate care until a casualty victim can be evacuated to a hospital. That is why Dr. Romans and Dr. Hartman are here."

"Seems to me we just need some type of shed with a roof on it for an aid station," a burly looking Army colonel interjected.

"With all due respect, sir," John said, "if we have something a little more sophisticated, the threat of permanent disability or death can often be avoided."

"Humph…well, yes, I suppose," the colonel allowed, *"Leftenant."*

The chilled reference to Naval rank across the table would take, Obadiah Hughes knew, about an hour to thaw among the other Naval officers sitting further up the table. It would be a long meeting.

The conference continued for three and a half hours, with the Army and Navy grudgingly giving way and coming to agreement. They finished when Wesley summed up the meeting in a few sentences of what was wanted, what was needed, and what could be done in the given time frame.

Wesley knew some of what he said was not welcome, but his commanding officer had made it clear he had a fairly free hand and would back him. Whoever had become nervous about defenses in the East in London was high up the chain of command to be given the autonomy he had. "Dr. Romans, Dr. Hartman, perhaps we could meet over dinner this evening and discuss your particular ideas based on what we've gone over here today," Wesley concluded.

"That sounds like a fine idea," Admiral Edwards interjected, glancing at

General Hughes. It was clear the two ranking officers in the room had conferred before the meeting and had made some command decisions based on the "*suggested cooperation*" orders given by higher sources in London. "I believe that is all for now. Thank you for coming, gentlemen."

Wesley caught up with John and Peter on the way to their temporary lodging. "Never build anything by committee. Especially one composed of Army and Navy brass."

"I believe you're right," Peter agreed. "I'm afraid I lost most of what was discussed by the time we left."

"I'm not surprised," Wesley said.

"Captain, if you don't mind me asking, do you by chance have a sister at a place called Helen's Landing?" John asked.

"As a matter of fact I do—Sally," Wesley answered, a little startled by the question. "Any special reason for asking?"

"We know her. She's a nurse at the hospital we've been attached to."

"You're not her friend, John, she's written about in her letters, are you?"

"John, your sins have come home to haunt you," Peter teased, starting to laugh.

"I've been the perfect gentleman," John said a little huffily. "We're friends."

"Actually, Sally has only commented she found you to be enjoyable company," Wesley reassured him, smiling a little at John's apparent chagrin. He dismissed the thought and changed the subject, thinking it would be a good idea to learn a little more about these men from the Navy. "I was going to suggest we go to the Raffles for dinner tonight. It will be the first decent meal I've seen in quite some time. My crew will be on leave for the next two days. They need to let off steam and unwind before we start a new project. Most of them were in Holland or Dunkirk before placing defenses in Britain during the worst of the Blitz."

"I understand you were at Dunkirk," Peter said.

"No, I only made it as far as the Meuse River the second day in Holland, before a stray *Gerry* fighter ran across me and some others on a bridge. They were moving out across it. I was scrunched over trying to connect a charge to blow it up. If I'd been standing, I probably wouldn't be here today. Next thing I knew I was on a destroyer called the *Mariah* crossing the Channel, with the German Luftwaffe chasing us most of the way."

"Helen Burns will want to meet you, I'm sure," Peter commented.

"Burns, the name sounds familiar."

"Andrew Burns was the first officer on the *Mariah* when you sailed with her. He's the commander now," John explained.

"Well, who's this Helen Burns you spoke of, his wife?" Wesley asked.

"His mother," John answered. "A pleasant woman who is in full command of her life, wouldn't you say, Peter?"

"Helen's a very nice woman. She and Jane and Sally have become rather good friends."

"She also is able to get her way, and you're glad to let her have it. A very unique talent. But, I do agree, Peter, Helen is a nice lady. And I emphasize the word lady."

"I see. I look forward to meeting her," Wesley remarked. "I certainly owe her son a debt of gratitude along with his ship. Well, gentlemen, until this evening then."

The three new acquaintances retired to the Cad's Alley after dining that first evening, and began an in-depth discussion about medical needs in the field. While the two doctors spoke about orderly sterile conditions to bring a patient back to health, the engineer countered with the brutal reality of the chaos during a pitched battle. Wesley knew first hand the ugliness of war and the break up to a government's infrastructure it caused. He also knew medical emergencies were the norm and not the exception during such a crisis. How then, he wondered, could they bring order to this one area, while the rest of the world fell apart and society's morês with it? These two doctors knew the answer, even though they didn't realize it now. The challenge was to dig deep enough to reach the prize buried within.

The pace increased after that first evening, leaving John and Peter a little astonished at the end of two weeks to find a plan in place and some initial drawings completed. The design was fairly simple but quite functional. The newly designed aid station could hold up to eight beds comfortably, leaving space for a small trauma and a minimally equipped operating room for those who couldn't wait to be moved to a larger facility.

John and Peter met with Wesley at the end of the two-week whirlwind of activity to discuss the preliminary drawings and answer any further questions. "I have to meet with my immediate superior tomorrow," Wesley said. "The day after that I would like to visit Dr. Jamison's hospital for a few days on my way north. I believe your suggestion about meeting with him would be helpful to finalizing these plans. It will also give me an opportunity to see Sally. I haven't seen her since she came here before the war started. I was originally going to take my leave and come out, but things didn't exactly work out that way."

"As far as seeing Dr. Jamison, Admiral Edwards told us yesterday we would be returning to Helen's Landing when we're finished here," Peter said. "We could help with any arrangements on that end."

"Very well, I'll leave it to you to set it up then."

John and Peter found Admiral Edwards in his office later in the day reviewing the last page of a file. "This is a good report," he said, tapping the folder. "I'd try to keep you on staff here, but I think your talents would be put to better use at Helen's Landing. These are your orders returning you to Dr. Jamison for now. We'll need to re-evaluate after some of these outposts are manned. The Army will want their own doctors; however, we may decide to have a Naval representative in place as well."

"Captain Vilmont requested a meeting with Dr. Jamison before going further north," Peter reported.

"It's probably a good idea. We'll contact Jamison from here to make the necessary arrangements. Unless the Army is feeling segregated this month, Vilmont can travel by ship with you the day after tomorrow."

CHAPTER 15

John, Peter, and Wesley left Singapore Harbor aboard the *Sheltie,* a flat bottom coastal gunboat with a crew of sixty, including the Chinese cabin attendants and her captain, on October 9 in company with three other ships in her class. The three men were temporarily assigned to the cramped wardroom that sported a crest of a Sheltie in motion.

The small shallow draft ships sailed the coastal waterways and estuaries, visiting modest settlements and larger villages that evidenced Britain's population spread throughout the Empire. The small fleet regularly showed the flag and instilled a sense of military strength that gave reassurance to British settlers, while discouraging the Malayan natives from reclaiming their land through violence.

Wesley learned significant differences existed between the Navy in Singapore and the Navy in England. The small ship was in perfect repair with brass fittings polished to a glowing shimmer, decks scrubbed, and the officers and men turned out in crisp uniforms, going about their business at a steady, almost ceremonial, pace. The boson piped Wesley aboard with considerable ceremony in comparison to what little he had seen in England aboard troop transports. He learned later the "Boatswain's Call of Piping the Side" is usually reserved for high-ranking British or foreign Naval officers. Since he was a captain from the Army, the Navy had put its best foot forward.

Wesley retreated to the wardroom when the *Sheltie* entered the Singapore Strait and spread the aid station plans out on a table for review, but his thoughts soon turned to England. The threat of an invasion seemed less likely now in Britain. When he was recalled early from his medical leave he thought an invasion might come at any time and feared for his parents' safety. He had little doubt that if the Germans crossed the Channel, they would move with the same lightening speed as they had in Norway and on the Continent.

The dreadful need to fire on French Naval ships at Oran in June, however, was another matter. Wesley understood the need to prevent the French fleet from falling into German hands after France fell. But to fire on the very ships that a few weeks before had been their Ally only further strained the relations between France and England.

Wesley believed there must have been a better alternative to the situation and briefly wondered why the French ships had not sought refuge in a neutral or British held port instead of remaining vulnerable to German confiscation. Their orders at the end surely could not have forbidden seeking a safe refuge. He wondered how history would judge the British decision. He decided it would probably depend on the outcome of this most recent world conflict.

"Captain Vilmont?"

Wesley looked up and saw a perfectly turned out Naval officer type was addressing him. "Yes."

"Sir, I'm Lieutenant MacVae. The captain has asked if you would join him for dinner this evening."

"Thank you, Lieutenant, it would be a pleasure." At least he hadn't forgotten the correct protocol taught in officer's training during more peaceful times.

"I'll inform him, sir. He dines at 1900 hours," MacVae informed him.

Wesley nodded, "Thank you, lieutenant," before turning to the plans he had spread across the table. The remainder of his unit arrived by air in Singapore the day before he sailed. The Army was transporting the men and equipment by truck to the north with his second in command, Lieutenant Arthur Nance, in charge. He expected them to be settled into barracks or temporary housing of some type by the time he arrived.

"Hello, are these the drawings for the aid stations?" John asked upon entering the wardroom.

"I've just been reviewing them to see if there's anything I can do to make any improvements. They have to be placed out of the line of fire, yet be easily accessible," Wesley explained.

"It sounds like a logistics problem," John commented.

"To some extent, yes. However, you have to understand the Army. They like things a certain way. When someone comes along and throws in a monkey wrench, they get nervous."

"I take it you are the monkey wrench."

"In a manner of speaking."

A Chinese cabin attendant opened the Captain's door to Wesley at precisely 1900 hours and invited him to enter. The small outer cabin was dominated by an oak table that lowered from an inner wall with four place settings precisely laid on an immaculate white linen tablecloth with the *Sheltie*'s crest embroidered at one corner. The cabin attendant answered a second knock at the cabin door, announcing John and Peter's arrival in dress whites. At that moment the Captain, a large red headed Scott with bushy sideburns, entered the room from the inner bedroom of his cabin suite.

"Good evening, gentlemen. I'm pleased you could join me," Captain MacNeill began with a slight brogue, returning John and Peter's salutes. "Would you care for a drink before we dine?" MacNeill nodded to the Chinese cabin attendant, whom quickly left to prepare the officers' refreshments. "Please be seated. I understand you're an engineer, Captain. It must be a most interesting field."

"At times it is," Wesley replied. "Especially when a project has been completed and you know you had a hand in it."

"Yes, I suppose it would have a sense of reward. A little like a doctor after a birthing, wouldn't you say?" Captain MacNeill remarked, looking to John and Peter.

"I'm afraid we haven't been involved in many births," John responded. "We do more diagnoses and surgery at present. But yes, there is a certain sense of euphoria after assisting in a birth."

"I see, but you agree with the metaphor. Well, shall we dine?"

Captain MacNeill kept a flow of conversation going throughout the evening with a skillful ease. The party was enjoying an after dinner brandy and imported Cuban cigars, when the conversation turned to the war with Germany.

"I don't believe they'll invade now," MacNeill commented.

"I believe you're right," Wesley agreed. "I am concerned though about this agreement among Germany, Italy and Japan."

"Do you consider Japan a threat to us here?" John asked.

"I don't know. Somebody is nervous enough to send my outfit here instead of North Africa where there is fighting now. I do know I'll like working much better without being shot at while I'm doing it."

"Come now, Captain, surely Japan is not considered a threat here. Singapore is an invincible fortress with her 18-inch guns to defend her from any attack by sea, and north of there you have the jungle to contend with. Only a fool would attempt that," Captain MacNeill voiced with conviction, echoing Eastern Command's consolidated opinion.

The small ships entered the harbor at Helen's Landing on the twelfth after an uneventful voyage. John and Peter invited Wesley to stay with them, since a rooming house was the only accommodations available in the village. After dropping off his bags, Wesley headed for the hospital where he found Sally with her head bent over a chart at the nurses' station. "Nurse, could you give me some directions please?" he quietly inquired.

Sally looked up with a feeling the voice sounded familiar. "Wesley! But, how are you here?"

"The Army works in mysterious ways. I said I was going to come and see you here. It just took a little longer than expected. Come here and let me look at you," Wesley grinned, before embracing her.

The two siblings went to the single waiting room across the hall, with both trying to talk at the same time. "Gosh, I can't believe it's you. You look so good. So, tell me about Mom and Dad, how they're holding up," Sally said in a single breath.

"You know Mom, always on the go. She does volunteer work three days a week to help sew things up for soldiers. Dad's been made a sergeant in the Home Guard. He takes it very seriously and salutes me when he's in his uniform as his superior officer. Of course, outside of it he reminds me he is still my elder."

"That sounds like Dad all right," Sally laughed. "It all seems so far away from here. I hope they take care of themselves."

"Don't worry, Sal, they're fine. And the farm is doing better than it has in years," Wesley reassured her. "Dad put in more fields anticipating shortages, and he was right. The Agricultural Office has been in touch with him and all the farmers in the parish to plant more fields."

"Was it very terrible, Wes? The fighting and all?" Sally asked a little diffidently.

"It was pretty dicey. A lot of good men were lost, Sal, in Holland and at Dunkirk. I saw London before I left. The damage was pretty heavy there."

"I still can hardly believe it's come to this. We heard rumors of peace overtures, and then suddenly the terrible air attack on London was announced."

"I'm afraid you can believe it. What I saw in Holland alone was enough. The Germans just kept coming, finding any weak point, and then exploiting it. I'm beginning to believe it will be a long siege before it's over. But, tell me, what about you?"

"There isn't a whole lot to tell. I really like being here and like the work as well. It's a little like being paid to be on vacation."

"What about John...Dr. Hartman?" Wesley asked.

"John? What do you mean, Wes?" Sally asked, crinkling her forehead in question.

"I met him and Peter Romans in Singapore. In fact, I'm bunking with them for a few days," Wesley explained.

"How extraordinary. You come half way around the world and wind up meeting someone from this tiny place. To answer your question, however, John is a very good friend. We enjoy conversing and sometimes share a meal, but romantically...no. He's just fun company. John will always be a loner. You have now performed your brotherly duty regarding my honor," Sally impishly concluded.

"Sal, you know I would never pry."

"I know. I just had to tease you like when we were kids together," Sally laughed. "But come, you must meet my roommate, Jane." Taking his hand, Sally pulled Wesley from the waiting room back across the hall and poked her head in the doorway of the tiny office behind the nurses' station. "Jane, you'll never believe this."

"Believe what?"

Sally stepped aside to show a tall sinewy man in about his late twenties to early thirties, with curling dark hair and very blue eyes. "This is my brother, Wesley. He's been assigned to Malaya. He just got in this minute."

As soon as she saw the two together, Jane knew they had to be related. "Hello, it's a pleasure to meet you," she said with a smile. "I've heard a great deal about you. It looks like you've recovered from your wounds. I'm glad for you. Sally was pretty worried there for a while."

"Yes, thank you. I hope what you've heard hasn't put you off. Sally wrote that you're from the United States," Wesley said.

"That's right."

"I hope we have a chance to talk a little about your country before I have to go north."

"I'd be pleased to tell you whatever I can. I'm from Michigan and grew up in Muskegon on Lake Michigan, one of the Great Lakes. I went to Hackly School of Nursing there before taking a nursing job at the University of Michigan Hospital in Ann Arbor after graduation. I'm sorry, but I'm not very familiar with a lot of the other states."

"I hope to visit someday to see your Grand Canyon. Maybe when the war ends I'll get there."

"I hope it will be very soon...for both of those things. I'm sorry to cut you short, but I have to make rounds. You two probably have a lot to catch up on. Why don't you go ahead, Sally? I can manage until the night shift comes on. It's only about twenty minutes," Jane offered.

"Are you sure? Thanks awfully, I'll see you later at home." Sally happily picked up her sweater and purse and led Wesley to the outside. "Come on,

Wes, let's go someplace and have a good catch up with a cup of tea and some cakes."

Jane's thoughts turned to the letters Peter had sent her that were filled with love and hope for the future when she left the hospital and wondered when he might be returning. She had been home about ten minutes, when there was a knock at the door. She opened it to find Peter standing before her on the other side. "Do I get to come in?"

"Peter! When did you get here? I can hardly believe it," Jane stammered, as she threw her arms around him. He drew her closer, kissing her until they were both a little breathless. "Oh, Peter, I've missed you so much. I read your letters over and over again."

"I missed you too, Jane. I never knew what I was missing when guys would get letters from their sweethearts."

Jane led him to the sofa where they sat snuggled close together, enjoying each other's nearness. "When did you get back?"

"About an hour ago. I wanted to see you alone, not at the hospital. Because the minute I saw you I wanted to kiss you," Peter said, doing just that.

Smiling, Jane leaned toward Peter and kissed him. He put his arms around her, caressing her as the kiss deepened, turning their thoughts away from having been apart. They pulled back after a brief time, not yet ready to cross the final boundary that bound a man and woman as one.

"You must have come with Sally's brother, Wesley," Jane said. "He came to the hospital to surprise her."

"Yes, I know. Wesley asked us not to tell her he was here when we were in Singapore. He wanted his arrival to be a complete surprise to her. In fact, he was the reason we were sent there."

"What do you mean?"

"We did some consulting with him before coming back to Helen's Landing. He's here to augment the Army's defenses and build aid stations at some of the outposts. The Navy apparently has something to do with it, so we were elected to go to Singapore and meet with him," Peter explained. "We came back as soon as we could."

Jane prepared a light dinner when the sun began sinking beneath the horizon, while she and Peter talked in relaxed compatibility. "I expect everyone is still at our place. Do you want to go there for a while?" Peter asked.

"I would like that. It will be like a party to celebrate your return," Jane happily agreed.

While waiting in Dr. Jamison's office Wesley thought about the last couple of days. The impromptu party on Friday evening had gone quite late into the night. He and Sally borrowed a small boat on Sunday and went around the bay, reminiscing and talking about their futures. But now it was time to get back to business. Wesley knew the Tripartite Pact that bound Germany, Italy, and Japan in itself was not a military threat, but it was a step toward an escalating and potential crisis.

"I'm sorry to keep you waiting, Captain," Dr. Jamison said, sitting down behind his desk. "I don't know why a perfectly intelligent and normal human being can't follow some simple instructions for his own medical well being. Sorry, didn't mean to go on."

"I take it you have a difficult patient."

"Mm, you could say that. Now then, what can I do for you?"

"As you probably know, the Army has been building reinforcements along the coast road and near some of the military encampments to strengthen our numbers and have defensive ability. We also have a need to build some functional aid stations, something like a mini-hospital, to support the additional troops and front line casualties that would occur during a hostile action, until they can be moved to a more sophisticated hospital setting," Wesley explained. "It was suggested I talk to you about the medical arena."

"How would they be staffed?"

"The preliminary design calls for a single ward that can hold up to eight beds comfortably with one Army doctor and two male nurses. There might be a second doctor or nursing assistant, but I don't know. A lot would depend on the circumstances at the time."

"For starters, you would need some way to maintain sanitary conditions. The climate here is conducive to breeding infection. Second, the layout needs to flow effectively, allowing movement either to the ward, the operating room, or the morgue. Don't look surprised. In an emergency situation, and I assume we are talking possible combat as well, moving the dead away from the sight of the living makes a difference in a patient's morale," Dr. Jamison pointed out. "It can even make the difference sometimes to a patient hanging on to life or letting life go."

"I never thought of that," Wesley said. "We talked about a small trauma room with a ward and small operating room. Peter and John were right. I'm glad we were able to talk."

"I take it they were called to Singapore for this purpose?"

"You have to understand the services. The Army brings in an engineer, so the Navy, not to be out done, brings in two doctors, since they have a vested interest in the medical structures. I would have to say their contribution had merit. I learned many valuable things from them," Wesley said. "Could you show me how the movement works here at the hospital?"

"Of course."

Dr. Jamison guided Wesley to the emergency entrance, and he soon understood how the various sections branched one from another that allowed access to flow smoothly.

"Thank you, I understand it better now. A little adjustment in the drawings should accommodate the need very nicely," Wesley said when they returned to Dr. Jamison's office.

"Glad I could help. Tell me, how is your shoulder coming along?" Dr. Jamison asked.

"It's pretty good considering. Most days I don't really notice it." Wesley was surprised Dr. Jamison knew about his brush with death.

"That's good to know. It can be a tricky area to work on. Sally was worried when she got your mother's telegram, so I made some inquiries to an old colleague friend in London," Dr. Jamison explained. "Helen Burns made the request, but I was glad to do it."

"I've heard that name. Her son was the first officer of the ship I was evacuated on I've been informed."

"Amazing! Andy's the commander now."

"So I've heard," Wesley responded, shaking hands with Dr. Jamison and thanking him again for his time.

Wesley sailed with Captain MacNeill on the seventeenth of October to Kota Bharu in northern Malaya to begin inspections and make improvements to defensive emplacements. His crew would be reinforcing current structures as well as constructing additional ammunition dumps and the proposed aid stations. He had some doubts about the Army's acceptance of the aid stations in the manner they were intended to function. There was a great deal of diplomatic jousting between the East and West currently but no direct hostilities to demonstrate a need for change.

CHAPTER 16

Aerial bombings over England ceased until November 14 when Germany struck once again with Coventry as the primary target. Fire fighters watched in helpless sorrow as intense swirling infernos raged across the quiet centuries-old village, destroying what had taken generations to build, when the bombing cut the town's waterlines. The Cathedral was the most mourned loss. The only part left to attest to the fifteenth century historical holy structure was the spire silhouetted against the night's sky. It was as if an accusing finger from God was pointing toward those who dared commit this sacrilege against His house. A great many were dead when the bombing was over, and a large portion of the town was damaged or destroyed.

Helen shut off the radio in Malaya after the BBC concluded the evening report. "All the lovely old places being destroyed," she sighed in sadness. "I just don't know what to think anymore. Andy was just a little boy when Ralph and I came here, and the war to end all wars was behind us. At least that was what everyone thought at the time. Now..."

"I'm afraid I don't know either, Helen," Martin Jamison responded. "I suppose the world depression had some impact. Germany protested long before the start of this war the punitive restraints set against her at the end of the last war, and the financial burden inflicted on an already shaky economic structure."

"But that surely doesn't justify the total destruction of England," Helen protested.

"Do you think that's the real reason for the war, Dr. Jamison?" John asked.

"In part maybe. I think it gave the catalyst for Hitler's rise to power. The German people needed something, or someone; to blame for the economic crisis they were enduring. Hitler pointed his finger and said, "Follow me," and they did.

"Yes, but they must have seen Hitler was leading them to confrontation," Peter reasoned.

"Some maybe and some could still have doubts. But Hitler gained power with each step he rose, until he gained control," Dr. Jamison explained. "I would guess most of Germany believes the war will end soon."

"Then they don't know the nature of the English," Sally pronounced, defiantly setting her chin.

"You're most likely right, Sally," Helen agreed. "We tend to apologize for our victories and glory in our defeats. Dunkirk is a good example. But God help anyone who treads on us too hard."

"But I don't understand targeting the town like that," Jane said. "It's as if they don't care what's destroyed; just so something is. Almost like a blood lust."

"It seems whenever we come together we end up talking about the war," Helen sighed. "Here it seems so far away, like someone telling a bad story."

"Yet, Sally's brother has been sent to build emplacements for reinforcements to be sent here," John pointed out.

"Surely, that's just a precaution," Helen protested. "I mean, who would make war here?"

"Hopefully no one. Now, Helen, about this idea of yours—how do you want to start?" Dr. Jamison asked, changing the subject.

Taking their cue from him, the others diverted the talk back to planning for an American Thanksgiving celebration. Helen thought it would be interesting to do something to commemorate the day to begin a year-long theme of recognizing different national holidays from around the world. Jane gave a brief summary about the Pilgrims and American Indians that celebrated the first Pilgrim harvest and what traditional foods were now served.

"I like the pumpkin pie part," Peter jested.

"You would," Jane laughed.

"It sounds delightful, a day to feast and celebrate harvest. Here we forget the season changes in colder climates. There's always something in bloom," Helen observed. "Of course, we do have the rainy season. Perhaps we could do a modified feast and serve in the cafeteria in costumes of the time."

"If you can get anyone to wear them, Helen," Dr. Jamison cautioned.

"Martin, you know there are always volunteers. I'm sure we can find some pictures of what we want and create something."

"Well, you only have two weeks to do it in," Dr. Jamison pointed out.

"Then I'll have to start first thing in the morning," Helen countered with spirit.

"We used to just make the oversized collars and hats to put over our street clothes in school," Jane interceded.

"You see, Martin, no trouble at all," Helen beamed. After making preliminary plans, Jane and Sally agreed to meet the following afternoon to go over what Helen could find and make final adjustments.

"Helen is like a general laying out battle plans," John remarked on the drive back to the village. "If she had been in England when the shooting war started, it might not have."

"Helen is a determined woman," Dr. Jamison agreed. "She's worked hard to keep us afloat. You're right though, she goes full steam once an idea has taken root."

"I hope she doesn't tire herself too much. She's not getting any younger. After her surgery last February, she needs to take it easier," Jane reminded them.

"You won't ever get her to really slow down. That's why I insist on her taking a holiday three or four times a year," Dr. Jamison explained.

"I like her," Sally added. "She's interested in life and not just passing through it. She takes part in it and enjoys it."

"I believe you have something there," Peter agreed. "Too many people do miss out on things because they don't take part."

A week passed with no further reports of heavy bombing raids over England. It appeared for now the air war was subsiding, and the news returned to events closer to home in the East. Peter heard on November 21 that the evacuation of American women and children from the Netherlands East Indies was almost complete. He wondered what, if anything, Jane might do.

"Did you listen to the early news reports today?" Peter asked Jane later that evening.

"Why, has something happened?"

"No, not really. I just heard American women and children were being evacuated from the Netherlands East Indies," Peter explained.

"Oh that," Jane shrugged unconcerned. "Yes, I heard it, but it doesn't really have anything to do with me. America isn't at war with anyone. Besides, we're quite a ways away from there."

"True. I just wondered if you were bothered at all by it."

"No, I can't say that I am. I like it right here," Jane said with a smile. "I especially like the company."

Peter reached across the table, taking her hand into his. "I'm glad," he smiled, looking into her glowing green eyes. "I rather like being in your company." Jane felt her heart beating faster, as the love within her grew deeper. It was a special moment to be cherished and remembered for a lifetime.

Japan Mobilizes Naval Reserves was the latest headline of the *Singapore Gazette* the day after the NEI reported evacuating American women and children. A Chinese dispatch on November 23rd reported 20,000 Japanese troops being moved out of the Yangtze River Valley to Shanghai, allegedly for transport to Formosa. On the 26th the local bi-monthly paper reported Japan was asking for control of Saigon, Tonkin, and the South China Sea coast.

"I would say things have become more serious according to the latest reports," Peter commented, when he finished scanning the articles while trying to eat a quick lunch between patients.

"It could be a show of force to gain diplomatic leverage," John said.

"I wonder," Tom Linn interjected. "It seems they are becoming more like Germany since signing an agreement with them. They have defied all entreaties from the West about China since first invading. And now it seems that Japan grasps for everything in her sight."

"I agree. Japan's interests appear more concentrated outside China lately. But I still wonder if it isn't a show of force to gain a diplomatic point," John mussed.

"Some point," Peter muttered, rising to go on rounds.

November 28, America's Thanksgiving Day, arrived with temperatures climbing into the mid eighties. Jane heard there was snow in Michigan. This was a far cry from what Thanksgiving was like in the United States. Families would gather around the tables of parents and grandparents delighting in the savory dishes that loving hands had prepared for them. Whether served on elegant china or every day plates, Thanksgiving was a time for feasting in America.

Jane had last celebrated Thanksgiving with Jim at his parents' home in Howell, Michigan. It snowed on Thanksgiving Eve, and they built a snowman on the front lawn under the early morning sun. Jane smiled to herself at the memory and wondered how Jim's father was holding up today. News came in late August that her mother-in-law had died in June. Her father-in-law wrote, "She kind of gave up after Jim died." Jane knew her mother-in-law's health was poor, and Jim had been her only child. She thought she understood. Jim's dad went on to say he was going to move in with his widowed sister in Florida now that his little family was gone. She hoped the two lonely siblings might find some comfort and companionship with each other. At least Jim's dad wouldn't rattle around the lonely house in

Michigan, now only filled with memories and unfulfilled dreams, during the cold winter with its short days and long dark nights.

Peter gave Jane the chance to talk out what she felt when the news reached her. She recalled sensing his unspoken concern that it would open the wound she had suffered at Jim's loss. "It's all right," she had said. "I've laid him to rest. I only feel sorrow over his father being left alone now."

Peter had held her to him then. "You'll never be alone, Jane. I'll always be here. I hope for his sake your father-in-law finds his own peace in time, and someone to share it with."

"Jane, come on. We'll be late," Sally summoned from the doorway. Jane shook off her reminiscing and went to help with the day's events. She was a little surprised by the impact of the traditional American decorations when she entered the hospital's cafeteria and the number of people attending the event on a Thursday afternoon.

"It looks just like the cafeteria did when I was in school," Jane gasped. "Helen, you're a wonder."

"Thank you, my dear. Frankly, you just have to know who to call on to use their God given talents and let them do something they enjoy in the first place. In no time, things are done."

The day concluded on a happy note when everyone sang "God Bless Our Native Land." The song fulfilled the British need to express patriotism in this troubled time, and it was a traditional American song as well.

"I still have to say I like the pumpkin pie best," Peter jested with a twinkle in his eye, as he and Jane walked to the harbor after the celebration concluded.

"Eat too much of it, and you'll have to order a larger waistband," Jane warned with a smile.

The young couple slowly strolled along the pier to watch the last of the sunlight reflect on the water, before sitting down on their favorite bench to wait for the sun to set beneath the sea. They briefly talked about the day, and then fell silent to watch the sun stretch its kaleidoscope of color across the water's rippling surface.

"Jane," Peter said, "I haven't much to offer right now. I don't even know how long the Navy may keep me here. But the thought of leaving here without you is unthinkable to me. I…Jane, I'm trying to ask if you will marry me." Peter felt he had botched it badly because of his nervousness and could feel the heat rising in his face.

Jane was silent for a moment, before looking into Peter's eyes with a wellspring of warmth. "Peter, I love you more than I can express in words. There was a time I thought I would never be able to know that feeling again. I found out after coming here I couldn't run away from myself and had to face things as they were. I'm glad though that I came because I found you. Yes, Peter, I will marry you."

Peter gratefully released the breath he unconsciously held and lowered his lips to Jane's, sealing the commitment they had just made to each other. Their lips briefly parted before coming together again, savoring the moment. Peter gently took Jane's left hand into his and slipped a diamond and emerald ring in the shape of a delicate white rose onto the third finger. "It was my grandmother's," he simply explained.

"Peter," Jane breathed; her voice barely more than a whisper, as emotion threatened to overwhelm her. "It's beautiful."

An American press release in December brought the unsettling news that Joseph Kennedy resigned as the United States Ambassador to Britain on November 6th to help President Roosevelt keep the United States out of the war.

"How can the United States not get involved?" John queried the doctor's lounge. "It's a substantial power with coasts on the Atlantic and the Pacific. I read yesterday in a Japanese paper that the loan the U.S. made to China brings them 'closer to the final test with Japan,' whatever that means."

"What can the United States do to make a difference?" Tom Linn inquired. "It seems they feel separated from European politics, and I don't believe they have an understanding of the Oriental cultures."

"They could help with supplies to Britain to fight the Germans anyway," John countered. "I don't understand why they're taking so long to give Churchill an answer."

There was no answer to John's question. The hospital staff felt caught up in world events that spiraled further out of control almost daily. A glimmer of hope shone briefly for some type of settlement in the East, when it was reported a Japanese delegation was en-route to Batavia, NEI to seek an economic accord between countries. Two days later it was announced Germany, Italy, and Japan had established a military and economic commission to implement their alliance.

"It seems when things start to look up, something else happens," Sally commented.

"What do you mean?" Jane asked.

"The news lately. Things are starting to happen in our own back yard. If you had told me two years ago I'd be concerned with international events, I would have said you were crazy."

"I don't think it will come to blows. After all, your brother was sent here to stiffen defenses and make things ready for more troops. That should discourage any real threat," Jane reasoned.

"I suppose so. I'm probably just letting Dad's last letter bother me. He's been with the Home Guard since Dunkirk and is still waiting for an invasion. Wesley said he didn't think that would happen now. He said the fighting has moved to North Africa. I think deep down Dad's a little disappointed."

"Disappointed about the Germans not invading?" Jane asked in some surprise.

"Well, maybe that's the wrong expression. I think Dad believed it was going to happen and had prepared himself to defend hearth and home. When it didn't happen, I believe he felt a little lost and didn't quite know what to do. I mean, they had wounded Wesley, and Dad wanted to give them what for," Sally explained.

"Yes, I can understand that," Jane acknowledged.

Sally gave Jane a mischievous grin after a few minutes of silence and turned to more personal matters. "So, tell me, have you and Peter set a date yet?"

"We're thinking in the spring, but it will depend on whether he gets transferred someplace else," Jane tentatively answered. "We just don't know yet for sure."

"I see. Maybe you need to just pick a date and trust the good Lord it will be okay."

"You might be right."

It was only a few days before Christmas when Jane and Peter sat on their favorite bench overlooking the harbor. "A penny for them," Peter elicited.

"I was just thinking about something Sally said the other day."

"What's that?"

"That maybe we should just set a date and trust it will be all right," Jane responded a little hesitantly.

"Do you have one in mind?" Peter asked, smiling at her.

"I've thought about April 20th. It was my parents' anniversary. I was only ten when they died in the accident, but I remember them being happy together. I don't know, what do you think?"

"I think it would be just fine."

"Are you sure? There isn't some other date that you would rather have?"

"The date has special meaning for you, and what ever day it is will be special for me from then on. April 20th sounds like a very good day to me," Peter continued with a smile.

"It will be like having my parents with me to be married on their anniversary," Jane confided a little misty eyed.

"We'll make the announcement on Christmas Day after dinner at Helen's, if that's all right with you," Peter suggested.

"She's become almost like a surrogate mother to all of us it seems. I like the idea of making the announcement there very much," Jane agreed.

"Merry Christmas, Helen," Jane gaily proclaimed when she came into Helen's sitting room late Christmas afternoon.

"A Happy Christmas to you as well. Welcome everybody." Helen had decorated with the traditional Christmas ornaments placed around the room and had a potted palm tree off to one side with a Santa train beneath it. The friends happily gathered in the festive room, enjoying the decorations and comfortable camaraderie shared between them and their hostess.

"This is a little like being home," Sally brightly observed. "We always had a train under the tree. Dad would play the conductor, saying all aboard, and Wesley would run the train around the tree. He was an engineer even then, only on a train instead of building things."

The meal was the feast Dr. Jamison had predicted, and everyone's appetite was well sated. But even on this day the war and the threat to their way of life was not forgotten. When Martin Jamison said grace, he asked for the fighting to end soon and world leaders to come to a concordant of agreement.

"I hope your prayer is answered, Dr. Jamison," John commented after dinner. "With Japan strengthening its alliance between Italy and Germany, we could see some hostility if Britain can't come to some kind of an agreement with them."

"You mean the military and economic commission they implemented a few days ago? I agree, but I think their interests are more in the East Indies. Primarily I believe Japan wants to gain more oil concessions and to regain most favored nation status," Dr. Jamison responded.

"If you're right, we could see the so called alliance crumble, leaving Germany with only Italy as an ally," Peter noted, instilling a little hope into the conversation.

"It could be a ploy as you say, Dr. Jamison, but they would have to be handled in such a way so as to save face," Tom Linn cautioned the others.

"Yes, you're most likely right, Tom," Dr. Jamison agreed. "Japan would not want to appear to be backing down because of pressure being put on them. She also wouldn't want to appear slighted by other nations in negotiations."

"Maybe something will come of the negotiations in Batavia," Peter said.

"I hope you're right, Peter," Jane commented.

"I think we should try to put the war and other concerns aside for today," Helen said. "Let's celebrate this day with something enjoyable. How about some Christmas carols around the piano?"

"Helen," Peter said, turning a little red, "Could I say something first?"

"Of course, Peter. What is it?"

"Well, Jane and I want to announce we've set a date of April 20th to be married."

"Why, that's wonderful! Now we do have something to be thankful for to add to our celebration," Helen enthusiastically responded.

"Jane! You didn't tell me!" Sally chided with excitement.

"Have you thought about where the wedding will be?" Helen asked.

"No, not really. I suppose at the little church," Jane replied.

"Why not have it here?" Helen suggested. "I have more then enough space."

"That's very generous of you, Helen, but we wouldn't want to impose on you," Peter interceded.

"Nonsense!" Helen responded with spirit. "Jane and I are friends. Besides, I would enjoy looking forward to something special like this."

"Well, Jane, what do you think?" Peter asked.

"Helen, if you're sure it wouldn't be too much for you, I'd love to be married here," Jane smiled. "It's so peaceful and lovely."

"That's settled then. Now let's enjoy some carols at the piano. Martin, will you play for us please?"

On the day after Christmas many people begin to plan for New Year's Eve. In Japan, on December 26, 1940 Emperor Hirohito opened the Japanese Diet with the customary one-minute speech. The BBC reported the content of the speech that evening after news about the African desert campaign.

"I hope the nations will come to some kind of agreement," Jane commented, as she and Peter listened to the wireless.

"So do I," Peter agreed.

Helen's Landing heard more disturbing news on December 29 over the BBC which reported London's financial district was bombed with incendiaries, causing over a thousand fires and destroying Guildhall.

"Germany again seeks to destroy London by fire. Guildhall is gone, and seven churches dating back to Sir Christopher Wren are burning as well. The walls of flame from this unholy act by Nazi Germany glow like daylight across the night's darkened sky. It is only a few short weeks since German planes destroyed God's holy temple in Coventry. The charred rubble from the Houses of God lay in deep smoldering piles with some saying it is a foretaste of *The Revelation to John*."

"It's terrible," Sally lamented at this latest German air offensive against England. "They just keep destroying everything."

"I expect we're doing some damage ourselves," John said. "At least I believe we're making some head way in North Africa. Have you heard from Helen how Andy is faring in all this?"

"Andy? No, I haven't. Oh, I do hope he's all right." Sally prayed that all the men fighting in the war were safe. She couldn't help wondering though about the *Mariah* and Andy Burns in particular. She reasoned to herself it was because Helen had become a good friend.

CHAPTER 17

Lieutenant Commander Andrew Burns was sitting across a small corner table from Lieutenant Quentin Patterson, MD, having a quiet Sunday supper. Doc had suggested his London club, which overlooked a private anchorage that was temporarily under the Navy's command as a place to relax and have an uninterrupted meal. The menu was limited, but the food was tasty. The aged chef brought out of retirement as the war escalated and younger men left their jobs to join in the fight had worked a small culinary miracle.

"It isn't up to pre-war standards, but I believe the chef is a bit more adept than our cook on board the *Mariah,*" Dr. Patterson commented, as he sipped his pre-war wine.

"You would know better than me, Doc," Andy noted.

"So, tell me, how does command sit after a few voyages?"

"You may well ask. I can appreciate Troy Edmon more than I can tell you," Andy responded with feeling. "You know, Doc, sometimes I'm amazed at what the men put up with. They're drilled until they perform like zombies. They're bombed and strafed by the enemy, given little rest or comfort, often lying down with damp blankets, and they still act on command, when they should be running for their lives. I expect though you're wondering about making the final commitment for them. It's what I've trained for most of my life. I know that sounds like a pat answer, but it is a truthful one."

"Yes, I suppose it is. I could say the same about medicine," Dr. Patterson thoughtfully reflected.

"You make life and death decisions every day, Doc. At least I have the benefit of traditions and regulations to draw from, along with the knowledge passed on by my previous commanders. I've learned something from each of my shipmates and not just from the officers."

"Gentleman," the elderly waiter diffidently interrupted. "I'm sorry to disturb you, but an air raid will be starting soon. You must go to the shelter."

"I didn't here any sirens," Dr. Patterson objected.

"We can hear the sound of planes coming outside, like last August. The sirens will sound very soon, I'm sure. Please, sirs, go to the shelter," the waiter pleaded with urgency.

"Lieutenant Patterson, we need to get to the ship," Andy ordered, automatically reverting to his role as a ship's commander. "Thank you for the warning, but we'll need to leave while we can."

"We're close to the harbor. It should only take a few minutes to get there on foot," Quentin Patterson responded, recognizing Andy's sense of duty and concern for his men at having the ship in danger and not being aboard. Shrugging at the decision to give up the safety of shelter, the waiter left them to seek it himself.

The two men hurriedly paid their bill and walked with purpose toward the harbor's main entrance gate. The mournful sound of air raid sirens disturbed the crisp winter night air, as Andy and Quentin Patterson showed their identification at the perimeter gate and joined other sailors rushing toward the quayside to catch the duty boat. Andy felt a momentary thrill at seeing the ship loom ever closer at her outer harbor anchorage, admiring her graceful lines even in this time of hurry to be aboard, when the first bombs began to drop on the city. He had always felt a sense of companionship when approaching the ships where he served, but the *Mariah* was different; more like a child he had to nurture and protect.

"Sir, Lieutenant Roden is on the bridge," the Officer of the Deck answered to Andy's inquiry. He was the new midshipman who joined after the *Mariah* had returned from meeting the *Orion.* Andy believed his name was Barnes.

"Very well, carry on," Andy ordered, returning Barnes' salute.

"Number One, how do things stand?" Andy asked, stepping onto the bridge.

"Sir, all guns are manned. And I ordered the engines brought to stand-by in case we're ordered to sea," Mason briskly responded.

"Good, we'll just have to wait and see. The men should all be aboard by now who were at the canteen," Andy noted.

"I see fires starting in the city," Mason reported, pointing toward the shore. Andy briefly watched the fires springing up across the city as another flight of enemy planes flew overhead, before giving the order to open fire.

A pall of smoke could be seen drifting over the capital when dawn broke across the London sky. The men aboard the *Mariah* heard over the wireless that the fires during the multiple airborne raids damaged seven century's old churches designed by Sir Christopher Wren the previous night.

"A dirty shame, 'hat's what I say, a dirty shame," Bert lamented to his friend Ernie.

"Them Germans, 'hey're a pack a dirty ferinners, what-cha 'spect," came the terse reply.

"To burn churches, why, it's anti-Christ, 'hat's what it tis, anti-Christ," Bert pronounced with feeling. Ernie had no response to this profound statement and could only shake his head in sad agreement.

"Number One, join me in my cabin," Andy ordered shortly after the attacks on London ended.

"Sir."

"We have received orders to sail on Saturday. The holiday leave will have to be cut short I'm afraid."

"I understand, sir."

"One other thing," Andy noted, looking up at his first officer.

"Sir."

"I'm ordering you to take leave as of noon today until 1800 hours Friday." Andy held up his hand when Mason started to protest that he needed the time to have the ship ready for sea. "What needs to be taken care of I will see to. Besides, it gives me the opportunity to better evaluate the junior officers' strengths and weaknesses," Andy explained, while also giving a lesson in command. "A dose of *the old man* once in a while keeps the men at their peak efficiency. And, I need a well rested first officer in the weeks to come."

"Yes sir, thank you. I'll leave a list of what needs to be done before I leave," Mason responded, with a grin spreading across his face. "Besides, I was taught in officer's training to never argue with my commanding officer."

"I'm glad to hear that," Andy lightly jested, before dismissing his first officer. He felt his choice of a second in command was sound at the time, and Mason Roden was proving that choice to be the correct one. The short break was a lesson as well as a kindness. Andy knew from experience that the first officer was the most harried soul aboard the ship. He had to keep the *Mariah* ready for sea at a moment's notice and be the commander's right hand, while at the same time act as a buffer between the crew and her captain.

Andy went out onto the deck the following Friday morning in search of Tim Parker. He found him with a new rating at the starboard 20-mm gun, patiently showing him how to strip and clean it and how to open the breech quickly to reload it when jammed. Tim spent hours with someone if they showed potential or interest in a job. His philosophy was simple, "If you're gonna do it, you might as well learn it right."

"Mr. Parker," Andy briskly addressed his warrant officer.

Looking up, Tim quickly came to attention and saluted when he saw his commanding officer addressing him, nudging the baby-faced rating to do the same. "Sir!"

"Have all enlisted personnel aboard by 1900 hours, we weigh at 0700 tomorrow," Andy ordered.

"Aye, sir. Is there anything else you need, sir?" Parker asked.

"Well," Andy drawled, "You might consider having the 20-mm gun put back together. It probably would be of more use that way."

"Aye sir," Parker chuckled.

"Carry on, Mr. Parker."

Returning the salute to Tim Parker and the open mouthed rating, Andy returned to the bridge to consult with his navigator. He had found that Brian Jones was high-spirited and possessed an uncanny sense of direction. He wondered if there might be some truth to the legendary Davy Jones, often called the *Spirit of the Sea,* with a possible ancestral connection to this Mr. Jones.

"Mr. Jones, review our charts for the Indian Ocean and South China Sea," Andy ordered. "We may be in need of some specific ones for island groupings as well."

"What ho! A tropical cruise, perchance to leave old man winter behind! I shall go through the charts right away, sir," Brian responded with irrepressible enthusiasm. "Are there any specific ones I should have on hand?"

"Be sure you have the last enemy positions for the Mediterranean Sea and the Island of Crete. We'll need Alexandria Harbor as well. Other than that, the ones I mentioned earlier," Andy told him.

"Aye sir, I'll get right on it."

Andy found the list left by his first officer to be fairly short. Mason had organized work parties while the *Mariah* was docked. The crew chipped away rust and peeling paint along the *Mariah*'s sleek hull where salt-water seas had eroded and peeled away her protective cover and finagled an unheard of slot to have her boiler cleaned. The new primer and dazzle paint applied to the hull gave her a different appearance, making her harder for the enemy to see on the open ocean.

Mariah took on fuel and ammunition while the first officer was gone and replenished her water supply. The task reminded Andy of when he had completed the same task during Dunkirk. It amused him a little when he observed Midshipman Barnes practice issuing conning orders to the empty bridge and listened for a few minutes before making his presence known.

"Not too bad, Mr. Barnes," Andy said, stepping onto the bridge, "But the quartermaster usually replies about then."

"Sir," Barnes had croaked, as his face turned crimson and his Adam's Apple bobbed up and down in his nervous surprise.

"Tell me, Mr. Barnes, do you hope to have a command one day?" Andy asked, smiling briefly to help ease Barnes' nervousness at having conversation with his commanding officer.

"Yes sir," Barnes whispered. Then, with a little more assurance, "Yes sir, someday," pausing a moment before he continued speaking with reverence. "A ship as beautiful as this."

"Yes, she is a beautiful ship," Andy agreed, momentarily sharing with this young beginner what all sailors felt about the decks beneath their feet. "Carry on, Mr. Barnes," he ordered, returning to his role as the ship's commander.

"Aye, sir."

Andy took time each day to observe the four new sub-lieutenants attached to the *Mariah.* One who had some experience with boilers and machinery was assigned to Mr. Thompson in the engine room. Lieutenant Thompson commented a few days later, "He'll do," which was a fair endorsement from the only other officer aboard who worked his way up from the ranks. Andy considered Kirk Thompson, along with Tim Parker, God's gift to the *Mariah.*

Three other new officers were assigned to the various needs of the ship according to their strengths and weaknesses. One was a little shaky but might stiffen up after gaining more experience. He would have to be watched more closely for now. Andy knew replacements were becoming scarcer, as increasing hostilities demanded more men and machinery. All the replacements appeared able to complete assigned tasks and delegate daily chores to the ranks. How the new officers would function in battle was a question yet to be answered.

It was a cold damp morning when the *Mariah* prepared to sail with the looming threat of a heavy snowstorm. The crew was at their stations when Andy stepped onto the bridge and addressed his first officer, "Number One." The previous evening the two men met to review the sailing orders and to bring Mason up to date on where the ship stood.

"Engines are on stand-by, anchor is up and down, sir," Mason reported.

"Very well, weigh anchor, all ahead slow," Andy ordered. "Course is 0–2-0."

"Anchor's away," came the quick reply.

"My course is 0–2-0, speed is slow," the quartermaster reported.

"Midshipman Barnes," Andy beckoned.

"Yes, sir."

"Mr. Barnes, take us to the harbor limits," Andy ordered, before stepping away from the bridge command position.

The blood drained from Barnes' face, as he stepped to the center of the bridge to take command of the ship, giving a choked, "Yes, sir," to orders given.

The first turn came, and with an effort Midshipman Barnes properly gave the first active duty bridge command of his Naval career. The quartermaster immediately made a crisp response, knowing, as Andy did, this was how an officer was made, starting with that first timid step. The young midshipman had found his voice as the *Mariah* approached the harbor limits, confidently addressing his commanding officer.

"Sir, we are approaching the harbor limits."

"Very well, Mr. Barnes, you are relieved," Andy solemnly responded, before stepping with authority back into the command position at the center of the bridge.

"Speed is slow, course is 0-4-5, sir," Barnes carefully reported.

Nodding gravely, Andy took back the bridge. He knew Midshipman Barnes would never forget this day, just as he had not forgotten the first time he took the bridge and conned his first ship out of the harbor. Young Barnes would have to grow into the job of commanding ships and men quickly to fill the increasing losses this conflict was bringing. Andy was sure those losses would increase by the numbers before it was over.

CHAPTER 18

The *Mariah* entered the English Channel at midmorning with orders to join a large convoy. She was to serve as an escort to the merchant freighters and troop transporters bound for North Africa laden with men and equipment. The brewing weather conditions promised a heavy snowstorm that would offer a double-edged sword of protection and danger. No enemy planes could fly today with minimal visibility through the low lying clouds, but the convoy might never see the danger coming if an enemy submarine spotted them.

The merchant freighters began to appear in twos and threes like ghostly shadows out of a swirling white void in the late afternoon. Nerves grew taut until the recognition signal was given to the challenge issued each time a new ship approached the convoy's swelling number of vessels.

Andy knew the troop ships scheduled to join the group at 1830 hours were filled to capacity with British and Canadian Army personnel who would be fighting Rommel's Army in the desert and ancient towns of North Africa. He wondered briefly if any would walk across the desert lands of biblical times where prophets were tested before God sent them out to deliver His message to the nations. He also remembered the stories of ancient armies rising up against God's enemies and wondered if the Allied armies would be found worthy in His sight.

Several days passed with no enemy activity which lulled the men into a false sense of security. Fog and cloud cover with intermittent snow squalls had concealed the long line of merchant and troop ships' southerly turn into the Atlantic. Increasingly warmer weather brought clear skies, leaving the lightly armed troop transporters and merchant freighters more vulnerable to the enemy's unmerciful offensive tactics.

Enemy sea and air attacks were ravaging the supply convoys crossing the North Atlantic, causing shortages in everything from cloth to fuel. *Mariah*'s crew heard over the wireless that food rationing in Britain would be reduced or increased weekly, as the situation demanded. The north-south passage was becoming more hazardous as well since the Tripartite Pact was signed. The Italian Navy was cruising in familiar waters with Axis air bases close by for enemy bombers to utilize.

"Planes three o'clock," a lookout yelled.

"General quarters, general quarters, all men to your battle stations," echoed throughout the ship, when Andy pushed the alarm to warn the crew that danger was approaching. The determination to not allow their shipmates to see their fear gave the men a look of cold unfeeling purpose, as they loaded the guns and brought them to bear to await the commence firing order.

"I see them, sir. They're turning off the port bow," Mason reported, pointing eastward.

"They'll line up to attack with the sun behind them," Andy stated. "Report to your battle station."

"Yes, sir." Mason knew it would be more difficult for the gunners to take aim with the sun blinding them.

"Here they come!" a gunner shouted, while he anxiously moved his finger closer to the trigger.

Two bombs straddled a troop ship, sending a shower of splinters across the lower decks that cut men down where they stood with no regard to rank. A second wave of dive bombers descended as the convoy continued its appointed course. The escorts brought every gun to bear in the effort to shoot the attacking enemy planes out of the sky and protect their charges. But one plane broke through the barrage and, in a twist of fate, sent a single bomb down a minelayer's smokestack that exploded in the boiler room. Thick black smoke instantly billowed skyward through a rupture where the hull was peeled back like a banana skin. The concussion from the blast set off the stricken ship's mines within seconds that finished the job in a blinding explosion that tore the ship apart and scattered her crew and broken hull across the ocean floor.

"Up 100, fire," Mason ordered, forcing his mind away from the total oblivion he had just witnessed.

"Right full rudder," Andy ordered, conning the *Mariah* away from the threat of any unexploded mines. The ship to his starboard, about 1,000 yards away, remained on course, running directly into a stray mine that broke her back on impact. "Steer 1-2-0," Andy ordered.

"Steering 1-2-0," the quartermaster calmly reported.

"Mr. Barnes, try to see if there are any survivors," Andy ordered on the heels of the routine reply.

"Aye, sir. Sir," Barnes cried out a moment later, "I see some men on the forward deck of the freighter. It looks like they're trying to lower a life boat."

Looking to starboard, Andy could see the stricken ship was settling. "Steer 1–4-0, reduce speed. Mr. Barnes, inform Mr. Parker to be prepared to take on survivors," he ordered.

"Yes sir," came Barnes' automatic response before he started down the bridge ladder to carry out his orders.

"Mr. Parker, Commander Burns said to prepare to take on survivors. He's turned toward and slowed," Barnes conveyed.

"We'll be ready," Parker assured the young midshipman addressing him. Though old enough to be his father, Roger Barnes was an officer, and Parker treated him with the same self-discipline he employed with all the officers. *This one wasn't too bad,* he thought. Tim also knew Barnes had passed the first test toward commanding a ship when he successfully conned the *Mariah* through the harbor. "You men there, lower the nets. Be ready to assist," he ordered, as the *Mariah* carefully approached the survivors.

The men in the water knew this was their only hope. No rescue boats would be lowered to save them with the threat of enemy planes returning and catching a ship unable to maneuver quickly. Some climbed the rescue nets using the last of their waning strength, before falling to the deck in exhaustion. Others were pulled up by waiting hands, with their burns and wounds roughly handled, until they could be lowered to the deck by the same hands now gentled after freeing a victim from the sea's hungry grasp.

Roger Barnes returned to the bridge after helping to rescue a badly burned man whose face was a swollen mass of hideous blisters and blackened flesh that hung from his body. Barnes tried to be careful not to hurt the man, but he screamed in tortured pain, as the agony of contact with his stricken body penetrated pulsing raw nerve endings. Roger turned away then, as bile rose in his throat, hoping to gain control of his emotions before reaching the bridge and Commander Burns.

"Sir, Dr. Patterson and Harris are with the survivors, there were twenty-three," Roger reported, tightly clenching his jaw in an effort to control his voice. He could still hear the echo of screams and smell the stench of charred flesh from the man he had tried to help.

"Thank you, Mr. Barnes, and well done," Andy acknowledged to Barnes' first experience with the human element of war. He remembered all too clearly a few months past his own cruel awakening that the ravages of war brought to humankind. It momentarily saddened him to realize he was becoming battle hardened to human suffering in the wake of so much tragedy during the past year.

When the planes moved off Mason returned to the bridge to report. "Sir, two enemy planes damaged. I've had extra lookouts posted in case another wave approaches."

"Very well," Andy acknowledged. "We'll have to wait and see. We could have some trouble, unless it comes yet today."

"Do you think U-boats will be waiting?" Mason asked.

"It's possible. If it were me, I'd choose a place where I could maneuver and had plenty of depth. Mr. Jones, where would you say there is depth and maneuvering room?" Andy asked.

"Here, sir, on the west side of Crete where there's better thermal layers. That is if you're thinking submarines." Brian Jones was beginning to understand his commander, and knew he liked a straightforward answer. Sometimes though, because of the anomalies the sea and weather conditions caused, there was no absolute answer.

"We should be approaching Alexandria before nightfall tomorrow," Andy thoughtfully considered. He knew the German and Italian forces now worked in tandem. Whatever the British believed about the Italian Army, their submarine force was something to be reckoned with. He was also learning to respect Brian Jones' abilities as a sailor and gave his opinion weight when reaching a decision. "If you're right, Mr. Jones, it could be a busy night."

The convoy bravely continued to sail toward its destination, as Andy thought about the ships and men already sacrificed in a war barely one year old. The intensity and savageness of the attacks on both sides in 1940 increased with the passing months. It appeared 1941 would continue on the same path, with the promise of even greater violence before this war would end.

"Commander, the lead escort signaled a possible sighting," he heard over the voice pipe in his sea cabin.

"On my way," Andy acknowledged, quickly scooping up his jacket and placing his hat, bearing the Lieutenant Commander insignia, on his head.

The *Mariah* was bringing up the rear of the convoy to keep an eye out for stragglers, or ships having mechanical breakdowns. The first day out one freighter kept breaking down and finally told to return to Harwich for repairs. Some freighters being used would already be in the breaker's yard and the metal melted down for use in new ships with the latest innovations if the current need had not outweighed that consideration.

Andy mounted the bridge and raised his glasses to scan the sea's surface for any irregularity before conferring with his first officer. "Has anyone else seen anything?"

"No sir, not since the initial report," Mason answered.

"Torpedo 2,000 yards off the port quarter," a lookout yelled, shattering the quiet.

"Left full rudder, all ahead flank," Andy ordered.

"Left full rudder, all ahead flank," the helmsman evenly replied.

"Sound general quarters. Mr. Barnes, signal the lead escort, am under attack, am taking evasive action," Andy continued, with the orders rolling off his lips as if making moves on a chess board. "Number One, have Mr. Parker prepare to drop depth charges."

"Aye sir," Mason acknowledged, as he left the bridge thinking about the sudden attack when they returned from Singapore in the early spring of 1940.

"Navigator, what's our depth?" Andy asked.

"Over 100 fathoms sir," Brian quickly answered.

Roger Barnes managed to send the signal, and then stood rooted to the spot. He had felt a wave of fear run through him when the lookout yelled torpedo, and still felt shaky inside. "How can Commander Burns be so cool, so positive of his next move?" Roger wondered. "He acts like it's just another exercise to be gotten through." He jumped, when an explosion near the front of the convoy rang through the darkness. A moment later the night sky suddenly turned into day which slowly dimmed to reflect the stricken ship's fires on the water's dark foreboding surface.

"Mr. Barnes, inform the lead escort am commencing depth charging," Andy ordered.

"Yes, sir," Roger responded automatically. The order brought him out of his reverie, instilling a sense of calm at the ordinary chain of command to perform his duty. He would learn over time that this was why the Navy drilled its men until the response was instinctive, despite a man's fear in battle.

The convoy started breaking up with ships turning away from each other in all directions, creating chaos for the escorts and targets of opportunity for the enemy. A merchant ship was torpedoed causing casualties, but the damage was mostly above the water line and it continued on course. A second escort laid out a grid pattern with the *Mariah* to depth charge the submarine responsible for the attack. They kept it up for two hours with inconclusive results.

The *Mariah* came alongside the torpedoed freighter during the night and took off some of the injured that required more than a pharmacist mate's attention. Andy sent extra hands to help the wounded ship's crew shore up the damaged hull in the hope she would be able to maintain the convoy's speed of eight knots and not be left behind as a vulnerable straggler, nor become a liability should the convoy elect to slow its speed to protect her.

Dr. Patterson was still attending to the wounded when the sun lifted above the water on its timeless journey across the sea. He had operated on six severely wounded men and was concerned he might have to operate again before reaching a hospital. He had saved one man's leg using a procedure developed by French doctors who had discovered the technique toward the end of The Great War. It amazed and troubled him that most medical advances were made to benefit mankind because a war made it necessary.

"Doc," Andy greeted, when he entered the infirmary at mid morning. "What should I tell the shore personnel to prepare for when we dock?"

"Hello Andy," Dr. Patterson tiredly acknowledged. "We'll need ambulances for at least eight stretcher cases. I'd like to go with the one. I'm hoping for hospital conditions if I have to operate again. We have thirty walking wounded to transport as well. How long before we dock?"

"Probably nine hours, if the Germans and Italians don't interfere that is."

"I see. How come Mason isn't here?" Quentin Patterson asked somewhat apprehensively. "He generally takes care of these details."

"I thought I'd see for myself, commander's privilege. I also wanted to see if you needed more hands for the time being."

"Troy Edmon taught you well, my friend. I think we're okay for now with what we have. I'll need some extra help when the walking wounded disembark."

"I'll see that you have the men you need," Andy assured him. "In the mean time, try to get some rest, Doc. We can't afford to have you out of commission." Andy waited for a nod of understanding before returning to the bridge.

"Harris, I'm going to lie down in the pharmacy for a nap. Call me if there's any change," Dr. Patterson said, after Andy left him.

"We'll be okay here for now, sir. You get some rest," Emil Harris urged. Harris had a fierce admiration for the doctor and would go to great lengths to see he took care of himself. Dr. Patterson had said he could easily become a male nurse, and Harris worked hard to live up to that high standard.

The *Mariah* continued steadily on course, while her lookouts ceaselessly scanned the sea and sky for any new menace. The strain was greater after the last two attacks, as fear crept into the crew's thoughts of yet another enemy attack occurring before reaching their destination. Rumors circulated overnight about convoys being mercilessly stalked in the North Atlantic between Iceland and England. The vision of sinking ships and desperate men in the water were still fresh in the crew's minds, leaving the uncomfortable thought that the same tactic could be used in the Mediterranean.

Smoke was rising from the waterfront when the *Mariah* entered the harbor limits, after an air raid ended an hour before their arrival. The enemy saw the approaching convoy on the horizon near the end of their bombing run and radioed their base to send more planes. Lady Luck was with the British though that day, with all the remaining German aircraft engaged on a mission to intercept a British aerial attack to the north. Once the gangplank was in place the wounded were quickly taken ashore the first to leave. Few were left to talk about their rescue, or those left behind in a salt-water grave with no marker and no proper ceremony to memorialize their lives.

CHAPTER 19

The *Mariah* came to life after spending an uneventful night. A rare overnight rain moving south off the Mediterranean into the northern desert prevented any enemy bombing raids, allowing the merchant ships to off-load their cargo without interruption. The merchant ships would soon take on goods for the return journey to feed a hungry British population, before the sailors, and their ships that survived, would be given a few days rest before the dangerous cycle began again.

"Leave is limited to inside the perimeter," Andy concluded, in the morning briefing. He was talking with Mason and Sub-lieutenant Anderson, one of the new officers who would be standing the next watch as OOD, before going ashore to turn in his report.

"Yes, sir," Mason responded.

Andy went through his mail after the briefing and found four letters postmarked Helen's Landing, Malaya. It always amazed him how the mail kept up with them. Two were from his mother and one appeared to be from Dr. Jamison, but the fourth letter had handwriting he didn't recognize. He was pleasantly surprised upon opening it to find a note from Sally Vilmont. She began by explaining the *Mariah* had rescued her brother, Wesley, when he was wounded in Holland. "*What a small world it is that my brother should wind up on a ship where you were the first officer,*" she wrote. She concluded by saying she hoped he wouldn't think her too forward by corresponding with him but felt it important to thank the *Mariah*'s commander and her crew.

Andy remembered a rather nice looking spirited nurse with auburn hair and a smattering of freckles across a rather cute, slightly upturned, nose when he had visited Malaya in the early spring of 1940. She had called herself "Nurse Sally" when he first visited his mentor, Martin Jamison. He learned later she was Sally Vilmont and had been one of his mother's nurses after her unexpected surgery. Andy wondered if it would be protocol to write back and decided to give it some thought.

His mother's letters were chatty and full of news about people he had grown up with. She also spoke about a wedding to be held at the house. Andy remembered the couple and what his mother had said, "*Mark my words, those two will be married inside another year.*" Andy thought she would be neck deep in preparations and loving every minute of it. Martin Jamison was right; she seemed to thrive on activity. His letter talked about current events and his growing concern about stability in the East with statements by Japanese officials affirming their intention to establish a "new order" in East Asia. Andy thought about this latest international development, and wondered whether their new sailing orders were related.

Andy sought out Dr. Patterson early that evening to ask how things had gone at the base hospital. He entered the infirmary to find the doctor propped back in his chair reading an American newspaper and sipping a brandy. "Hello, Doc. I see you're catching up on your reading."

"Have you seen this yet? I must say if what I've just read is true, it's certainly a round about way to lend aid to your friend and ally," Dr. Patterson answered by way of greeting.

"What does it say?"

"Here, read it for yourself."

FDR sends Lend Lease Bill to House and Senate the headline read in large bolded print. The article continued, stating on Friday, January 10, 1941 President Roosevelt introduced a multi-billion dollar bill to the United States House of Representatives and Senate proposing aid to Britain through a lend-lease program. The report emphasized the British were fighting to restore democracy in Europe against an aggressive and dictatorial rule, outlining the fall of Eastern European countries to Germany and the past year's fighting in Norway and Western Europe.

"Well, what do you think, my friend?" Dr. Patterson asked.

"The aid might be of value if it comes soon. But if their Congress sits on it, it could be too little too late," Andy thoughtfully answered. "According to news reports, not all Americans want to get involved. This may be the compromise: send equipment, not men."

"It could be," Dr. Patterson agreed. "What did you need when you came down?"

"Just thought I'd find out how things went at the base hospital today. I know you were concerned about a couple of the men."

"We won one, but lost another," Dr. Patterson replied matter-of-factly.

"I see. Could we have done anything more before we docked?"

"No, not really. The human body is a marvelous machine, but it can only take so much abuse before it quits working. The only thing that would have saved the man was to not be shot at to begin with. And the only way for that to happen is to not have a bloody war," Dr. Patterson responded with feeling. Then, taking a deep draw on his pipe, he exhaled slowly. "Sorry about that, not your fault. The politicians started this a long time ago. But thank you for allowing me to let off steam."

"Any time, Doc. Get some rest, tomorrow will be a better day."

Andy was finishing up with Lieutenant Thompson regarding the engine room status the following morning when Mason and Dr. Patterson appeared as ordered. "The fueling was completed yesterday evening," Thompson reported. "Engines are purring like kittens. I checked the shafts myself, and they look to be okay, sir. I don't think the mine that went off under the freighter did any damage to us. The freighter probably absorbed the shock."

"Carry on then, Mr. Thompson," Andy ordered, dismissing him to return to the knobs and dials he watched like an anxious father at his daughter's first recital.

"Sit down, gentlemen. There's coffee if you'd like," Andy invited, pouring a cup. Most people believed the English drank only tea, but in the morning Andy liked a good strong cup of Navy coffee. "I asked you both to come so I would only need to go over this once. As you know, we've been doing convoy duty since the end of last August between here and Britain. We now have orders to sail to Singapore in company with six other ships and a second escort leaving this evening. The Admiralty hasn't told me why the change from our usual duty, I can only speculate."

"It makes sense, sir. I mean, we would be able to fill them in on the latest tactics being used," Mason reasoned.

"Yes, that's possibly the reason for the change. Doctor, your job will be to insure the infirmary is ready for what ever is in store, as always. Number One, all liberty is canceled in preparation to sail."

"Yes, sir. Our stores are being delivered at 0930. We're second on the list. There wasn't a lot, and it should all be stowed away in ample time," Mason reported.

"Good. Doctor, what about you?" Andy asked.

"What supplies I need are coming with the rest of the stores, except the narcotics. I'll have to sign for those at the base pharmacy. If I go over this morning, I should be back in about an hour."

"I'll walk with you as far as the admiral's office after we finish here,"

Andy said. The conference continued another twenty minutes, with details from the fresh water supply to ammunition reviewed to ensure the *Mariah* was completely self-sufficient once she put to sea.

With practiced precision, the *Mariah* entered the Mediterranean Sea at dusk on the first leg of her journey. Clouds could be seen in the distance when they left the anchorage with the smell of rain in the air. The seas looked choppy, but not threatening, when the ship turned east toward the Suez Canal to meet the gathering convoy.

"Looks like rain coming in," Brian Jones commented.

"Number One, post extra lookouts," Andy ordered. "Be sure they stay alert both sea and sky." He knew the low-lying clouds and increased wind would soon ground enemy planes, but the possibility of a submarine attack was very real.

"Right away, sir."

The winds became more intense, when *Mariah* and her charges turned toward the Suez Canal where two other ships joined them. One was clearly carrying British troops. The other was the minelayer, *Victoria,* making her first voyage with a new commander, which would serve as the second escort ship. Andy noted that, unlike the journey between England and North Africa, the *Victoria* carried no mines in her cradle while she served as an escort vessel.

Mason had the midnight to four watch that night and felt a twinge of sympathy for the soldiers, as he observed their ship corkscrew through the seas. He thought most of the Army troops would be sea sick from the irregular motion, causing the inner ear to lack a sense of balance. He felt blessed that particular affliction had never affected him.

About 0230 Andy came to the bridge, when he sensed a change in the ship's motion. "Number One," he acknowledged, before looking over the log and reviewing the chart. Looking skyward, all Andy could see were angry clouds rushing toward each other on a collision course of opposing wind directions. Violent waves crashed against *Mariah*'s hull, as she fought to hold her course. Andy could see water cascading off the lifeboats of their nearest companion ship, as the increasingly turbulent sea reached toward the sky.

"Number One, have the duty personnel string life lines along the decks and pull the watch keepers back to shelter," he ordered. "We don't want to lose anyone."

"Yes, sir. What about the others, sir, should we signal them to do the same?"

Andy raised his glasses to scan the nearest ships and saw someone in khaki leaning over the rail of the troop carrier fall, when a towering wave washed across the deck. The rapid flow of receding water carried the flailing soldier toward the deck's edge until he crashed into a gun mounting. "Bloody fool," Andy muttered, while he continued to watch the sea soaked soldier crawl to safety and disappear below. "It appears you better. Our Army brethren are apparently unfamiliar with the sea and her rules. It looks as if the *Victoria* is already starting," he concluded, watching the ship beyond the troop carrier through his glasses.

The impact of rain driven sideways by howling winds at dawn dulled a man's brain and pelted his face like needles. Watch keeping was kept to the relative safety of the bridge when the decks below became too dangerous, even with lifelines, for men to walk upon. A submarine couldn't attack in these seas unless her captain was beyond reason. Andy had not seen a storm this severe in several years.

"Sir," Midshipman Barnes called out, "The troop ship is signaling."

Mason quickly brought up his glasses to see what they were saying. "What is it, Number One?" Andy asked.

"Their pumps are failing. Can we send any over," Mason replied after a moment.

"Heaven have mercy! How in these seas?" the rating on watch exclaimed.

"Quiet there," Parker gruffly reprimanded.

"How indeed," Andy softly breathed. "Mr. Parker, go below and ask Lieutenant Thompson to come to the bridge. Maybe we could rig something like a boson's chair to ferry the pumps over."

"Reporting as ordered, sir," Thompson briskly stated, coming to attention.

"At ease, Lieutenant. Has Mr. Parker filled you in?" Andy asked.

"Yes, sir."

"What do you think, can we do it?"

Thompson rubbed a hand over his chin in momentary thought before answering his commander's inquiry. The idea when Parker had first told him about it seemed daft. Now that he saw the other ship's decks being brutalized by the seas, he knew they had to try. "I believe we can, sir, if we put enough sea space between us," he affirmed, while instilling a note of caution. "We could fire a weighted rope over using a Vary pistol. It should give us the distance we need. We'll have to be careful not to ram her though. Have to keep a close eye to the helm," he warned.

"How soon can you be ready?" Andy asked.

"If Mr. Parker had a couple-a men help bring the equipment, about thirty minutes. Normally, we could do the job with a whip rope from a lower yardarm. We can't work from the lower deck though. The seas would be too high."

"What about from here?" Andy asked.

"It's about the right range. Yes sir, I think it would work," Thompson surmised, eyeing the troubled ship once more.

"Make the necessary preparations then," Andy ordered.

"Yes, sir," Thompson crisply responded, as he saluted and left the bridge to assemble the necessary tools and equipment.

"Mr. Barnes, signal, *Will be attempting to send over pumps soon.* Then tell the *Victoria* to have all other ships take station 2,000 yards ahead of us," Andy ordered.

Thompson told his junior officer about the upcoming attempt to send equipment across in the heavy seas to the troubled troop carrier. "Be sure you keep a close eye to the engines. Make sure the bridge gets a quick response when they call for more or less power, or we'll lose the chance and very possibly the ship as well."

"Don't you worry, Mr. Thompson, we'll keep things under control here," his second assured him. Nodding, Thompson motioned to Parker and the two ratings with him to gather up the tools and head for the bridge.

The tense excitement of the moment crackled throughout the ranks, as the time to initiate the makeshift plan approached. Crossing himself, Thompson lifted the Vary pistol and took careful aim before he fired. A length of narrow line spun out to trail behind the attached heavy weight catapulting out toward the sea.

Wind-whipped swells reached upward with curling hook-like fingers trying to snatch the slender life-giving cord from the air as it passed across the void between the ships with astonishing grace, tracing a thin curly line through the air. The heavy wrench pulling the slim cord to the stricken ship fell with deceptive speed onto the upper deck of the other ship. Anxious hands drew it secure before the sea could snatch the thin cord away in its cruel appetite for the unwary. Once the lead line was secure, the crippled ship's crew drew the heavier rope across in preparation to making the transfer. The troop ship's elderly captain watched with a careful eye, hoping the Navy was up to the challenge the sea was meting out this day.

Andy watched when the first pump started across the void to be sure it was moving smoothly. The small cargo swung wildly in the opposing winds while the two ships' crews worked to make the transfer. The *Mariah* was buffeted with intermittent winds from opposite directions, making her drift one direction then change and slide in another, as she rode the increasingly unpredictable swells. It took ten minutes of careful movement over angry seas to send the first pump across. It seemed an eternity for Andy, as he made constant minute adjustments to course and speed to keep the *Mariah* in check with the seas. Three pumps made the precarious journey before disengaging and putting some distance between the two ships. The simple signal from the transporter, "*Thanks mate, we can make it now,*" was enough to satisfy *Mariah*'s crew.

The seas began to quiet and the rain started to abate by nightfall, as the small convoy moved out of the storm. Dr. Patterson and Harris were kept busy throughout the day with a steady stream of the unlucky. "I don't know if I make a good sailor. I find rough seas to be most unpleasant," the doctor pronounced that evening.

"Doc, at least you're dry down here," Mason laughed at the understatement. "Up on the bridge you get all wet."

"That's what I mean," Dr. Patterson replied with an impish grin.

Intercepted radio reports kept the crew informed about England and Churchill's appeal to the United States a week after President Roosevelt sent the Lend-Lease Bill to the American Congress. The officers and crew listened and wondered how long it might be before help would be offered.

"At least Churchill is keeping the issue before the public," Mason commented.

"I hope it does some good in the United States," Dr. Patterson noted.

The crew was not idle during this easy passage through the Suez Canal and into the Persian Gulf enroute to meet a convoy out of Australia at Jakarta. Drills were stepped up to hone any rough edges off emergency response times. Andy smiled when he remembered Dr. Patterson's comment, "I finally get back to the tropics and instead of lounging on the deck dreaming of native beauties, I'm on the deck simulating casualties and fire control. I knew I should have joined the Army! At least they get to camp out." The men had a good laugh from it, and Andy knew it was the doctor's way of relieving some of the grumbling at having to drill.

The *Mariah* had a quiet, almost boring, passage through the Indian Ocean and Java Sea, sighting only one ship in the distance that appeared to be Portuguese. She dropped her anchor on February 5, 1941, in Singapore Harbor after sailing with the first convoy to bring reinforcements and equipment to the Malayan Peninsula.

CHAPTER 20

Wesley Vilmont and his engineering crew were inspecting battle emplacements at Pattani Baharu on the northeastern Malayan Peninsula by March 1, before moving on to the newly improved airstrip at Kuantan Airfield. A mini-hospital, as Wesley called it, was being built to Army/Navy specifications several map clicks south of the airfield along the coastal highway. The change required a design change to build cabins, kitchen, and sanitary facilities to house and feed the support personnel and medical staff that would serve at the facility. The Army reasoned the improved aid station would serve a greater number if situated at a central location near a port and not impose a burden on current military facilities.

It was also pointed out the locations outlined allowed easier access to coastal facilities, since the Navy would be using the aid stations from time-to-time and provide a means of evacuation in the unlikely event it should become necessary. The Army, with Naval concord, noted that some coastal communities had rudimentary medical facilities in place, which were adequate for emergency use. And, for those areas that did not, the aid stations could serve the civilian population if not situated on a regular Army base, thereby justifying construction costs.

"Sir, we're loaded and ready to move out," Lieutenant Arthur Nance reported.

"Thank you, Lieutenant," Wesley acknowledged, gazing at the newly erected structures one more time.

"Sir, is something wrong?" Arthur asked.

"I've been an Army engineer since I graduated from college. It's always what I wanted. This is the first time I've felt my superiors were dead wrong." Wesley knew he shouldn't voice these concerns to Arthur, but he also knew his second in command was a different breed from most Army lieutenants. He felt a certain sense of kinship had grown between them in their common goal to bring modern ideas into the Army's defense modes.

"Command may reconsider in time and place another aid station at the airfield," Arthur said by way of encouragement.

"I wouldn't count on it. Once the Army reaches a decision, it nearly always stands. I think too they don't believe what happened in Norway and Europe can happen here." Turning away from the scene, Wesley resumed his commander's role. "Our orders are to inspect the defenses at Kota Bahru then move south on the coast road. We'll be checking the work the civil engineers did for the most part. I've met with them since we've been here, and they seem to be on schedule."

"Captain, this crew will be on schedule," Arthur assured him. "Sergeant Aimes is a stickler for detail, but he doesn't let it slow him down."

"I'm glad to hear that, lieutenant."

Wesley knew Arthur was working for a large engineering firm with ties to an American company when the war started. He had also discovered Arthur was fluent in three languages, including Japanese, during the time they had been together in Malaya and that he was a very good engineer. Wesley found those who had not taken Arthur seriously at first soon learned he was persistent, despite his small frame, and usually right. Arthur had earned the respect of his sergeant and with it the respect of the men.

Wesley and his crew, which consisted of Arthur Nance, fourteen enlisted men, and Sergeant Aimes, traveled the coast road, stopping sometimes to look at unexpected bays and sandy beaches.

"These are very picturesque places. A resort would go well at some of them," Arthur commented.

"Yes, very lovely," Wesley agreed. "Unfortunately, it is also difficult to defend all of them."

"Do you think we'll have to?" Arthur asked.

"Probably not right away, maybe not at all. But I'd feel better if some of the beaches weren't so close to a major thoroughfare. Japan has become more aggressive since she signed the Tripartite Pact. Now they talk of a *new order* in East Asia, whatever that means."

Wesley turned to gaze across the small inlet where they had stopped and could picture a resort with women and men lying on the beach. *That is how it should be,* he thought. "I don't know," he reflected aloud. "It seems like a chess game, with each side trying for checkmate."

"I did see in a recent newspaper where Japan's Diet gave up the right to examine cabinet policies publicly as long as their government doesn't change any election laws," Arthur noted. "Even with the internal policy changes though, everything still falls back to their Emperor."

"I wonder if he's really paying any attention to what's going on in the government," Wesley grumbled. "I heard on Saturday the Japanese government announced rice would be rationed. I was under the impression they grew more than enough to feed their population. Japan seems more interested in the Netherlands East Indies right now though than in any food shortages caused by embargoes being imposed by the West. Japan certainly isn't going to give up in China from the looks of things, and the West isn't going to lift any embargoes without some kind of compromise there."

Wesley's crew stopped at small outposts along the main coastal causeway, checking with on-site civilian project engineers over the next week. Existing emplacements were inspected and arrangements made for ammunition dumps and checkpoints to be completed. Wesley and his crew spent a night at one of the new outposts about half way between Kota Bahru and Kuantan. The sandy beach at the tiny inlet resembled many others along the coast. *Arthur was right. A quiet resort would go well here,* he thought.

Wesley lay in his bunk that night thinking about the build up of arms in Malaya and wondered what had really prompted it. The public believed that Singapore was an invincible fortress with its big guns pointing to the sea. They also believed the jungles of the Malayan Peninsula to the north made invasion by a hostile army impossible. Wesley knew as an engineer, looking at it purely as a technical problem, neither assumption was true. He also knew the build up of arms here, when there was a fighting war in other parts of the world, meant someone high up the chain of command had to be worried. *But who?* he wondered.

Wesley's thoughts drifted to the village where his sister lived, which sent a chill through him, when he began to question whether she and her friends were really safe. Helen's Landing could accommodate ships as large as destroyers, with its naturally deep waters that would be coveted and targeted for capture as quickly as possible by an invading army. He smiled to himself when he recalled that Sally had talked nonstop while he had rowed a little boat around the bay. He began to mentally formulate a plan for tighter defenses there and a few other villages like it and thought Arthur would have some ideas as well. He believed there might be receptive attitudes toward making the deep water harbors more secure if it was pointed out the Navy needed the facilities to keep the Army defenders better supplied in a crisis.

Wesley's crew completed the inspections along the coastal road on the eastern seaboard and made recommendations for further improvements. The harbor at Kuantan was a busy one and needed better defenses to help protect it from attacks by air and sea. Wesley thought all the major harbors should be mined, not just the recently announced fifty by eighty mile radius around Singapore. But again, he was regarded as an alarmist. "This isn't France," he heard again and again.

"Captain, for what it's worth, I agree with you," Arthur told him after the most recent denial.

"Right now, I wish you were a general," Wesley had replied. "We might as well pack up and move on to the northwest and Panang. Perhaps the wind will blow differently there."

"You would think after the fall of Norway and Western Europe, attitudes would be different. I don't understand it," Arthur said.

"I suppose part of it is that those places seem so far removed from here, something you read about or hear on the wireless," Wesley explained. "As one general in Singapore said, only a fool would attack through the jungle."

With question in his eyes, Arthur quietly asked, "Do you believe that, sir?"

Looking into Arthur's eyes, Wesley understood the implications behind the simple question. He also understood why the perception about Singapore and Malaya were believed as gospel truth from generals to British civilians. The idea of bringing troops through the jungle was considered foolhardy in the accepted traditions of warfare. Taking a moment to reply, Wesley sought out the right words.

"From a purely theoretical standpoint, it is completely possible," Wesley stated. "The jungle would present difficulties in some areas. But with the right equipment and air support, yes, it could be done," he concluded. "Malaya and Singapore could become stepping stones to the oil in southern Sumatra and Malaya's tin mines in the north would be a natural resource prize."

With a sense of relief, Arthur nodded. "I agree with you, sir. If there is an attack against British holdings in the East, it will involve Malaya at some point."

Wesley and his crew arrived at Panang on Sunday evening to the news the British Fleet was shelling Genoa, Italy. Speculation was that an invasion would be next. On Monday the first RAF bomber group assigned as a defensive measure in northern Malaya flew out of Singapore en-route to their base close to the Thai border.

"I think I know why we spent so much time on that airfield now," Arthur said. "You noticed those planes went north this morning but never came back south again."

"I noticed," Wesley said. "Sergeant Aimes, we're to erect another mini-hospital outside the city, preferably near a decent roadway with access to the harbor. I want you to take a couple men and do some reconnaissance."

"Right away, sir," Aimes responded, standing ramrod straight and saluting.

"We'll be here a few weeks to complete the project with the civilian workers, and then we move south following the western coast. My sister is a nurse in one of the villages about 120 miles north of Singapore," Wesley told Arthur. "I've sketched out some preliminary defense plans for the deep water harbor and surrounding countryside. I'd like you to go over them and note any suggestions you think are relevant."

"Yes, sir," Arthur replied, "I'll start on them this evening."

CHAPTER 21

Andy was surprised by the unprecedented summons on a Saturday to downtown Naval headquarters shortly after the *Mariah* arrived in Singapore. The structured protocol had instilled a more civilian oriented routine of Monday through Friday daytime business hours, with Saturday and Sunday becoming the dreaded duty rotation time in the slower paced Eastern Command. The war in England and across the Atlantic was considered only a nuisance to watch-keepers, something that was on the other side of the world.

The small fleet of shallow draft river boats permanently stationed at Singapore sailed the coastal waters and up the narrow estuaries to little known settlements further inland, showing the British flag. The unchanging weekly routine allowed the officers and men to relax three nights out of seven in their shore-side homes, while British settlers throughout the region felt a sense of safety from rebellion by the Malayan population.

Andy remembered visits during his childhood and was able to accept the fading traditions more easily than some that were recently rotated out of the war zone to Singapore. The build up of forces in the East had begun to siphon ships away from the quick, sometimes desperate, battles at sea in the West. The abrupt change to peacetime regulations with an admiralty out of touch with the new realities of war was unsettling to many of the recent warriors now transferred here.

Several other officers were in the Admiral's outer office when Andy reported to the Admiral's Aide. He feared the worst, but quickly realized the personnel milling about were too relaxed, appearing more annoyed than anything at being called in on a Saturday. "I was called right out of my tennis match," one commander was saying, as another shook his head in sympathy. Andy shared a look with the *Victoria*'s commanding officer and wondered what the summons could mean.

"The Admiral will see you now, gentlemen," the aide announced, ending Andy's speculation shortly after his arrival. "About bloody time," he overheard someone breathe, as he entered what in the West would be the war room.

Andy had the feeling he should prostrate himself before the admiral with the ritualistic drama that was unfolding. The Admiral Singapore entered through a side door within a few minutes and mounted the podium, as everyone in the room rose to acknowledge his presence.

"Gentlemen," the Admiral said in his carefully modulated voice, "please be seated. As you know, we have been placed on a higher alert status since the current unfortunate circumstances across Europe and England, and the fighting that has spread into North Africa." Andy thought *unfortunate circumstances* the understatement of the century. *The admiral should have been at Dunkirk in May or London in August and September. Then he would know the meaning of unfortunate circumstances, and more,* he briefly surmised.

"Japan has since signed the Tripartite Pact with Germany and Italy, with whom we are currently at war," the Admiral continued. "Therefore, after careful deliberation and consultation with the Admiralty in London, the decision has been made to mine a sea area fifty miles by eighty miles around Singapore and north into Malaya to increase defenses in and around Singapore and the surrounding area. My aide will distribute specific orders with regard to each ship's role in the operation to commence at 0700 Monday. That is all." The Admiral snapped the folder shut he had in front of him and, picking it up, left the same way he came without further comment.

"I have each ship's orders here," the aide announced. "Please pick them up from the table as you leave the room." A shuffling of feet followed the instructions, as the various ships' commanders rose from their chairs and began to file out. Andy heard grumbling about the ungodly hour set, and the general consensus Churchill and his foreign policy, along with the First Sea Lord in London, were interfering with their well-ordered lives.

Midshipman Barnes was the OOD that Saturday and snapped to attention when Andy boarded the *Mariah*. "Have Lieutenant Roden sent to my cabin when he returns from the city, mid," Andy ordered, while returning Barnes' salute.

"Aye, sir," came the instant reply. It was clear to Barnes that Commander Burns had something on his mind by the quick orders given before he left the deck instead of asking for the boarding officer to report, as he usually did when returning from shore.

Andy went directly to his cabin and broke open the packet he brought back from the admiral's conference. He returned everything to the envelope when he had reviewed the contents and placed it in the ship's safe. The sun was beginning to settle beneath the horizon when Mason returned to the *Mariah* and reported to Andy's cabin.

"Sir, reporting as ordered," Mason said, saluting.

"At ease, Lieutenant. Come in and sit down," Andy invited, returning the salute.

"Thank you, sir."

"Care for a gin?"

"Yes, thank you, sir."

Andy sat down and raised his glass before informing Mason of their orders. "We have orders from the Admiral Singapore," he began, causing Mason to raise his eyebrows slightly as Andy continued to explain. "We're to sail with our companion from North Africa, the *Victoria,* up the western coast of Malaya a distance of eighty miles north. We will then commence laying underwater mines, while journeying back south again to Singapore Harbor."

"Has something happened to take this step, sir?"

"Nothing I am aware of other than the Axis Pact last September. The operation will be announced at a news conference by the admiral tomorrow."

"I see," Mason slowly acknowledged, while contemplating the unforeseen explanation of events.

"Singapore is a different breed from the rest of the world, lieutenant. I remember as a boy thinking it a paradise of big ships and heavily mustached men who sailed them into wondrous adventures. I also know that protocol is strictly adhered to, thus the announcement. But I can't help wondering if it won't cause more harm than good right now."

"Sir, I have to agree with you about this causing a further rift in our negotiations with Japan. I wonder how they will react."

"Indeed. I would have to say *react* is the definitive word. However, these are the orders at present."

"What will our function be, sir?" Mason asked, returning to the immediate needs of his commander and the ship.

"The *Victoria* will lay the bulk of the mines. We are to *lend support* and will have mines to dispense as well. I don't need to tell you to enforce safety precautions. You know all to well the consequences."

"Yes, I sure do, sir. I'll inform Dr. Patterson he'll be needed along with the other officers to assist with the no smoking precautions until we're rid of the mines. When will the loading begin?"

"We load on Monday starting at 0700. We should be underway shortly after that. Tim Parker has worked with them before. The last time was at Holland just before Dunkirk began."

"I'll inform him of the orders, and we can work together," Mason said.

"You know, in civilian life he would be at least a vice-president in a company. I don't think there's much Tim doesn't know about this ship or its crew."

"You may be right. But don't try to recruit him to Lloyds just yet."

"I'll try to restrain myself for the duration."

"Carry on, Number One," Andy ordered, appreciating his first officer's abilities and sensitivity to the current situation. He knew this was a serious step being taken that would have international ramifications and firmly believed Japan would protest the move and drive the wedge even deeper between the East and the Western allies.

"Look alert there. I ain't got no plan to be leavin' this here world just yet," Parker stiffly ordered. He and Mason were carefully watching while the mines the *Mariah* would carry were brought aboard. The loading had started several hours earlier, with the *Victoria* taking on her lethal cargo that morning. Even with the awnings spread to keep the sun from beating down on the deck, the day was hot and humid, and tempers were short.

"Daft, that's what tis, daft, loadin' mines when a man's 'ands are wet from sweatin' wit the 'eat," Bert gruffly complained.

"Yer tell 'em, Bert. Yer goes right up ta yer soo-peer-i-or an tells 'em," Ernie retorted.

"Yer a..." Bert's instant rebuttal began.

"You two, pay attention to what yer a doin'," Parker snapped, watching a moment to be sure his order was followed.

It was late in the day by the time the mines were secured to Parker and Mason's satisfaction. "Nasty things," Parker said, "Always hated 'em."

Mason understood the potential danger to the ship if anything went wrong and thought it odd something that looked so innocent could be such a volatile menace. Just one he knew could damage a hull; even sink a ship if it exploded in the right spot. He also knew nothing would be left if anything went wrong with what the *Mariah* had on board.

The *Victoria* and *Mariah* set sail early Tuesday morning, following the route outlined in the orders that included a grid map with instructions of exactly where to lay the mines. Andy knew it was important to follow the map precisely. Otherwise, their own ships wouldn't know where the mines were located. He remembered the conversation with his high-spirited navigator the previous evening and thought Brian Jones would certainly earn his pay with this.

"Mr. Jones, these are the charts we'll be using for the operation," Andy indicated.

"A grid. I should be able to follow this with one eye shut," Brian had commented, while reviewing the charts.

"If you don't mind, lieutenant, I'd just as soon you kept them both opened," Andy confided.

"Not to worry, sir, we'll put the little darlings right on the money," Brian assured his commander.

The *Mariah* and *Victoria* turned north in the Malacca Strait along the western coast of Malaya to reach their assigned area and began the tedious operation of laying out the mines. Brian checked and rechecked the chart, signaling the *Victoria*'s navigator, and then checked the grid map against the main chart for their exact position before any mines were released. The operation continued into the late afternoon, with half the mines dispersed by first call to dinner to lay in wait for some unsuspecting enemy ship. Andy wondered briefly who that enemy might be.

"Sir, the *Victoria* has signaled she's having difficulty releasing the mines," Mason informed Andy in his sea cabin half way through the early evening watch. "Her commander believes one of the rollers has slipped out of place. He is requesting a return to Singapore for repairs."

"We're close to the *Lauren.* They have just about everything needed for repairs. If they don't have it, they can make it in their machine shop," Andy responded.

"I didn't realize she was near here. I thought the *Lauren* had gone to Australia," Mason replied.

"I saw a map just inside the open door of the admiral's office with the ships out of Singapore and their present location. She's sitting in the outer bay at Helen's Landing," Andy informed his first officer with a steady look.

"I'll signal the *Victoria,* sir," Mason said.

"Send a signal to Singapore outlining the situation first," Andy ordered.

"Sir?" But as the security implications became clearer, Mason nodded, "Yes, sir, I understand. I'll signal Singapore for instructions right away."

Andy watched this latest lesson of peacetime Naval structure being quickly understood, and once more felt his choice of a second in command to be the correct one. Technically an officer in the *Wavy Navy* for the duration, Mason was quickly adjusting to a peacetime Navy in a brewing cauldron of discord.

Shaking the thoughts from his mind, Andy turned his attention to the mines still on board. He knew half the village could be wiped out by docking at the pier if anything went wrong, so the *Mariah* and *Victoria* would need to anchor well apart in the outer bay at Helen's Landing. He smiled briefly to himself at the thought of anchoring in the bay where he had day dreamed during his boyhood about the adventures of the ships coming and going that anchored in the deep water bay.

Singapore soon replied to Mason's inquiry, advising the two ships should continue on to Helen's Landing where the repair ship *Lauren* would be informed of their situation. The *Mariah* and *Victoria* turned their bows north and set a course toward Andy's boyhood home. "It's a deep water natural bay," he commented to Brian.

"According to the chart, the depth is enough to accommodate the *Mariah* with room to spare. Yes indeed, a very nice harbor for us," Brian acknowledged.

Yes, a nice harbor, Andy thought, *one that would be coveted if war came to disrupt the quiet life there.*

CHAPTER 22

Andy rose early Wednesday morning to join the *Victoria*'s commander and first officer to discuss procedure and assure that necessary repairs were underway. Upon returning to the *Mariah,* Andy sought out Quentin Patterson. "Doc, how would you like to see a perfect replica of a British seaside village in the heart of the tropics?"

"An offer I cannot refuse," Doc responded with a grin.

Quentin Patterson was surprised when he stepped onto the pier to see how much the waterfront did resemble the small towns and villages that dotted the English seashore. The storefronts along the main thoroughfare bore the same common names seen from Liverpool to Scotland. He and Andy walked further into the village where they saw several Army trucks stopped at a crossroad. "Where you from?" Doc hollered out.

"Down under, mate," came a cheerful reply.

"They're from Australia!" Dr. Patterson exclaimed. "Wonder when they arrived in this neck of the woods? They can't all be from the small group that we met in the Java Sea."

"I wonder where they're headed, and why now," Andy speculated.

"A good question," Dr. Patterson agreed, lighting his pipe. "Where we headed?" he asked, after they turned onto the gravel roadway leading to the edge of town.

"There's someone I want you to meet while we're here," Andy replied.

The road they followed brought them to the village hospital before disappearing into the thick tree line. They entered a side door and found Sally at the nurse's station concentrating on a chart. "Nurse Sally, is Dr. Jamison in today?" Andy quietly asked.

Sally looked up in surprise and directly into the twinkling mischief behind Andy Burns' eyes. "Andy? I don't believe it! Helen didn't say anything about you coming here."

"It's nice to see you again also," Andy grinned.

"Dr. Jamison just finished morning rounds. Why don't you go knock on his door," Sally suggested.

"I'll do that. Come on, Doc."

Andy opened the door with the small name plate, Martin Jamison, M.D., when he heard "come" in answer to his firm knock. Martin Jamison was discussing the next fund raising event with Helen, when he stopped in mid sentence. "Well, bless my soul!"

"What is it, Martin?" Helen asked, as she turned in her chair.

"Andy!" she exclaimed in surprise, rising from her chair to embrace him with a mother's affection.

"Hello, Mother, I didn't know you were here, too."

"Ahem," Dr. Patterson said, clearing his throat.

"Sorry, Doc. Mother, this is Lieutenant Quentin Patterson, our ship's doctor."

"But, surely, you're not old enough to be this old salt's mother," Dr. Patterson said, lifting Helen's hand to his lips. "A true pleasure, madam."

"Dr. Patterson," Helen responded, in her best societal tone at the gesture.

"Doc, this is Martin Jamison..." Andy started to say.

"Martin? Martin Jamison from London Hospital class of 1917? It's me, Quentin Patterson. Remember?" Dr. Patterson asked, with searching eyes. "We shared a cadaver together in anatomy class before we stumbled around in basic training during the last war."

"Bless my soul. Quentin?" Dr. Jamison questioned, in disbelief at seeing his old school mate in Helen's Landing. "After all these years. I thought you were a big shot surgeon on Harley Street. How on earth did you wind up here?" he asked, warmly shaking Dr. Patterson's hand.

"Always wanted to go sailing, so I joined up for the duration in '39," Dr. Patterson responded with twinkling eyes.

"I see you haven't changed you're line about wanting to become a sailor. Helen, watch out for him. He's got a different line for every female he meets," Dr. Jamison jokingly warned.

"I take it you two know each other," Andy said.

"Ever since medical school," Dr. Patterson affirmed. "You've done all right, Martin. This hospital is a great accomplishment. I read that you had established a hospital in the outer reaches of the Empire, but I didn't realize it was here. I remember when we graduated that you wanted to bring medicine out here, and it appears that you did just that."

"You didn't do so bad yourself from what the medical journals report," Dr. Jamison responded.

"My moment of fame," Dr. Patterson sighed. "Ah well."

"So, what brings you here?" Dr. Jamison asked.

"We came in company with another ship, a mine layer," Andy replied. "I assume you've heard the announcement out of Singapore."

"Yes, I heard it," Dr. Jamison acknowledged. "I have to say I believe it will be another provocation and perceived as a loss of face to the Japanese if they don't respond."

"You could be right, Martin," Helen said. "I don't understand the government's need to be one up, so to speak. I know you have to do as ordered, Andy, but I wish there was no need for this."

"We may be picking the hateful things back up next week for all we know. If the Admiralty in Singapore had been at Dunkirk or seen some of the London fires, they'd be a bit more cautious about what they tell the press. Why..." Dr. Patterson began with a rising voice, and then stopped looking a bit sheepish. "Sorry, didn't mean to get on my soap box."

"That's all right, Quentin. I would have to agree about the Admiralty out here. Many just don't believe what happened in Europe could happen here. I just wish there was..."

Martin Jamison was halted in mid sentence when a sudden loud booming shook the window panes and shocked the ears, as it filled the air with its frightening presence, before receding with thundering echoes that reverberated repeatedly back toward the sea. Andy's eyes narrowed in the knowledge there was only one force on earth capable of such a sound that made him cringe. *Pandora's Box,* he thought momentarily, before reverting to his role as a Naval commander facing a possible catastrophic situation.

"That came from the harbor," Andy said in a hard flat voice.

"Andy, what is it?" Helen asked, with a rising fear starting to invade her senses at the look on his face.

"Stay here, Mother. Lieutenant, we need to get back to the ship now," Andy ordered in his no-nonsense commander's voice, thinking of the *Mariah* and what might have happened.

"I'm coming with you," Dr. Jamison firmly asserted. "We can take my car. It's faster."

The three men stopped at the nurse's station long enough for Dr. Jamison to leave instructions to send John and Peter to the harbor as soon as they returned from the Peterson's. A swirl of black smoke could be seen in the distance rising over the bay and harbor as they got into Martin Jamison's '32 black sedan.

"It doesn't look big enough to be the whole load," Andy stated, trying to see through the billowing black smudge that encompassed the outer harbor.

"What do you mean?" Dr. Jamison asked.

"The mine layer was having trouble with one of her racks. We off loaded the mines still on it, so the *Lauren* could make repairs. Something has gone wrong," Andy explained. Something must have gone terribly wrong to cause an explosion large enough to rattle the hospital's windows from the outer harbor limits. Andy wondered what he might find when they got to the harbor, if there was anything left to find.

"There's the *Mariah,*" Dr. Patterson said, pointing toward the harbor.

"What about the *Victoria* and *Lauren?*" Andy asked. "Do you see them?"

"Too much smoke. I can't tell," Dr. Patterson answered.

The three men quickly boarded the motor launch at the pier and headed straight for the *Mariah.* Coming along side, Andy mounted the boarding ladder and was met by Mason Roden. "Report, Number One."

"We're still not sure, sir. The repairs were underway and seemed to be going well. There was a flash behind the *Victoria* just before the mines that were transferred to her launch exploded. The concussion from the blast caused a burning torch to fall over on the *Lauren,* coupled with falling debris, starting a fire on the upper deck. I've sent men over to assist and told them to bring the injured back here. The *Victoria* sent a messenger to say she has damage, but how much is still being assessed. Apparently her radio is also out of commission for now. By some miracle the mines in her second rack didn't go up," Mason concluded.

"You heard, Doc?" Andy asked.

"Yes. We better be ready for broken bones and burn cases. Probably have some smoke inhalation, too," Dr. Patterson said.

"What can I do, Quentin?" Dr. Jamison asked.

"We'll probably both be needed to operate when the injured are brought aboard. What we need is someone to help Harris."

"I told Sally to send John and Peter as soon as they get to the hospital. If someone could meet them and bring them here, they could prep the worst cases and help with the burn cases," Dr. Jamison said.

"See to that, Number One," Andy ordered. "Send Midshipman Barnes to assist the doctors and have Mr. Parker report to me."

"Right away, sir," Mason crisply replied.

Martin Jamison listened with interest while Andy assessed the situation and gave orders to bring it under control. He noticed the change in Andy's usual easy-going demeanor become a man in full and confident command of a dangerous situation.

"Parker, reporting as ordered, sir."

"At ease, Mr. Parker," Andy ordered. "I want to know the effect, if any, this had on our cargo aft."

"The load is secure, sir. I looked it over myself. Fortunately we're facin' the *Victoria,* so the super structures took what concussion there was. If them mines left on the *Victoria* go, well, then it could spell trouble," Tim concluded.

"Thank you, Mr. Parker. Be ready to bring the injured on board. We'll have two more doctors coming shortly. Lieutenant Patterson and Dr. Jamison, from the local hospital, are preparing the dispensary now. We may have to move some to the village hospital later. If we do, we have to do it from here. I don't want to chance getting those mines any closer in than they are already."

"Yes, sir. I'll put a detail together," Parker offered.

"Have them report to Midshipman Barnes. He'll be assisting the doctors with their needs," Andy ordered.

"Aye, sir."

John and Peter quickly set to work on the burned and bleeding men lying in rows of threes and fours across *Mariah*'s deck, after a brief run down by Roger Barnes. The quiet mummer of "*easy there friend*" was heard from unknown sailors staying with a badly injured man until help arrived, or the soul left its earthly ties, leaving the maimed and broken house where it had lived behind.

Andy assessed the situation on the *Victoria* and *Lauren,* assigning men to help with the remaining casualties after the stubborn fire was extinguished. Others from *Mariah*'s crew were left to help with temporary repairs aboard the *Victoria* until she could return to Singapore and be put into dry dock, with a priority to rig a temporary antenna to get her radios back on the air. While this was being accomplished, the more difficult task of ensuring her hull's integrity was intact began. The *Lauren* was more fortunate, with her damage appearing to be confined to the upper deck. The mines left on the *Victoria* though were a worry. Andy would recommend Singapore send a mine tender to remove their remaining mines before the *Mariah* took the *Victoria* in tow for the return journey.

"Whew, I'm not as young as I used to be," Quentin Patterson groaned.

"My aching back," Martin Jamison responded in turn.

"The two youngsters seem to have things in hand for now, Martin. Let me offer you a gin before I see what we can find to eat. Operating always makes me hungry."

"You seem to have a fairly quick routine here, Quentin. Was it like this in the Atlantic and the Channel last year with the German attacks?"

"Sometimes," Dr. Patterson reflected. "Most of the time it was pretty boring punctuated with periods of intense panic."

"I see. I'm becoming concerned about all the build up of forces here. An

Army captain visited a few months ago about building better aid stations. In fact, he was brought from Holland to England on this very ship. You operated on him for a shoulder wound. His name is Wesley Vilmont, the brother of one of my nurses."

"There have been so many. I'm afraid I don't remember him," Dr. Patterson said, with a touch of sadness in his voice.

"I don't doubt it, Quentin. I remember the end of the last one in France, the war to end all wars. Hah! I can't remember most of the faces though now, just their wounds," Dr. Jamison reflected, looking into his empty glass. "You said something about eating. I'll have to get back soon for evening rounds."

Helen was waiting when Martin Jamison and Quentin Patterson arrived at the hospital. "How bad is it, Martin?"

"It could be worse. The damage is limited to Navy ships, two of them anyway. Andy's still on board the *Mariah* making arrangements with Singapore to remove their load of mines before he can attempt to tow the other one back to Singapore. Quentin offered to make evening rounds with me here before we plan how many beds we'll need to prepare. Singapore has already made initial contact with me about that and wants Quentin to be the Navy's medical liaison. John and Peter are still on the destroyer."

"What can I do to help, Martin?"

"Not much for now. Let Jane and Sally know the situation. They'll need to cover A and B wards tonight. We'll have to open C ward tomorrow for the men who need immediate hospital care that will be brought here. I'll talk with them later about special nurses," Dr. Jamison explained briefly. "We'll need the volunteers to man the kitchen and help get the beds ready as well."

"I'll see to that," Helen offered.

"I'll leave the details in your capable hands then, Helen, thank you."

Preparations were made when morning came to move the most severely injured to the local hospital. "We've rigged special slings to lower them to the launch. The two doctors that stayed last night will go with the worst ones," Midshipman Barnes reported to Mason.

"It sounds as if you have things well covered," Mason approved.

"Thank you, sir. One of the men thought of the sling idea and using canvas to make it out of," Barnes replied. "Commander Burns said to be ready this morning, so the men worked through the night."

"I'll fill him in, carry on," Mason ordered.

"Yes sir."

"Signal from Singapore, sir," the messenger reported.

"Thank you, carry on." Andy motioned Mason to enter while he scanned Singapore's orders. "It seems the hospital has a contract with the Navy for emergencies," he said after a moment. "Singapore has contacted Dr. Jamison to alert him about the situation and to prepare for any casualties needing immediate hospital care. It appears Dr. Patterson will be our liaison."

"I guess we stopped in the right place," Mason said.

"How are preparations coming along to move the injured men?" Andy asked. "The sooner we do that the sooner we can concentrate on the rest of it."

"Everything is ready. Hartman and Romans are supervising the transfer now," Mason reported. "Barnes did all right. Seems he improvised a rigging to accommodate our need. He and the men worked through the night to get it ready."

"Singapore is sending a tug to assist with preparations to tow the *Victoria* to dry dock," Andy related. He paused a moment before continuing. "I'll not forget the dedication to duty performed by the men and officers during this crisis."

"The first patients are coming in about five minutes," Sally alerted Jane, while she was briefing the auxiliary staff.

"We're ready here," Jane assured her, before returning to the auxiliary nurses that had not been called on since the blasting accident the previous year.

New patients were brought in the rest of the morning and carefully placed in the waiting beds. The most severe cases were gently lowered, using Barnes' canvas sling, to the waiting launch for transport to shore. The men that could perked up a little at having real female nurses fussing over them.

The day passed with the hospital showing an unprecedented amount of activity not seen since the construction accident the previous year. By nightfall the new patients were settled into their beds and the staff into a busy routine.

British newspapers and the BBC reported on Thursday that Tokyo newspapers were stating the Japanese would be forced to take counter-measures if the British continued their activities in Southeast Asia in response to the underwater mines dispersed around Singapore. The British responded by insisting they were only taking measures to protect their interests.

"They had to make some response I suppose. I doubt we've heard the last of it though," John commented, after switching off the radio in the doctor's lounge.

"After what happened last week, I should think the government would be less enthusiastic about provoking them," Sally responded. "I don't see the reasoning behind putting those horrible mines in the water. Those poor men that were killed and so many hurt over it."

"Yes, I know. I can't say I like it much either, but I suppose they think it will prevent what happened in Europe. After all, Japan does have a treaty with Germany and Italy," John pointed out.

"I know. I just think there should be a better way."

"What say we try to forget about the news for now and go see the picture show that came in last week?" John suggested.

"That sounds like a winning idea," Sally agreed.

CHAPTER 23

March came with little breaking news about the war in Europe. Jane and Peter were oblivious to most of this, as they looked forward to their wedding day. When Helen asked Jane who would give her away, Jane said she hoped it would be Dr. Jamison. She remembered his compassion for her pain and grief when she first came to Malaya. She was grateful that he allowed her to talk about her short marriage and Jim's death without pressuring her to let him go before she was ready. His wisdom had helped to bring her back to the living and restore her faith in God's love, which instilled the courage to love once again. *Yes,* Jane thought, *Dr. Jamison has been like a father to me in so many ways. He should be the one to walk with me on my wedding day.*

"Do you want me to ask Martin?" Helen asked, when Jane looked a little hesitant the day she and Peter and Dr. Jamison were visiting to finalize the wedding plans.

"No…no, I think I should. He's just so busy, and I don't want to impose. But I can't think of anyone I'd rather have."

"All right, then. Martin and Peter will be back from inspecting the garden soon."

Helen had proposed the ceremony be celebrated in the formal garden, using the large octagon gazebo as the focal point. Dr. Jamison and Peter had gone out to look over the area and decide how best to arrange seating for the guests.

"Well, ladies, do you have everything in order?" Dr. Jamison asked, when he and Peter came through the dining room's French doors.

"Just about, Martin. I believe Jane has something to ask you," Helen said, giving Jane a smile of encouragement.

With her cheeks feeling flushed, Jane took a deep breath. "Dr. Jamison, it would mean a great deal to me if you would consent to give me away."

"Bless my soul, child, I would be honored. Thank you, my dear," Martin Jamison agreed with a smile, before kissing her cheek.

"Well, that's settled," Helen said. "Now then, Peter, John is to be best man you said," and made another check mark against her list. "Let's see, flowers, catering, Fr. Finney, music, invitations are out. I think we're ready for a beautiful day."

"Helen, we can't begin to thank you for..." Jane got no further before Helen tut-tutted her, stating she was enjoying every minute of it.

Helen and Dr. Jamison went to the sitting room following afternoon tea in the gazebo to hear the early news broadcast.

"This is the BBC reporting from London," the announcer began. "Today Whitehall announced the first contingent of 50,000 British troops was landed in Greece. Mr. Churchill states..." the newscaster continued, giving the official statement released with the public announcement.

"It seems that Britain is looking to bring Hitler down," Dr. Jamison said. "I wonder if she can."

"It seems the war is always casting its shadow over us," Helen sighed.

The weeks of March passed, with Japan announcing the Imperial Rule Assistance Association had gained the support of the Japanese Army. The United States announced on March 22, 1941, the welcome news that the Senate Committee had unanimously approved the seven billion-dollar Lend-Lease Bill.

"Well it's about time," John said. "With us going into Greece and also fighting in North Africa, we'll need the aid."

"I wonder how long before anything is sent?" Peter asked, voicing the question on many a British supply officer's mind.

"It better be fairly soon. I heard this new ruling party in Japan is more fascist, like the Nazis in Germany. That could make things hotter around here, especially now that the Japanese Army has pledged their support to the new party."

"You don't seriously think that makes Japan a threat though, do you?"

"I'm not sure anymore." John hesitated a moment before explaining his reasoning. "They have the support of the Army, but the Emperor hasn't been quoted anywhere as giving his blessing to the new party. But he might not have the kind of power we think he does."

"But I thought he was considered almost a god," Peter objected.

"Even God has been ignored by some. Sodom and Gomorrah come to mind," John responded, before he left to check on a new patient. The thought that Japan's Emperor might be only a figurehead with no real power left Peter to wonder about Japanese politics, and what direction Japan's politicians would choose.

"Hitler said there would be fiercer attacks at sea this year. I thought he was just trying to make noise, but now I don't know," Dr. Jamison said after hearing on the early news about the Battleship *Malaya* being in New York for repairs under the lend-lease agreement. He and Quentin Patterson were listening to the BBC after examining the last of the Navy's patients remaining at Helen's Landing. Dr. Patterson had been sent by Admiral Edwards in mid April to supervise relocating the injured men from the *Victoria* to Singapore to complete their recovery or for transfer to a long-term facility in Australia.

"I can tell you it was fierce enough before. We saw some pretty nasty stuff," Quentin Patterson told his friend.

"Yes, I thought so from what I could gather out of Andy's letters last year. How was the trip back to Singapore from here?" Dr. Jamison asked.

"A lot less tense once those bloody mines were gone. The *Victoria* managed to get one of her boilers going the second day out and could make about four knots. She limped into Singapore Harbor and was put in dry dock for initial repairs."

"What about Andy? The Admiralty at Singapore have anything to say?"

"Kept us waiting almost a week," Dr. Patterson replied, pursing his lips in disapproval. "More for affect most likely. Darned fools wouldn't know how to put out a fire in an outhouse between them. They finally decided it was *an unfortunate inciden*t and let it go at that. Told Andy he had taken all the appropriate precautions and nothing more."

"I see. Well, I believe Helen is expecting us for dinner. I guess we should be going," Dr. Jamison said, setting his glass on the side table. "Quentin, for what it's worth, I agree with you. Andy made good decisions in a crisis. Singapore clings with quiet desperation to the colonial existence that was carved out here. The Navy is a part of that. The current situation is a threat to that existence, and the *Mariah* and her crew are visible reminders of that threat."

"I suppose," Dr. Patterson grudgingly conceded. "Still think they could be a bit less awkward though."

Dinner with Helen had a soothing affect on Quentin Patterson as they talked about everything from the servant situation to the most recent international events. He found her views to be insightful and recognized a strong intelligence behind that feminine facade.

The evening ended after the three dinner companions listened to the nine o'clock evening news. Not much was said about the fighting in Greece or the Army's strategy in North Africa. The British government was keeping information at a minimum for the present and newscasters were hard pressed to deliver any of the attention grabbing headlines from a few months past.

"Thank you, Helen, for a most enjoyable evening," Quentin Patterson said at the evening's end.

"You're most welcome, Quentin. It's too bad you won't be here through Sunday. We have a wedding planned, and I look forward to a day to celebrate and forget about the war."

"Then I wish for you a day that will have only happy memories," Dr. Patterson gallantly stated.

"I'll see you Friday evening, Helen," Martin Jamison said as he prepared to leave.

On Sunday morning Jane could see the landscape stretching out below the house to where it slipped downward to meet the water's edge from the bedroom that Helen placed her in Friday evening. Helen told her the room was prepared for a daughter, but it wasn't meant to be. The wedding rehearsal on Friday evening had been fun, and she witnessed a side of Dr. Jamison that she had not seen before. He was kind as always. But he also had joked and laughed, making the rehearsal less stoic and relieving the nervousness that Jane had started to feel.

The wedding party gathered around the radio following the rehearsal to hear the BBC nine o'clock news broadcast. "The RAF in Singapore has revealed United States pursuit planes are arriving here to strengthen our air and Naval defenses," the announcer began.

"I'll be," John said. "Could it be part of the Lend-Lease scheme I wonder?"

"Well, if nothing else it might keep the wolves at bay for now," Peter interjected.

"Shh, there's more," Helen said.

"This reporter has learned American forces will be landed in Manila during the coming week to augment the Philippine Army. Whitehall has applauded this commitment to increase America's presence in the East, stating it will give strength and stability to western interests throughout the region. This is the BBC, Singapore Station, reporting."

"It appears America may be looking more closely at her interests in the Pacific," John commented, when the broadcast ended.

"That could help to make things more stable here," Dr. Jamison remarked. "Of course, it could have the opposite affect. I guess all we can do is wait and see."

"Let us pray to the Almighty the governments of these misguided countries will come to their senses and end this immoral fighting," Fr. Finney fervently invoked.

Wait and see, Jane thought. The waiting was over for her and Peter. Today they would be married for better or worse until death parted them. Thinking about the vows she would make today took Jane back to Ann Arbor and another time she had said those words. Death had parted her from Jim, and now she was here on her wedding day about to take that same sacred vow. *Will death come again and part us? I survived it once,* Jane thought, *I can't again. If death comes, let it be me.* She felt guilty after thinking it, knowing that it was selfish. Peter said she would never be alone again, and she had to believe and trust in him to be there for a lifetime.

Jane saw the white silk dress with the embroidered bodice and pale pink sash that she would wear today and remembered the excitement at finding the perfect dress. "But Jane," Sally had said, "It's the perfect look," when they had poured over the catalog from Singapore until the pages were limp and wrinkled. It had taken her a week to decide. Then, on an impulse, she filled out the order form and mailed it before she changed her mind again. She told Peter what she had done, and he said she looked wonderful to him all the time. Jane smiled to herself when she thought about it. All that fuss over a dress, when all that really mattered was marrying Peter on this special day.

Knocking on the door, Helen peeked in, "I thought you might be awake. I brought us some coffee and toast to begin the day."

"Helen, that was kind of you. You've been so wonderful through all of this," Jane said.

"It's been my pleasure. Now, let's drink our coffee and relax a little before the rest of the house is awake. I checked on Sally, and she's still sleeping soundly."

"The coffee is good," Jane commented. "I watched the sun rise this morning and thought about the past few years."

"There have been a lot of changes for you since coming here. I expect it took some getting used to."

"Yes, there were changes. I told Peter about it." Jane turned her head to look out the window without really seeing the view. "I told him about Jim, what happened," she quietly went on, before turning back to look at the friend she was confiding in. "Helen, I love Peter. I didn't think I would ever be able to say that again after Jim died, but I've been given a second chance at happiness."

"But something is troubling you."

With a sense of shame at her lack of faith, Jane confessed her fear of death snatching away that second chance, leaving her lost and alone again. "Have you told Peter about this?" Helen asked.

"Yes," Jane whispered. "He knows."

"And what did he say?"

"That he wouldn't leave me alone. That we would have a life together," Jane said, her eyes starting to fill with tears.

"I'm sure he's right, my dear," Helen asserted with conviction. "You had a terrible experience at a very young age, but it's time to give it up to God and look to the future. You and Peter love each other, and today is the beginning of a long and happy life together. You'll look back one day and wonder where all the years went."

"Do you really believe that, Helen; that we'll grow old together?" Jane asked, trying to rid herself of further doubts.

"Yes indeed," Helen reassured her. "I believe it with all my heart and soul. Now you just stop worrying and trust in God's grace for the future." Smiling now, Jane reached out a hand to her friend, who took it in recognition and comfort before rising to prepare the household for the coming day.

"Are you ready, Jane?" Sally asked. "I'm so nervous you'd think I was the bride."

"I'm ready. What do you think? Am I okay?" Jane asked a little anxiously.

"You look wonderful," Sally confirmed.

"Come in," Jane called out, when there was a knock at the bedroom door.

Dr. Jamison came through the door and smiled. "Jane, you look lovely. Both of you are enough to stop a man's heart. They're ready downstairs. I left Peter in John's care for now."

"Thank you, Dr. Jamison, and thank you for being here today. It means a great deal to me."

"Shall we?" Dr. Jamison asked with a gentle smile, extending his arm to her.

Fr. Finney stood a step above the wedding party in his white robe and vestments, holding an open Anglican Prayer Book in his hands, as his gentle smile rested on Jane and Peter, when Dr. Jamison responded, "I do," to the age-old question, "Who gives this woman to this man?" He then invited the bride and groom and their attendants to come before the altar at the center of the gazebo to take their wedding vows in the presence of God.

The ceremony was from the Church of England tradition, and the vows were said with the couple facing each other while holding each other's right hand. Father Finney blessed their wedding bands as they repeated the words, *with this ring I thee wed*, before taking his *stole* to wrap around their joined right hands as a symbol of *tying the knot.* He then declared, "In as much as Peter and Jane have taken solemn vows in the presence of Christ, by the joining of hands and the exchanging of rings, I pronounce that they are husband and wife. In the name of the Father, and of the Son, and of the Holy Spirit, Amen," Fr. Finney intoned, making the sign of the cross over their joined hands. "Those whom God has joined together let no man put asunder." He then invited the newlyweds and their guests to share the bread and wine of communion, making it their first act as a married couple. The ceremony ended with the church soloist singing "Because" before Peter kissed his bride.

The reception was a whirlwind of congratulations and well wishers, leaving Jane a little overwhelmed when she realized the great number of friends who were attending this special day in her life. She attributed this to Helen encouraging her to become involved in activities, drawing her out of the protective shell that she had wrapped around herself.

"Peter, it's been a perfect day. As long as I live, I'll never forget. I love you so very much," Jane told him with smiling eyes, while they were dancing.

"Nor will I, darling. I wonder though when we can make our escape?" he teased with an impish grin.

Looking at the expression on Peter's face, Jane started to laugh. "I believe after we cut the cake. From what I've been told, it is proper protocol for the bride and groom to cut the first piece. I understand it's considered very bad form to leave before that."

"We wouldn't want to be known for bad form. I think Helen is signaling to us now," Peter said. "Perhaps we should see what she wants. It could be time to cut the cake," he went on to say, appearing innocent which left Jane trying to stifle an outburst of giggling, as she led Peter to Helen's side.

"My dears, I know you were going to go to your bungalow tonight, but I have another option for you to consider. There's a cottage on the seashore below the house that's secluded and quiet. Ralph and I used to go there sometimes to be alone. If you wish, you're welcome to use it for a retreat."

"Jane, what do you think? It would keep the pranksters away. I fear John has something up his sleeve," Peter said.

"Helen, you've done so much already. I don't want you to fuss."

"Jane dear, it's no trouble. Hannah cleans it weekly and keeps fresh food there. I still go sometimes when I want to be alone, to think, or just remember. Ralph and I had some of our most enjoyable times there," Helen assured her.

"I didn't realize. It sounds like a wonderful place to start a new life," Jane agreed.

"That's settled then. Come now and cut your cake before we send you on your way."

Jane stood on the veranda with her back turned to the wedding guests to send the bridal bouquet into the waiting outstretched hands of the village's single young women. The bouquet went high into the air before gracefully falling toward the earth and landing in Sally's hands as if aimed in her direction. "I don't believe it," she declared, "I don't even have a steady boyfriend," bringing laughter from the well-wishers, before Peter and Jane ran through a cloud of rice to the waiting borrowed car and the start of a new life.

"Helen said we would come on it suddenly if we followed the path from the hospital," Peter said. "Wait, what's that up ahead?" They came to a quiet little bay after a few more steps, where the sea lapped at a small strip of sandy beach with a small duplicate of a Tudor style house tucked into the first trees beyond the shore. Jane gasped at the sight of the Victorian decor when Peter opened the door, and the open staircase leading to the upstairs bedrooms.

"Boy, if this is a cottage," Peter said, "I wonder what the boat house is like."

"It's beautiful," Jane said a little breathless.

"May I carry you in, Mrs. Romans?"

"Mrs. Romans. Oh, Peter, that sounds so lovely."

Sweeping her slender body into his arms, Peter carried his bride over the threshold, and then kissed her, before carefully standing Jane on her feet. They walked hand-in-hand through the main level living area and kitchen then up to the bedroom, where Helen had a servant secret their suitcases. Peter held Jane close to him, stroking her hair, before bending to kiss her, as she melted into his arms.

They decided to change for a swim at sunset and found the water refreshing, before lying on a blanket to watch the sun lower beneath the sea, murmuring words of love before their lips slowly came together. The last rays of sunlight shone on them when they gave themselves to each other, experiencing the selflessness of being one. "I wish time could stand still," Jane sighed. "It's so lovely here with you." Kissing her, Peter took Jane's hand and led her into the house.

CHAPTER 24

"I've reviewed the drawings for Helen's Landing," Arthur informed Wesley in mid-May.

"And?"

"Sir, if I could suggest a few modifications, I think it would be most effective in defending the area," Arthur began, while opening the storage tube.

"That's why I wanted you to look at it. I thought you might have some ideas." Wesley leaned over the unfurled drawing and began scanning the symbols, noting several upgrades to the original plan.

"Not having seen the lay of the land myself, my suggestions are contingent on the practicality of carrying them out," Arthur explained. "However, if we moved this emplacement to here," he continued, pointing to the map overlay, "it would cover the cross road as well as a possible land assault to the harbor."

"Yes, I see what you mean. What about an amphibious assault?"

"I believe it might come to the north or south along one of these short sandy beaches where there's less resistance. A lot of small inlets around there."

Too many uncharted little beaches altogether, Wesley thought while studying the drawings more intently. "What if we put in defenses at each side of the bay? That way we've covered the harbor against a threat as much as possible."

"It's quite feasible," Arthur agreed. "We need to do some reconnaissance to find the best locations for building battlements before any specific sites could be chosen."

"We should be done in Kalang by the end of the week," Wesley concluded. "A day or two to pack up, then we can move south and have a better look."

The third week of May 1941 found the *Mariah* resting at anchor in Singapore Harbor, where she had remained since returning from Helen's Landing. Dr. Patterson was relaxing in the wardroom reading the latest newspaper reports after spending a few days in the city.

"Doc, you're back!" Mason declared when he came into the wardroom. "I see you survived the big city."

"Contrary to popular belief, I came through unscathed."

"Hello, Roger old boy, why so down in the mouth?" Mason asked when Midshipman Barnes entered the wardroom.

"You should ask," Roger groaned. "I've just been informed I am to correct all of our signals. It will take forever," he sighed, throwing his hands in the air and dropping into a chair.

"Tut-tut," Dr. Patterson soothed, clucking his tongue. "No rest for the young it seems. Cheer up, me boy, it could be worse."

"I don't know how," Roger moaned.

"Well, you could be doomed to be a reporter," Dr. Patterson told him.

"What?" Roger asked, wrinkling his brow.

"The good doctor is skeptical of those who report world events," Mason explained. "I do have to say though, Doc, the reports from the Yanks are encouraging."

"I suppose. It says here that the American Legion Executive Committee is urging convoys be organized for delivery of war materials to Britain. On the other hand, our Ministry of Economic Warfare has been pushing to have Axis funds in the United States frozen. And, according to Thursday's paper, their government hadn't made a commitment when the paper went to press."

"Doc, let's have a gin and see what the BBC has to say about today," Mason suggested. "Something for you, Roger?"

"A ginger ale would be nice, thank you," Roger wistfully sighed.

"One ginger ale and two gins it is," Mason said, as he switched on the wireless set.

The White Cliffs of Dover was concluding before the announcer came on the air. "This is the BBC reporting. Today it was announced that British and United States oil companies in the East Indies will renew contracts to supply Japan with 1.8 million tons of oil a year."

"Boy!" Roger declared, "That's a tall order."

"British forces continue fighting in the deserts of North Africa against aggressive Axis resistance," the short broadcast continued. "Mr. Churchill pledged in his latest communiqué England would continue her fight to restore the wrongfully occupied territories to their rightful owners. This is the BBC, Singapore Station, reporting. Good evening."

"That should keep the Japanese happy," Roger said. "I mean 1.8 million tons of oil."

"Perhaps," Dr. Patterson allowed. "It could, on the other hand, give the Japanese a reserve, allowing them to exercise an offensive action to take possession of the supplier."

"On that cheery note, I'm for bed," Mason said, as the party in the wardroom broke up and headed for their bunks.

Wesley and Arthur toured the harbor front at Helen's Landing shortly after their arrival. They soon concluded that antiaircraft guns could be placed between the harbor and village to gain the most effective vantage point against air strikes, and shore batteries could be constructed to the north and south along a three-mile strip to hinder invasion by sea. An ammunition dump would be constructed a few miles north of the village to supply defenders, while protecting the community from a devastating explosion should there be an accident. Each man knew the plans hinged on approval from Army headquarters in Singapore.

"Helen's Landing already has a good working hospital, and it has ties to the Navy for some reason," Wesley said. "What I want to do is go to Singapore and speak with General Hughes and possibly his Navy counterpart, Admiral Edwards. If they would agree, we might be able to set this up as a model and see what happens."

"It's worth a try, sir," Arthur encouraged. "The plan has merit."

"Right now I'm going to see Dr. Jamison. He was helpful in the final design of the improved aid stations," Wesley reasoned. "I would welcome his input on this. He knows the community and can give us some idea about how receptive the people here might be."

"I'll take a look around to see if there are any likely spots for other harbor and land defenses," Arthur offered.

"Come," Dr. Jamison invited, when Wesley knocked on the open office door.

"Hello, Dr. Jamison, I'm not sure if you remember me. We only spoke the one time a few months ago."

"Of course, you're Sally's brother, Wesley. So, how have the improved aid stations come along?"

"You may well ask. That's one of the reasons I came to see you. The Army liked the idea; however, not for placement on their bases, but well away to protect them from enemy attack."

"I see," Dr. Jamison responded, rubbing the bridge of his nose. "You said it was one of the reasons you came. I gather there are others."

"Yes sir. My second and I have prepared a tactical defense plan for Helen's Landing. I'd like to have your opinion about it and any suggestions you might have. If Army Command accepts it, the plan would be a model for the area," Wesley explained.

"I'm no engineer, but I can tell you that folks around here like their quiet life," Dr. Jamison cautioned. "They also know the harbor needs protection. We had an incident a few months ago with a couple of Navy ships anchored out in the bay. I think it made folks here more aware of its vulnerability should tensions become more strained on the international scene."

"Will you look the plans over, sir?" Wesley asked.

"Sure I will, for what it's worth. I'll tell you what I think about it tomorrow. I will also tell you not to lose faith. It takes time to change time-honored traditions, but it can be done," Dr. Jamison noted. "Now, tell me how your shoulder is holding up. By coincidence it was an old medical school friend of mine who operated on you. He's in Singapore right now on the very same ship that took you across the Channel."

"Maybe I'll be able to thank him in person," Wesley said. "I plan to visit Singapore and speak with my superior about the plans after you review them."

Dr. Jamison took Wesley's drawings with him to meet Helen that evening and discuss the final arrangements for the annual fundraiser.

"What's that, Martin?" Helen asked, when he arrived.

"Oh just something Wesley Vilmont asked me to look at," Dr. Jamison explained. "Is everything in place for tomorrow?"

"Martin, of course it is. Sally and Jane have been real troopers. I believe it should be a smashing success. Shall we eat and then listen to the news?"

"That sounds good, Helen. It's been a busy day."

"You should take a prescription from yourself and get some rest. A few days away might put the bounce back in your step."

"Perhaps."

At nine o'clock the two friends went into the broad-windowed sitting room that overlooked the sea and turned on the evening news. "This is the BBC reporting. On Wednesday last, Mr. Churchill received a vote of confidence in the House of Commons by a margin of 447 to 3. This has been declared an overwhelming approval of his leadership abilities during this time of unprecedented challenge to our great nation," the announcer began.

"At least there seems to be solidarity now, unlike a year ago with Chamberlain," Dr. Jamison commented.

"On another front," the announcer went on, "German and Italian representatives are reported to be in Tokyo, Japan for a conference regarding the Axis Pact. To date no comments are being reported about the conference agenda, or its outcome. This is the BBC, Singapore Station, reporting. Goodnight."

Rising to shut off the radio, Helen looked troubled.

"What is it, Helen?" Dr. Jamison asked.

"I'm not sure. Just an uneasy feeling about Japan meeting with Germany and Italy. I…I can't explain it really."

"Maybe these will put your mind at ease," Dr. Jamison said, tapping the container with Wesley's drawings.

"What do you mean, Martin?"

Opening the cylinder, Dr. Jamison spread out the overall sketch of Helen's Landing, explaining that the unfamiliar markings were proposed defenses for around the village and harbor.

"What is this to the north, Martin?" Helen asked.

"They're called tank traps. I believe the purpose of all this is to surround the village with defenses to protect the deep water harbor we have here."

"I see," Helen thoughtfully commented. "I truly hope it doesn't come to that."

"So do I, Helen, but it could be a deterrent to discourage invasion by hostile forces as well. The plan has to be approved in Singapore before any construction could begin," Dr. Jamison pointed out.

"We've had several convoys of trucks going through with every manner of Army troops. I wonder how many soldiers it would bring here and where they would stay."

"What do you think?" Wesley asked Martin Jamison the next morning.

"It is a good overall defense of the area. If it were built, where would the troops that man the outpost be lodged?"

"There's an abandoned farm about five miles northeast of here. Arthur, my second, inspected the buildings and believes they could be repaired to house the necessary personnel," Wesley responded.

"The old Charmical place," Dr. Jamison acknowledged. "It's been empty about seven years. They moved to Australia. The house and servant quarters were pretty sturdy as I recall."

"May I tell my superiors in Singapore that you support the plan, sir?" Wesley asked.

"You might mention I've seen the drawings and relate I found the overall plan to have merit, for what it's worth. I would also mention the proposed place to lodge the personnel needed to man the outposts as well."

"Thank you, sir. I appreciate you taking the time to see me," Wesley said.

"When will you leave for Singapore?"

"Right away. I'll report to my immediate superior and ask if we can present this to General Hughes."

"I see. Well good luck to you," Dr. Jamison said, shaking Wesley's hand.

Dr. Jamison called John, Peter, and Tom Linn into his office after morning rounds and told them they would be on their own for a few days while he went to Singapore on business that required his attention. The three young doctors told him the hospital would be fine while he was gone. They also told him he should take a few days to relax.

CHAPTER 25

"Rear Admiral Jamison to see Admiral Edwards," Martin Jamison told Eric Edward's aide early Monday morning at Singapore's Naval headquarters. Dr. Jamison never gave his rank much thought, but decided there were times when rank did have its advantages.

"Martin Jamison, as I live and breath," Eric Edwards enthusiastically declared. "What pried you out of Helen's Landing?"

"Hello, Eric, how are you?" Dr. Jamison responded with a smile, shaking his friend's hand.

"Fine...fine. Things at the hospital okay? You usually don't leave there unless something really important comes up. I believe the last time was in 1938, when you went to the United States to raise more funds," Admiral Edwards said, eyeing his friend more closely.

"I had some business to attend to in Singapore, and I wanted your opinion about this Axis conference in Tokyo."

"Well Martin, I really don't know any more than you do. What do you think?"

"I believe Germany might be seeking some warm water ports in the East, and Japan fills the bill. I don't think Hitler gives two hoots about the Emperor's opinion or the Japanese military, but he wants the use of the docks in Japan's port cities."

"I suppose that's possible," Eric Edwards allowed.

"I also think if Germany gets a toe hold in the East it could threaten all of

Malaya," Dr. Jamison continued. "And I know that opinion is in the minority here."

"Yes, for the most part it is felt that Malaya and Singapore are safe from any aggression by the Axis alliance. A few dissenting voices take exception to that opinion. Where is all this leading to, Martin?"

"I'm not sure, Eric. I just have concerns about our current fragile peace."

Eric Edwards steepled his hands in front of him waiting for further comment, but Dr. Jamison said no more. "So, how long will you be in Singapore?" he finally asked.

"About a week, a little R-and-R. Thought I might get you to have dinner with me one night while I'm here."

"Be glad to, let me check my calendar. How about Wednesday?" Admiral Edwards suggested, glancing up at his friend.

"That will be fine, Eric. Tell me, is the *Mariah* still here?"

"In the harbor, why?"

"I thought I might stop to see Andy Burns, her commander, and Quentin Patterson, an old friend and colleague, while I'm here."

"That's right, you know Lieutenant Commander Burns."

"He grew up at Helen's Landing. The village is named for his mother you know. His family was one of the first to settle there." Dr. Jamison noted. "Since the war started, Andy's been involved at Holland and Dunkirk and handled the recent incident in our little corner of the world. But you probably already know that from his record."

"I believe you're trying to tell me something," Admiral Edwards observed.

"Only that he's a good officer. We're very proud of him at Helen's Landing. Well, I better be on my way. I'll see you Wednesday evening; say 7:30 at the Raffles."

"That's fine, Martin, 1930 hours at the Raffles," Admiral Edwards confirmed, using the ingrained British Navy 24-hour timeframe.

Eric Edwards decided to see what Martin Jamison was hinting at after Martin left his office and instructed his aide to bring the personnel file for Lieutenant Commander Andrew Burns. He read Andy's file with interest after noting the unspecified commendation dated 1940 and had to admit he was a good officer. The incident with the *Victoria* appeared to be something he could not have foreseen. He noted Andy's intervention to bring the situation under control as the ranking officer was efficient and well executed. He made a notation that a Letter-of-Commendation be placed in the file along with a recommendation to the Command Board that Lieutenant Commander Burns be promoted to commander. Eric Edwards shook his head and smiled to himself as he set the file aside when he thought about how Martin Jamison made his point without censuring the Navy's high command.

Dr. Jamison received a quick response when he requested transport to the *Mariah*'s anchorage as Rear Admiral Jamison.

"Rear Admiral Jamison requests permission to come aboard," he called out, after stepping onto the boarding ladder's lower platform.

"Permission granted," Roger Barnes responded a little nervously. This was his first admiral as OOD. He was fortunate Tim Parker was nearby to make quick arrangements for the boson to pipe the unknown admiral aboard. Saluting the flag and the OOD at the top of the landing stairs, Dr. Jamison asked to see Commander Burns.

"Mr. Parker," Roger formally said, "inform Commander Burns Rear Admiral Jamison wishes to see him." Saluting, Tim Parker quickly walked across the deck in search of his commanding officer. He found him with Dr. Patterson in the infirmary with his feet propped up, drinking a cup of tea.

"Sir," Parker said, "Rear Admiral Jamison requests to see you."

"Rear Admiral Jamison? It can't be," Andy said, looking at Dr. Patterson. "Do you mean Dr. Jamison?"

"He just said Rear Admiral Jamison, sir," Tim answered.

"Very well," Andy responded.

"If it's Martin," Dr. Patterson began with a widening grin, "I want to know where he stole the uniform."

Andy went to the wardroom where Roger informed him he had placed the unknown admiral and found Martin Jamison waiting for him in a rear admiral's uniform. Taken by surprise, he saluted and invited him to have a seat. "Dr. Jamison, what brings you to Singapore?"

"Just a little break is all. Your mother said to say hello and to see how you are. Mothers are great worriers you know."

Smiling, Andy nodded his understanding. "Yes I suppose they are," then paused a moment before diffidently asking, "Sir, are you really a Rear Admiral?"

"Very much so. That is in the British Navy Medical Reserve anyway. I suppose you wonder how it happened. Well, when the hospital started twenty years ago, we needed funds, and the Navy needed a place that could supply emergency hospital care for those who couldn't wait until their ship got to Singapore. One thing led to another, and here we are."

"I suspect there's more to tell," Andy said. "What brings you here today?"

"Wanted to check on the men I treated after the accident for one thing; also, wanted to see you, my friend. Thought we might get together with Quentin and do the town before I return home."

"I'd like that very much," Andy agreed, smiling at the thought. "I believe I need a break from routine."

"Then we shall before the week is out. Now then, may I see the men we treated?"

"Certainly. I'll take you to the infirmary and have them sent down. Doc is going to have a conniption when he learns that you outrank him," Andy concluded with a grin.

"Quentin will adjust. I recall from our medical school days that he has great recuperative powers," Dr. Jamison stoically reassured him.

"Don't you salute superior officers, Lieutenant?" Martin Jamison sternly asked, upon entering the infirmary.

Looking unsure, Quentin Patterson threw a perfect Navy salute. "Martin, if this is a joke I'll have to come up with something special."

"It's no joke," Andy said.

"Really?" Dr. Patterson asked, looking confused.

"Quentin, I'm afraid the Navy made me an officer, and it came to this," Dr. Jamison said somewhat apologetically.

"Well I'll be," Dr. Patterson drawled.

"Admiral Jamison wants to examine the men he treated after the accident," Andy said.

"That should be easy enough," Dr. Patterson responded. "I'll have Harris pull the files for you."

"Thank you. How did the trip from Helen's Landing to Singapore go with the last of the men, Quentin?"

"For the most part pretty well. Sending the two special nurses helped. A couple of the men experienced some added discomfort with the travel arrangements. Besides, a sailor prefers a boat ride to overland transport any day. What should I call you anyway, Doctor or Admiral?" Dr. Patterson asked uneasily.

"Martin is good, unless we're with a bunch of uniformed regulars. Then we would have to go by the book." Looking relieved, Dr. Patterson went to find Harris.

The rest of the day Dr. Jamison reviewed charts and examined the men who were treated at Helen's Landing. Some wore external scars that would be with them the rest of their lives, but the psychological scars were not as easy to judge. He closed the last file shortly after 1800 hours and leaned back in the creaking wooden desk chair with a sigh.

"How do they look to you, Martin?"

"Physically, I believe fairly well. I sense some tension about a repeat of what happened. But it's only natural after a trauma to have some apprehension."

"They have a real sense of loyalty to the *Mariah* and her commander," Dr. Patterson pointed out. "Some of these men have been with her through it all."

"Admiral, doctor, Commander Burns asks if you would join him for the evening meal," Sub-lieutenant Anderson formally asked from the infirmary doorway, standing at attention.

"Quentin, okay with you?" Dr. Jamison asked.

Nodding assent, Dr. Patterson rose out of his chair and set his glass down. "Thank you, Sub, I'll show the admiral the way," he said in dismissal.

"Yes sir," came Anderson's crisp reply accompanied by a stiff salute.

"Martin, you've got the youngsters all in a flap with that uniform. They'll lay in their bunks tonight and quiver with excitement at having had a real admiral aboard their ship," Dr. Patterson grinned.

"I invited my First Officer, Mason Roden, to join us as well," Andy said when the two doctors entered his outer cabin.

"A pleasure, Admiral," Mason said, saluting and shaking the offered hand.

"Thank you, Mr. Roden. Don't be fooled by the uniform. I don't know much about shipboard routine. The rank is more a formality for the Navy. It does come in handy from time to time though," Dr. Jamison allowed.

"For instance when you mention something to other Admirals, sir?" Andy suggested, with a small smile and a knowing look.

"Perhaps. Well now, this looks good," Dr. Jamison said, moving toward the fold down table set with *Mariah*'s mascot china on a linen tablecloth bearing the ships crest.

Andy asked about the recovery of the crew who were injured in the recent accident. Both doctors concluded the men were healing well from their injuries, most of which came from fighting the stubborn fire on the *Lauren*'s deck.

"And the *Victoria?*" Andy asked.

"I believe there are a few who won't be returned to active duty," Dr. Patterson put in.

"Is that true, sir?" Andy asked.

Looking straight at him, Dr. Jamison truthfully answered, "It's true. I examined three men yesterday afternoon that will have permanent disabilities. One has lost his sight. I thought at first it was from the shock of the blast, but now it appears the optic nerve was damaged. Two other men I examined may be returned to shore duty after long-term physical therapy."

"Have any of the other men lost their sight, sir?" Mason asked.

"No...no," Dr. Jamison answered. "The burns were quite severe and have caused tissue and muscle damage. In time, a great deal of it, they should regain mobility. However, they will be severely scarred. I still hold out hope that some sight may be regained in the right eye for the man I mentioned earlier. We'll have to wait and see."

"Commander," Dr. Patterson said, "you did everything possible to prevent anything happening. The crew has a great deal of faith in you."

"That's true, sir," Mason added. "I think they would follow you anywhere."

"Thank you, lieutenant, doctor. I hope we've each learned from this to prevent a reoccurrence. The *Mariah* and her crew will be called on to serve again I believe. She needs to give her best when the time comes," Andy emphasized.

"Is there something in the wind?" Dr. Patterson asked.

"I'm not sure. Admiral Edwards hinted at something involving a call he had from General Hughes' headquarters, when he summoned me earlier today," Andy answered.

"General Hughes contacted Eric, did he?" Dr. Jamison asked.

"I have a feeling you might know more than you're letting on, sir," Andy said.

"Only what I read in the newspapers or hear on the nine o'clock news. Sometimes folks stop in for a chat at my office, but that's not really anything to speak of," Dr. Jamison replied off-hand.

"I can't say I'm terribly impressed with newspaper reporters or the evening broadcasts, Martin," Dr. Patterson put in, with a snort of indignation.

"Dr. Patterson has an aversion to reporters in general," Mason explained to their guest. "He told Roger Barnes recently that being a midshipman was superior to being a reporter."

"I see. Well, gentlemen, I must return to shore. I thank you for a most informative day," Dr. Jamison said, setting his coffee cup down.

"I'll see you to the deck," Andy offered.

"Commander, I'll be in touch later in the week to arrange a time to meet with you and Lieutenant Patterson ashore," Dr. Jamison formally said before stepping over the side to the boson's whistle.

"Andy Burns tells me you spoke with him, Eric," Martin Jamison remarked, when he met Admiral Edwards at the Raffles Hotel on Wednesday evening.

"I reviewed Lieutenant Commander Burns' file and found him to be a competent officer. I recommended a Letter-of-Commendation be placed in his personnel file regarding the handling of the incident at Helen's Landing, along with a recommendation he be promoted to commander based on his overall performance as a commanding officer," Admiral Edwards responded matter-of-factly. "He may well make admiral one day if he continues on his present course."

"A very proper and insightful summation."

"Yes...well, I thought you would approve. I had a meeting with General Hughes today and one of his engineers, a Captain Vilmont. I met Vilmont a few months ago when the improved aid station project began. It was a most interesting discussion."

"Was it?" Dr. Jamison asked with interest. "Wesley appears to be a dedicated young man from what I've seen. His sister is one of my nurses."

"Interesting. Martin, is there anyone you don't know something about?" Admiral Edwards pointedly asked. "Our young captain is very earnest about his plan. I will say he made a credible presentation, giving valid reasoning for the defenses he wants to install."

"How did General Hughes respond?"

"He listened and asked some very insightful questions, as well as seeking certain technical clarifications. We're going to meet again tomorrow morning to discuss it further. Tell me this; are the people at Helen's Landing concerned for any special reason about having greater defenses?" Admiral Edwards probed with searching eyes.

"I wouldn't say so much concerned as having a certain sense of awareness. Protecting the harbor and surrounding area could be of value in an emergency."

"How are the two doctors I sent you working out?" Admiral Edwards asked, clearly not wanting to get into a deeper discussion about Wesley's proposal.

"Very nicely. We were especially glad to have them in the recent emergency and last year when we had the construction accident," Dr. Jamison answered, sensing his friend's reluctance to talk further about defenses at Helen's Landing.

"Dr. Patterson said the conditions were similar to combat," Admiral Edwards mentioned. "I wondered how they responded."

"You mean did they freeze at all in the emergency. The answer is no. The reserve status while they are with us has helped make their services more natural for the population we normally serve. Most folks think of the hospital as belonging to them, along with the harbor. The Navy's interest is usually pushed to the back of their minds, until recently anyway."

The conversation turned to catching up on people both knew and the increased submarine attacks in the Atlantic, along with reference to the American lend-lease bill regarding the planes recently sent to Singapore. "I don't know much about them, but I'm told the airplane is supposed to be the weapon of the future," Admiral Edwards skeptically noted. "We'll have to wait and see. I'm not convinced the Navy is quite finished yet. With Army units being sent north and Naval forces patrolling the shorelines, we'll have to call on your hospital more for services, Martin. The Army wanted to send one of their own doctors, but the Admiral Singapore and I informed them with three doctors from the Naval Reserve, and the local man as well, that it wouldn't be prudent at this time. We did suggest they send some qualified staff to the new aid stations Vilmont designed, not just a hastily trained medic."

"If C ward is opened, we'll need more nursing staff," Dr. Jamison pointed out.

"We thought of that and decided to send four male nurses to augment the staff. You'll still run the hospital as always. However, the Navy is in a position right now that we need to activate the military wing outlined in our agreement," Admiral Edwards said. "General Hughes will probably be in contact with you sometime soon regarding the Army's interests."

"I thought C ward might be opened before much longer. Tensions are building, I know."

"It's been an interesting evening, Martin," Admiral Edwards said, as the two friends bid each other goodnight. "I'll keep you informed as details are worked out about opening the military ward at Helen's Landing."

"I'll expect to hear from you, Eric. Until then, we'll start making arrangements on our end to have things in place.

"Very well, Martin," Admiral Edwards acknowledged, before leaving the hotel shaking his head at the varied number of people Martin Jamison knew.

Dr. Jamison made arrangements on Saturday to meet Andy and Dr. Patterson in the opulent lobby of the Raffles Hotel at 1830 hours. "Andy, Quentin, glad you could make it. Thought we might have one of those famous *Singapore Gin Slings* before we dine."

"By jove, Martin, that is a superior idea," Dr. Patterson responded with enthusiasm.

Heads turned as the three men entered the dining room when people noticed the two uniformed officers being seated. The young single, and some married, women whispered to each other about the younger one with the rugged wind blown features that surrounded the intense blue gray eyes.

"So, I said to the man, 'I don't want to buy the thing, just take a ride in it,'" Dr. Patterson was saying about his experience with a taxi driver when the waiter arrived.

"You do quibble over price in Singapore," Andy laughed. "I can remember coming to Singapore as a boy when Dad was alive and the feeling of excitement at being here. We used to have a wonderful time. I have to admit that I still feel a certain thrill when visiting."

"How did you get here from Helen's Landing?" Dr. Patterson asked.

"Paddleboat. Remember, Dr. Jamison, when it came into the harbor how people would stand and watch the goods being unloaded, and then it would take on passengers and sail away. I thought as a boy it must be very exciting to travel up and down the coast, stopping at all the different towns."

"The paddleboat still services some of the settlements along the coast and up the small tributaries. But not as many people travel on it since the coastal road went through," Dr. Jamison said.

The three men went into an alcove in the hotel lobby after a meal only the Raffles could create to enjoy an after-dinner cigar, a brandy and listen to the nine o'clock news.

"This just in," the announcer dramatically began. "The British government has declared a state of emergency in the Malayan State of Selangor, after three rubber plantation strikers were killed in a clash with the Army." The men looked at each other in surprise and waited to hear further details.

"Few facts are being released about the incident at this time," the announcer continued. "But one can only speculate that tempers between civilian workers and Army personnel have reached well beyond the breaking point, which has resulted in the unfortunate death of three of His Majesty's subjects. This is the BBC, Singapore Station, reporting."

"That doesn't sound so good," Dr. Patterson said, when the broadcast concluded. "We're supposed to be in Malaya to keep the peace, not incite what could become a riot."

"Indeed," Dr. Jamison agreed.

"I wonder what went wrong," Andy said.

"It's hard to say. Some folks resent the Army's presence and see it more as an infringement upon them," Dr. Jamison commented.

It was after eleven before Andy and Dr. Patterson returned to the *Mariah,* where Mason Roden met them on the deck. "What is it, Number One?" Andy asked.

"Sir, we've been put on alert because of the state of emergency at Selangor," Mason reported. "We have not received any sailing orders."

"Very well. Unless something more happens, we probably won't receive orders until Monday. In the mean time, restrict leave to inside the perimeter," Andy ordered.

"Yes sir."

Monday morning new orders were sent for the *Mariah* to expect two passengers, along with their sailing orders. "We take on two passengers at 1800 hours and return to Helen's Landing for a fortnight, before sailing further north to patrol the Malacca Strait. We are to return to Singapore on or about the 30th of June," Andy informed Mason.

CHAPTER 26

Martin Jamison entered Singapore's downtown Naval headquarters on Monday morning and was quickly escorted into Eric Edward's office, where he found Wesley Vilmont and General Hughes waiting for him. "Martin, come in, we've been expecting you," Admiral Edwards cheerfully invited.

"Admiral, General Hughes, Wesley," Dr. Jamison greeted them, looking quizzically at each in turn.

"I see you know Captain Vilmont, Martin," Admiral Edwards noted. "That's good. It will make General Hughes' request to have him work with a Naval officer easier to accommodate."

"What do you mean, Eric?"

"General Hughes is asking for the Navy's input regarding the most effective deterrents to enemy attack of desirable deep water ports along the Malayan coast. Since Helen's Landing meets the criteria with its harbor and immediate coastal waters and has peripheral military ties, it was thought to be an ideal location to work together on the problem."

"I see, but how does that involve me?" Dr. Jamison asked. "I'm a doctor and have little knowledge about these matters."

"That's true, Admiral Jamison," General Hughes replied. "However, we believe you are the perfect choice for the role of liaison between the Army and Navy, not to mention the general public. We certainly don't want another ugly incident like the unfortunate occurrence in Selangor last week. Your military rank is a marked advantage, and, as a leader within the civilian community, you have the ability to intercede should there be any difficulties."

"Well, Martin, you do know the area, and you can be persuasive if need be," Admiral Edwards put in. "I have the orders here bringing you to active duty for the next sixty days. You'll find sailing orders as well to join the *Mariah*. She's leaving for a routine patrol, but will break her voyage to spend a fortnight at Helen's Landing. I believe Commander Burns will be most helpful with suggestions about the harbor. Captain Vilmont will be accompanying you on the first leg of *Mariah*'s voyage as well."

"I believe that covers everything, Admiral Edwards," General Hughes said, rising from his chair. "Captain Vilmont and I will finish our meeting, and then he can report to Admiral Jamison."

After a short discussion about local laborers to work with Army personnel on the project, Wesley and General Hughes closed their briefcases and left the office. After waiting to the count of ten, Eric Edwards burst into laughter.

"What's so funny, Eric?" Dr. Jamison frowned.

"Martin, if you could have seen the look on your face when I told you about being called to active duty," Admiral Edwards responded, still chuckling and wiping tears from his eyes.

"I can't say I find it amusing, Eric," Dr. Jamison woodenly replied. "What about the hospital? I'm needed there, not to be some fancy paper pusher."

"Yes, well, you'll still be at the hospital. You do have to admit coming here with an agenda. I just flushed it out a little. Seriously Martin, I need someone on the spot to run interference if trouble starts brewing with the locals. The Navy does not wish to be drawn into an incident like Selangor, and General Hughes certainly doesn't either."

"And this way I can officially ask questions," Dr. Jamison acknowledged. "What was all this talk about Andy?"

"He's familiar with the area and has first-hand knowledge about harbor defenses. Vilmont may be an engineer, but he's not a sailor," Admiral Edwards firmly emphasized. "You can't put tank traps on water."

"Very well, Eric," Dr. Jamison sighed in acceptance. "I'll try to keep the peace. When do Wesley and I report to the *Mariah*?"

"By 1800 hours, that's 6:00 p.m. in case you've forgotten the basics. They have orders to sail at 0700 tomorrow."

The *Mariah's* OOD saw the harbor boat approaching and wondered if it was some of the crew returning and how drunk they might be. Sub-lieutenant Gaines had found being a low ranking officer less than the experience he had expected. He thought he would be in ocean battles that sank German ships when he joined the *Mariah,* not sent to this backwater pool of iniquity. He resented even more the continuous drills when nothing was happening. Gaines frowned when the harbor boat came alongside a little too fast and threw brackish water onto the boarding platform before it stopped. He saw a civilian and someone who appeared to be from the Army stepping onto the lower platform to the boarding ladder.

"Permission to come aboard," Dr. Jamison called out.

"Who are you?" Gaines asked, frowning again.

"Rear Admiral Jamison and Captain Vilmont of the Army," Gaines heard in reply to his question that by rights should have chased away these interlopers.

"Have you some identification, Admiral?" Gaines asked, with a touch of sarcasm. *Admiral my foot,* he thought. He had spent the day touring Singapore when Dr. Jamison had visited the *Mariah* the previous week and, therefore, did not recognize him. *Where's the uniform? Probably a drunk trying to put it over on the Navy, admirals don't board a ship without a uniform,* he reasoned. *Well, it won't cut any ice with me.*

Mason overheard part of the exchange and came out onto the deck to investigate. "Trouble, Sub?"

"Just a couple of drunks claiming to be an Admiral and an Army Captain," Gaines replied.

Mason's eyes went a little wide when he came close enough to see who was at the landing. "Admiral, welcome aboard, sir."

Dr. Jamison returned Gaines and Mason's salutes before extending his hand to Mason. "A pleasure, Lieutenant. I'd like to introduce Captain Wesley Vilmont from the Army."

"It's a real pleasure to be here," Wesley said, shaking Mason's hand. "I owe a great deal to this ship and her crew."

"Wesley was at Holland," Dr. Jamison briefly explained.

"It was the *Mariah* that brought me back to England," Wesley told Mason. "I don't remember very much about the voyage. I heard at the nursing home the Germans strafed the rescue ships half way across the Channel."

I remember it all too well, Mason thought, before addressing Dr. Jamison. "Admiral Jamison, what brings you here?"

"We're to join you for the first leg of your journey," Dr. Jamison replied, handing Mason the orders to sail with them. "Is Commander Burns aboard by chance?"

"Yes sir. Please, come with me," Mason said, leading the newcomers toward Andy's cabin.

Mason opened a cabin door bearing the simple brass nameplate, Commander Burns, a gift from the ranks when the promotion came through the previous day. Looking up from his desk, Andy saw Dr. Jamison entering along with someone in an Army uniform he didn't know accompanied by his first officer. "Dr. Jamison, what brings you to us?" he asked, rising to greet the unexpected visitors.

Passing along the orders, Dr. Jamison said, "I've been shanghaied into service I'm afraid."

Andy scanned the orders and realized he was in the presence of a superior officer. Quickly saluting, he said, "Admiral, welcome aboard, sir."

"Thank you. This is Captain Wesley Vilmont from His Majesty's Army Corps of Engineers."

"A real pleasure, Commander," Wesley said, warmly shaking Andy's hand. "I doubt you would remember me, but the *Mariah* and her crew saved me at Holland. I hope Dr. Patterson is still with you. He did a smashing job patching me up."

"You were wounded then?" Andy asked.

"A stray Messerschmitt had a few rounds left and let loose on a bridge we were going to blow. I heard later that my second got the job done," Wesley responded with satisfaction. "I hope to spend some time consulting with you before you leave Helen's Landing."

"What about?"

"Wesley will be designing defenses for our harbor," Dr. Jamison interjected.

"You were raised at Helen's Landing and witnessed what happened in Europe. That knowledge can help us in our quest to have a better defensive strategy," Wesley explained.

"I'll have to think about it. Number One, see that our guests are taken care of," Andy ordered.

"Yes sir. Admiral, we have a cabin available for your use. Captain, you're welcome to bunk with me."

"That would be fine," Wesley agreed. "When I've put my kit away, might I see your Dr. Patterson?"

"I'll take you there myself," Mason offered.

"Doc, you have a visitor," Mason said at the wardroom doorway.

"I heard Martin was here doing his admiral thing again," Dr. Patterson noted. "I still have trouble thinking of him in that role, but then I knew him when."

"It's not the admiral, Doc. This is Captain Wesley Vilmont from the Army. He asked to meet you."

"Doctor," Wesley beamed, shaking his hand energetically. "This is a great pleasure for me. I can finally thank you for the smashing job you did fixing me up."

It was the first time Mason could remember seeing Quentin Patterson at a loss for words. "Ah, you're welcome."

Smiling, Wesley explained, "I'm not surprised you don't remember, sir. I was wounded in the shoulder in Holland and you operated on me."

"Oh, I see," Dr. Patterson nodded. "I'm sorry to say there were so many, it's hard to keep track of who was who and put a face with them."

"I understand, believe me. Far too many were wounded or lost," Wesley said with feeling. "But that was then; hopefully something was learned from it."

"One can always hope. I wonder sometimes the way we seem to go back and forth in North Africa," Dr. Patterson replied. "Still, the *Hun* was kept out of Britain."

"I think the RAF and their Spitfire had something to do with that," Wesley pointed out.

"I'm sure you're right," Dr. Patterson agreed. "We were in the Channel last August and September. The cover was thin sometimes, but it did the job. Now..." He got no further before Midshipman Barnes came in. He informed the three men Admiral Jamison and Commander Burns wanted them to report to Commander Burn's cabin.

"I thought we could have a bite to eat and discuss the *Mariah*'s role in your plan, Captain," Andy said. "Admiral Jamison and I have discussed it, and I believe there may be some suggestions we could make. I think our Mr. Parker and Lieutenant Thompson would be helpful to you as well."

"That's great, Commander. My second has been getting the quarters in order for the men it will take to man the outpost while I've been in Singapore," Wesley responded. "Arthur is a first rate engineer and made several additional suggestions to the initial plans before Dr. Jamison saw them. I'm sure we can implement any suggested improvements."

"Dr. Jamison, you've reviewed the drawings, sir?" Andy asked.

"Yes, briefly. I thought it might be helpful to involve a Navy man, though I didn't think I would have quite so direct involvement myself."

"By jove, Martin, you do get into some interesting situations," Dr. Patterson commented.

"I might have gotten in too deep this time, Quentin. They made me take sixty days of active duty over this," Dr. Jamison forlornly explained, causing Quentin Patterson to throw back his head and howl with laughter at this unexpected explanation that left the cook's assistant, who brought their meal, to wonder what kind of party these officers were having.

"You mean you're on active duty now, sir?" Mason asked.

"I'm afraid so. Don't ask me to sail the ship, I'm a doctor who got shanghaied," Dr. Jamison dolefully sighed, shaking his head once again at how Eric Edwards had so skillfully orchestrated this turn of events.

"I would welcome your presence on the bridge tomorrow when we leave the harbor, sir," Andy invited.

"Bless my soul, I should like that," Dr. Jamison responded to the honor of being invited to join the bridge crew. Though an admiral and technically allowed access to any area of the ship, an invitation to the bridge by a ship's commander was a prestigious Naval courtesy.

Martin Jamison stood on the bridge early the following morning and marveled at the sheer size of the destroyer. He could see her four torpedo tubes positioned innocently on the deck until armed with their sinister cargo that could sink a ship. He briefly wondered what would happen if the East couldn't find a middle ground, and these weapons were brought to bear. He shivered slightly at the thought. He stood back from the forward part of the bridge, trying not to be in the way, and watched with admiration while ratings and officers moved back and forth with a sense of purpose that resembled a choreographed ballet.

"Engines on standby, sir, anchor up and down," Mason reported.

"Very well, anchors away, raise the flag," Andy ordered.

The *Mariah* passed a minesweeper and paid tribute with the boson trilling his whistle, before the other ship's boson trilled her whistle in reply. The ceremony of *leaving harbor* continued, as the *Mariah* slowly edged toward the sea with the British flag billowing proudly overhead. Martin Jamison found the ceremony involved to have a soothing affect, giving men a sense of pride to exercise time-honored traditions.

"Admiral," Andy said, "please join me."

"Magnificent," Dr. Jamison breathed, as the night's darkness released its hold over the sea to the morning sun's brilliant shades of transparent silver and gold reflecting off the crystalline surface, while the harbor unfolded before him. The empty ocean beckoned the ship to enter where sea and sky melded together on the distant horizon.

"It is a beautiful sight in the early morning to guide your ship out of the harbor with the sea softly summoning her," Andy agreed, as the two friends shared the moment to wonder at God's awesome creation. Martin Jamison watched in fascination while the *Mariah* transcended into her natural element, when she entered the Singapore Strait, and the first watch began.

"Char, sir?" the young mess man asked, after the men were dismissed from leaving harbor.

"Thank you, son, don't mind if I do," Dr. Jamison smiled. "Commander, I thank you for a most interesting and moving experience. I believe I'll leave you to it and go to the dispensary."

"You're welcome, sir. Please feel free to join the bridge crew any time."

Thursday morning the *Mariah* once again dropped her anchor in the deep water bay at Helen's Landing. The *Lauren* was no longer there, and she had the anchorage to herself for the time being.

"Dr. Jamison, it's good to have you back," Jane said when he appeared at the nurses' station. "Was your trip restful for you?"

"Until I was shanghaied, it was going quite well."

"Sir?"

"Oh, nothing, Jane, just a little humor. Are things all right here? No major crises while I was away?"

"Everything was quiet. Peter said last night the closest we came to an emergency was when Mrs. Thomas had her baby almost before they could get her to the delivery room."

"Evelyn had her baby, did she? I was beginning to think it just didn't want to see this old world. What did she have, boy or girl? I suppose I should go see her when I get changed."

"Six pound, seven ounce girl. They named her Patricia Ann."

"Dr. Jamison! You're back," John declared in some surprise, when he came around the hallway corner.

"So it would seem. I have some things to attend to, and then I want to see you and Peter. Give me about an hour," Dr. Jamison instructed, before going down the hall to his office.

"I wonder why he's wearing that uniform," John thoughtfully mused.

"I thought it was something he picked up in Singapore," Jane answered, crinkling her eyes slightly in question.

"Those were admiral's stripes on his sleeve. You don't wear them unless you're entitled to," John replied. "I know he's a reserve, but why the uniform?"

The rest of the day Jane pondered what John had said about Dr. Jamison being in uniform. She hadn't thought about Peter still being attached to the Navy, and other than the time he had been called to Singapore, the Navy seemed to have forgotten about him. Now she wondered again if Peter would be called away.

That evening Peter was his usual cheerful self but did notice Jane seemed distracted. "What's on your mind?" he asked.

"Just something John mentioned today."

"What was that?" Peter prompted.

"About the way Dr. Jamison was dressed when he came back today."

"Oh that," Peter said, starting to laugh.

"I don't see what's so funny."

"Sorry," Peter apologized, still smiling. "It seems while he was away Dr. Jamison went to see his friend, Admiral Edwards, about Wesley Vilmont's defense plans, at least indirectly. One thing led to another, and he was made the liaison between the Army, Navy and the local population. Admiral Edwards brought him to active duty for sixty days until the project is finished."

"John said there were admiral stripes on his sleeve. Is that true?" Jane asked.

"Dr. Jamison is a Rear Admiral in the British Navy Medical Corps Reserves. Technically, he's my superior officer as well as John's." Starting to laugh again, Peter told her, "He says he was shanghaied."

"So that's what he meant this morning," Jane said, starting to laugh. She hesitated in further thought before speaking again. "Peter, do you think we'll be all right here? I mean, with all that's happening and now Wesley's increased defenses?"

"I think so. I'm quite sure the Navy would evacuate us if there was any real danger."

"Even with all this build up the Army has done and more coming all the time?"

"We're medical people and kept well away from where any shooting might be. They would evacuate us before it came to that, I'm sure," Peter reassured her. Taking her hand, Peter drew Jane to him, gently holding her close and kissing her. "Don't worry, darling, I'll be with you. I love you," he murmured, once again seeking her lips.

"Peter," Jane whispered, before closing her eyes as he caressed her slender body. "I do so love you."

CHAPTER 27

Wesley's defense plan began to take shape as soon as the *Mariah* dropped her anchor at Helen's Landing. Andy and Brian Jones reviewed the coastal chart before drawing a comprehensive blueprint with helpful suggestions by Parker and Thompson for additional shoreline fortifications along a five-mile strip north and south of the village.

"I not only owe you for saving me in Holland," Wesley remarked late Saturday evening, "I am also grateful for your help here, Commander Burns."

"Please, call me Andy. Most folks around here do."

"All right, Andy," Wesley agreed with a smile, "I'm Wesley or Wes to most." Both men felt a sense of camaraderie beginning to grow between them.

"Come," Andy responded to the unexpected knock at his door. Midshipman Barnes entered looking dazed and colorless, bearing a radio message that loosely hung in his left hand. "What is it, Mid?"

"Sir," Roger began in a barely audible voice, "The *Hood,* sir, she was sunk in the Denmark Strait by German battleships. My...my brother, sir, he was aboard her."

"Easy there, sailor," Andy softly counseled, as he gently removed the flimsy sheet of flash paper from Roger's limp hand.

Roger Barnes was valiantly fighting the emotions that threatened to overwhelm him in the presence of his commanding officer. His older brother, Tom, had been like a father to him after theirs died in the 1930s influenza epidemic. *How will I go on now that Tom is gone?* he wondered, before looking up to see Commander Burns watching him and drew himself up so as not to place a shadow on Tom's memory.

The war had once again touched the *Mariah,* Andy reflected. His body tensed when he realized the loss of life as he scanned the Navy's brief signal with the cold official words. "Over 1,400 men," he said aloud, before recognizing the valiant struggle Roger Barnes was making to ward off the terrible blow the terse message had delivered to his soul. "I'm truly sorry, Mr. Barnes," he consoled, placing a hand on Roger's shoulder. "Report to Dr. Patterson, and tell him I sent you."

"Yes sir, thank you sir," Roger croaked, before leaving the cabin and stumbling slightly as he made his way to the dispensary.

Andy gave Wesley a bleak look after Roger left them. "Doc will get him through this. It would take away his dignity to openly mourn his loss in front of me. All those men," he breathed, still in shock that the *Hood,* a heavy battleship, was lost.

"It's hard to take in. We had considerable losses in Holland. But it's unreal to think of so many in a single moment," Wesley quietly said, as he began to grasp the magnitude of the loss.

"What ho, young Barnes, what brings..." Dr. Patterson cheerfully started, and then stopped when he saw the white face and dazed expression.

"Commander Burns sent me," Roger started to explain, but the grief of his loss could no longer be denied.

"What's happened?" Dr. Patterson quietly asked, placing a gentle hand on Roger's shoulder.

"I'm sorry, sir," Roger shakily whispered. "The *Hood,* sir, she's been sunk with no apparent survivors. My..." he started to say, but then had to take a breath before continuing. "My oldest brother, Tom, he was aboard her."

"I see," Dr. Patterson slowly responded. "I'm sorry, Roger. It's not much, but I am truly sorry."

"Thank you, sir," Roger softly acknowledged, before giving in to his grief.

"Here, drink this," Dr. Patterson instructed after a few more minutes passed, handing over a glass containing two fingers of brandy. "It will help to sustain you a bit."

Roger sat with Dr. Patterson throughout the night watch, telling him about his older brother and how he had always looked up to Tom. Quentin Patterson listened with infinite patience to the small everyday incidents from a childhood that caused the bond between the two brothers to gain strength and endurance, asking simple questions when Roger flagged. *Roger Barnes should be with his family immersed in familiar surroundings, with the local parish priest to offer words of comfort and hope,* he thought. But these were abnormal times, and Quentin Patterson was fairly certain this would not be the last time he sat with a crewman because the war had short-changed another life.

"I just had a letter yesterday," Roger brokenly said.

"It might not be much, but it is something to remember him by over time," Dr. Patterson noted.

"Yes…yes it is," Roger sighed.

The following Sunday evening the officers not on watch were gathered in the wardroom having a gin and talking about the war in the Atlantic, when the discussion turned to the *Hood.*

"I still have trouble taking it in," Sub-lieutenant Anderson commented.

"I heard the German battleships *Bismarck* and *Prinz Eugen* were both involved. The *Hood* was out gunned with both battleships attacking, otherwise it might have been a draw," Sub-lieutenant Humes reasoned.

"Humph," Gaines grumbled.

"You have another opinion, Sub?" Mason asked.

"Laxness on the part of the gunners," Gaines bluntly stated.

"How do you figure that?" Mason asked.

"It's apparent, since it has been reported that the enemy escaped unscathed. It just proves a rating needs hard discipline," Gaines asserted, with full confidence in his belief.

"Excuse me," Roger said, leaving the room.

"Mr. Gaines, if I were you, I wouldn't advertise that opinion," Dr. Patterson cautioned.

"Those men gave their lives defending not only their ship but England as well!" Sub-lieutenant Humes passionately imparted. "Why, Midshipman Barnes lost his brother on the *Hood.*"

"Sometimes you come up with the daftest notions, Gaines," Sub-lieutenant Perkins said, causing Gaines to excuse himself from the wardroom.

"Is it true, sir?" Anderson asked after Gaines had left the wardroom. "Was Roger Barnes' brother on the *Hood?*"

"It's true," Mason interjected. "He was a gunnery officer who was commended in the past for his service by the *Hood*'s captain. Doctor, would you have time to see me before retiring?"

"Of course, come along by all means."

Quentin Patterson let loose with a series of epithets when the dispensary door closed before pouring out two brandies. "What are we going to do about that buffoon?" he finally asked, still somewhat heated about Gaines' apparent lack of all sensitivity. "He's a menace, not to mention being a bloody fool."

"I know, Doc," Mason sighed, shaking his head. "I've come down on him and so has Commander Burns. He simply doesn't seem to understand it's the men's loyalty you need, especially now."

"Well, thanks for letting me spout off anyway," Dr. Patterson responded, resigning himself to the apparent impassé regarding the unpopular Mr. Gaines.

"Any time, Doc."

Monday morning found Dr. Patterson waiting for Martin Jamison to return to his office. "Quentin, I wasn't expecting to see you."

"No, probably not. Martin, I need some advice, and I believe you are the only one who would be qualified to give it."

"All right, I'll do my best," Dr. Jamison offered. "What seems to be the problem?"

"Suppose you had a situation that caused a sense of unease among your staff, but your hands were tied to do anything about it. Would you allow it to go unchecked and continue to erode, or perhaps find a way to rid yourself of it?"

"A difficult dilemma. Is there such a situation?"

"Let us say the pot shows signs of boiling," Dr. Patterson evaded.

"I see. Well, it's always best to have harmony, but it isn't always possible. People do have off days you know. I assume we're talking about a person and not an event."

"A very unpleasant one."

"Unless you have authority, and I assume you don't, there really isn't much you can do, Quentin," Dr. Jamison pointed out.

"I'd like to give him a little something, so I could tell him his appendix was bad."

"I'm afraid we can't do that, my friend," Dr. Jamison cautioned.

"I know, Martin, but I feel better having unburdened myself."

Admiral Jamison took the motorboat out to the *Mariah* later that afternoon, knowing that Andy and Quentin Patterson were with Wesley on shore. He talked with the men and paid attention to their body language and indirect comments, as he mentioned various officers.

"Commander Burns now, 'e's capital, 'e is," Bert approved. "Never treats ya likes ya was beneath 'im. Ain't that so, Ernie?"

"Oh, yes sir, 'e's a tops, 'e is," Ernie agreed. "That Lieutenant Roden too. 'Ee talks and makes a man 'ave pride in wot 'e does. Shares a joke now an' then too 'e does."

"What about your other officers?" Dr. Jamison asked.

Sniffing some, Bert debated how much or little to tell. The admiral was Commander Burns' friend, but he was an admiral. He finally opted for the ratings safe reply and sought neutral ground. "Most a them's okay. Not as capital as Commander Burns, but then they's not 'ad the 'spirience yet. Like children still needin' some 'elp from their mums."

"Hrump," Ernie snorted. "Those 'ose willin' to take suggestion 'hat tis."

"I see," Dr. Jamison responded, while gaining insight by what was left unsaid. He knew from experience that the two men would not comment further about their superiors, who in the civilian population would be called their betters. "Thank you, gentlemen."

"What-a-ya mean spoutin' off?" Bert irritably asked, after the admiral was out of earshot.

"What-cha mean? I didn't say who it twas," Ernie retorted.

"Parker, why are those men loafing there? Get them back to work before I bring them up on defaulters," Gaines heatedly ordered.

"Right away, sir," Parker responded. Martin Jamison shivered when he noticed the cold hatred toward the unfeeling taskmaster in Tim Parker's eyes, as Parker went to reprimand the men that he had just spoken with.

"Have to watch them every minute or they slack off. Is there anything else you need, Admiral?" Gaines asked.

"No, I've seen enough for today."

Martin Jamison pondered the situation upon returning to shore. The following afternoon he believed he had worked out a solution acceptable to the Navy and in the *Mariah*'s best interest and put in a trunk call to Admiral Edwards.

"Martin! I say, how are things going up there?" Eric Edwards enthusiastically greeted his friend.

"Quite well, Eric, quite well," came the scratchy response over the tenuous telephone connection. "Tell me Eric, do you remember speaking about the need for an assistant to your aide?"

"Why yes. Don't tell me you've found someone, Martin. I'd have to question your motive after bamboozling you," Admiral Edwards lightly responded.

"On the contrary, Eric. I've found the assignment most interesting."

"Uh-huh. So, who is this person you've found?" Admiral Edwards asked, letting a touch of suspicion creep into his voice.

"He's a sub-lieutenant named Gaines. I believe he would be much more useful at a shore post to tell the truth, Eric."

"I see, and where might he be now?"

"Right now he's serving on the *Mariah,*" Dr. Jamison answered matter-of-factly.

"But she's to leave there at the end of the week," Admiral Edwards objected. "It would leave her short an officer."

"Not if a deserving young man were dispatched by airplane, say in the morning, from Singapore. It could return with the other young man," Dr. Jamison suggested in the practical voice of reason.

"I see you have it all worked out," Admiral Edwards responded, waiting a moment in thought before continuing. "Very well, I guess I owe you for pressing you into service. Not that you didn't deserve it, mind. I do have someone who came to me last month from England. To tell the truth he stinks as a clerk. I'll have the orders cut and make the necessary signals. And Martin, I trust this is the last one for a while."

"I think you can count on it, Eric," Dr. Jamison assured his friend.

"Very well then," Admiral Edwards agreed.

"I'll send in a progress report on the other business the end of the week," Dr. Jamison said, before he rang off.

"Mr. Gaines, report to Commander Burns," a voice ordered over the *Mariah*'s tannoy speaker the following afternoon.

"Gaines, reporting as ordered, sir."

Have to hand it to him, Andy thought, returning the perfect salute. *At least he can get protocol right if nothing else.* "Mr. Gaines, I have a signal from Singapore that orders you to report to the airfield at Umbai at 1000 hours tomorrow. You will be flown to Singapore and are to report to Admiral Edwards."

"But sir, I didn't put in for a transfer," Gaines objected.

"Nor did I ask to have you replaced," Andy replied.

"Then, I don't understand," Gaines said somewhat puzzled.

"Sometimes the Navy places a man and then decides he would be of greater use somewhere else; though I don't know the reason here. I will have to say some of your service has been very good, especially in organization," Andy said. "On the other hand, where the men are concerned, there is need for improvement. Discipline is important and has its place, but it must be applied in a manner that maintains the dignity of the disciplinarian and those receiving instruction," Andy noted. "I'll have Lieutenant Roden make the necessary arrangements to see that you are taken to the airfield." Extending his hand, Andy said, "Good luck to you."

Taking the proffered hand before formally saluting his superior, Gaines realized for the first time he wouldn't be missed by his shipmates. He still wasn't convinced that hard discipline wasn't the key to gaining the desired outcome with the rank and file. The men were, after all, supposed to respond to orders from those with a higher rank. *I hope my next post isn't a destroyer, or, worse, a battleship. I don't really like being at sea,* Gaines thought as he prepared to pack his belongings.

Andy left the ship with Dr. Patterson Wednesday evening to join his mother and Dr. Jamison before the *Mariah* sailed. "Mother," he said, affectionately kissing her cheek, "it's good to see you. I hope to get up to the house tomorrow for a few hours before we sail."

"That would be splendid. I would like that very much," Helen beamed.

"Mrs. Burns, lovely as always," Dr. Patterson greeted. "Martin."

"Thank you, doctor, but I thought you agreed to call me Helen."

"As you wish, Helen."

"Admiral," Andy said, saluting and shaking the offered hand. "Thank you for the invitation."

The party retired to Dr. Jamison's restful native Malayan furnished sitting room that brought out the vibrant color and rich native woods. His houseboy served after dinner coffee, before sliding the double doors to the dinning room together, leaving the doctor and his guests to their conversation. The good doctor, he thought, spent too much time at the hospital. It was good for him to have people in and entertain.

"At least no one was seriously hurt on the *Mariah,*" Helen commented about the previous February's incident, when the discussion turned to the *Mariah* and her crew.

"No, the *Mariah* was very fortunate," Andy agreed. "The *Victoria* wasn't as lucky."

"She was able to return to Singapore under her own power. I know you mean the men though," Dr. Jamison said. "I'm still unable to comprehend the *Hood* and the loss of life with her."

"At least the *Mariah* and her crew were well away from it," Helen emphasized.

"I wish I could say no one on board was really touched by it," Andy responded.

"What do you mean, Andy?" Dr. Jamison asked.

"The midshipman who was given the signal to bring to me lost a brother on the *Hood,*" Andy explained.

"How dreadful!" Helen declared with feeling. "What an awful way to learn you've lost a loved one. This terrible war. I wonder when it will end."

"Perhaps when the politicians find better ways than shooting at each other to solve their differences," Dr. Patterson responded.

Changing the subject, Dr. Jamison asked, "What was the business with the Army Land Rover yesterday morning? It looked like one of your people in it, Andy."

"One of the sub-lieutenants was recalled to Singapore rather suddenly, and another sent to replace him before we sail. It was a bit unorthodox. I was lucky Wesley could loan us his vehicle to drive to the airstrip."

"Good riddance, I say," Dr. Patterson interjected. "He wasn't the most pleasant fellow."

"What about the replacement?" Helen asked.

"His record seems all right, nothing to suggest poor performance of any kind," Andy responded. "He was a gunnery officer in the Mediterranean before being sent to Singapore and saw some pretty heavy fighting there before his sloop was sunk."

The evening ended with talk about the success of the hospital fundraiser. "We really did quite well," Helen said. "Of course, Jane and Sally were a big help in organizing it. Sally's brother, Wesley, was there representing the Army, but he was called away before I had a chance to meet him."

"With the fortifications that are being constructed, it was good for Wesley to show interest in the town's events. I'm just sorry he was called away before meeting some of the locals," Dr. Jamison said.

"I hope your better defenses never come to the test, Martin. This conference in Tokyo with the Axis countries is a worry," Dr. Patterson said.

"At least Churchill was given a vote of confidence, and the government isn't haggling with itself like it did after Norway," Andy commented.

"Germany was kept from invading England though," Helen interjected.

"Yes, but it was close. The invasion of Holland at a time our government was in turmoil gave the Germans an advantage," Andy pointed out.

Helen mentioned the cottage before they said good night. "I told Peter and Jane to use it from time to time to escape everyday life and enjoy the beauty of paradise."

"I'm glad to see it being used more," Andy approved before saluting Dr. Jamison and once more shaking the offered hand. "Good night, sir, and thank you for the enjoyable evening."

"I hope there isn't a serpent in paradise," Dr. Patterson remarked in the motor launch on the return trip to the *Mariah*.

"What do you mean, Doc?" Andy asked.

"This conference in Tokyo, I hope it isn't a step toward hostilities breaking out in the East," Dr. Patterson explained.

"If the rumors about Russia hold any truth to them, it could be they're talking about the possibility of the Soviets joining in with the Axis countries. Russia did sign a non-aggression treaty with Germany in '39," Andy reminded him.

"That could mean an entirely new set of problems. I don't believe the world is ready to see a fourth country become part of Germany's bid to conquer a major portion of it."

"Britain may still have something to say about that," Andy grimly replied, as the launch came alongside the *Mariah*'s boarding ladder.

CHAPTER 28

Helen watched the *Mariah* weigh anchor early Saturday morning from an upstairs window and turn north into the Malacca Strait. She whispered the *Sailor's Prayer,* while signing the cross, asking God to grant *Mariah*'s crew a safe voyage while she watched the ship disappear over the horizon.

The nine o'clock news broadcast on Saturday evening reported the Japanese delegation made a formal proposal to the Netherlands and Britain in an attempt to break the trade negotiation deadlock. The Japanese Foreign Minister, however, the day before was quoted as stating that Japan would carry out her obligations with her Tripartite partners. *Doesn't their government know what it wants?* Helen wondered.

Wesley's defense plan was nearing completion in June. The abandoned Charmical plantation was fully restored under Arthur's direction and ready to accept the Army troops that would man the outpost. The antiaircraft guns and checkpoints around the harbor were in place, and the outlying defenses were taking shape. "Sir, the defenses are shaping up nicely. I believe we will have a credible presentation after this to give to Singapore," Arthur commented, when he and Wesley inspected the latest emplacement and found it satisfactory.

The BBC reported in early June that Japan had signed a commercial agreement with Russia for mutually most favored nation treatment and barter exchange of goods. London and Stockholm, on the other hand, were reporting Nazi troops concentrated along the Soviet frontier, leaving a few people in the area wondering whether Moscow's agreement with Tokyo was the first step toward bringing Russia into the Axis alliance.

"A most perplexing development," John commented, when the broadcast regarding this new development between Russia and Japan ended.

"Why do you say that?" Peter asked.

"Only that you wonder if Hitler wants a friend to his east and will honor the '39 pact he made with Stalin, or if he has a more sinister motive."

"I see what you mean. He's anti-Communist, but Japan has a trade agreement with Russia. And Japan is Germany's ally." Peter cocked his head to one side a moment in thought, and then smiled slightly when he spoke. "I wonder what Stalin is thinking?"

"Churchill is probably wondering the same thing," John surmised.

The Japanese and Dutch trade negotiations were in danger of breaking down by mid June. A Japanese spokesman revealed during a radio interview that the Dutch reply was *very unsatisfactory* when Japan demanded the right to share in the Netherlands East Indies' economic exploitation.

"Another blow to the easing of tempers and loss of face," John remarked, after switching off the latest broadcast.

"It's almost as if Japan is battling with itself," Peter commented. "One group wants to talk, and the other doesn't."

"Japan is at a crossroads," Tom Linn explained. "To lose face would be an insult to their Emperor, but to become the aggressor may also be unacceptable." Tom Linn's summation appeared to explain the situation on both sides of the ocean, as the diplomatic corps worked with one hand tied and armies prepared themselves for battle.

Jane and Peter entertained their first guests on Sunday, June 22, 1941, with a small dinner party. The newlyweds felt a special anticipation that Helen and Dr. Jamison, who had done so much to make their wedding day memorable, would be their first guests along with Sally and John.

"My dear, you and Peter have done wonders with this place," Helen complimented her hostess after accepting Jane's invitation to tour their home.

"Thank you, it did turn out well," Jane agreed, with a new homeowner's pride in the finished product. "Sally helped to pick out the curtains. Peter and I had fun painting it. I'm not sure though what got more paint, the walls or us."

"Your first home is especially enjoyable to decorate and make it your own. Not to mention the fun that can be had while doing the work."

Jane served a traditional American Sunday dinner of roast chicken on the newly sanded and varnished dining table that was salvaged from disposal. She continued the American theme with the traditional June dessert: strawberry shortcake.

"That was delicious," Dr. Jamison complimented. "Peter, you better be careful or your waistline will increase by the inches."

"Tomorrow it will be rice with no sauce to make up for today," Peter laughed. "Jane says doctors are terrible about watching their diet, so she watches it for me."

"Yes, and if you're bad you shan't have the offer of seconds on dessert," Jane put in.

"See what I mean," Peter impishly jested, pulling a long face.

"You sound terribly abused," Sally bantered.

Conversation flowed between the generations, with topics discussed from the church organist appearing a little inebriated at the late Sunday Evening Prayer Service, "too much Communion wine," Peter interjected, to the more somber developments lately with Japan.

"I really do wonder what they want," Helen said. "Their government agencies seem to contradict themselves. One talks of negotiating, while another says they see no common ground."

"Most likely a piece of the pie, as the Americans say," John suggested.

"You're picking up American slang quite well, John," Jane commented. "Seriously though, I believe President Roosevelt will encourage Congress to do whatever is necessary to carry out the lend-lease program with Britain, while trying to keep some semblance of peace in the Pacific."

"He may have trouble there, Jane," John cautioned. "Japan has an element that is reported to be itching for a fight, and it's growing stronger I think."

"It's nearly nine o'clock, should I turn on the news?" Peter asked, thinking it would help turn the conversation away from its current direction.

"A splendid idea, Peter," Helen affirmed.

The radio emitted squeaks and high pitched squalling before settling into a steady hum until the tubes warmed up, before Peter adjusted the dial in time to hear the announcer begin.

"This is the BBC reporting. When it was thought a fourth nation might be added to the Axis partners, an all out offensive by German armed forces invading Soviet Russia began today instead," the announcer boldly stated, and then paused a moment for his listeners to absorb the dramatic statement.

"What?" Helen gasped.

"Unbelievable," Dr. Jamison breathed, somewhat stunned by this new development in the world order.

"Reports are sketchy at the time of this broadcast regarding damage and loss of life caused by the Nazi planes that bombed several Russian cities, including Kiev, Odessa, and Minsk. The aerial attack was soon followed by German armored ground troops crossing into Soviet territory," the announcer continued. "Hitler claims the, and I quote, 'Russian betrayal' of the 1939 pact has caused Germany to declare war against her eastern neighbor. There is no word as yet from Moscow about this blatant act of aggression, or the rumors Mr. Churchill tried to send a warning to Mr. Stalin that Hitler was preparing an attack against the Russian nation. Our sources in Japan were unavailable for comment, and no official statement has been forthcoming by this Axis partner. The trade agreement so recently signed between Japan and Russia may now be in jeopardy over this latest betrayal by Japan's ally, Nazi Germany. This is the BBC, Singapore Station, reporting."

Everyone sat in stunned silence after the broadcast ended; trying to take in the latest report that Germany once again was striking out against her neighbor. Only one year had passed since the swift fall of Norway and Western Europe and the British rescue of Allied troops on the beaches at Dunkirk. The question now was whether Russia would follow in 1941.

"Russia is a large country. They may stop them," Sally said without conviction.

"I hope you're right, but I wonder. Germany sailed through Europe mighty fast last year," John pointed out.

"All we can do is wait to see what develops in the next few weeks," Dr. Jamison reasoned. "The Russians are stubborn, and Stalin won't give ground very easily."

"The conference of the Axis countries couldn't have addressed this," Peter commented. "Japan wouldn't have made the trade agreement with Russia. I wouldn't think so anyway."

"Perhaps it will make the Japanese reconsider their decision to break negotiations in the Netherlands East Indies, and with whom they align themselves," Dr. Jamison said.

"That would be a step toward offering peace," Helen hopefully suggested. "It could lead to both sides feeling satisfaction and a willingness to compromise."

It was apparent by the end of the week Germany would not be easily stopped, as she gained ground on Russian soil, coming within fifty miles of Minsk. Another blow to the hope of negotiated differences came when the Japanese Trade Commission sailed from the Netherlands East Indies without an agreement and set no date to meet with western representatives in the foreseeable future. The last Sunday in June the Japanese Prime Minister stated he saw no reason why Japan and the United States could not remain friendly.

"America won't back down," Jane stated with conviction, after the latest broadcast. "Japan doesn't understand the American attitude."

"That seems to be the problem," Helen responded. "The East and the West don't understand each other at all." She and Jane were at the cottage talking over a cup of tea after listening to the afternoon broadcast a week after

Jane and Peter's dinner party. Jane had offered to help repaper the guest bedroom when Helen mentioned she wanted to spruce the rooms up a bit.

The afternoon news broadcast on June 30 reported the French Vichy government had broken diplomatic relations with Russia. "Not unexpected since Germany pretty much dictates what they will do," John commented in the doctor's lounge afterwards.

"It does make me wonder if Stalin was hedging his bets by initiating relations with the Vichy government in the first place, and then lost when Germany invaded," Peter remarked.

Jane and Peter were relaxing in their sitting room on the Fourth of July, after compromising over America's Independence Day. Teasing, Jane said, "Why Peter, we always had fireworks and parades and picnics. People put their flags out for Independence Day," giving emphasis to the word independence and laughing at the long face he pulled.

"My dear, the British are noted for taking their defeats with dignity. Of course, the colonies are still a bit uppity about their unfortunate misjudgment in parting with king and country," Peter drolly responded to Jane's comments. Then, unable to stop himself, he burst into laughter. It was decided by mutual agreement that a picnic on the waterfront would be in order before returning home in time to hear the nine o'clock evening news broadcast.

"This is the BBC, reporting from Singapore," was announced just as Peter tuned in the wireless set. "In an address to the nation and world today, Mr. Wilkie of the United States Navy is quoted as saying he was quite certain that before long the great force of the American Navy will be, and I quote, 'brought into play' to ensure delivery of aid to Britain. President Roosevelt's speech to the American nation on their national holiday reiterated America's determination to assure delivery of goods to the British people. Mr. Churchill, in response to Mr. Roosevelt's speech, thanked the American people for their support and urged America to continue the life giving lend-lease plan. This is the BBC, Singapore Station, reporting."

"It seems celebrating your holiday is in order today," Peter said, switching off the set.

"I would guess there's a lot of support for Britain in the U.S. right now after Germany turned against Russia," Jane surmised.

While Jane and Peter talked in their sitting room, Wesley discussed the evening's BBC broadcast with Arthur Nance and John Hartman. "Well, I must say, it's good to hear the Americans are finally starting to take things more seriously, Arthur said.

"The way things are going with Japan it wouldn't hurt to have a few of those supplies sent here," John emphasized.

"I would like to see a more up to date fighter plane out here," Wesley agreed. "I've been told the Japanese Zero is a good airplane and difficult to out maneuver with what we have now."

"It would also give some needed air support to ground troops," Arthur pointed out.

"The Spitfire made a difference last year against the Germans. Dunkirk would have been a debacle without what air cover we did get," Wesley noted.

The men talked for some time about Russia's inability to halt the German Army and Hitler's unnerving audacity. It was the general consensus that Hitler wanted to rule a large portion of the world and would crush his neighbors at every opportunity to reach that heady goal. Europe was half way around the world from Malaya though, and the discussion eventually turned to local concerns and the British troops to be stationed at Helen's Landing. The Army high command concluded since Helen's Landing contained heavier fortifications that British troops were preferable to the Australian troops outlined in the project's planning stages. "Give the people traditional troops, and they're more likely to accept the changes," Wesley quoted to John and Arthur from Singapore's directive.

After a busy week, Wesley and his crew completed the final stages of construction. He walked around the last shore emplacement one more time, before starting toward the hospital to meet Sally, along with Jane and Peter, to relax beside the seashore. Sally had wiled away his initial reluctance, using a course of reasoning that was hard to deny, as she had so often done during their childhood. "Come on Wes, it will be fun. Besides, you can't work all the time," she had said. "I've hardly seen you while you've been here." Wesley had given in and said he would meet them on the hospital lawn by noon.

"Wes, over here," Sally called out.

Waving, Wesley walked over to the patio where recuperating patients often sat to look out at the ocean. "Hello! Am I late?"

"Only a little. Did you bring your bathing trunks?"

"And a towel, mum," Wesley replied, with an impish grin.

"Jane and Peter will be out in a minute. We convinced Helen Burns to come along as well."

"I haven't had a chance to meet her. I understand she's an interesting person to know."

"Here they come now. Hello, Helen, I'm so glad you decided to join us. Before we go, I'd like you to meet my brother, Wesley."

"Mrs. Burns, a pleasure," Wesley smiled, taking the proffered hand.

"It's nice to meet you, Wesley. Sally's talked of you often."

Wesley was a little surprised when the small party took a wide well worn path that appeared to just go off into the jungle with no apparent purpose. The wall of trees ended after a few minutes at a small expanse of sandy beach with gentle waves lapping the shore, not more than sixty feet in width. He wondered briefly how many little beaches like this dotted the Malayan coastline.

The afternoon was spent lazing on the beach between dashes into the cool inviting water. The friends pointed out birds diving toward the sea in search of fish and saw a group of Proas, the Malayan version of a Chinese Junk, go by in the distance, with their bright colored sails fluttering in the breeze. The warm tropics lived up to the reputation of being a paradise, leaving the war and threat of more aggression forgotten in this magical environment. The little group reluctantly returned to the hospital lawn at the end of a delightful afternoon to meet Dr. Jamison and John at teatime.

"Martin, you missed a perfectly lovely afternoon," Helen greeted her long-time friend, when he appeared to share tea and cakes with the returning swimmers. "I can't remember when I've felt so relaxed."

"Perhaps I should prescribe it from time-to-time for my patients that tend to overdo and are in need of a restful vacation."

"Perhaps," Helen allowed.

"Sorry I'm late," John briefly apologized, taking a seat at the outdoor table. "Since Mr. Smyth was persuaded to follow a doctor's orders, getting through one of his examinations takes quite some time."

"A job well done," Peter interjected with a smile.

"Tea?" Sally asked.

"Yes, thank you," John accepted, taking a biscuit off the tray. "So, did everyone have a good swim?"

"Very nice," Jane confirmed. "Next time you have to come as well."

That evening Wesley and Sally joined Jane and Peter at the little restaurant in town. The radio played the latest songs from England until the evening news began.

"This is the BBC reporting. Late reports today from our remote sources confirm the Japanese government took control on Friday last of that nation's financial establishments," the announcer began. "All private Japanese banking institutions have now become virtual subsidiaries to the Bank of Japan, as the new government bureau has been named by Japanese officials. In further updates from the East, it is reported the Japanese Army began today to move troops and equipment from Tonkin in northern Viet Nam, south, toward Saigon, that country's capitol city. And now a word from our sponsors," the announcer said, before the latest dry goods store commercial began.

"Fighting continues in Russia with German troops pushing toward Moscow against a stubborn and tenacious Red Army," the broadcast continued at the conclusion of the live advertisement. "Little detailed information is available, other than the estimates of mounting casualties, as Soviet citizens defend their native soil. This is the BBC, Singapore Station, reporting. Goodnight."

"I don't like the sound of the latest developments in Japan," Wesley said.

"I don't understand. Did their government just take over the banks?" Sally asked.

"That's what it sounds like," Wesley confirmed.

"But that means no one has any say about how their money is used outside the government," Jane objected. "The Japanese government could just take everything and use it any way they want."

"You still don't hear anything about their Emperor," Peter noted. "I wonder if he realizes what's going on."

"He must," Wesley said. "They don't do anything without his okay. Those people worship him. I'm concerned about this drive toward Saigon as well. After the aborted negotiations in the NEI, it could be a step toward further aggression in the Pacific. Saigon has a good sheltered seaport."

"Japan wouldn't be a serious threat here though, would they? They're still at war with China," Sally reasoned.

"That might be, sis, but it will bear watching for further developments," Wesley responded to the somewhat naive logic behind the false sense of security that so many British citizens held.

CHAPTER 29

The *Mariah* was at sea when German forces crossed onto Russian soil. "The question about what the German Army was doing at Russia's western border is answered," Mason remarked, when the *Mariah* received a signal about the invasion.

"I wonder if Hitler's Army will sail through Russia as quickly as it did Western Europe," Andy questioned. "It would give Germany a coastline to exploit in the Pacific."

"That would link Germany with her ally in the East if the Russians don't stop them," Brian Jones calmly pointed out.

"Yes," Andy agreed. "It would more readily open the East for the Germans to link with the Japanese."

"Not a pleasant thought," Mason observed. "No, not pleasant at all."

The group anchored in Jakarta's large harbor a fortnight before weighing anchor once more and entering the Java Sea. *Mariah*'s orders had kept her crew busy updating oceanographic charts and maps of the tiny islands scattered throughout the region, venturing inshore as close as possible without grounding to sound the depths of little known coves and bays. "Keep a close watch on the fathometer," Andy cautioned, when it seemed the ocean bottom was rising to meet them. "We don't want to run aground."

"You can depend on it, sir," Lieutenant Brian Jones assured him. "I wouldn't want to get off and push," he grinned, bringing a chuckle from the bridge crew.

Mariah turned her bow toward Bangka and Belitung Islands on the final leg of her journey, taking the Gaspar Strait into the South China Sea. Dozens of islands sprang from the sea, with some no larger than a city block. Others contained growing British and Dutch settlements sporting valuable harbors that shipped oil and vital raw materials to their mother countries. Shifting depths brought by the continuous rise and fall of the tides and constantly changing ocean currents were carefully documented, as they approached Singkep at the southern island cluster leading to Singapore.

The crew heard upon arrival in Singapore the third Wednesday in July that the United States had mined the Manila and Subic bays in the Philippines. "Looks like the Americans are getting serious," Anderson commented that evening in the wardroom.

"About time," Dr. Patterson replied.

The wardroom conversation that evening revolved around Churchill's claim the British had achieved air equality with Germany thanks to the American lend-lease agreement. News came the following week from Russia that Moscow was being heavily bombed, along with the announcement that Stalin had officially been installed as the Commander and Chief of the Red Army.

"Hitler better beware," Dr. Patterson remarked, after hearing about Stalin's promotion. "I've heard he is ruthless toward his enemies and seeks revenge in as unpleasant a manner as humanly possible."

"The Germans may have a tough time when winter sets in if they don't reach their objective by fall," Mason noted.

"All the more reason to hope Stalin is true to form."

"What-cha readin', Doc?" Mason asked, entering the wardroom late on Friday afternoon.

"Just the latest headlines, what you can believe anyway."

"What do they have to say this time?"

"There's quite a bit of rhetoric, and our British and the American press are printing harsh responses. But basically it looks like things are deteriorating," Dr. Patterson began. "Our esteemed Foreign Secretary Eden refers to Indochina by stating, let me see here, oh yes here it is. '...Certain defensive actions have been enforced in Malaya because of the Japanese threat to our territories.' Japan of course has to respond, so they have frozen not only British but American assets as well."

"I know the Japanese have been at odds with the Americans and us, but isn't it a bit extreme to take that kind of action?" Sub-lieutenant Davis commented, entering the conversation for the first time. He had only been with the *Mariah* since their most recent voyage and was still feeling his way. The funny thing was he had no idea what had caused the sudden change of assignment after the ship had sailed from Singapore. Not that he was complaining. He hated shore duty.

"There's more," Dr. Patterson continued, peering over the top of his glasses and tapping the paper.

"Don't tell me," Mason interjected, "we froze Japan's assets, tit-for-tat."

"You got it," Dr. Patterson affirmed. "The worrisome part though is the Americans."

"Why do you say that?" Davis asked.

"They banned oil sales, breaking their sales agreement with Japan. In time, if Japan can't buy it, they'll try to take it. Then you have a shooting war instead of a war of words."

"We may be out of the frying pan and into the fire the way things are going. At least in the Channel and the Mediterranean you knew for certain where you stood," Mason commented, just as Midshipman Barnes came into the wardroom looking for the first officer. "Lieutenant Roden, Commander Burns wants to see you, sir."

"Thank you, Mid," Mason acknowledged, rising to see what was needed.

"Come," Andy called when Mason knocked on his cabin door.

"Sir, reporting as ordered," Mason said, saluting.

"At ease, Lieutenant, care to sit down?" Andy invited, indicating a chair.

"Thank you sir."

"We have received orders to sail tomorrow evening with the *Victoria* and two other ships to Hong Kong, after first stopping at Manila," Andy informed him.

"Manila! That is a surprise."

"We are to confer with the American fleet, what's there, about the current situation, and then move on to Hong Kong. We are going to show the flag, as Admiral Edwards put it, in an effort to deter hostilities from breaking out. Heaven knows we don't need to be fighting on another front, especially now," Andy emphasized. "As to the ship, where do we stand?"

"All the supplies are replenished, and we took on fuel when we returned from Java," Mason reported. "I had planned to have fire and general quarter drills over the next few days. Being here has made the men begin to forget."

"They would soon remember if we were sent to the Atlantic. Carry on with the drills while we're at sea. They'll grumble, but we need to keep our edge."

"Yes sir, I plan to include casualty and rescue as well."

"Good idea. I know the pace at Singapore is much slower than in London, but we need to be at our peak readiness when called."

"We were just discussing the current situation in the wardroom. Doc believes Japan might seek possession of oil fields in the East since the Americans have banned the sale of oil to them and, in effect, broken their sales agreement. He said Japan could strike out and that would begin a shooting war here. I'll be sure the drills continue, sir."

"You do that, Lieutenant, you do that."

If Quentin is right, and he often is, Andy thought after Mason left him, *Japan could begin an offensive to take the oil and other commodities she so desperately desires. We'll need a lot more Mason Rodens if Japan strikes in the Pacific, especially if Germany overruns Russia and sails from her Pacific ports.*

Alan Samuels watched the small group of Naval ships leave Singapore Harbor from his boardinghouse bedroom window, being careful to note that the vessels leaving the harbor were the same ships he had seen coming and going over the last few months. Alan looked around the cheap, sparsely furnished room, where his few worldly possessions lay on the old four-poster bed after the ships passed out of sight. His mother's death in a pedestrian accident had left Alan on his own since the age of fifteen. Alan's mother was a woman of color and his father an English sailor who, according to his mother, had left when he was an infant. He was a tall, slender, white skinned outcast in both the Malayan and White cultures, with dark oriental eyes and course black hair, as well as being a bastard by birth. He especially hated the name he had been given because it sounded British and reminded him of the English father who had refused to claim him.

Alan learned during the eight years he had been on his own how to survive in a system rigidly divided. His malevolent hatred grew and festered year by year like an untreated cancer that made him ripe for recruitment when a Malayan businessman, working for the Japanese Embassy, approached him two years earlier. He was told that Malayan trade would increase throughout the area if he passed on a few minor shipping observations.

The same aging businessman had contacted Alan the previous week. He said the Japanese had another job for him. "You have an eye to detail," the man had said. "We want you to go north along the western coast and take notice of what is there."

"What are you looking for?" Alan asked and for a moment feared he had gone too far by asking.

The man's dark piercing eyes gazed at him, as if trying to see inside his mind, and, finally, to Alan's relief, he answered, "Anything unusual or out of place."

Alan nodded agreement to the proposition with a small grin that reflected the intense malice he held against the British population. He was told tickets for the local steam-wheeler and an envelope with cash for his needs would be at the shipping office the following week. He was then given instructions about how to pass on the information at the end of the journey. After another assenting nod from Alan, the man, whose name Alan did not know, left him. Alan believed more than trade was involved but was beyond caring. The only thing he could think about was ridding Malaya of the British.

The *Mariah* entered Manila Bay on August 10th after sailing through the South China Sea and into the Serasan Strait, drawing as near into Sarawak Island as possible before turning northeast toward the Philippines. Her crew once again mapped the diminutive dots of land that sprang up out of the sea, recording position and depth close to little-known shores.

"Lieutenant Patterson," Andy formally summoned at the wardroom doorway the day after *Mariah*'s arrival at Manila. "The captain of the American destroyer anchored here has extended an invitation to dine with him this evening."

Quentin Patterson glanced doubtfully over the top of the American newspaper he was reading. "You're quite certain they want me?"

"The invitation is for me, my First Officer, and our Medical Officer, that's you, Doc," Andy informed him. "We are to be there at 1800 hours. I believe the Americans have their evening meal a bit earlier than our customary dinner hour."

"Ah well, you can't blame them really. They lost their sense of propriety when the colonies left king and country behind," Dr. Patterson allowed with twinkling eyes.

Captain Davidson formally received his British visitors on the main deck with all the pomp and circumstance befitting visiting foreign Naval officers to an American vessel before the party adjourned to his cabin.

Jerry Davidson had to duck when entering his cabin to get his six foot four inch frame through the cabin doorway to avoid scraping his bristled red hair against the upper doorframe. A formal dinner table was precisely laid with a Navy blue linen tablecloth, bearing the destroyer's monogrammed initials, beneath the bone china embossed with the United States Navy Seal. However, being an American ship, no spirits were kept on board. Andy had foreseen this circumstance and produced two bottles of French wine he had procured in Singapore from a small but well regarded vineyard when he learned the *Mariah* would visit the American base.

"Commander Burns, that was excellent forethought," Captain Davidson said. "I thank you for the wine. It will be a fine complement to our meal."

"My pleasure, Captain. I'd like to introduce my First Officer, Lieutenant Mason Roden, and our Medical Officer, Lieutenant Quentin Patterson."

"Gentlemen, a pleasure. This is my second in command, Lieutenant

Horace Gregory, and our doctor, Lieutenant Lawrence Baker. Well, shall we be seated?"

Jerry Davidson contemplated his visitors over after-dinner coffee before moving the conversation to the evening's business. He felt in his bones the United States would soon be allied with these men in the Pacific against the Japanese and most likely in the West as well against German and Italian forces. The British had fought and lost in Norway and Europe the previous year, but he had done his homework about this crew and hoped the stories were true.

"I understand you were sent to observe our defenses in the area. Is that correct, Commander Burns?"

"Basically, yes. We've been putting defensive measures in place for some time now and building up troops on the Malayan Peninsula and Singapore."

"And you want to know if we're doing the same," Davidson bluntly stated.

"I don't know as I would have put it quite that way," Andy said.

Waving his hand, Jerry Davidson dismissed the need for circling the issue. "The time has come to be up front, Commander. America has begun to take more serious defensive measures here. Mining the bay is one of them. We could be in it with Japan the way things are looking at any time. As to land defenses, I couldn't say, I'm not a soldier. But General McArthur is, and he is in command. I do know Japan has made an indirect threat, stating she would get rubber, tin, and oil in the South Orient despite the de-facto embargo against her by the United States and the British in Malaya. So, as I said, anything could happen."

"I saw that in the American newspaper Dr. Patterson was reading," Mason remarked. "It said the claim was made by a Japanese newspaper."

"Every day brings about more hostility. Monday they stopped steamboat service to the United States, stranding several hundred Americans," Dr. Baker pointed out.

"Their reply to the embargo most likely," Dr. Patterson surmised.

"Yes, that could be the reasoning," Dr. Baker agreed.

"I understand you've been at sea the past ten days," Captain Davidson said. "Have you been able to listen to any of the news broadcasts either out of Singapore or Hong Kong?"

"Not for a few days," Andy acknowledged. "We try to keep up with current events, but there are times when we aren't in a good location to receive them."

"NBC will be broadcasting from Manila shortly. Let me see if I can tune it in for you," Davidson offered.

The NBC chimes sounded, announcing the top of the hour when Jerry Davidson turned up the radio's volume. "This is NBC news in Manila reporting with the weekly review," the announcer began. "Today, in a London broadcast to the women of America, Britain's Queen Elizabeth thanked the United States for her aid to the British cause. In other news this past week, Japan has suspended steamship service to the United States stranding over 600 Americans. Informed sources tell us intense discussions are taking place within our government to ensure the safe exit of our citizens from Japanese soil. On the other side of the Atlantic in the House of Commons, British Foreign Secretary Eden stated quote, 'Action by Japan against Thailand is a provocation of hostility toward British holdings.' It is believed numerous troops are beginning to arrive near the Thai/Malayan border and are seen by United States and British authorities as a threat to Singapore and a matter for concern. A Japanese spokesman answered from Tokyo, stating the United States and British warnings regarding Thailand are unwarranted. The Australian Naval Minister, however, countered by implying the question of peace or war in the Far East depended upon Japan. I don't know folks, but it sounds like tempers are getting the better of diplomacy. Good night from NBC," the announcer concluded, as the familiar chime sounded once again.

Jerry Davidson turned the radio off and looked somewhat bleakly at the others. "I fear if even half of it is true, war will come our way, and soon."

"A war Britain isn't in the best position to fight with her resources already stretched thin," Andy acknowledged.

The discussion turned to Russia and Germany's threat to Moscow before the evening drew to a close. "Stalin is tenacious. If Russia can hold the *Hun* away from Moscow a little longer, their winter may do the rest," Lieutenant Gregory stated.

"I have heard you don't want to spend a winter there. I believe diplomats sent to Moscow look for any reason to be away during the worst winter months," Mason noted.

"Captain Davidson, this has been a most interesting evening," Andy said, at the close of the evening's discussion. "We thank you for your invitation and a delicious meal. If it could be arranged, I would like to speak with your Army counterpart before we leave the area."

"Lieutenant Gregory will make the necessary arrangements for tomorrow morning, Commander Burns. Perhaps we'll meet again in our travels."

"If we do, the gin pennant will be up," Andy assured him.

"What was that all about?" Dr. Patterson asked, during the return trip to the *Mariah.*

"We were looking each other over," Andy answered. "We're already in an alliance with the Americans because of the lend-lease they created. We'll be allies in a war situation if tensions with Japan continue, and I believe in other theaters as well. If Japan strikes, the Americans will declare war, and we will join her according to Churchill. They would then have little choice but to ally themselves with us in Europe and Africa as well."

"But that would mean a total world war," Mason objected. "The one with Germany and Italy is quite enough without having it spread."

"It hasn't happened yet, maybe it won't," Andy indicated. "But I don't hold out much hope."

CHAPTER 30

Alan Samuels disembarked the narrow triple decked coal driven paddle wheeler at Helen's Landing and walked along the pier. He had two hours before the boat sailed further north while the shipment of special order items out of Singapore was off-loaded onto the docks. The Army used much of the cargo space to move less immediately needed provisions that pre-empted civilian cargo. Tempers among land and business owners were growing short as essential tools and fresh merchandise once again did not ship out of Singapore. "Sorry sir, we can't control how much space the Army might need," he overheard a ship's officer telling a complaining Englishman.

Alan left the dock area to walk the short distance to the main street. He noticed the English landlords had tried to create a village in the image of pictures he had seen of Britain's seaside resorts. *Why do they not just leave?* he wondered. *They do not appreciate the natural beauty here and try to make it look like England.* He walked further into the village and saw reflections in shop windows that showed the newly placed harbor defenses and a number of British troops behind him at the crossroad. He continued to slowly walk along the street, peering into windows and looking about, trying to decide which way to go, when the decision was made for him.

"Now then, what might you be wantin' hangin' about here?" a soldier sternly asked.

Alan's eyes did not meet his inquisitor's when he answered, submitting to the British authority as expected. "Nothing sir, just seeing the sights before the boat leaves."

"Well, move along now. You can't be dilly-dallyin' around here," the soldier ordered.

Alan's blood seethed within him as he walked beyond the northern edge of the village where the vegetation grew thicker before turning back into jungle. He noticed something out of place through the thickening trees but could not get close enough to make out what it was. Alan turned around and walked with purpose back toward the harbor, fearing that he would miss the boat, when a truckload of soldiers traveling north passed him at the edge of the village. He stopped a moment to view a larger building that seemed out of place and read the hand painted wooden sign that identified it as *Helen's Landing Hospital.* It seemed an odd place for a hospital this size to be located. From what he could tell, the village appeared to be a small and insignificant little settlement with no visible signs of mining around it or large cash crops to ship out to the homeland.

A British family of five was boarding the small paddleboat when Alan approached the gangplank. He stood at the rail watching the dock activity and overheard a lopsided dialogue, which clearly indicated the wife was not going to give in to her husband's reasoning.

"I tell you, Margaret, you're overreacting. Just because British troops are concentrating at the Thai border in the north doesn't mean anything will happen here," the husband argued. "It's just a precaution, I tell you."

"I don't care, George. We're taking the children to mother in Sydney. The twins were to go there next school term anyway," the woman named Margaret retorted.

"Well, taking the paddle-wheeler to Port Dickerson first is a waste of time," the husband, George, countered. "We would be better off to await its return from the north and take it to Singapore. And shipping off over half our belongings to Australia is just plain silly."

"We've been through this before. It's settled," Margaret asserted. "We can catch the steamer at Port Dickerson that goes to Singapore directly and from there the ship to Australia."

"All right…all right, you win," George sighed in exasperation. "We'll do it your way. Bradley, come along now."

Moving away from the rail, Alan inwardly smiled at the exchange. *The man is weak,* he thought. *But at least they are leaving.* He did not believe the family would be returning after hearing what the overbearing wife had said.

Andy spoke with an Army Colonel in Manila and was given a general briefing about defenses in the Philippines before the *Mariah* left Manila Bay with her sailing companions and turned toward Hong Kong at sunset. Mason noted ships through his glasses in the breaking morning light three days into the voyage, when a lookout reported ships off the starboard bow moving east to west in company.

"Navigator, what is their location?"

"Here sir," Sub-lieutenant Anderson responded, indicating a point on the chart.

Mason briefly wished that Brian Jones, with his uncanny ability to accurately pinpoint their location on a sea chart at any given time, had the watch. Looking again with his glasses, he could make out the Japanese flag on the masthead and the distinctive silhouette with the raked back smokestacks, unique to Japan's Navy. There appeared to be two destroyers, a minelayer, and some other type of ship he couldn't identify that were soon over the horizon. "Did you make note of the contact and location?"

"Yes, sir," Anderson answered.

The *Mariah* dropped her anchor in Hong Kong's busy harbor two days after sighting the Japanese ships on a Friday afternoon. "I've given twenty-four-hours leave in rotation to the men. I feared mutiny had I not done so," Mason reported with a smile.

"A wise decision," Andy agreed. "We sail Thursday morning for Singapore, following the Vietnamese and Malayan Peninsula coasts at a respectful distance. We might sight those ships you saw a few days ago."

"They haven't been seen returning, but we could easily have missed them," Mason said. "It's a big ocean."

"True. I don't think they've returned though. I have a feeling we'll run across them again."

Dr. Patterson found Andy in his cabin speaking with Mason about the ship's many needs. The *Mariah* was like a demanding wife that was never quite satisfied as her captain and first officer worked to keep her in fighting trim. "There you are then. Are we going to see the sights, my friend?"

"Yes, Doctor, that we are," Andy replied. "Mr. Roden, you're welcome to join us."

"That's right, me boy, we shan't lead you too far astray," Dr. Patterson assured, with a twinkle.

"An offer I cannot refuse," Mason countered, falling into the lighthearted mood.

Andy pointed out different attractions to his companions while strolling through the business and marketing districts. He noticed subtle changes since his last visit as a new sub-lieutenant before the hostilities between China and Japan began. It struck Andy that Hong Kong with its proximity to the mainland and the conquering Japanese forces would quickly become vulnerable if hostilities broke out between the British and Japanese.

Andy led his companions to a night club frequented by British officers when he visited Hong Kong as a young sailor.

"Spirits and dancing girls," Dr. Patterson approved. "A right compatible combination."

"I've never seen anything quite like this," Mason said, looking around slightly awe struck by the bustling waiters and scantily dressed entertainment.

"Another chapter in your education," Dr. Patterson lightly noted.

Andy took in the patter while he looked around the room noticing several empty tables. The party moved on to a late night show in the nightclub district to round out the evening before returning to the *Mariah,* and again the establishment was not crowded. It was well after midnight when the three men approached *Mariah*'s gangplank where Sub-lieutenant Davis saw them over the side.

"Davis, all well?" Andy asked.

"Yes, sir, very quiet."

"Very well, carry on." Davis was sure Dr. Patterson was a little tipsy along with Lieutenant Roden. He wasn't so sure about Commander Burns. He appeared perfectly sober.

The *Mariah* raised her anchor to leave Hong Kong behind after her short visit, setting a westerly course toward Viet Nam. Andy watched the bustling harbor filled with ships from all corners of the British Empire begin to drop into the horizon. He wondered when he might return to this port that conjured up so many writers' imaginations about intrigue and mystery, and what he might find if the Japanese came there as well.

The *Mariah* was sailing parallel with the east coast of Viet Nam, when the lookout's shout broke the early morning quiet. "Ships to starboard." Mason steadied his binoculars on the moving dots that took shape as they moved closer before summoning Andy to the bridge, stating ships had been sighted.

"Where are they, Number One?"

"About ten degrees off the starboard bow, sir."

"Yes, I see them now," Andy acknowledged. "Looks like your destroyers on a return voyage."

"The other ships aren't with them," Mason noted. He watched the Japanese destroyers pass in the opposite direction and briefly wondered where they had been and the purpose of their mission.

"Mr. Jones, plot the location and mark it on the chart. Show the last known direction they were headed," Andy ordered.

"Aye, sir. I have the plot marked," Brian responded, looking out toward the distant sea. "They appear to be moving northeast at present. I wonder if they're marking us down as well."

"More than likely they are," Andy matter-of-factly replied.

"A little like ring-around-the-rosy," Brian commented.

Yes, Andy thought, *a game that ends, "ashes-ashes, they all fall down."* He wondered if it was an omen of things yet to come and shivered for a moment, before resolutely returning his thoughts to the present. "Keep a close watch," he ordered. "I expect there will be more ships as we get closer to Saigon."

"Yes sir," Mason briskly responded.

The *Mariah* and her sailing companions followed a course parallel to the eastern coast of Malaya, rendezvousing with a group of patrolling gunboats before returning to Singapore. The group arrived in time to hear on the BBC that the Soviets had informed the Japanese Ambassador that any interference with normal trade between the United States and Russia would be considered an *unfriendly act.*

"Considering the Russians are at war with Germany, Japan may not give much credibility to that warning," Dr. Patterson commented at the end of another evening broadcast about the rapidly failing diplomacy in the Far East.

"If Japan does interfere, it would be a breech of the trade agreement they have with Russia, wouldn't it?" Roger Barnes asked.

"Maybe in a round-about way. I don't believe Japan will be concerned over any trade agreement with Russia if Japan and the United States have a conflict. They'll most likely decide they can take whatever Russia may have had to offer," Dr. Patterson replied.

Mason found Brian Jones and Dr. Patterson conversing in the wardroom sipping a gin and tonic and tossed a folded paper into Brian's lap. "Take a look at that and tell me what you think."

Brian could see it was a map when he unfolded the paper, but something was odd about it. "This is a map of Japan," he said, after taking a closer look. "According to this though, it shows their possessions include all the islands and coral reefs bound by the Sprately Islands in the west, Half Moon Shoal to the east, North Danger Reef, and Swallow Reef in the south."

"Exactly," Mason agreed. "It came out last week."

"You mean they just drew up a map and put in what they wanted?" Dr. Patterson incredulously asked.

"That's what it looks like," Mason confirmed. He was fully aware this latest action would be perceived as a hostile threat against the West and a snub toward the diplomatic community.

CHAPTER 31

It was late September, and Jane's thoughts drifted back to Michigan where the trees were beginning their colorful fall display. Her heart had ached for the familiar when she first came to Malaya, but Jane couldn't really say that she was homesick for Michigan now. It was Jim that she missed, not the place where they lived. This small Malayan community had brought her healing and welcome friendships and, in time, a new life with a second chance to love and be loved.

Jane and Peter listened to the daily news broadcasts hoping to hear that an agreement was made to break the tensions threatening to destroy their home and the quiet life they and their friends enjoyed. They learned Britain had sent a ship to Japan at the end of August to remove all British subjects who wished to leave. Japan responded by sending her own ships to Britain, Malaya, India, and the Near East to bring back several hundred nationals. It seemed to Jane the more she listened to the news and hoped for a break in the diplomatic stalemate, the more unstable the Far East became. *I didn't even know Malaya was here a few years ago,* Jane thought. *Now I don't ever want to leave.*

The first of November Japan took the position that she would break her perceived encirclement by force if necessary, bringing another blow to the hope for a peaceful resolution. The following day the BBC reported that Japanese citizens were building air raid shelters. Each new event brought greater tension to the diplomatic sessions and pushed the Japanese and Western negotiators further apart.

"Peter, do you think the Japanese seriously believe we would attack them?" Jane asked at the end of another troubling broadcast.

"I don't know, Jane. Maybe the air raid shelters are just to reassure their people."

John was following not only the news out of Japan but the United States as well. He found the Americans an enigma and wanted to gain some insight into their responses to events. An unknown attacker sank an American freighter the day before in the Red Sea. John wondered if it had been mistaken for a German or British supply ship. *But, surely, they must have been flying their nation's flag,* he thought. *How could a mistake like that happen? Were the Germans trying to provoke the United States or had some British ship really mistaken it for an enemy?* A few days later John was in the hospital lounge with Peter and Tom Linn listening to the afternoon radio newscast.

"This is the BBC, Singapore Station, reporting," the announcer began. "Today America's President Roosevelt announced he has ordered the United States Navy to shoot on sight any submarines or surface raiders in waters deemed necessary for America's defenses. United States Naval Secretary Knox reports that convoys are being escorted in all United States defensive zones. It is believed by informed sources that this action is in response to the recent sinking of an American ship in the Red Sea. President Roosevelt reminded listeners that the United States is a neutral country in this most recent world conflict, sighting the attack on an American ship as a heresy to all sailors." John turned off the radio when the news ended and a soap commercial jingle began.

"Does this mean the Americans are coming into the war?" Tom Linn inquired.

"How do you mean?" Peter asked.

"They say they are escorting convoys and will shoot at attackers," Tom explained.

"I've been trying to follow the Americans to some extent," John responded. "They haven't declared war on anybody. But they don't appear to like being shot at either."

"I wouldn't like being shot at," Peter interjected.

"What I mean is they seem to have a certain amount of complacency regarding Europe. But they don't want anyone to interfere in their eastern territory," John explained.

"Is it true British ships are being repaired in America as well?" Tom asked. "I read this in an American newspaper and wondered if it could be true."

"Jane still receives the *New York Times,* and there was a story in it about

British ships being repaired under the Lend-Lease Bill," Peter told them. "Apparently quite a few."

"It's almost like they were dipping a toe in the water over lend-lease, and now the whole foot is in," John observed.

Alan Samuels left the paddle steamer at Panang and checked into the small waterfront hotel as instructed. He laid on the sagging iron bed, letting the slow turns of the overhead fan cool his naked body from the afternoon's oppressive heat and humidity.

Alan reviewed in his mind the things he had seen while moving along the western coastal waters of the peninsula. The glimpses of guns and the number of soldiers at Helen's Landing puzzled him. The small village didn't appear to be much different from other settlements along the coast. Alan thought back to the hospital he saw there and wondered if it along with the harbor might have some significance. *Maybe the British Army has something to do with the larger hospital,* he thought.

Alan wished the day would pass so he could meet his contact. He thought it sounded like a spy thriller, *meet his contact,* and daydreamed about being a spy, like in the thrillers he read. Alan didn't believe they wore the kind of disguises described in the stories, but he did believe they led an exciting life.

Eventually he drifted into a light sleep, waking with a start when the sun began to set. He listened with his eyes closed for a moment with the feeling someone was in his room. In his semi-confused state he couldn't be certain. He decided after coming fully awake that it must have been a dream stemming from his earlier thoughts about spy stories. He pushed the thought aside to splash some water over his face and neck before dressing. Alan gathered up his room key and carefully locked his door to leave the hotel and walk down a side street toward the small cafe on the next street to keep his rendezvous.

The man from Singapore had noiselessly unlocked the outdated door latch to Alan's room and entered to find his naive prey sleeping in unsuspecting innocence. He made a small noise as he left to begin the lessons this amateur would need to learn to survive.

The man watched from across the street to see if anyone followed the half-caste he had recruited and cultivated over the past two years, carefully stroking his ego to inflate Alan's self-image. It had been child's play, almost too easy. Alan's hatred of the British was ingrained so deeply he had no insight into the fact that he was being used by yet another would-be conqueror. The man from Singapore hoped to up the stakes. What he learned from Alan this night would be the first step. He waited half an hour before entering the cafe himself, giving a lesson in patience.

"Good evening, my friend," the man from Singapore softly greeted, taking the seat across from Alan.

"You!" Alan started in surprise. "I thought you were still in Singapore."

"Now I am here," the man quietly replied. "How was your excursion?"

"Interesting," Alan noncommittally answered, plainly showing that he did not like being surprised like this.

"Oh, how so?"

"Just a lot of interesting things to see and hear," Alan evaded, thinking that he too could be mysterious.

"I see. And what kind of interesting things might that be?" the man asked, not showing his annoyance at the obvious game being played out by this unskilled amateur.

"Oh, say the family leaving Malaya for an extended period of time, the amount of things the Army moves using up cargo space and making the British aristocracy angry, and a place called Helen's Landing," Alan loftily replied.

"What about this place is so interesting?" the man asked, with a touch of interest.

"There seems to be more soldiers than normally would be in a place like it. I saw some big guns at what appeared to be a crossroad near the waterfront. The soldiers were British and made me leave, said I couldn't dawdle by them." Alan could still vividly remember the soldier and openly showed his disgust. "The other settlements had some Australians who were a lot friendlier, at least until the British overlords came along. They didn't have as many soldiers or guns though."

"Did you see anything else at this Helen's Landing?" the Singapore man asked.

"I am not sure. When the soldiers made me move along, I walked just beyond the northern edge of the town by a coastal road. I saw something through the trees, but I couldn't tell what it was," Alan truthfully answered. "I also saw a much larger hospital, like in the bigger cities only on a smaller scale. I could not find out more about it. Maybe it has something to do with the soldiers. I had to get back before I missed the boat."

"It sounds like you had a most interesting journey that was filled with many noteworthy attractions."

Thinking to himself about his next statement, the nameless man decided it would be best to continue along the lines that further trade was in serious jeopardy. "I am afraid all this build-up in defenses and the kind of hindrances imposed with all the back and forth embargoes will destroy all the trading markets," he tried.

"The British are the cause of all this," Alan hotly responded. His hands began to shake, as he continued with anger flushing his face. "They will bring more suffering before all this is settled. They should go away and take their oppression with them."

"It may be they will one day," the man offered off-hand.

"Not unless they are made to," Alan retorted like a sullen child.

"You may be right," the man responded, watching Alan closely. "It may come to force by other interests to push the British out of Malaya, for the sake of trade."

"You mean a war," Alan bluntly stated.

He may be a little brighter than I first thought, the man from Singapore thought to himself. *Let us see if he jumps at the bait then.* "Would you be opposed to an invasion by outside interests to clear the way for trade?" he asked.

"Are you serious? If the British were forced out, the oppression would end. For that, I would welcome the liberator. I only wish there was something I could do to make it happen."

"Maybe there is," the man allowed, again watching Alan's reactions closely.

"What do you mean?"

"I would like to introduce you to someone who thinks as you do. That it is time for a change, time for the Englishman to go home."

"When can I meet this person?" Alan eagerly asked.

"Soon. I will make the arrangements. Meet me here in three days time at the same hour," the nameless man instructed. "Until then enjoy the sights."

"Why so long?" Alan asked somewhat impatiently. "Can't you just take me there now?"

"Patience, my friend. These things take time," the man soothed.

"Very well, but I do not see why it must be so long a wait."

The man from Singapore was pleased with his manipulation of this naive pawn. He hoped Tonaka would be pleased as well with this latest recruit. His hatred of the British ran even deeper than Alan's. Tonaka's father was also English, but unlike Alan's mother, who it appeared was a willing participant in his conception, the arrogant son of a British ambassador had ravaged Tonaka's mother. The boy was sent back to England shortly after committing the act, leaving Tonaka's mother to bear the shame of his birth and the ridicule of her family. His Japanese stepfather never let Tonaka forget the shame and humiliation the English had inflicted on his innocent mother. *Yes,* Raja thought to himself, *Tonaka will be pleased with Alan Samuels.*

"Mrs. Burns," Wesley said, "it is very gracious of you to invite us to your home."

"Yes indeed," Arthur echoed. "Thank you very much."

"It's my pleasure. Martin, have you completed your task with the Navy?"

"As a matter of fact I have, Helen. I sent the final report to Eric this morning."

"It was good to have you involved, sir," Wesley acknowledged.

"Helen's Landing hardly seems to notice what's been done," Arthur noted. "Except for more soldiers around, people seem to be going about their normal daily business."

"All this talk about war preparations is depressing," Helen sighed. "I've often wondered why people can't get along. I don't really believe any nation's population wants war and all its devastation." Changing the subject, she smiled. "I believe I hear the dinner bell sounding. Shall we, gentlemen?"

"Mrs. Burns, that was the finest meal I've had since before I joined up," Arthur declared, when they returned to the sitting room.

"Here, here," Wesley agreed.

"Helen, you've done it again, as always," Martin Jamison concurred.

"You'll make me blush, but I thank you. Would you like to hear the news while we have our coffee?" Receiving assenting replies, Helen turned on the radio to allow the tubes to warm up before turning up the volume when the broadcast began.

"This is the BBC, Singapore Station, reporting. According to recent intercepted dispatches, Hitler's Army claims to be less than 100 miles from Moscow. No announcement has come out of the Russian capital to date regarding the accuracy of this bold public statement to the German command by German forces at the Russian front.

"Meanwhile, on another part of the globe, the Japanese Embassy in America announced on Saturday last an agreement has been reached through the United States State Department to allow the repatriation of some 2,000 Japanese to their homeland. This singular diplomatic understanding has not, however, opened the door to further talks between the United States and Japan about the Axis alliance and territorial boundaries in the East. This is the BBC, good night."

Wesley was the first to break the silence that followed the broadcast. "It appears Russia is having difficulties."

"So it seems," Dr. Jamison concurred. "I wonder what will happen when their winter comes. I've heard they can be quite severe."

"It would depend on how well equipped the Germans are to deal with it," Arthur replied. "From an engineering stand point, it would mean keeping engines running and wheels and tanks moving. If they freeze up, it could be a long winter."

"What are you thinking about, Helen?" Dr. Jamison asked.

"I was wondering why Japan finds it necessary to bring those people out of the United States. It's almost as if the Japanese government is preparing for further break downs in its talks."

"I know what you mean," Wesley said. "I read last week the Japanese government broke all diplomatic relations with the Polish government in London."

"I think Japan's government wants and believes war is the answer," Dr. Jamison noted. "The only thing stopping them is the Emperor right now, and that could change."

"Let us pray he will continue to stop them," Helen interjected.

"I would have to agree with that," Wesley concurred, before setting his saucer and cup on the small table next to his chair. "Mrs. Burns, I thank you for your hospitality. Arthur and I must return to the barracks to check on preparations to move south for a few weeks before returning to Helen's Landing."

"Sergeant Aimes probably has things in quite good military order by now," Arthur commented with a smile.

"You're most likely correct in that assumption," Wesley grinned. "There's no slacking in the ranks with Sergeant Aimes in charge."

"You'll be stationed here then?" Dr. Jamison asked.

"At least for the next few months. I might be able to spend Christmas with my sister this year."

"If you're here," Helen said, "we'll all celebrate it together."

"The birth of the Christ child, the Messiah, the embodiment of peace and God's love toward man, celebrated in the midst of a spreading war," Arthur softly reflected.

"Man's own enigma. Even Jesus was rejected by man," Dr. Jamison responded to Arthur's quiet observation.

Helen sat for some time after the men left thinking about the snippets of news and Andy's last letter. He said for the first time that he had some concerns about her safety. Most people she knew weren't concerned and believed what they were told—that the Japanese certainly would not dare to approach Singapore by sea with its big guns and that jungle warfare was impossible. Helen knew from Andy, and now Wesley, jungle warfare was possible. She decided to write to an old friend in Australia to start making some practical arrangements if the need arose.

Alan rode the weekly bus to Kuala Lumpur and took accommodations at a boarding house, as Tonaka had instructed. "It is time for a change to free the East from the strangle hold the West has inflicted, especially the British colonialist," Tonaka concluded at their first meeting. Alan's eyes had told the story when Tonaka spoke, and Tonaka knew he had Alan in his grasp. This naive boy was one more tool for him to use and discard at will, until the tyrant was vanquished. Surely he would then be seen as truly Samurai in the eyes of his Japanese family and become a hero to the nation where he longed to be accepted.

Alan looked out onto the main road in Kuala Lumpur from his rented attic room through the limp pieces of faded dingy cloth that passed as curtains. He had chosen the boarding house because it was located near the center of the capitol city. It was late morning and several Army trucks with soldiers passed by going north just as Alan began to turn away from the window. He tried to count how many trucks were in the convoy and whether soldiers or equipment was being transported to tell Raja when he saw him. Tonaka had revealed Raja's name to Alan, saying it was an act of trust between them. Alan had decided then there was more than trade involved. Otherwise, the movement of soldiers wouldn't be of any importance.

Alan left the capital for Port Dickerson after a few weeks, making sure he could stop for a few days in Kelang. He took a room as was expected of a half-caste in a shabby waterfront hotel and at the prescribed hour went to a cafe to meet with Raja.

"I see you are prompt, my friend. Let us walk on the waterfront," Raja suggested, leading Alan out to the wooden walkway. He talked of trivial things until reaching the expanse of busy piers and crowds of dockworkers unloading cargo before turning to business. "What can you tell me?"

"Only that a great many soldiers are being sent to the north. Trucks passed through the capital for three days with Indian and Australian troops. I saw two trucks with British troops earlier today," Alan concluded, making a sour face.

"How could you be sure?" Raja asked.

"They wore skirts and had bagpipes. They got out in the center of town and did some kind of demonstration before moving on," Alan explained.

"You mean they were Scottish," Raja corrected.

"Scottish, British, they're all the same. The one in charge was British, I'm sure." Alan's tone brokered no tolerance of the differences. To him they all were the enemy.

"Did you notice anything unusual?" Raja asked, diverting Alan's thoughts from the perceived slight.

"The bus I rode went through a check point at most of the small settlements. Just a jeep in the road and the bus driver says he's going to a town and they wave him through. More soldiers might have been close by, but I did not see them. Kelang looked like it had more big guns around. I saw many airplanes coming and going. I could not keep count. They went up in the air then turned around and came right back, and then did the same thing all over again several times, just taking off and landing again," Alan reported more briskly.

"You're very observant," Raja complimented, stroking the fragile ego. "Now to new business. Tonaka was interested in what you said about this Helen's Landing. He would like you to go there and see what you can find out about this place."

"It might take some time," Alan cautioned. "Certainly more than a traveling half-caste would spend there."

"You could say you are looking for work," Raja suggested. "It would seem normal."

"Yes, they would let me mop their floors," Alan bitterly acknowledged.

"Be patient. The British will not always be here," Raja soothed.

"The sooner they are gone the better."

His hatred will eventually consume him, Raja thought about Alan on his journey to meet Tonaka. He sighed, thinking it was too bad in a way. Alan might be trainable except for this unharnessed flaw.

The bus wound its way over the snaking jungle roadway that was cut into existence by the sweat and blood of the Malayan people to provide the British overlords access to Malaya's rich natural resources. Raja watched the countryside pass by, remembering the hardships endured growing up during that time of change. He learned to trust no one, especially the Englishmen who had come to his homeland and were taking Malaya away one cargo load at a time. The Japanese would most likely be no different he thought, but their money was sufficient to give him a few luxuries in his old age.

CHAPTER 32

"Alan, would you go to emergency please?" Sally instructed the newest janitor.

"Yes, ma'am."

"Dr. Hartman, Dr. Jamison wants you to meet him in B ward," Sally called, when she caught sight of John.

"Thank you, nurse," John acknowledged with a grin and a wink.

"That man is incorrigible," Sally told Jane, when she returned to the nurse's station.

"What man?"

"John. He's such a tease."

"A letter came for you today," Jane said, handing it to her.

"Wonder who it's from? Well I'll be!" Folding the letter, Sally put it in her pocket after absorbing each word that was written on the two short pages and started humming, as she fussed around the nurse's station.

"Okay, I'll bite," Jane said. "Who's it from?"

"Oh, just Andy, you know, Helen's son."

"Andy Burns? I didn't know you two were corresponding."

"Just some friendly letters. It's not like we've gone out or anything."

"I see." Jane decided after watching Sally fidget about the tiny nurse's office and accomplish little more than moving a chart about that it might be more than a few friendly letters.

Jane and Peter walked along the harbor front that evening as they had their first night together. "I always love coming here," Jane sighed contentedly. "Our special place. At least I think of it that way."

"It is special," Peter softly murmured, giving her a kiss.

Jane and Peter sat for some time in contented silence. They gave little notice to the people around them while the sunlight slowly gave way to the approaching night. They did, however, notice one other person also watching the rising moon. "It looks a little like the new janitor, what's his name? Oh yes, Alan," Jane commented.

"Wonder what he's doing wondering around in the dark," Peter said, trying to get a better look at the pier's edge.

"Maybe the same thing we are, enjoying the sunset," Jane reasoned.

Alan watched Jane and Peter slowly stroll out of sight after the moon rose. He had walked around the pier and harbor as much as he could without drawing attention to himself, waiting to discover what else might lie farther along the water's edge. But the doctor and nurse had stayed on the pier a long time upsetting his plans. Alan decided to go back to his rooming house and wait until early morning, when few people were around to wonder about his presence.

"Hi, Alan," Jane greeted the new janitor when he came around the corner by the nurse's station. "How are you today?"

"Hello, Mrs. Romans. I am well, thank you."

"Oh, Alan, were you down by the harbor last night? Peter and I were watching the sunset and thought we saw you."

Thinking to himself he had as much right to be there as anyone, Alan decided not to deny it. "Yes, I too watched."

"Next time come and join us. You're always welcome," Jane invited.

"Thank you, I will try to remember that." Alan did not believe for a moment she was serious about him being welcome by her husband or friends, knowing in the English society his kind were never welcome in the white man's circle.

"Maybe Jane will have something to say about the remark out of Tokyo," John said, coming out of the lounge.

"Which one?" Peter asked. "They make one about every other day it seems since Tojo came to power."

"The one about the United States and Japan coming to a parting of the ways and the Imperial Navy itching for a fight," John explained.

"She's not very political. She did tell me once it wasn't a good idea on Japan's part to make the general public in the United States get up in arms. She said the Americans would only give so far, and then, as she put it, *look out.*"

Alan heard the two British doctors talking before turning down another hallway and was surprised to learn Mrs. Romans was an American and briefly wondered what had brought her to Malaya. It would explain her difference from the others. Being married to an Englishman though made her part of the British system.

Wesley waited nearly an hour before the aide outside General Hughes' Singapore office told him the General was ready to receive him. He stood at attention giving a parade ground salute when he entered the General's inner sanctum with his eyes looking straight ahead. "At ease, Captain," Hughes casually commanded, returning Wesley's salute.

"Thank you sir," Wesley said, assuming the accepted at ease position, feet apart, hands behind the back, eyes focused on the white washed wall behind and slightly above the general. He quickly took in the British flag to his left and a paper strewn desk with the straight back wooden chair behind it where Hughes sat, facing away from the broad window overlooking the parade ground, before giving his full attention to his Commanding General.

"I wanted to see you regarding Helen's Landing," Hughes began. "I spoke with Admiral Edwards this morning. It appears the citizenry there is basically unaffected. According to Admiral Jamison's final report, the people of Helen's Landing seem to feel secure. And for once the Army and Navy were able to work in harmony. Housing the men outside the town is also working out well it appears."

"Yes, sir," Wesley briskly answered.

Obadiah Hughes eyed Wesley a moment, wondering briefly what kind of officer he had standing before him. Vilmont adhered to accepted regulations to the letter. Yet it seemed he also had a mind of his own. He had effectively used the Army's chain of command, and even involved their rival service, to construct the controversial defense plan now in place at Helen's Landing. Hughes was concerned with Japan's withdrawal from the negotiating table and Germany's proximity to Moscow. He put the troubling thoughts aside and looked again at the officer standing before him.

"General Sir Archibald Wavel, British Commander of the Indian Army, will be in Singapore on Sunday," Hughes stated. "I want you to brief him on what you did at Helen's Landing. My aide, Higgins, has a copy of the final map you completed."

"Yes, sir. When do you want me to brief him, sir?"

"Higgins will fill you in after the general arrives. Report in with him at 0800 hours on Tuesday," Hughes ordered.

"Yes, sir."

"Captain, for what it's worth, it's a good idea even though most of my counterparts tend not to think as I do," Hughes allowed in a rare moment of sharing a confidence.

"Thank you, sir," Wesley replied, looking straight at his general for the first time.

"You're dismissed, Captain," Hughes ordered, returning to his role as a commanding officer.

Coming to attention, Wesley saluted his general before leaving Army Headquarters to visit the *Mariah*. He had grown to respect the tall quiet man who seemed to have a glint of humor in his eyes that could turn to steel when encountering command decisions. He believed they were becoming friends. Midshipman Barnes escorted him to the wardroom to join Dr. Patterson and Mason Roden. Wesley remembered Barnes was the one whose brother went down with the *Hood* the day he was in Andy's cabin revising the blueprints for Helen's Landing.

"What's the Navy coming to?" Dr. Patterson demanded in mock alarm. "They're allowing the lowly Army into our revered sanctuary now."

"Pay him no mind, Captain," Mason grinned, rising to shake Wesley's hand. "Doc's been on the deck too long in the sun."

"Yes, they don't understand my delicate nature and make me drill! Can you believe it?"

Laughing, Wesley relaxed onto the offered chair. "It must be the gin pennant is up after such a grueling experience. Mind you, in the Army we have to camp out in tents during exercises, enduring rain and cold, and sometimes we even have to get dirty. Might I be allowed though to buy you both a gin to ease the trauma that has been inflicted upon you? Seeing as how I'm only a lowly Army captain though, they might not take my order."

"Bless you, me boy," Dr. Patterson expounded. "We'll make an honorary officer of you, and you may drill with us and learn from your betters how to stay out of the mud." After a pause, he added, "At a lower rank, of course."

"Of course," Wesley replied, with a grin.

The wardroom Wesley found was a place where the officers were able to relax to some degree. Quentin Patterson was an exception, being able to appear totally uninhibited. Wesley was starting to think some of this was an act on the doctor's part to help his fellow officers unwind.

"Sir," Mason said, getting up when he spotted Andy at the wardroom doorway. "Please come and join us."

"Thank you, I believe I will. Wesley, how are you my friend?"

"Just fine, thanks," Wesley responded, shaking Andy's hand. "I've been enjoying your marvelous gin and tonic."

"May I get you one, sir?' Mason asked.

"Yes, I believe I will partake. Thank you, Mr. Roden. I see Wesley has survived the wardroom initiation."

"The Army would take away my bars if I allowed the Navy to get the better of me," Wesley jested. "The offer to buy a gin was a simple enough bribe to ensure the Navy was pacified."

"Hah!" Mason hooted.

"Careful, my friend, the natives may turn," Andy warned.

"True, when in Rome," Wesley said, raising his glass.

Andy was trying to fall into the light heartedness of the wardroom, but Quentin Patterson noticed he clearly had something on his mind. "Admiral have a lot to say?"

"New concerns over the Japanese. Tensions are growing."

"I see. And?"

"Doc, I wouldn't be surprised to see the United States and Japan go to war."

"What makes you say that?" Wesley asked.

"Admiral Edwards said the Japanese released a statement earlier today that unless the United States ends its economic blockage that they will have to seek out vital goods and raw materials in self-defense," Andy explained. "He is especially concerned about the tone of the statement."

"What else did the Admiral say?" Wesley asked.

"The United States is looking to amend their Neutrality Act to arm merchant ships."

"That sounds like they're getting ready to gear up for hostilities," Wesley noted.

"If America goes to war with Japan," Andy said, "Britain will be drawn in. The natural resources they're looking for, oil and tin and rubber, are out here. Some of it right in Malaya with the tin mines in the north."

"Not a pretty picture at all," Dr. Patterson concluded. "In fact, a bloody ugly one."

"It does explain one thing," Wesley remarked.

"What's that?" Andy asked.

"Sometime next week I'm supposed to brief General Sir Archibald Wavel, British Commander of the Indian Army, on the defenses at Helen's Landing," Wesley explained. "If they're beginning to think Japan will strike, maybe the Army will want more land defenses than they have at present."

Looking to close the talk about Japan, Andy asked Wesley how long he thought he might be in Singapore.

"Probably not more than a week or two unless something comes of the briefing General Hughes wants me to give Wavel," Wesley told them.

"Then what?" Mason asked.

"For now, I'm to be at Helen's Landing to oversee the personnel and evaluate the effectiveness of the deployment."

Andy met Wesley in Singapore on Thursday before his return to Helen's Landing. He told Andy about the briefing with General Wavel and his belief the general wasn't interested in any changes. Wesley made the observation that he believed most of the Army was under the impression Malaya and Singapore were invincible, adding if they had been on the ground in Holland they wouldn't be so complacent. Andy listened and nodded agreement, stating there were those in the Navy who thought the same way.

Andy reflected that attitudes in the East were similar to the beliefs in 1939 before the defeat in Norway and the fall of Western Europe. It didn't appear Russia was faring any better than Belgium, Holland, or France had in their brief struggle against the Nazi war machine. He wondered if Singapore would be the next Dunkirk, only with the Japanese this time. No friendly shores awaited a beleaguered retreating Army and Navy a day's sailing away across a natural deep body of water here. Java or Australia, several sailing days away, would be the closest to receive anyone if the worst happened.

CHAPTER 33

"Martin, the new janitor, Alan I believe his name is, seems to do a very good job," Helen remarked.

"Yes, I've noticed that also. I'm thinking about asking if he would like to try his hand at becoming an orderly."

The two friends were sitting in the small hospital cafeteria sharing a cup tea, while Brahms' 2nd Symphony softly played over the old wooden cased Victory radio in the background. Helen came to discuss the possibility of providing an evening of entertainment for the Army personnel stationed at the converted Charmical plantation.

"It must be awfully monotonous to only go from their barracks to their work station and back to the barracks again. Even when they have a day off, Helen's Landing offers very little in entertainment. The community should do something to make the Army feel appreciated. After all, they are here for our benefit."

"What do you suggest?" Dr. Jamison asked with some cautious interest.

"Maybe we could put together a fair and hold it on the hospital grounds."

"What kind of fair?"

"The usual I suppose, Martin. You know, horse shoe contests, water games, fishing for prizes, food of course. All the things we did as young people, nothing really extravagant."

"It would make Eric happy to see the Navy taking an active role in keeping up the moral of their Army brethren," Dr. Jamison thoughtfully considered.

He looked at his friend a moment with a slight smile. "I believe you might have thought about this before today."

"It's settled then. I'll start putting it together in the morning. Now to the..." she got no further, before Dr. Jamison held up a hand and turned up the radio's volume.

"...Yesterday the Japanese government's Finance Minister reported to the National Finance Council that Japan intends to force Britain and the United States to retreat from East Asia. Mr. Churchill responded to this perceived threat from London today, stating if the United States becomes involved in a war with Japan the British would declare war within the hour. The Japanese have responded that they regard Mr. Churchill's warning as a plot to draw the United States and Japan into war against each other. This is the BBC, Singapore Station, reporting."

"It doesn't get any better does it, Martin?" Helen sighed, as the broadcast concluded.

"It doesn't appear to, Helen."

"Martin, if you think it would be better not to make any plans right now I'll hold off."

"No, go ahead. The men will enjoy it. And, they may be called on before long to defend us against hostile actions."

"I can't understand why the people of Japan don't speak out. Surely the average citizen doesn't want to see a war begin."

"They may believe there is no choice. The Japanese citizenry could very well believe the western allies are threatening their way of life."

Helen contacted her friends in the hospital guild on Wednesday to start putting together plans for a fair. The majority of the guild members were enthusiastic about the idea of welcoming British troops. "All we really need to do is use the booths we already have for the Christmas bazaar and make different placards for them," one member suggested. Helen sat back after a short time and let the ideas flow back and forth. As she had always said, people liked having something to plan and look forward to. All they needed was a catalyst to get things started.

"I tell you, Martin, it's uncanny," Helen said, when the plans were finalized.

"How so, Helen?"

"The people here seem to look at this fair as only another social event. They don't appear to understand what's going on around them. I spoke with Jon and Lucy Harris the other day. Jon is convinced that nothing will come of the perceived threat by Japan."

"They may realize the threat is there, and this is a way to put it out of their minds," Dr. Jamison reasoned.

"You mean bury their head in the sand. I was going to ask Alan Samuels to be sure to come to the fair, but I haven't seen him. He seems to be so quiet and nonverbal. I thought it might draw him out a little."

Martin Jamison realized Helen was once again looking to take another waif under her wing. It had certainly made a difference to Tom Linn when Helen befriended him a few years after Andy went away. Now he was becoming a fine doctor. Martin Jamison knew Helen's influence in Tom's life had made a difference. "Alan will be back on Monday. This is his weekend off."

Alan took the early morning bus to Kuala Lumpur and once again secured a room at a small hotel near the waterfront that catered to his class. He met Raja in the late afternoon at a nearby park.

"How are things going, my friend?" Raja asked, as he and Alan strolled along a pathway.

"Quite well. The British hired me to mop their floors, as I said they would."

"Tonaka said you would find a way. It seems he was right," Raja offered in an effort to appear pleased with this development. "Tell me, have you learned any more about this Helen's Landing?"

"I have confirmed that anti-aircraft guns are in place. I had heard of them being around Singapore and larger ports and around where airplanes are kept, but not at such a small and unimportant town."

"Do they have any mining nearby? That would make the village a more valuable possession," Raja reasoned.

"Nothing, I tell you. They only ship coffee and sugar to warehouses in Singapore. The only other thing of any significance is their precious hospital. Guns point out to sea for about five miles north and south of the harbor along the shoreline as well. The hospital nurses and doctors say it is to stop an invasion from the sea and help keep the harbor open," Alan continued. "In the surrounding jungle, mine fields are laid out and something called tank traps."

"That's quite extraordinary. How were you able to find out these things?" Raja was skeptical about what Alan was telling him.

"Soldiers guard where the mine fields are to keep anyone from wandering into them. The guns I saw when I went fishing," Alan explained simply.

"Tonaka will be interested to hear about this. Are there any other points of interest?" Raja still thought the report exaggerated and would tell Tonaka so when he repeated Alan's observations.

"Only a fair for the British soldiers," Alan responded in agitated disgust. "The hospital people say it is to welcome them to the town."

"It would be something to attend if there is a way," Raja encouraged.

Alan's face became flushed and his voice rose in contempt at the suggestion. "What on earth for?"

"Soldiers talk among themselves. You may hear something of interest," Raja pointed out.

"That may be, but I am sure none like me will be attending," Alan bitterly stated, closing any argument to the contrary.

His judgment is clouded with bitterness. His deep hatred of the British will not be easily channeled into a useful tool of organized resistance against the West. It is too bad really, Raja inwardly sighed. *If he isn't exaggerating, his observations are quite good.*

Raja was to meet Tonaka the following night. At least this raw recruit had brought him something that might be of significance to report. Alan couldn't explain though why this particular settlement had such a modern hospital or any reason for the extensive gun emplacements. *If Alan would just listen to reason and set aside his prejudice, he might find the answer,* Raja thought.

Tonaka watched the land drop from sight, as the small passenger steam ship headed east into the China Sea on the first leg of his return voyage to Japan. He would change ships twice before completing his journey to friendly territory. With what Raja had brought him, coupled with his own observations, he believed his superiors would be pleased. He was puzzled about the place called Helen's Landing, which was reported to have greater defenses around it. Raja assured him there was nothing of value there. *Then why the heavy defenses?* he wondered.

The unanswered questions nagged at the edges of his mind as he reviewed British defenses on the Malayan Peninsula. The north had a great build up of troops but little in the way of armor or experience to back them up in a hard fight. Indian and Australian soldiers arrived without tanks, heavy artillery, or motorized transport, and carried outdated rifles. Tonaka believed the troops were soft and would not offer the resistance the British were trying to convince his government, and their own citizens, would be available at the Thai border should Japan choose to cross into Malaya.

Newspapers and British radio reported the following week that Emperor Hirohito had formally opened the Japanese Diet the previous Monday, urging cooperation with Premier General Tojo's government. The Diet quickly passed a resolution on Tuesday supporting an East Asian Cooperative Sphere as a national policy.

"I wonder what that means," Tom Linn said, putting the local bi-monthly paper down.

"What's that?" Peter asked.

"This East Asian Cooperative Sphere Japan is talking about all the time. I wonder what it means."

"I guess expanding their economic interest outside their home waters from what I've heard."

"Yes, but how far?" Tom asked, with some concern. "They seem to have their eye on all of Indonesia."

"What about Indonesia?" John asked, when he came into the lounge.

"We were just talking about the latest reports out of Japan," Peter explained. "We were wondering what the East Asian Cooperative Sphere might encompass."

"A very good question. One I imagine a great many political analysts are asking as well," John remarked. "Not to mention the Army and Navy."

"From what little I've read, it looks like Tojo's government is getting everything it wants," Peter noted.

"So it would seem. It appears the hardliners there are in power and intend to use it," John commented.

"People don't seem to notice though," Tom observed. "They're going about their business as usual here. Earlier today I heard a store owner talking about his intended Christmas stock."

"Yes," John agreed. "People generally prefer to see everything as normal until something forces the issue. Right now that could prove to be a fatal flaw."

Tonaka stood on the hill overlooking Tokyo Bay as the sun began to make itself known across the surface of the sea. He had traveled to the Japanese Embassy in Saigon after reaching friendly territory and reported his findings in Malaya to a low level diplomat that operated as Japan's intelligence contact. Upon receiving the questionable report, which did not tally with previous observations, he was summoned to Tokyo Intelligence Headquarters by the quickest transportation available.

Tonaka flew as the only passenger on a bumpy uncomfortable two engine mail plane into a base in southern China. He was met the same day by an Army transport plane and flown to Tokyo. Seasoned intelligence officers at the central office questioned him in detail about his findings and Helen's Landing specifically. Tokyo wanted particularly to know more about this new source and how reliable the information might be. Tonaka related all he knew about Alan Samuels, including details of his own face-to-face meeting with him. He also told his interrogators in his opinion the information was true, partly because Raja had also passed through the area in question and confirmed the soldiers were there.

Tonaka learned upon his arrival in Japan the Diet had supported all thirteen bills presented by Premier General Tojo's government. Based on the provocations demonstrated by the Americans and the British, Tonaka believed Tojo was right. It pleased him the Diet, his country's highly respected governing delegates, had voted in favor of Tojo's government. He was even more elated that his revered Emperor supported General Tojo and the Diet in its decisions.

Tonaka smiled, as he watched Japan's powerful Naval force leaving Tokyo Bay from a hilltop overlooking the harbor. He knew other ports throughout the island nation were witnessing a similar event. He was given the honor to observe this awesome day in history before returning to Malaya by his superiors as a reward for his devoted service to Japan and her Emperor. *The world will soon recognize Japan for the great nation she is and deny her no more what is rightfully hers. Even Hitler and Mussolini will be awed by their Axis ally,* Tonaka thought on this 25th day of November 1941.

The fair was in full swing, and it appeared everyone there was enjoying the fun. "Come on, Sergeant, you can do it," some of the men were cheering, as the older man took aim at the target with the dart gun. Another booth had a ring toss set up where several soldiers were trying to win the shiny trinkets attached to the posts. The horseshoe games proved to be a popular competition, with the clang of a ringer every now and then bringing cheers from the onlookers.

"Mrs. Burns, this is really super. I know the men appreciate the effort put forth by all the folks here at Helen's Landing who worked on this," Wesley said when the two sat down at one of the gaily decorated tables scattered across the lawn after Helen introduced him to several landowners from the area.

"These men are here because of us. I also know most of the towns' people here don't think anything could ever happen. They believe the men will be moved on eventually."

"And, what do you think?" Wesley asked out of curiosity.

"I don't really know. I do know things look pretty bleak right now. These men may have to defend us."

"Then you're more observant than most."

"Hi," Sally cheerfully greeted, coming up to Helen and Wesley.

"Hello, Sally, you look very pretty this evening," Helen said.

"Why, thank you. I've come to steal my brother away for a bit if I may."

"You two run along and enjoy yourselves."

Alan stood a little distance away listening to the exchange. He was on the verge of making an excuse to not attend when the older woman stopped him in the hospital corridor and said he should come here tonight. Raja's words, *soldiers talk among themselves,* came to him then and he accepted. Alan had learned so far the kind of guns that were along the shoreline to deter landing craft, and about the artillery defenses a short distance inland, when he overheard the gun handlers debating which gun was a better weapon against an enemy.

Dr. Jamison came out the hospital's side door onto the patio and sat down. "Well, Helen, it looks to be a success."

"That's good to know. One always wonders if everything will come off all right."

Alan walked along the roadside later that evening trying to locate where the artillery placements were located before he met with Raja again. He heard an Army truck coming at one point and stepped into the first line of trees out of sight before the headlights picked him out. He was interested, and sure Tonaka would be as well, to learn the nurse called Sally had a brother who was the British Army officer in command of defenses around the village. At least enduring the time spent in the English woman's company had yielded some useful information.

Alan stopped short about three miles north of the village when he heard voices coming from a bend in the road and cleared his mind of the fair to observe what the British forces had in place. He had nearly stumbled headlong into the Army guns he saw through the trees and undergrowth thinking about other things. Alan smiled to himself, pleased that he had found what he wanted. He returned to Helen's Landing after watching and listening for half an hour to the soldiers and what the sergeant had to say before the night watch settled in.

The news out of the East became more ominous in the week following the fair every time the radio was turned on or a newspaper picked up. The Americans were demanding Japan's withdrawal from the Axis and renouncement of further aggression to settle the mounting diplomatic concerns. Japan's reply was complete dismissal of the stipulations as impossible to accept. In the meantime, Britain maintained her support of the United States' demands to the Japanese.

"We seem to get farther and farther apart each time one or the other makes a statement," Peter said.

"Neither side wants to admit it could be wrong to any degree," John replied. "It's just a matter of time now before they stop talking altogether."

"You mean they'll resort to force," Peter flatly stated.

"I believe it will come to that before much longer, yes," John confirmed. "I heard officials in the United States believe they'll be at war with Japan eventually. They're too far apart on the issues."

"If Churchill is to be believed, and I think he is, that will mean us too," Peter grimly stated. "After the losses in Norway and Europe, and now the evacuation of our forces in Greece, England would be at war on every part of the globe."

"Not the *Phony War* of '39, that's for sure," John observed.

Shaking his head as he stood up, Peter left John at the outdoor table in its picturesque setting on the hospital patio overlooking the sea. Malaya, even with its alluring tropical beauty, could not stir optimism in either of them as they contemplated the future.

CHAPTER 34

Christmas lights glowed with celebratory invitation in Singapore's shop windows and ships in the harbor glistened with a freshly polished luster on Friday evening, December 5, 1941. The city basked in the knowledge the battleships *Prince of Whales* and *Repulse* rode at anchor in the most desirable port in the East. The quayside donned a rainbow of color, as harbor boats whisked women in evening gowns and sparkling jewels, along with men in formal attire, to be received with generous ceremonial tradition aboard Britain's two most impressive ships. The guests were wined and dined with the best the Navy could provide, while orchestras played under freshly stretched awnings that shielded the decks from the damp night air.

The battleships and their support vessels were sent by the British government to Singapore in the effort to promote a strong British Naval presence in the East. Judging by the jubilant reception, the King's subjects were embracing the appearance of great power the battleships bestowed on them in the belief Japan would surely not dare to challenge such a powerful and fearful Naval force.

"What do you think of her, Doc?" Mason asked, as they toured the *Repulse.*

"She's big enough that's for sure, and she bristles with tiers of guns. I saw the dispensary. Makes ours look like a closet."

"Midshipman Barnes seems enthusiastic," Mason observed.

"Roger? He's fascinated with the thing. I heard him say except for the

Mariah he'd never seen anything so resplendent," Dr. Patterson responded with twinkling eyes.

"I'd hoped to tour the *Prince of Whales* as well, but we sail early tomorrow morning. Maybe when we return."

The boson piped *Mariah*'s salute when she passed the two massive battleships early the next morning, having it returned by their buglers, as she made her way out of Singapore Harbor. Andy felt a certain thrill, a sense of deeply steeped tradition, as he conned the *Mariah* past the *Repulse* and *Prince of Whales* with their buglers sounding the answering salute. The aircraft carrier that was to sail with the battleships would give these great ships credibility and make the battle group a formidable foe. Andy had heard she might still be coming after repairs to her hull were completed from the grounding accident during sea trials off South America.

"Sir, crew is secured from leaving harbor. First watch is closed up," Mason reported.

"Very well, carry on, Number One," Andy responded, then returned to his chair on the bridge and thought about the last few months spent based out of Singapore. He believed when the orders came it would be a short reprieve from the Atlantic and Mediterranean to update the Eastern fleet on German tactics. He had found instead the tour to be more like peacetime assignments before the war with Germany began. Even as tensions rose, many did not believe war would threaten British holdings in the East. Andy was certain Japan was primed to strike out at her perceived enemies. He questioned if the British could determine where the strike might come before it happened. And if they could, would the Allies be able to contain it with the defenses that were in place?

"Course to steer is 0–7-0," Mason ordered.

The helmsman deftly turned the ship at the order and responded an instant later when the *Mariah* settled into her new track. "My course is 0–7-0."

"Very well, carry on."

"Aye, sir."

"We should be there in a few hours," Andy commented. "Ransan is just across the strait. We turn north to Bengalis and sail around the island to the Bengalis Strait. Once there, we chart its depth and return to Singapore. It shouldn't take more than a few days time."

"We've been doing a great deal of charting lately," Mason noted.

"The Navy does most of the charting and mapping at sea. Charting new territory is one of its primary functions. Commerce often makes decisions based on our findings about where to locate new operations."

"So, in a sense we're a bit like the first explorers to new territory, and before long industry follows to provide the goods we need to stay," Brian remarked.

"I would say that's a fair analogy," Andy agreed.

The *Mariah* reached the assigned area and began the survey work which continued into the next day and evening. Mason was standing the midnight watch, when a signal was handed to him by the radioman on duty. "Why so grim?" he asked.

"The message, sir," the man replied, with a sad face.

Quickly scanning it, Mason's body went rigid and his blood ran cold by the time he had finished. Blowing into the voice pipe, he waited for Andy to respond.

"Burns here."

"Sir, message from base. Singapore has come under air attack by the Japanese. All ships are to come to a first alert status," Mason reported.

"So, it's happened. All right. You know the drill. I'm on my way."

"Yes, sir, I know the drill," Mason quietly acknowledged, allowing his voice to reveal his sense of sadness.

"Now hear this," came over the speakers. "Man your battle stations. This is not a drill. I repeat this is not a drill."

"What's that?" Dr. Patterson groggily asked.

"Sir," Harris said again, touching his shoulder. "We have to come to battle readiness."

"A drill at this hour!"

"No sir. I think it's the real thing this time."

Quentin Patterson lowered his head with a look of despair, before gazing up again at Harris. "I see, let's get things organized then," he quietly ordered. "I'm sure when he has time, Commander Burns will let us know what's happened."

"It looks peaceful enough," Andy said. "We'll be south of Kundur when we emerge from the strait. It could be a tight fit if the Japanese have any ships hanging about."

"Sir, we could turn east before Mendol and swing around Tupang. That would bring us out here," Brian suggested, tracing a finger over the chart.

"Not far from where we started. That would allow us to see if any Japanese ships are close to Singapore from the west," Andy commented, scanning the chart. "My guess is that the planes were carrier-based and came out of Saigon or someplace near there. We should know in a day or two at the most."

"Sir," the radioman said. "There's another signal."

Andy glanced through the message then read it aloud to the bridge. "Hong Kong was also attacked along with several American possessions, including the U. S. Naval Base at Pearl Harbor, Hawaii. We are to maintain radio silence. There aren't any damage reports yet."

"Okay you men," Parker barked, "let's look alert there. Remember what you learned before." Parker was at the starboard 20-mm gun checking the ammunition supply and the gunners' readiness. Many of the crew were novices to combat who had replaced veterans rotated to Australia to serve on ships returning to England. Looking up, he saw a mess man coming with a fanny of cocoa for the men. *Commander Burns doesn't forget his crew, even now,* Parker thought. *Edmon taught him that in the Atlantic and the Channel.*

The *Mariah* returned to Singapore Harbor without incident. She found it looked empty with the *Prince of Whales* and *Repulse,* along with their support ships gone. The group had sailed like avenging lions with orders to repel any Japanese troops landing in northern Malaya where reinforcements had come ashore at Kota Bharu. Other ships in the vicinity were warned to make way for *Force Z.*

"Engines off," Andy ordered.

"It doesn't look like there's any damage to the base," Mason said taking in the immediate vicinity.

"It must be more in the city," Andy reasoned. "We're to report in with Admiral Edwards at Naval headquarters upon arrival. He wants to see both of us. We'll probably be able to tell more when we get closer to the city's center."

"I'll have the whaler lowered sir."

"Mr. Jones, you have the watch," Andy ordered.

"Aye, sir."

Grim-faced men walked with purpose in a flurry of hurried activity outside the Admiral's office, where Andy and Mason overheard people talking about the multiple Japanese attacks while they waited.

"Looks like their battleships are all but sunk right in the harbor," one man said.

"I heard some of their cruisers and destroyers went along with them," another put in.

This was the first information Andy or Mason had heard about the damages to shipping at the United States Naval Base in Pearl Harbor. They looked at each other for a moment asking the same silent questions before Admiral Edwards' aide came and led them into the admiral's inner sanctum.

"Come in Commander, Lieutenant," Eric Edwards briskly ordered.

"Thank you sir," Andy responded, as he saluted.

"Sir," Mason echoed, saluting.

"At ease men, sit down. We have things to cover."

"Thank you, sir," Andy acknowledged, taking a chair and indicating one to Mason.

"I'll come to the point, Commander," Edwards began. "Even though most of the base believes the *Repulse* and *Prince of Whales* will squash the attack by Japan, I don't want to bet everything on one resource."

"I understand, sir. As my mother says, 'don't put all your eggs in one basket,'" Andy quoted.

"Yes, well, an apt metaphor I'm sure. I'm sending you back into the Malacca Strait. If Japan gets a foothold in Malaya, they'll push south and west to take the rubber plantations and tin mines. If they get that far, you can bet shipping will follow," Eric Edwards reasoned.

"That would be the most logical next step for them," Andy agreed.

"Commander, you know the area better than nearly anyone here and the most likely places a landing could be attempted."

"Yes, I know a good deal of the western coast," Andy confirmed. "My family took many trips up and down it when I was growing up."

"That's why I'm sending you. Lieutenant, I want you to make yourself as informed as possible as well," Edwards instructed, looking at Mason for the first time.

"Yes, sir," Mason stiffly acknowledged.

"It's not just the usual, you may have to take command," Eric Edwards said, taking in the stiff demeanor. "I'm also sending the *Victoria.* I want you to bring her officers and navigator into the full picture as well."

"When do we leave, sir?" Andy asked.

"Tomorrow night. I know it's a quick turn around, but right now it's necessary.

"We'll be ready, sir."

"Very well, carry on."

"Yes, sir," Andy responded, before he and Mason saluted and left the admiral to attend to the innumerable tasks open warfare had brought to another part of the world.

"I see you've been ashore as well, Doc," Andy noted at the quayside, when he and Mason returned to the harbor, indicating the package under Dr. Patterson's arm.

"Had to resupply while I had the chance. Stopped at a quiet little place and heard all about the attack." Dr. Patterson airily indicated, making no attempt to hide his anger and contempt about the situation.

"I get the impression there's more to tell," Andy prompted.

"Seems no one was around to turn off the lights when it happened. The Japs just came along and had everything in the city lit up for them," Patterson informed them.

"You mean no one was on duty?" Mason incredulously asked.

"Apparently the chap that was supposed to be there had something better to do the other night. I understand the Army has taken over now. Of course, that's closing the gate after the cow is already out."

Sub-lieutenant Davis was in the wardroom when the men returned to the ship engrossed in the daily paper. "Hello, Davis, what has you looking so intent there?" Mason asked.

"What? Oh, I was just reading about the attack on Pearl Harbor in the United States."

"Did I hear you say Pearl Harbor?" Dr. Patterson asked, coming into the wardroom.

"Yes, sir. I was just reading in the paper here about it," Davis explained.

"I caught the opening of their President Roosevelt's speech. He said, 'December 7, 1941 is a day that will live in infamy,'" Dr. Patterson quoted.

"According to this, Japan gave no formal document severing all relations with the United States before the attack," Davis summarized. "The Embassy representatives brought the document with Japan's formal diplomatic intentions after the fact to the American President."

"You mean they had the unmitigated gall to perform such an act without first severing all talks?" Mason asked in stunned disbelief.

"That's what it says here. It also has the speeches from Mr. Churchill and the rest declaring war on Japan," Davis continued.

"Yes," Dr. Patterson said with a touch of sarcasm, "Greece, the Netherlands, and the Free French have all followed with Britain in declaring war on Japan, along with the Americans. Seems they're all up in arms about America being attacked like that, even more so than the attacks on their own possessions in the East. If America had come in before Europe fell, it might have been different."

"You can't change the past, Doc. Anyway, they're well in it now. They won't have much choice but to declare war on Germany as well," Mason noted, and then grinned a little. "I bet Churchill slept well last night. He's wanted America in this right along.

"Signal sir," the radioman said.

"Thank you, that will be all," Andy responded.

"Yes, sir."

Opening the page Andy read the message.

> Japanese reinforcements landed at Kota Bharu. STOP. Heavy fighting. STOP. Kota Bharu air base in jeopardy. STOP. END.

The following day *Mariah*'s crew was busy with preparations to sail on a war footing. Unlike some ships stationed at Singapore, the *Mariah* was a war veteran and her crew soon fell into the quickened pace. A dispatch was brought to Andy late in the afternoon while reviewing preparations with Mason and speaking with Lieutenant Thompson about the engine room, which momentarily turned his skin pale.

"What is it, sir?" Mason asked in concern.

"The *Prince of Whales* and *Repulse,* they've been sunk," Andy breathed.

"Both?" Mason asked in stunned disbelief.

"Someone must have made a mistake," Thompson objected. "Why, they're the finest ships around. They can't be on the bottom."

"Number One, send an inquiry to base headquarters and ask for confirmation," Andy ordered.

"Yes, sir, right away."

"That will be all for now. We sail at 2200 hours," Andy concluded.

It was late in the day before Mason received the terse reply, *confirmed,* to his inquiry regarding the status of the battleships. He went in search of his commander to deliver the stark one-word message and found him and Quentin Patterson quietly talking in the infirmary.

"Were they wrong?" Andy asked when he spotted Mason hovering in the doorway.

"I'm afraid not, sir. They're both gone," Mason quietly answered.

"Who's gone?" Dr. Patterson asked.

"I guess you didn't hear. It's all over the ship by now. The *Prince of Whales* and *Repulse* were sunk by Japanese torpedo bombers earlier today," Andy explained, running a hand over his face before continuing. "I'll inform the crew after we've sailed."

The Mariah sailed north into the Malacca Strait to follow the Malayan Peninsula's western coast with orders to seek out and destroy enemy shipping. The *Victoria* sailed along side her after being restored to complete fighting trim, leaving her painful experience the previous February a distant memory in the ship's log. Andy made a brief announcement about the loss of the *Repulse* and *Prince of Whales* after the ships were settled into the zigzag sailing pattern that war made necessary.

"First the *Hood,* and now the *Prince of Whales* and *Repulse,*" Roger Barnes quietly murmured.

"Did you say something?" Parker asked.

"No, not really. I was just thinking about those two ships and the *Hood,*" Roger answered, looking out to the horizon.

"It's hard to take in; them bein' gone I mean. Just don't seem quite real," Parker reflected.

"Yes, not quite real," Roger wistfully sighed.

CHAPTER 35

Dr. Jamison was sleeping when the attacks at Singapore and Kota Bharu occurred. An insistent knocking in the predawn hour at his front door woke him before hearing urgent voices and then a knock at his bedroom door. Slipping on his dressing gown, he opened the door to his manservant and John Hartman. "What is it? An accident?"

"No sir," John began. "Singapore has been attacked by air, and urgent messages are coming in from the Northern Provinces that Japanese soldiers are invading across the Thai border near Kota Bharu."

"It's finally started then. The diplomats weren't able to circumvent Premier Tojo's hard-line government. Have there been any further attacks reported since these initial ones?"

"Not that I know of, sir. I'm sorry to wake you," John apologized. "But I thought you would want to know."

"You did the right thing, John."

"Sir…sir, wake up, sir," Arthur urgently called, shaking Wesley's shoulder.

"What is it?" Wesley mumbled, still half asleep.

"Sir, the Japanese have attacked," Arthur reported.

Coming fully awake, Wesley swung out of bed and reached for his pants. "Where and in what strength?"

"Land invasion across the Thai border near Kota Bharu, and Japanese aircraft bombed Singapore. No damage reports yet," Arthur reported.

"Kota Bharu air base," Wesley surmised. "They'll go for the air base. Have there been air attacks in the north?"

"I don't know, sir. The reports coming in are pretty sketchy."

"Okay. Bring the unit to first alert," Wesley ordered. "We'll be on a war footing before nightfall."

Soldiers moved with purpose when they went to their posts as Helen's Landing started another day. Alan noticed the change and wondered what had suddenly caused the British soldiers to have this transformation in attitude. He learned the reason when he arrived at the hospital. *So, the arrogant British are worried,* he thought.

Helen came into the hospital at midmorning and found everyone in the doctor's lounge. "What's going on, Martin?"

"Helen! I'd forgotten you were coming."

"So it seems. Why is everyone in here?"

"You haven't heard?"

"Heard what, Martin?" Helen asked, looking bewildered.

"We're at war with Japan," John told her. "They invaded at Kota Bharu and also bombed Singapore."

"What?"

"I'm afraid that's not all," Peter said. "They hit the American Naval base at Pearl Harbor, Hawaii, and several other American possessions, along with Hong Kong."

"They don't know what they've started," Jane told the others, unconsciously twisting her wedding band. "The United States will retaliate. The nation will be up in arms and in the end won't show any mercy after this."

"We were hoping to hear more on the hourly news update. But all they're saying is where fighting broke out and that there are some casualties," Sally said. "Wes might find out more later on today. He's bound to be in touch with his headquarters."

"I guess all we can do is wait," Jane sighed.

"You're right, Jane," Dr. Jamison agreed. "Let's get back to work. We may be called on for support."

The news about the fighting in the north kept getting worse as the days passed, coupled with the announcement the *Prince of Whales* and *Repulse* were lost at sea. The Army couldn't hold Kota Bharu or the air base and had fallen back. Wesley's mini-hospital to the south of the base was swamped with more than 300 wounded passing through, before it too was evacuated.

"Martin, Eric Edwards here."

"Yes, Eric. How are you?"

"Worried," Eric Edwards bluntly stated. "The Japanese are pushing west and south in Malaya. We're losing ground fast. I'm bringing you, Lieutenant Hartman and Lieutenant Romans to active status. I need one of them at that aid station of Vilmont's near Kalang. And Martin, watch out for yourself up there."

Eric Edwards rang off, and Dr. Jamison called John and Peter into his office. "John, Peter, take a chair. I've just heard from Admiral Edwards. We're to be placed on active duty affective immediately. John, I'm sending you to the outpost aide station outside Kalang to help with the overflow of casualties. Route them through here for evacuation by sea to Singapore," Dr. Jamison ordered. "Evacuate back to here if it comes to that. It's the only direct order I'm going to give you."

"I understand, sir. When do I leave?" John asked.

"As soon as I can arrange transportation with the Army. I understand they are sending an Army surgeon as well. I'll get in touch with Wesley and let you know. That's all for now."

After Peter and John left his office, Dr. Jamison wondered if he would ever see John again. He knew he had sent John north instead of Peter because Peter was married to Jane. He hoped he wouldn't have to live with the possibility he had sent a young man to his death, or worse.

Peter told Jane that evening he was brought to active status earlier in the day and about the order for John to report to the outpost near Kalang. "And Dr. Jamison and I will be working with the more severe cases before they're evacuated to Singapore," he concluded.

"I thought you would be taken out of the mothballs, so to speak," Jane said. "Peter, do you think we'll have to leave here?"

"I don't know. If things get worse, we might. If the Army can hold them, then I would say no. I'm not sure is all I can tell you right now."

"I understand. I just hope that if we do have to go we can leave together is all." Jane looked softly into his eyes for a moment, as a gentle smile settled across her face. "I was going to wait until Christmas Eve, but I want to tell you now. I'm fairly certain we're going to have a baby by summer."

"Do you mean you're pregnant?" Peter asked, momentarily stunned by the unexpected news.

"Yes," Jane softly answered.

"You've made me the happiest man in the world!" Peter stammered before sweeping her into his arms.

"Peter, you're pleased then? I mean...you're not upset we didn't wait longer, especially now?"

"Upset? Jane, I couldn't be happier," Peter assured her, before holding her close to him again. "Darling, I love you. And now we're having a baby. In the midst of war and hatred in the world, you're creating a miracle of hope for the future."

"It's why I wondered if we would have to leave. I want our baby to know his father, the kind of man he is, gentle and caring," Jane whispered in a shaky voice.

"We'll find a way Jane. We'll find a way," Peter softly reassured her before kissing her with all the feeling and emotion welling up within him.

The *Mariah* and her companion cruised along the northern coast of western Malaya in the attempt to provide a protective shield against more Japanese soldiers being set ashore. If the British Army could establish a line of defense there was still time to halt the enemy. He briefly wondered how the folks at Helen's Landing were holding up with the knowledge the Japanese Army was swiftly advancing its southerly push toward Singapore.

"Planes, eleven o'clock off the starboard bow," the lookout shouted.

"Signal the *Victoria,* sound battle stations," Andy calmly ordered.

"Close up," Mason ordered. "Wait for the order to fire. Watch your aim, remember the drills."

Gunners could make out the *Rising Sun* insignia on the wings before the order to fire was given. The 20-mm gun came to bear when a torpedo plane targeting the *Mariah* came within range. In a twist of fate a single 20-mm projectile struck the torpedo detonator the enemy plane carried with enough velocity of force to cause the firing mechanism to activate itself. The ensuing explosion enveloped the enemy plane in an eye-searing fireball that fell into the sea. *Mariah*'s gunners cheered at the minute victory before roughly being told to watch their front for the next one.

Enemy planes swarmed over the *Mariah* and *Victoria,* as ships came into view over the horizon. The *Victoria*'s gunners brought down another plane and sent a second away with smoke pouring out of the engine compartment. "Make our course 0–6–5 degrees," Andy ordered. "Prepare to engage with torpedoes. Set depth for three feet," he ordered. "Fire one...fire two," he ordered when the enemy ship filled his sights. Andy watched for a moment to be sure they were running on course before bringing his sights to the second target that was already turning away from the danger speeding toward it.

"Watch your front," Davis ordered, when some of the crew watched the torpedoes racing toward their target. "Guns to bear four o'clock...fire," he barked as another wave of planes dove toward the *Mariah* and *Victoria* like a flock of falcons protecting their young.

"Harris, hold this here. That's it," Dr. Patterson said with less urgency. "Have to stop the flow of blood. I think it clipped an artery. Put a tourniquet on it until we can get it slowed down. There, that's better. See what's happened to him over there."

"He's dead, sir," Harris reported. "The front of his skull is gone."

"Leave him then," Dr. Patterson ordered with a sigh. "Let's get this man below."

Ba-Wham

A shock wave came across the deck, causing Dr. Patterson to lose his balance and fall to the deck. Sitting up, he looked around thinking the ship had been hit.

"Are you all right, sir?" Harris asked with concern.

"Yeah, I'm all right. What the devil was that, anyway?"

Andy watched the torpedoes hit their target. The ensuing explosion, fueled by high-octane gasoline and cases of ammunition, caused the transport ship to break apart in a matter of minutes. A slick of burning oil and a few timbers were all that was left to mark the grave.

The second ship was attempting to move away from the sudden danger. *Victoria*'s guns managed to strafe the enemy vessel several times causing fires to spread across her decks as it steamed toward the horizon. Andy saw for an instant what looked like a torch moving along the deck then fall into the sea. He belatedly realized it was a man on fire, just before the ship disappeared from view.

Suddenly, the sea and sky were empty. "Signal the *Victoria* to report damages and casualties," Andy ordered.

"Yes, sir," Roger responded and began flashing the signal lamp. "She says four casualties, one dead, sir. No damage."

"Does she need medical assistance?"

"No sir, not at this time," Roger replied, after receiving the *Victoria*'s answer.

"Very well. Mr. Jones, bring us back to a course toward Panang Island," Andy ordered.

"Course to steer is 1–7–0 degrees," Brian answered.

"All right, let's get this cleared away," Parker ordered. "We want to be ready for the next round."

"Just like last year," Bert commented to his friend.

"What-cha mean?" Ernie asked.

"Planes a comin' at us again. Just like when we was in the Mediterranean and the Channel afore it," Bert explained.

"What-cha 'spect wit the Japs bein' in wid Hitler," Ernie retorted.

"Yeah, guess yer right," Bert agreed.

"Mr. Parker," Davis said.

"Sir."

"When the casings are cleared out, have a new supply of ammunition brought up in case we get hit again before nightfall," Davis ordered. "This close to the air base they might have another go at us yet today."

"Yes, sir," Parker briskly responded.

"And, Mr. Parker," Davis said, as Tim Parker stood waiting for him to finish, "good shooting."

"Thank you, sir. All right, you heard the Lieutenant, get it done."

Waiting to the side, Mason overheard the brief exchange. *This is the moment Sub-lieutenant Davis becomes a member of Mariah's crew,* he thought. Mason knew Tim Parker would see to it the gunners under Davis gave him everything they could. He exchanged a few words with Davis before receiving his report and moved on to the next station. Ten minutes later Mason returned to the bridge to report *Mariah*'s readiness to meet the next challenge.

CHAPTER 36

John and Captain David Jergen, an Army surgeon, traveled north with Wesley and his engineering crew against a torrential flood of terrorized refugees fleeing south on a harrowing ride to the aid station near Kalang's harbor. Enemy planes rained unending torrents of deafening gunfire into the fleeing hordes of frightened humanity, leaving the roadway littered with the bodies of young mothers and their children to lie beside the old and infirm. Civilian and Army vehicles were bombed indiscriminately, and then pushed aside by the survivors in the urgency to evade the enemy's unrelenting push through the Malayan Peninsula.

The first few weeks at the outpost John and David Jergen rotated the on-call duty and spent many evenings over a chessboard engaging in conversation from medicine to politics. The recent enemy onslaught to encircle Kuala Lumpur had changed that. The harbor had become untenable in recent days, and it was up to the Army to evacuate anyone leaving the aid station now.

"The ones with the green tags on the beds go tonight," John briefly explained to the Army sergeant who would lead the hospital trucks to Helen's Landing. "I had the cook make up some sandwiches and a thermos to take along."

"That was right nice a-ya, mate," the Australian sergeant acknowledged, grinning through three days growth of heavy beard.

"Try to go as easy as you can," John cautioned. "Some of these men have some pretty serious injuries. I wouldn't move them yet, but the air strikes are getting worse every day. Kalang's harbor is inaccessible after the last two days of enemy bombing. Now the Japs are concentrating on the road along the coast. I'm not sure how long it will be open for the trucks to get through."

"Don't you worry none, sir. We'll get 'em ta yer hospital," the sergeant firmly assured him.

"I expect you will," John grinned.

"Trucks get here okay?" David Jergen asked when John passed the operating room doorway.

"Yeah, they're loading now. He the last one?" John asked, glancing at the man being taken from the operating room.

"For now at least. I'll get him settled in if you'll check the patients that are left."

John nodded his agreement and turned into the small ward to examine the few remaining patients that were too critical to chance moving. He was acutely aware that before long the choice might not be a medical consideration if the Japanese weren't halted soon in their advance through Malaya.

"We're loaded up, sir," the Australian sergeant told John a half hour later.

"All right then, Sergeant. You should be there by dawn. Good luck."

Wesley pulled up to the outpost just as the trucks were leaving and called out to John's retreating back. "Hello, Wes, what brings you here?" he asked, walking over to the mud caked Land Rover.

"John, I need you to come with me," Wesley said with some urgency.

"Why? What's wrong?"

"Lieutenant Nance, Arthur, my second. He's been hit pretty badly. We've done what we can. The medic said not to move him any further until a doctor could take care of him. So I came here, hoping you could come."

"I'll get my bag."

John quickly explained to David what Wesley needed before hurriedly adding surgical supplies to his medical bag and jumping into the Land Rover. "What happened?" he tersely asked as they pulled onto the road.

"We were setting charges at the northern approaches to Kalang. Arthur was near a land mine he was preparing to place, when we were strafed and it exploded," Wesley explained in a clipped voice. They stopped a few miles north of the aid station outside a small building about the size of a cow shed. "We brought him in here."

"John slowly removed his stethoscope, carefully contemplating the minimal options the circumstances presented, after examining Arthur. His labored breathing and falling blood pressure were ominous signs of multiple life threatening injuries. "I don't know, Wes. I don't like the sound of his lungs, and there's internal injuries causing blood loss and shock."

"Is there anything you can do?"

"I'll see if I can clean this up some. The rest…I'll have to operate," John bleakly explained.

"You tell us what you need, and we'll set it up for you."

John spent the better part of the night operating on the small battered body beneath his scalpel. He knew the aid station would be the location of choice to operate, but he did not believe Arthur would survive the trip to get him there. The chances even now John knew were pretty slim that Arthur wouldn't die before he finished. The sun was rising on another day of war when he finally sewed the outer skin closed. He carefully bandaged the surface wounds before lowering his facemask and looking over at Wesley who volunteered to assist.

"All we can do now is wait. I've given him something to keep him under until we can move him to the aid station. The war is over for him for a very long time," John said matter-of-factly.

"Yeah, I guess it is," Wesley acknowledged, and then went outside to empty the contents of his stomach. He wondered how doctors and nurses could do that day after day, acquiring a new respect for their profession. Taking a deep breath, Wesley went back into the shed. "What do you think?"

"His pressure is up a little. That's good. And he seems to be breathing a little easier," John cautiously responded. "I was afraid at first he had a collapsed lung. We need to get him to Helen's Landing for proper care. He may need more surgery before he can be moved as far as Singapore."

"I guess he'll see Sally for Christmas then."

"I'd forgotten," John quietly said. He realized the day would have no meaning to him this year.

Alan rode in the back of the Land Rover in the early hours before dawn with three others that were to meet the Army trucks carrying the newest batch of wounded at the northern checkpoint. His job was to record a victim's blood type and place it on a wristband where doctors and nurses could easily find it. Raja had told him Tonaka would be coming through sometime soon and wanted to be shown the defenses around Helen's Landing, and Alan wanted to see how the checkpoint worked.

"You did a good job, Alan," Peter said.

"Thank you, Doctor Romans. I would like to go again if I am needed."

"I'm sure you'll be needed," Peter grimly assured him.

Alan grudgingly realized Raja was right again. *If they trust me, I'll be able to go anywhere and can show Tonaka whatever he wants to see,* he thought.

Christmas morning broke with rain and low clouds, grounding enemy airplanes and slowing the Japanese advance for a few hours. The falling rain seemed to reflect the subdued mood of the remaining residents at Helen's Landing where a prayer vigil for peace was held in place of the usual Christmas

Mass celebration. It ended with the parish solemnly singing "Silent Night." Fr. Finney planned to shepherd as many of his flock as possible to Singapore by the last paddle boat to leave Helen's Landing at midnight, allowing the parish this last Christmas in their homes. Jane and Peter were able to meet Helen at the village church before returning to the hospital.

"I'm coming to the hospital, too," Helen said. "The kitchen staff will need help with the wards being full."

"Dr. Jamison is going to move as many as possible to Singapore by ship tonight," Jane told her friend. "He thinks only three will have to remain here still."

"What about the lieutenant from Wesley's unit?" Helen asked.

"You mean Arthur Nance," Peter said. "He's in no condition to be moved yet. Dr. Jamison and I had to operate again yesterday morning to remove his spleen. Right now it's touch-and-go."

"Sally's with him this morning," Jane explained. "He's barely opened his eyes since he arrived. Dr. Jamison is very concerned."

"Maybe Martin will let me sit with him for a while. Arthur came to the house for dinner once with Wesley and Martin. He was such a nice young man, so appreciative and pleasant to talk with. It would give the nursing staff a break, and I'd like to do something to help him."

That evening Helen, Sally, Jane and Peter, Tom Linn, and Dr. Jamison gathered in the cafeteria to share a short time together in recognition of Christmas. Unlike the year before, the meal they shared was simple. Peter finally broke the silence.

"Jane and I have a little news to share. All right, darling?"

"Yes, it should be today," Jane quietly agreed.

"What is it, Peter?" Sally asked.

"Well, we just thought this was the right day and all." Peter's face began turning red, as he looked for the right words to tell these special friends the news about their impending parenthood before Jane rescued him.

"Peter and I are having a baby in the summer."

"That is good news, especially now," Helen said, smiling at them. "Congratulations, my dears."

"Jane! It's wonderful!" Sally exclaimed. "I'll have to write Andy and Wes to tell them."

"Andy said the two of you were corresponding," Helen said. "I'm glad."

"We've become good friends."

"Martin, you haven't said anything," Helen commented.

"Well, of course, I'm happy for the two of you. I'm just not happy about the fact I'm going to lose one of my best nurses," Dr. Jamison responded putting a smile on his face. He didn't say anything about the growing concerns he had regarding the increasing air raids and advancing Japanese Army or the rumors about Caucasian women being tortured and raped. He did wonder how he would convince these three women he felt responsible for to evacuate to Singapore and possibly on to Java or Australia. Now the reason was of even greater urgency.

CHAPTER 37

Andy concluded the Christmas Mass from the Naval Church Services Prayer Book and replaced his hat before wishing the crew a Happy Christmas. The cook had somehow managed to create a festive dinner from the meager supplies in the galley, penetrating the ship with the smell of fresh baking bread. Mouths watered at the thought of something besides a hastily eaten sandwich and tea ladled from a bucket. Arrangements were made to have three sittings to allow everyone time to enjoy this Christmas feast after his watch, providing the Japanese didn't interfere.

Dr. Patterson came to the bridge to report on the latest casualties after the service concluded. "So, I think they'll be okay for now. They were lucky it was a dud," he finished, referring to the bomb that had fallen near the forward gun position the day before. The bridge crew watched in fascinated horror when the Japanese pilot dropped his bomb directly overhead. It seemed to fall in slow motion until it hit the deck with a sudden force, bowling two men over when it landed. The expected explosion never came though, and the hideous device was carefully rolled over the side.

"I would guess they feel lucky to only have two broken arms and some abrasions between them," Andy judged, when Dr. Patterson concluded his report.

"I would say you're right, considering they both could be dead."

"Message, sir," the young telegraph rating said, handing Andy the folded paper.

"Hong Kong is surrendering to Japan," Andy grimly told the others after reading the short stark message that so greatly changed the balance of power in the East. "The Japanese will be able to concentrate on Malaya and Singapore now."

"It looks like Norway and France all over again," Dr. Patterson sadly commented.

Early in the morning the Sunday after Christmas a lookout spotted small boats in the distance. "They're landing craft," Mason reported lowering his glasses.

"The ship they came from must be just over the horizon," Andy reasoned. "We're close to Ipoh here and the tin mines. They probably are going to try to take them. We'll have to see if we can't upset their plans."

The *Mariah* fired a volley from the forward 4.7-inch guns into the landing craft catching the enemy off guard. Japanese soldiers splashed in the water trying to swim toward shore when another barrage of gunfire fell in their midst bringing a painful death.

A Japanese support ship appeared a moment later with her guns spitting fire. One volley after another flew toward the British ship that had brought the Angel of Death to their comrades. Andy ordered the torpedoes made ready while he engaged the smaller ship in battle. *Mariah*'s guns returned fire, volley-for-volley, as he aligned the attacking ship in his sites. He watched the torpedoes follow a straight path and hit the enemy ship with a flash that sent geysers of water into the air before reversing *Mariah*'s course when Zeros approached from the west.

"Two planes incoming at ten o'clock," Parker hollered, pointing toward the attackers as the 20-mm began shooting until one plane fell to the sea. Another flashed overhead, as its guns showered the deck with bullets before climbing for another pass with *Mariah*'s tracers chasing after it.

"Shoot," Tim ordered, when a third plane came toward the ship. The enemy pilot kept up a continuous volley of cannon fire aimed across *Mariah*'s decks as the Zero made its approach. Andy saw the threat and ordered a sharp turn to throw the pilot off his course. The Zero's bomb fell near the station where Tim Parker was located, causing an explosion that rocked the ship and bomb splinters to fly out in a lethal spray. Ernie, a gunner under Tim and Bert's mate, suddenly fell to the deck in writhing pain with a bomb splinter wedged in his chest.

"Medic," Tim shouted before putting another man at the vacant gun.

"Hang on, mate, I'll git one fer ya," Bert vowed, bringing his gun to bear and firing a hail storm of tracers after the plane that had caused this tragedy to fall upon them.

The final attack came from four planes diving out of the lowering sun.

Gunners flexed their waiting fingers in nervous anticipation until Andy ordered all guns to fire. The din of gunfire and scream of the diving planes was reminiscent to a demon's howl emanating from the bowels of God's fiery pit described in countless sermons down through the ages. Another bomb exploded along side, sending out a shower of splinters that cut down anything, or anyone, in their path, before the attacking Zero cart wheeled over the wave tops in the distance.

Mason went around the ship when the stand down sounded to inspect the damage and saw Dr. Patterson and Harris on the main deck tending to the wounded. Mason watched when one man was carried off with a large splinter sticking out of him and another taken a few minutes later with his head bandaged. Tim Parker came up with a bandage around his arm.

"You've been wounded," Mason said in concern.

"Just a scratch. Splinter grazed it is all," Parker shrugged unconcerned.

"How bad is the damage here?"

"One of the guns is loose at its mountin'. Fire damage is minimal, more smoke than anythin'. Railin' got twisted pretty bad along here where that bomb bounced some before it fell into the sea 'stead a crashin' through the deck. We got lucky, sir, it just grazed us some." Parker reported as Sub-lieutenant Davis approached.

"Sir, the other guns weren't damaged. Everything appears to be localized to this area. I've sent some men below to check the integrity of the hull."

Returning to the bridge, Mason gave his report. "I'll go below and look for myself, but preliminary reports indicate the hull is intact. We'll have to make repairs to the gun mountings and rail, but the ship came through pretty fair."

"We'll stay on this course until we're further south before turning east again. I'm going to make for Helen's Landing. Dr. Patterson reports some of the casualties need a hospital soon, and we can make our necessary repairs. The *Victoria* can meet us there," Andy said. "I just received a message her last recall to Singapore was to take on more mines after completing her present task and to join us once again. Carry on, Number One."

"Yes, sir." Mason thought about the *Victoria* as he made his way below decks and hoped her experience with mine laying in the Malacca Strait would be better than the last time.

"Lieutenant Jones, I want you to plot a course that brings us into Helen's Landing at dusk," Andy ordered.

Bending over the chart for a few minutes and checking his watch, Brian began laying out the required course and speed to bring them to their destination at the desired time. "Sir, I recommend we follow this course at twelve knots," he indicated, with his finger on the chart. "We should be there right about dusk."

"Very well," Andy acknowledged, ordering the course and speed change.

Mariah dropped her anchor at Helen's Landing just as the sun was taking its final plunge into the sea. A green flash of light shown across the distant water a micro-second before darkness overtook the day inviting the moon to rise. But tonight the war that no one wanted held *Mariah*'s crew in its grip, and the natural phenomenon went unnoticed.

"Bring those torches. Cut this part of the rail away here," Mason ordered, when the cutting torches were brought to the deck. "How long do you figure, Mr. Parker?"

"Shouldn't take more than about an hour or two for the rail. Have to repair the mounting bracket here for the gun and check it for damage."

"Mr. Davis, I'll leave you and Mr. Parker to it here," Mason said in clipped tones. "I'll have some sandwiches sent so work can continue uninterrupted. We have to be battle ready by daylight."

"Yes sir, we'll be ready," Davis affirmed. "Maybe we can jury-rig the damaged 20-mm if we have to until we can get it remounted."

"Do what you can, Mr. Davis," Mason ordered.

"You heard the First Officer, let's get it done, men," Parker barked at the waiting work crew.

Andy went to the hospital after a brief rest at 0500 hours to check on *Mariah*'s wounded crewmembers and found Dr. Jamison in his office. "Andy, have a seat."

"Thank you, sir. I came to see what the status is on my crew."

"Most are in fair condition, considering. They should be back on duty in a couple of weeks and can rejoin you in Singapore. The one with the splinter in his chest, your gunner, and the man from the engine room are another matter."

"How bad is Ernie?'

"Peter and I spent a good deal of time removing the splinter. Quentin did the right thing to wait. It punctured the sac around the heart and actually cut into the heart muscle itself, partially severing an artery and damaging a valve," Dr. Jamison explained. "The point acted like a cork. If Quentin had removed it when you were under way, your gunner most likely would have bled to death. He won't be able to serve on a ship again though. The damage is too severe."

"I see. He was a good gunner. What about George, our engine room mate?"

"He's nearly as bad. The bullet did a lot of damage when it passed through, and it grazed a lung as well. I don't dare move him for a few days at least."

"Thompson said he's a good man. They'll both be missed." Andy walked by the nurse's station when he left Dr. Jamison and saw Sally with her head bent over a chart.

"Hello, Nurse Sally."

"Andy," Sally softly breathed, looking up into the tired face that held a faint flicker of mischief in the eyes. "How...I mean, when did you get here?"

"I was just checking on the status of our wounded that were brought in last night with Dr. Jamison."

"You look all in. Would you like something to eat? The kitchen is open. I was just going to have some breakfast."

"That sounds good," Andy agreed.

Sally told Andy about Arthur Nance and of Wesley going to the north with John when they sat down at a table near the open French doors to the patio with their scrambled eggs and toast. Andy found himself pouring out his concerns about the Japanese advance and the Army and Navy's inability to halt them, "They keep moving south." He told her about the *Mariah*'s battles the past few weeks and the severity of the attacks by the enemy. "They seem to have an endless supply of men and machinery."

Sally listened as Andy relieved his frustrations and concerns about the deteriorating situation and saw the sadness in his eyes while he told it. The sun was coming up when Andy stopped talking about his misgivings and looked at the woman sitting across from him listening with uninterrupted attention. "I've been monopolizing the conversation, I'm sorry."

"You needed someone to tell it to. Thank you for letting me be that person," Sally softly replied.

"I have to get back, but may we talk again?" Andy asked, returning his attention to the present needs of his command.

"I'd like that."

Andy looked for a moment into Sally's attentive eyes and thought how nice it would be to have the time to talk when there was no rush to return to an injured ship at war.

"Sir," Mason said upon Andy's return. "We've received orders to return to Singapore."

"What's our status?"

"Port side railing is cut away and temporary repairs made. The aft 20-mm gun is inoperable at this time on the port side, and the mounting has been removed for repair. Hull integrity is intact," Mason reported.

"We'll have to risk it. If we stay here, we'll be a sitting duck once we're spotted," Andy said. "Be ready to sail in half an hour."

"Yes sir," Mason replied with a salute before heading toward the work crew on the deck.

Alan watched the *Mariah* leave the bay and noticed something didn't look quite right on the one side, like it was missing something. Alan had also seen the ship's commander leaving the hospital brush the cheek of the nurse Alan knew as Sally with a kiss and then hurry away. *Typical of the British to show no emotion,* he thought. *Keep a stiff upper lip at all cost.*

The news out of Malaya kept getting worse with each passing day. The British were heartened when the Army was able to repel an attempted landing in the lower Malayan State of Parak in early January. The tide of battle soon changed again in favor of the Japanese, and British forces were compelled to withdraw to positions further south. By January 6, 1942, British command in Singapore was forced to announce withdrawal in Parak. The Japanese were now less than 200 miles from Singapore and drawing ever closer to Helen's Landing.

CHAPTER 38

Brilliant rays of sunlight were reaching out to dispel the sea's nighttime onyx face when Jane pushed aside the bedroom curtain to the sound of thunder. Another rumbling crash quickly followed by several more woke Peter with a sudden start, "What the…"

"The guns are firing near the harbor I think," Jane told him, trying to remain calm. "I can see smoke and some flashes. Peter, maybe we should pack some things in case we have to leave."

Peter tossed aside the bed sheet and came to look over Jane's shoulder to see Japanese planes climbing away from the harbor and moving toward the north. "We better get dressed," he finally said. "We'll be needed at the hospital."

Jane turned away from the window and began the morning ritual of laying out her nurse's uniform. "Peter, would you help me please? I can't seem to get this zipper undone."

"What's the matter; is it stuck?" he asked, feeling her flinch at the touch of his hand. "Jane, are you all right?"

Jane feared she would become hysterical if she answered Peter's query and only gave a slight nod without looking at him before he gathered her into his arms, sensing her distress. "We'll be all right, my love," he gently reassured her. "I should have sent you to safety before now. But I believed things would be okay. I thought the Navy would move us before they got so close."

"I'm all right now. The guns frightened me is all. Peter, I want us to stay together. I'm more afraid of being separated from you than I am of the war," Jane quietly responded, looking into his troubled eyes.

Japanese planes flew over the village in a procession of assaults, dropping bombs and strafing the harbor in an attempt to penetrate the defenses that kept the hospital busy with the increasing number of casualties. Planes, damaged by the steady anti-aircraft fire, fell indiscriminately into houses and the surrounding jungle, igniting unchecked fires while frightened citizens fled in panic throughout the day adding to the chaos. By nightfall the toll of dead and injured was mounting.

When Alan entered the door to his boardinghouse that evening he saw two of his fellow boarders preparing to escape to Singapore removing what they could carry in a single car. "They'll never take the city," he heard them say. Alan went to his room and stretched out on the bed, picking up the espionage thriller off the nightstand he had been reading and soon fell into a light sleep. He woke with a start in the darkness when he felt a hand over his mouth and then pressure on his chest.

"I've come to see what you can tell me," Tonaka said in an even voice.

"Tonaka!" Alan breathed in surprise.

"Yes, my friend."

"But how did you get here?" Alan asked still feeling disoriented.

"It is of no relevance. It only matters that I am here."

"Yes, of course, you took me by surprise is all," Alan responded, trying to sound nonchalant.

"So, what have you seen?" Tonaka asked, as he stood up beside the bed.

"Quite a bit. The checkpoint is heavily defended. I saw two big guns, artillery they called them, north of the settlement. There might be more. I told Raja about the guns and mine fields. He has not contacted me for some time, but he has probably been busy."

"Yes, Raja has been busy," was all Tonaka said. "Can you show me these things?"

"Yes, but not until tomorrow. At night there is a curfew after nine o'clock," Alan explained.

"I will have to stay out of sight until then."

"You can stay here," Alan offered with a smile. "I am the only one left. The others have fled in fear. I will stay as well if you like."

"No. You must keep your normal routine, otherwise it might draw attention," Tonaka reasoned.

Alan was anxious for the daylight hours to end and worried that nothing should happen to his boardinghouse with Tonaka there. The anti-aircraft guns fired constantly throughout the week, seeming to surround the village in a brutal storm that fell into an eerie silence when darkness overtook the day. The air was filled with the smell of burning underbrush and pinpoints of light glowed in the night from the surrounding countryside where bombs had destroyed homes and warehouses. He was preparing to leave the hospital a few days after Tonaka's arrival when Sally caught up with him.

"Hi, Alan," Sally greeted him, a little out of breath. "I have to make a stop next to your boardinghouse and thought we might walk together. With all that's been happening, I just thought we might be safer."

Caught off guard, Alan was at first dismayed but agreed to walk with her. The short walk to town was strewn with destroyed houses and streets riddled with bomb craters. As horrendous as the damage was, the devastation near the waterfront was worse.

"It's a terrible shame to have all this destruction," Sally said when they turned into the main street. "If whoever is in charge would have listened to my brother, Wes, this might never have happened."

"I do not understand," Alan said looking puzzled.

"Wes had a plan to defend all over Malaya as heavily as here. But the powers that be said it wasn't necessary. As it is, Helen's Landing is the only place outside of Singapore and a few of the larger towns with any real defenses to hinder the Japanese from taking anything they want," Sally explained.

Tonaka pulled back from the window a little farther when Alan and Sally approached. He had explored the boardinghouse and surrounding buildings during the short lulls between air strikes to find drawers and wardrobes left open throughout the village. Articles of clothing and important papers precariously hung from cupboards and half closed desk drawers where frightened residents had packed in haste and left the rest behind.

Alan entered the house and found Tonaka waiting for him at the foot of the stairs. "Who was the woman you were taking to?" he casually asked.

"Her name is Sally. She's a nurse at the hospital. Her brother was in charge of building the defenses here."

Tonaka raised his eyebrows a little at the unexpected answer before speaking again. "How did she come to be with you tonight?"

Alan chuckled at the irony of his reply. "She thought we should walk together, that it would be safer. If she only knew."

Smiling faintly, Tonaka agreed. "You said something about her brother."

"Yes. It seems he wanted to put the same kind of defenses that are here all over Malaya, but his superiors were against it. He was told it was not necessary."

"Interesting. Did she say anything else on this walk under your protection?" Tonaka probed.

"Not really, only that if her brother would have had his way the rest of Malaya would have the same kind of defenses that are here. As it is, this is the only place outside Singapore and a few larger towns that is so heavily defended," Alan casually answered. "Come to the kitchen, and I will prepare us something to eat."

Helen heard the sound of a car motor coming up the curved drive and shook herself out of the reverie that she could not change. A messenger had delivered a note earlier in the day from Martin Jamison, saying he was concerned about her being alone in the house now that the servants had fled and suggested that he and Sally should come and bring her into town. Helen looked down one more time at the single head stone where a fresh bouquet of flowers rested before turning away to walk through the wrought iron gate of the family burial plot.

Sally saw Helen coming from her husband's grave and thought this had to be a difficult time for her, remembering the one time Jane had talked about leaving her home in Ann Arbor to come to Malaya. Jane had gone to visit Jim's grave to say goodbye, but the words never came. It wasn't until nearly three years later, when she met Peter, that she was able to begin to say good-bye to him. "Jim was with me in my heart," Jane had said. *It must be ten times worse for Helen to leave all the years of memories. Jane is young and has found that special love again,* Sally thought. "Helen, I'm so sorry," she said as she approached her friend. "This has to be a sad time for you. I wish things were different."

"I do too, Sally. But we have to face trouble when it comes," Helen said, linking her arm through Sally's. "One day it will be better I expect. Martin's waiting; we better go."

Martin Jamison watched the two women—one young, the other older, yet bonded by something unseen—coming across the lawn arm-in-arm and waited a few minutes before speaking. "Helen, do you have things ready? Would you like me to start putting them in the car?"

"I packed some things and put them in a safe place. Someday maybe I can come back for them. I shipped several things to the warehouse in Australia before the Japanese invasion began. I thought there would be time to do more or that a peace agreement might be reached at the last moment. I have two large trunks and a box is all, Martin. Oh, and there's three crates with food supplies."

"If you've forgotten anything, we can come back tomorrow," Dr. Jamison gently responded.

"Thank you, Martin, but I haven't forgotten anything. I brought the family album, and the rest is in here," Helen said, placing a hand to her heart.

"You'll be back one day. I'm sure of it, Helen. We both will," Dr. Jamison said, softly squeezing her arm.

"How close are they, Martin?"

"I'm not going to sugar coat it. You wouldn't want me to. At five o'clock this afternoon they were closing in on Kuala Lumpur. If they take the capitol, they'll be half way down the western coast," Dr. Jamison frankly told her.

"Wes and John," Sally said, showing some alarm. "They're not far south of there."

"I've already decided to contact John and tell him to evacuate back to here. He'll need a day to move out the casualties, and then come himself," Dr. Jamison explained. "The engineers will have to bring him and any new patients. They're the only ones with any trucks left near there, and getting a ship in now is out of the question.

Dr. Jamison managed to convince the two women over the past few days to stay together at the cottage during the crisis to be closer to the village and to keep them from being on their own. Not being optimistic, he thought they would be safer together. He saw Helen and Sally settled in before mentioning Ralph Burns' boat still stored in the nearby boathouse.

"I believe the *Angelica* is sea worthy, Martin. Remember? Andy had her worked on while he was home in 1940. He thought the next time he was here he would take the *Angelica* out with some friends. Do you really think we'll need her?" Helen asked, somewhat concerned.

"I don't know, but it couldn't hurt to look her over," Dr. Jamison said. "I have to get back to the hospital for now. I'll see you both in the morning."

"Helen, what's the *Angelica?*" Sally asked after Dr. Jamison left.

"A boat Ralph built a few years before he died. He was always saying, 'Helen, I'm going to build you a millionaire's yacht,' and he did."

"A yacht?" Sally asked in surprise.

"In a manner of speaking. Ralph built it to sleep up to twelve people and put a marine engine in it, but he also put in a large holding tank for fish. It looks more like a cross between a large tugboat and a trawler really. Ralph thought if you were going to be out on the water you might as well do something useful. I miss him still," Helen wistfully sighed, looking softly into the distance for a moment. "I don't know what he would have said about all this."

Sally reached out to touch Helen's hand for a moment before asking whether they should see if the boat was sea worthy. Helen opened the small side door to the nearby boathouse and lit the kerosene lantern kept on the shelf. The *Angelica* was raised out of her berth showing the signs of the recent restoration Andy had completed on her hull. The new ropes and pulleys holding her above the sea's destructive elements attested to the seaman's love for his ship and a healthy respect for the sea's power over man's feeble instruments to tame her. "I think she's all right," Helen quietly said, before dimming the lamp to leave the *Angelica* alone in her tranquil resting place.

CHAPTER 39

Eric Edwards did not mince words when he told Andy he needed the *Mariah* to keep the enemy at bay for as long as possible, when she returned to Singapore to resupply her ammunition and make hasty repairs. She put back to sea two days after her arrival while the final welds were still warm.

Mariah's orders were to join the *Victoria* and another minelayer to provide protection against the relentless air strikes and fire on coastal enemy positions. The sister ships were to lay underwater mines in an effort to slow enemy troop landings at little known beaches along the western sea coast. *Victoria*'s companion ship lay on the ocean's hard floor now, after disintegrating in an instant blinding explosion when a Japanese bomb detonated among her remaining mines. The one survivor, who was blown over the side, was now at Singapore's overflowing Naval hospital.

"Fuel tanks are topped off and repairs to damage from that last one are completed. Dr. Patterson has returned from the hospital," Mason concluded.

"Very well," Andy acknowledged.

"Sir, have you heard from Helen's Landing?"

"Not since yesterday. Martin Jamison is resourceful though. If there is a way out, he'll find it…I hope."

"I'm sure he will, sir. We know the town is still held by the British. They could get out by sea," Mason encouraged his commanding officer.

"Yes, it's possible. The *Angelica* is seaworthy. It wouldn't be the easiest trip. But it could be done." Andy looked up to see a rating hovering nearby and turned his attention back to the ship.

"Message, sir," the replacement telegraphist mate said.

"Thank you, that will be all," Andy crisply responded. He briefly thought about how quickly a person could be replaced. To Eastern Command it was just an open slot to be filled. "We're to report to the Admiral. He has a job for us," he told Mason, looking up from the brief message.

"I'll have the whaler lowered, sir."

Eric Edwards met Andy and Mason at his office door when they reported in to Admiralty headquarters and immediately ushered them into his office. "I'll get right to the point. The enemy is continuing to push forward. Unless something happens soon, they will be at our doorstep."

"What do you want us to do, sir?" Andy asked, knowing he wasn't going to like the answer.

"Frankly, I need you to go into the islands just south of here and search out any enemy ships that are close to the shipping lanes. If you can clear a pathway through them, we might stand a chance," Admiral Edwards evenly stated.

"A chance, sir?" Mason asked, a little bewildered.

"I believe we're to be the scout ahead of the wagon train, as the Americans say in their westerns," Andy candidly remarked.

"You have the idea, Commander," Eric Edwards grimly confirmed.

"You mean evacuate Singapore?" Mason asked in surprise. "I thought after the *Bengal Princess* was bombed and sunk, a defenseless ocean liner carrying women and children, that there wouldn't be any more big ships."

"There won't be, Lieutenant. Just a string of smaller craft filled to capacity."

"How soon, sir?" Andy asked.

"If they get across the Muar River, they're less than 100 miles from the city. The bombing runs have increased already. You sail tonight, Commander," Admiral Edwards vigorously answered, trying to sound confident. "The orders will be sent over to you shortly. Gaines is preparing them now."

"We'll be ready, sir," Andy assured his admiral.

Andy stopped a moment outside Admiral Edwards' office when he saw Sub-lieutenant Gaines engrossed in his work. He wondered if Gaines thought about the *Mariah* and her crew while he prepared the sailing orders that could sink her.

"Lieutenant," Andy said to Mason once they were outside the building, "I believe we have time to stop by the Raffles for one of their famous Singapore Gin Slings. It may be a while before we have the opportunity again."

"You're on, Commander," Mason responded.

The two men took a taxi to the hotel and passed through the lobby into the Cad's Alley where they found a small corner table. Andy didn't say anything until the drinks were served and the waiter left them.

"I asked you to come for two reasons, Lieutenant."

"A private talk you mean," Mason confirmed.

"Yes, we're less apt to be interrupted. First, I wanted to tell you it's been a real pleasure serving with you," Andy quietly began.

"Sir, I...thank you," Mason responded, at a loss for words.

Putting up a hand, Andy continued. "We've been handed a difficult situation this time. I wondered if you understand just what it could mean."

"You mean the *Mariah,* or in general?"

"Both, really, but I was thinking more about the *Mariah,*" Andy said.

"I think we'll probably keep going south once we leave here," Mason reasoned. "I would guess we may serve in somewhat the same capacity we did in France during the summer of 1940."

"Except it's about 500 miles to friendly shores," Andy noted.

"Yes...I see what you mean. Is that what you meant when you said we were the scout?"

"I believe in the Army they call it taking the point. Whatever it is, it means being the first to find the enemy," Andy indicated. "If anything should happen, if I can't continue, I'm counting on you to find them."

"I understand, sir, but I would prefer that we do it together."

Smiling a little, Andy started to reply when there was a commotion at the doorway. "There's a couple-a those fancy Navy types," a fairly drunk middle-aged man loudly told his companion. "Why aren't you out shootin' Japs 'sted a swillin' gin in here," the drunk yelled out in a slurred voice.

"Sir, I think maybe you should leave. You've had a bit too much to drink," Mason tolerantly advised.

"Leave, should I? Navy's nothin' but a bunch a snivellin' cowards. Can't even stop a bunch a slant eyed Japs from invadin' our shores," the drunk shouted.

Getting up from his chair, Andy came up to the man and leaned in close to his right ear. "I'd be careful what I said about those whose job it is to defend you," he quietly murmured. "They may decide against it."

"Why you," the drunk bellowed with the stench of alcohol strong on his breath and clothing. "Don't threaten me with your drivel," he yelled in a fit of rage shaking a fist in Andy's face. "You and your kind taken a man's possessions and tellin' him it's for the common cause. Bunch a no good thieves," he shrieked with spittle dripping onto his chin as he swung a fist toward Andy's jaw.

Andy sidestepped allowing the momentum of the drunkard's swing to cause him to fall with a crash to the floor. Andy and Mason walked out, leaving the moaning drunk on the floor of the bar as the police, summoned by the doorman, came through the hotel lobby.

"I wonder what his problem is," Mason said, when they were outside.

"I would guess we've commandeered something from him the Navy feels a need for. He looked familiar, but I can't place him," Andy said. "There will be a lot more commandeering if the Japanese keep coming. The Navy will need all the boats and supplies they can lay their hands on to evacuate the city."

The *Mariah* slipped out of Singapore's harbor, picking her way through the wrecked ships and debris left behind by the continuous enemy raids. Dusk was settling over the sea when she made her first turn in search of the enemy war ships that could destroy any convoy attempting to leave the area.

Andy considered the job ahead after the ship settled into her sailing routine, feeling fairly certain enemy ships were somewhere close by waiting to sail unchallenged into Singapore Harbor. He would thread the *Mariah* through the islands and into the many deep-water coves and small bays using every advantage available to become the stalker and not the prey. If he was careful, and lucky, the *Mariah* would come through the looming conflict and not become a statistic that laid beneath the sea's whimsical surface until the oceans gave up their dead on *the last day.*

CHAPTER 40

"Tie off that bleeder," John ordered. "That's better. What a mess, let's get it cleaned up." He read Dr. Jamison's three-hour-old evacuation order after operating on an Australian corporal who had been shot three times before hitting the ground. "We're to evacuate all the casualties to Helen's Landing by whatever means available tomorrow," he told the others. "It looks like Kuala Lumpur is falling to the Japanese."

"With all the artillery fire we've been hearing, it had to be closing in on us," David noted.

"Let's get these men in the trucks," John ordered the evacuating personnel the next afternoon. "David, good luck. I'll be following in a few hours."

"I'll see you at Helen's Landing. Until then," David said shaking John's hand.

John and Jeffery, the single male nurse who volunteered to stay behind, watched the last hospital truck with the big red cross painted on the roof pull onto the road and proceed south until it was out of sight. John and David had flipped a coin for who would stay to pack the remaining supplies and evacuate with the engineers that were placing the final defenses. John called tails, but it came up heads. "That's all right," he had said, "I found the trip north to be most interesting. I'm sure the Army will provide something to put a little excitement into the trip back."

The hairs on the back of John and Jeffrey's necks stood on end as a sense of fear filled them when the sound of a truck approaching the outpost became more distinct three hours after the hospital evacuated. Wesley pulled up to the aid station with what was left of his crew with his sidearm in his lap ready to shoot. He recognized John with someone he did not know emerging from the trees across the compound and slowly un-cocked his gun.

"Where's the rest of your crew?" John asked through the driver's window.

"Two more are in the back with injuries. My sergeant got it earlier today," Wesley responded in even tones. "The rest were killed yesterday."

"I see. We've got what's left of the medical supplies over in those trees. Maybe I should take a look at your men before we go."

"You won't have time," Wesley flatly replied. "We set some traps, but it won't hold them for long."

Wesley's despair, and the urgency to move out, was almost tangible as John sensed the need to hurry. "Help us get the supplies loaded. I'll see what can be done on the way."

The sun was starting to set, bringing an uneasy darkness over the land when the first booby-trap exploded in the distance. The truck carrying the last British personnel to evacuate the area pulled away from the outpost as a second explosion echoed across the jungle floor. "Give it all she's got, corporal, they're getting close," Wesley ordered.

The truck swayed on the uneven tarmac that followed the coastline, sometimes giving glimpses of the sea, and at others cutting through the nearby jungle foliage, giving the two wounded soldiers a bumpy ride. Wesley ordered the truck to stop at the halfway point to Helen's Landing just before the road opened to the sea again.

"Why did we stop? Is something wrong?" John asked when Wesley came around to check on his two injured men.

"No, just switching drivers. How are they?"

"About all we could do was clean up and redress their wounds for now. I gave them something for the discomfort. They should be all right if we reach Helen's Landing soon. How long…"

John got no further, as Wesley held up a hand and drew his side arm. "Listen," he whispered, when a low moaning was heard from close by. "Stay here," he firmly ordered before signaling his men to join him.

The three men moved cautiously forward while carefully listening for the moaning sound to be repeated, covering about 200 yards when Corporal Moore found the source of the eerie sound. "Over here, sir."

Wesley joined Moore near a ditch at the side of the road where two Army trucks, bearing bright red crosses, laid on their side with bodies strewn around them. "Get Dr. Hartman and bring the truck up," Wesley ordered.

John checked for any signs of life, recognizing the trucks as the same ones that left earlier in the day that brought a feeling of foreboding over him. The moaning sound drew him to the cab of the second truck where David Jergen was trying to pull his tortured bleeding body through the truck's shattered windshield. "Over here, I found someone. Bring my bag." Corporal Moore hurriedly brought John's medical bag and started to gag when he saw half of the driver's head was spattered across the dashboard.

"Help me get Captain Jergen to the truck," John ordered bringing Moore out of his momentary trance. "Careful, try not to jar him," he cautioned.

"He the only one left?" Wesley asked.

"Yeah, the rest were in bad shape to begin with. I doubt they knew what hit them," John grimly replied.

"The driver?"

"Dead."

"Let's get going then," Wesley ordered. "There isn't any more we can do here. We can't give them a proper burial and let the Japs know we were here. I'm sorry. I put their dog tags in my kit. At least their relatives will know what happened to them."

Climbing into the cab, Wesley turned to Corporal Moore and Private Jones. "Did you set it then?"

"Yes sir. It should take out quite a few when it goes."

"At least they won't have died in vain. Drive us out of here, private," Wesley ordered.

"Yes sir," Jones responded, putting the truck into gear.

It was nearly midnight with clouds covering the sky when the small group of survivors pulled up to the emergency room doorway. John quickly went in and returned with help to bring the three injured men inside. "Tell Admiral Jamison we're here and ask him to come down," he ordered the lone male nurse on duty.

"Yes, sir."

"John, good to see you got back all right," Dr. Jamison smiled when he came to the doorway. "We haven't seen the other trucks. Did you send the patients by boat after all?"

"The other trucks didn't make it, sir. We found them on the way here," John briefly explained. "They were strafed by an airplane it looked like. There's one survivor, David Jergen. He's hurt pretty bad."

"Okay, let's see what we can do. Nurse, get Dr. Linn and Dr. Romans down here, they should be sleeping in the lounge. Then have Ferguson prepare the operating room." Dr. Jamison ordered. He wondered what the world was coming to when a clearly marked and defenseless hospital transport was attacked.

John and Peter were drinking coffee with Dr. Jamison when Helen and Sally came to the small cafeteria as the rumbling sound of artillery resumed its malevolent echo throughout the village. Helen's Landing was experiencing the full impact of the Japanese war machine probing the defenses for a weak point to exploit and penetrate into the surrounding countryside.

"John, you're back. Is Wes here?" Sally asked a little anxiously.

"He's sleeping right now in the empty ward," Peter answered.

Alan listened while he mopped the floor to the conversation between the British civilians and staff who remained at Helen's Landing. He thought Tonaka might be interested in this latest development, especially after what he had learned about British defenses on their reconnaissance the night before and tried to carefully follow what was said.

Jane and Tom Linn watched over the few remaining patients through the day to allow the others some needed sleep. Late in the afternoon the remaining British citizens met in the cafeteria to make some necessary plans. Planes still bombed the defenses and harbor area and strafed the roadways. The anti-aircraft guns were still manned, but it had become apparent the Japanese were going to by-pass Helen's Landing for now. The latest word from Singapore was of a Japanese landing ten miles beyond them on the western coast earlier in the day.

"They're trying to cut us off. Then they can move in at their leisure," Wesley said. "The only way is to leave by sea, but it would have to be after dark."

"The *Angelica* is capable of crossing the strait. Ralph and I did before he died," Helen said.

"That was some time ago," Dr. Jamison reminded her. "Is the *Angelica* in any condition for that now?"

"Andy had the hull reworked last year during his visit. Remember Martin? Someone would need to check the engine. We'd need fuel too, more than the tank can hold. I remember we had to refuel before we came back," Helen replied.

"How many are left in the hospital?" Peter asked.

"There's the gunner from Andy's ship, Ernie, and one of his engine room ratings, George. Let me see, Arthur Nance and the three John and Wesley brought in last night. That's six patients," Dr. Jamison said.

"We can get fuel yet today. Dr. Jamison, is that engine room rating, what's his name, George, is he mobile?" Wesley asked.

"He's up and starting to move around. He's pretty weak though."

"We don't have a choice. If he can guide one of my men through it, we can make sure the engine is working properly."

Helen led Wesley and his two men down the jungle path to the boathouse where the *Angelica* was carefully stored. "The double doors over there open out to the strait."

"What's this here?" Wesley asked, pointing at the stern.

"Oh, Ralph put a holding tank for fish there in the back," Helen explained.

"It looks big enough to hold at least three drums of fuel, sir, maybe four," Corporal Moore indicated.

"My dad would jury-rig his movin' trucks with petrol drums on long trips. We tied 'em down tight and ran extra fuel lines to pump right ta the main tank," Private Jones told them when he saw the holding tank.

"Private, you just got yourself a job," Wesley said with a slight smile.

"Yes, sir, I can fix it up right proper for us," Jones nodded showing a toothy grin.

"I believe we can make this work if we start right away," Wesley indicated, when the group returned.

"I'll leave the technicalities to you, Wesley," Dr. Jamison said. "Just remember, we have to move the patients with care and be able to keep them stable. We'll need to take as many medical supplies as possible."

"I understand, sir."

The next day it was verified Helen's Landing had been temporarily bypassed when it was picked up on the short wave that Johore was the only Malayan state still under British rule. George, the *Mariah*'s engine room rating, easily guided Wesley's man through replacing cracked hoses and making adjustments to the fuel flow and carburetor until the engine fell into a steady rumble before the gears and steering assembly were checked and appeared to be working properly. "A right smart little craft," George said when they finished just before he slid to the floor in a faint of exhaustion.

The only British troops left at Helen's Landing were the four artillery and anti-aircraft gunners who had volunteered to stay behind as the final defenders. Wesley ordered them to evacuate with the hospital staff, bringing any portable guns they could. "We'll put the STENS we have on the craft at first light, sir. We'll work our passage," the sergeant assured him.

Wesley knew the journey ahead would be dangerous, and that their chances were marginal. He remembered the day he had talked with Dr. Jamison about the aid stations and what Martin Jamison had said about not taking away a patient's hope. Wesley thought this was the same thing and resolved to keep the hope alive, so the remaining staff and patients he felt responsible for wouldn't give up and put themselves at the mercy of what was proving to be a pitiless conqueror.

CHAPTER 41

The last remaining citizens of Helen's Landing gathered in the hospital cafeteria when darkness covered the village to pass the night together, as never before noticed sounds began to echo out of the nearby jungle's blackness. "It's all right," Wesley reassured everyone when Jane and Sally started at the eerie noises. "It's when the sounds stop that something is wrong." Martin Jamison realized Wesley's depleted crew and four Army soldiers were all that stood between them and the Japanese, should the enemy arrive before they could evacuate the remaining hospital staff and their patients.

"We have to leave by nightfall tomorrow. The men not working the anti-aircraft guns can help move the remaining medical supplies out in the morning," Wesley said.

"I can't find Alan anywhere," Jane said in concern after searching the empty hallways.

"He must have fled with the others hoping to get to Singapore. No one is on the streets," Wesley told her. "Corporal Moore and Private Jones just finished a sweep around the hospital and surrounding area with our four Army friends and saw no one."

"I hope he'll be alright," Helen said. "I thought he understood he was to go with us."

"The British are trying to leave," Alan told Tonaka, nearly bursting with pleasure, when he entered the empty boardinghouse.

"How?" Tonaka tersely asked.

"They have a boat hidden they plan to escape in. I heard them talking earlier about getting it ready," Alan explained with a grin. "It means no one will be here to stop the Japanese Army from coming in and taking the town. That is good news, is it not?"

"Yes, that is good," Tonaka agreed, coming closer to Alan. Tonaka thought in a way it was too bad, but he had his orders. The lightening quick thrust of the long narrow doubled edged knife took Alan by surprise, as Tonaka pushed the razor sharp blade with an upward motion into the heart. "You have outlived your usefulness to us, as Raja did. If you would betray the British and your fellow countrymen, you would betray us as well in time," he explained to the sad question in Alan's eyes before his life faded away. Tonaka decided to wait until close to dawn before he went to see for himself about what Alan had told him regarding the remaining British in the village.

"Arthur," Wesley softly said, "we're moving you to a safer place now."

"I'll be okay, Captain. Look out for the others. Set the charges," Arthur murmured, before drifting back into a deep, drug induced sleep.

"Does he know where he is?" Wesley asked.

"Sometimes," Sally answered. "What did he mean by, 'set the charges'?"

"I'm not sure. We were setting land mines when he was hit. Maybe he thinks we're still there," Wesley surmised.

The medical supplies were packed as tightly as possible to be added to the food and fresh water being hastily boxed for the final trek to the boathouse. Tonaka watched from his leafy perch in amusement at these hasty preparations when he noticed the one called Sally disappear again into the hospital. He brooded over what Alan had said about her brother being an officer in the British Army and her lover a Navy commander. He could use his pistol and shoot them, but it wasn't enough to satisfy the deep well of hatred he bore against the British. He wanted to hurt, to humiliate. Tonaka watched until no one was in sight and drew his pistol, before slipping from his hiding place to noiselessly step through the open hospital door. He followed the sound of a woman tunelessly humming to a small room where a female back was turned to the doorway that he entered.

"I only have one more box of syringes to put in, and this is ready," Sally said, expecting to see one of the Army men when she turned with a smile which slowly faded, as the color drained from her face when she saw an oriental stranger holding a pistol in the doorway. "Who are you?" she breathed.

"It does not matter," Tonaka replied indifferently.

"Get away from me," Sally ordered, asserting a firmness she did not feel.

Tonaka laid aside the pistol, never taking his eyes off the British woman he had trapped within his reach. An evil grin curled the corners of his lips when he saw the mounting fear building in Sally's eyes. "What do you want?" she asked barely above a whisper.

"Only what your kind wanted," he hissed and then grabbed her in a vice-like grip. He felt a heady rush of elation at the power he held over this British whore mingle with a profane sense of pleasure to finally avenge his mother's shame.

Sally fought and struggled against the hold her attacker had on her and tried to kick, but her legs were pinioned against the wall by Tonaka's body. The sound of material being ripped filled the small room as he twisted the front of her blouse in his hand and tore it away. Sally's hand came free, and she raked Tonaka's face with her nails, drawing blood, earning a hard backhanded swipe across her face that caused a swelling bruise to appear on her left cheek. Tonaka sought to strip her remaining clothing away to savagely rape her in vicious retribution for his mother's dishonor, before he mercilessly disfigured and tortured her until he eventually killed her.

Sally's breathing became ragged fear filled gasps as panicked tears stung her face when she felt Tonaka's hot breath against her bare skin. She knew he would rape her, and worse, when she remembered the terrible stories that had filtered through from the north about Japanese soldiers raping and torturing British and Chinese women caught in their drive to the south.

She kept hoping one of the men would return and save her from this terrible monster that was hurting her. Panic rose in her throat when she felt her attacker opening his fly, but the scream would not come. She managed to free her left hand again, and then she remembered the pistol lying on the shelf.

Sally's panic filled eyes darted to the narrow shelf, trying to see where the pistol laid. She carefully reached out her trembling hand to slowly feel along the shelving in fear that her attacker would notice. Her terrified eyes darted back to Tonaka momentarily, as her body struggled against his hold, until she felt the cold steel of the small barrel against her hand. Her shaking fingers struggled to turn the gun to grasp it, as her mind wavered between fear and hysteria, when she closed her hand around the pistol's ivory grip. Tonaka sensed the sudden danger and grabbed for the pistol, as Sally struggled to work the firing mechanism. She felt the small protrusion of the trigger beneath her index finger, when Tonaka's larger hand painfully closed around the small smooth hand of his victim. The gun suddenly fired with a deafening roar that echoed against the tiny supply room walls, sending Tonaka reeling backward with a look of shock. Sally continued to work the trigger until there were no more bullets and the hammer clicked uselessly on the empty chamber.

She watched in horror when her attacker slowly crumpled to the floor where a widening pool of blood formed around his lifeless body.

"Those were gun shots! Come on," Wesley hollered with urgency to the Army sergeant that was with him, while instinctively drawing his side arm. Running to the open storeroom door, they found Sally, looking deathly pale, staring at the body on the floor, with the pistol still gripped in her hand. Her hair was in disarray and her blouse and shorts were ripped and nearly torn away. Her face and arms showed heavy bruising, and the stranger's blood was spattered across her nearly naked body. Wesley was carefully reaching out to remove the pistol from Sally's limp hand when John came running onto the scene that stank of spent gunpowder, blood, and fear.

"Is he dead?" Sally faintly asked through trembling ashen lips.

Leaning over the body to feel for a pulse, John slowly got up and nodded his head. "He's dead," he quietly answered.

"He kept saying he was avenging his mother," Sally said in confusion before her entire body started to quiver.

Taking in her torn clothing and the bruising, John concluded whomever this was had tried to rape her. "Sally, honey, give the gun to Wesley now," he gently instructed. "That's a girl," he softly complimented when she complied. John knew once the shock wore off she could easily become hysterical and struggled to remain calm. He took a blanket off the shelf and wrapped it around Sally's shoulders before carefully leading her out of the room. "Take her to the boathouse and stay with her," John firmly ordered Jeffrey, his male Army nurse companion from the abandoned aid station. "Make sure Helen and Jane are there also."

"Yes, doctor. Come along, miss. We'll get you all fixed up and take care of that nasty bruise," Jeffrey encouraged as he gently drew Sally to the outside.

"It's a Japanese made pistol, and he is definitely oriental," Wesley pointedly said.

"Then it's time to get everyone into the boathouse," John concluded. "We're out of time."

"Sergeant, grab that box. Come on, let's get out of here," Wesley urged. John grabbed a last armful of linens and followed Wesley and the sergeant out the emergency room door and down the jungle path to the cottage.

"Ah, there you are. One more trip should do it," Dr. Jamison said. "Jane and Helen are helping Tom and our male nurses store things now."

"I'm sorry, sir," Wesley responded, "There won't be anymore trips. We're out of time."

"What do you mean?" Peter asked.

"Sally was attacked a little while ago," John briefly explained, pausing a moment. "By a Japanese."

"Is she all right? I mean…did he," Dr. Jamison tried to ask as a sinking feeling came over him.

"No, she has some bruises where he attacked her and is pretty shook up. She shot him before he was able to force himself on her," Wesley evenly answered. "Right now we all have to get to the boathouse before any more show up."

"You're right, Wesley. Peter, help me with these cases," Dr. Jamison said, as they all headed toward the door.

"How is she?" Dr. Jamison quietly asked Helen about the small bruised figure he saw lying on the bunk.

"She has some nasty bruises, and she's frightened. At least she finally stopped shaking. Tom gave her something to help calm her down. Martin, we have to leave before it's too late."

"I know. We're leaving in a few minutes."

"Okay, let's get the engine started before we open the doors. The sun should be about gone. Wesley, when I tell you, push the doors open from the bow," Dr. Jamison instructed, taking the seat at the wheel.

"Yes, sir, I'm ready," Wesley acknowledged.

The boathouse doors opened to the last rays of light, giving the false image of heaven's transparent gold reflecting off the water's glassy surface, when the *Angelica* entered the Malacca Strait. Once the land fell away, Wesley dismissed the gunners he had stationed at the stern and went to the small bridge where Dr. Jamison was guiding the boat on a westerly course.

"I figure we have a better chance if we cross the strait before heading south," Dr. Jamison said, pointing to the chart. "We should be less likely to run across any of the invading forces."

"Where do you think we should head for?" Wesley asked.

"I thought here to the Bengalis Strait," Dr. Jamison indicated, pointing to the chart again with his finger. "The mouth leads to a narrow channel running between Bengalis and Paden. We'd have to cross open water at Rangson, but we would have another channel to bring us out by Tupan. We'll have to listen to the short wave to tell us where to go. Singapore if we can. Otherwise, we'll have to island hop until we can find a relatively safe port or run out of fuel."

Wesley agreed it seemed to be the best route after looking at the chart and comparing it to the map of the area from his gear. "I'm thinking we might want to hold up someplace during the day and travel at night," he suggested. "At least planes would be less likely to spot us."

"She should be waking up soon," Jane said. "It wasn't a strong sedative."

Sally was lying on the narrow bunk with a cold compress on her bruised cheek when she opened her eyes and saw Helen sitting next to her. "Are we on the boat now?"

"Yes. How do you feel?" Helen quietly asked.

"I killed a man…Helen, I killed a man," Sally said in despair at the act of taking the life of another human being.

"You didn't have a choice. He would have killed you eventually," Helen softly said.

"Yes…I suppose he would have," Sally slowly reflected. "I don't ever want to have to do that again."

"I don't believe you will be in that kind of situation again," Helen tried to reassure her.

"I think I want to go out on the deck and get some fresh air."

Jane and Helen helped Sally to her feet and took her to the small deck at the rear of the boat where they watched the distant shoreline. Tiny pinpoints of light briefly lit the sky and disappeared before a bright flash followed by a loud booming suddenly reverberated in tumbling waves across the water from the direction of Helen's Landing.

"What was that?" Jane asked in subdued awe.

"I believe they found our little surprise," Wesley explained, coming up behind the women. "I suddenly remembered what Arthur was referring to when we moved him."

"What do you mean, Wes?" Sally asked.

"We had talked about the possibility of having to evacuate when we built the defenses, and how to quickly destroy them. Set the charges meant activate the booby traps. Looks like it worked," Wesley said with satisfaction.

Light was starting to brighten the eastern sky when the *Angelica* entered the narrow channel between Bengalis and Pedang. The *Angelica* slowly followed it until they found a small inlet where the jungle met the sea. Tying up to a nearby tree with branches overhanging the water the refugees of Helen's Landing watched the sun rise on a new day.

CHAPTER 42

The Army gunnery sergeant on watch was closely monitoring a pair of Zeros as they faded from sight when Wesley walked onto *Angelica*'s deck after waking to the sound of airplanes passing overhead at mid afternoon. "How many are there, sergeant?"

"Looks to be only two so far, sir. They ain't spotted us far as I can tell."

Wesley looked up when a second pair flew over on a heading toward the Malayan Peninsula. "I expect they were just looking at the lay of the land. They're too high to see anything our size tucked into the shoreline like we are. Keep a sharp eye out. Call me if you spot anything unusual."

"That I will, sir," the gunnery sergeant assured him.

Wesley looked at the empty sky once more and wondered what they would do if the *Angelica* was spotted. He feared if discovered the three women would be raped by more than one soldier before being killed, or worse, left alive to be tormented, while the remaining men were forced to helplessly witness the defiling before their own agonizing journey to the grave's silent rest. Dr. Jamison was the senior officer, but he had put Wesley in charge of their defenses and the strategy to find a way to friendly shores. "You're far more capable at this sort of thing than I am," he had said during their discussion about the *Angelica*'s next move.

"Dr. Jamison," Peter quietly called, gently touching his shoulder, "sir."

Martin Jamison opened his eyes and was disoriented for a moment before he came fully awake. "What is it?"

"Sir, I think Captain Jergen is getting worse. His blood pressure is down, and he's running a fever," Peter reported.

"I better take a look at him."

Jane was bathing David Jergen with cool water in an attempt to lower the fever when Martin Jamison came to the narrow bunk and reviewed the notes for the past few hours before examining David and carefully checking his abdomen. "We have to go back in," he said, looking concerned. "I think its peritonitis. We must have missed a puncture in the bowel somewhere."

"Where do you want to do it?" Peter asked.

"We'll have to see where we can set up an area to operate," Dr. Jamison answered, taking in the confined space. "Jane, would you ask Wesley to come down please?"

"Right away, Doctor."

Jane found Wesley on the small upper deck talking to Sally with his arm around her shoulder. *They must be talking about yesterday,* she thought becoming reluctant to interrupt but knowing she had to. "Wesley, I'm sorry to interrupt. Dr. Jamison needs your help with a medical emergency."

"All right. We'll talk again, sis."

"You go ahead, Wes. I'm okay, really."

"I'm sorry I had to intrude, Sally," Jane apologized after Wesley had gone.

"It's all right. What's happened?"

"Captain Jergen is getting worse. Dr. Jamison thinks they need to operate again." Jane hesitated, feeling a sense of uneasiness at broaching yesterday's terrible event. She finally decided her friend needed an opening to help relieve the trauma and looked with compassion into Sally's eyes as she reached out to gently touch her friend's hand. "Sally, I don't quite know how to say this, but can I help somehow?"

"You just did, Jane...you just did," Sally whispered with a faint smile. "I think Helen was right, that he would have killed me given the chance. Wesley said he thought so too. I just wish there had been another way."

"We'll need to move on as soon as we can," Wesley said, after Dr. Jamison explained the situation. "How long do you figure the surgery will take?"

"Anywhere from two to five hours, maybe longer. We won't know until we go in and look."

"It's about six o'clock now. We should be underway by midnight," Wesley cautioned.

"I can't leave him the way he is, he'll die for sure," Dr. Jamison emphasized. "At the least we can give him a chance."

"We set up a discarded table in an old shed for John to operate on Arthur. We have more here to work with at least," Wesley thoughtfully replied. "I agree, we have to do what we can, sir. My concern is if we have to get underway before you're finished that the area is secure enough to not endanger the outcome."

"We should be all right if we're wedged in tight enough so the operating table won't move, even with the boat underway."

Wesley quickly took in the limited options while thinking about the many dangers around them and his own hope to get this small band of refugees to safety. David Jergen was a part of that small population. Dr. Jamison was right; they had to try to save him. "The passageway should be narrow enough to wedge a table into. We can curtain it off and secure a meal tray for your instruments. I can put a lantern overhead for more light. It will be tight, but it will work."

"Get it set up," Dr. Jamison concurred. "I'll get the rest of what we'll need."

Thirty minutes later the minuscule operating room was ready. Dr. Jamison and John entered the small area gowned and gloved where Jeffrey waited to begin the risky procedure.

The rest of *Angelica*'s passengers waited while the low mummer of voices escaped the curtained off enclosure as the two doctors proceeded with the tedious job of finding any more punctures in the bowel after closing the initial tear they had found. It was well after midnight when John closed the outer skin and placed a sterile dressing over the incision before David was transferred to a bunk in one of the small private cabins under John's close supervision.

"How did it go, Martin?" Helen asked while the others anxiously awaited the answer.

"I think we got everything, but he's terribly weak. I don't know what way it will go. It's up to the *Almighty* now. John, that was good work. Thank you for your help."

"You're welcome, sir. He's a fighter. I could tell that when we first found him. We spent a lot of time together at that outpost. I believe we were becoming friends." Martin Jamison nodded his understanding, recalling how he and Quentin Patterson had shared their lives over twenty years ago in that other conflict.

The Army gunners keeping watch were relieved to hear the operation was over and they would be moving on soon. The jungle sounds coming from the nearby shore reminded them of the previous night and the *Angelica*'s narrow escape. Helen and Sally made hot tea and sandwiches while Jane monitored David Jergen's blood pressure and checked the intravenous drip. He opened his eyes briefly and groaned before falling back into a deep sleep.

The *Angelica* traveled the narrow waterways from one small inlet to the next during the darkest nighttime hours. They hid under cover throughout the day until the small group of refugees reached the southern portion of islands off northern Sumatra and anchored in a small estuary at Tupang to study the map.

"There's a channel type bay at the southeastern side of Kundur we can hold up in until tomorrow night. If it looks clear, we can make for Singapore. Otherwise, we'll just have to see," Dr. Jamison said looking at the chart.

"Either way, it puts us in a better position," Wesley agreed. "We might have to take it a short hop at a time. We haven't seen any Japanese ships around, but they have to be somewhere close by. Right now I'd sure like to see the *Mariah* and Andy Burns."

The *Mariah* had followed a circuitous course to search the tiny islands and bays in the chain of islands to the south of Singapore. Enemy planes flew unchallenged that brought the anti-aircraft guns into continual use against the hit and run attacks before the Zeros moved on to more important targets. The Muar had been crossed, putting the Japanese only ninety miles from Singapore. Andy was sure the Japanese Navy would be on hand to sail into Singapore Harbor in triumph before much more time passed.

Andy's thoughts briefly turned to his mother and Sally and the others at Helen's Landing. *Did they get away?* He pushed the thoughts aside to concentrate on the immediate future. There would be time enough later to think about other things if he lived. *Where is the Japanese Navy now?* he wondered. The only thing they had found were the remains of small boats that had been strafed by enemy planes, killing the occupants whose bodies were left to the elements of nature. They had buried a group of these this morning at sea. One was a child not more than six or seven.

Dr. Patterson rapped on the sea cabin door, interrupting Andy's thoughts. "Andrew, I came to see how that splinter wound is healing." The day before a splinter had flown up during a strafing and embedded itself in Andy's arm. Dr. Patterson cleaned and bandaged the wound after finding the bone was bruised and put the arm in a sling. The plane was sent away smoking, giving Andy a moment of satisfaction that his nemesis wasn't infallible.

"Looks like it's healing nicely," Dr. Patterson said after replacing the dressing. "How does it feel?"

"Pretty good. Just a little soreness when I move wrong is all."

"Good. It should be good as new in a couple of weeks." Pausing a moment, Dr. Patterson asked, "Any news?"

"None. They could be in Singapore though and I wouldn't know about it," Andy responded, knowing what news was being asked about.

"As I recall from our days in the Army together, Martin is quite capable in a difficult situation. They most likely are enjoying a good meal and a glass of gin right now," Dr. Patterson cheerfully said.

"You're probably right, Doc. Come," Andy responded to the light tap on his cabin door.

"Message, sir," a rating reported while extending the flimsy sheet of flash paper.

"Send the first officer here," Andy ordered after quickly scanning the short message.

"Yes, sir."

"What is it?" Dr. Patterson asked.

"Recall to Singapore."

Andy reported to Admiral Edwards without delay when the *Mariah* arrived at Singapore Harbor. "We have to put a company of Army troops ashore here," Edwards explained, pointing at the map just north of Butu Pahat. "We'll be sending some Marines along as well."

"How soon, sir?" Andy asked.

"You and the *Victoria* sail in company. You'll provide protection as well as fire on enemy shore defenses prior to the landings. You leave tonight to be in position by dawn. As the senior officer, you will be in charge of the affair."

"We'll be ready, sir. My first officer was seeing to rearming as soon as we arrived." Clearing his throat, Andy asked, "Have you heard from Admiral Jamison, sir?"

"No. I wish I could tell you something, but I haven't heard from him for a few days now," Eric Edwards stoically answered. "There's a rumor a small boat left the area of Helen's Landing shortly before a large explosion occurred, but it hasn't been confirmed."

"Thank you for being frank with me, sir."

"You deserve honesty at least. Martin is my friend too," Admiral Edwards said. "He also lands on his feet, so don't give up hope."

"I won't, sir," Andy replied, rising to leave.

Andy considered what he had been told on the way back to the *Mariah*. *If the rumor was true, it might be the* Angelica. *But where was she now? And, if it was the* Angelica, *is Sally with Ma and Dr. Jamison?* He pushed the thoughts aside when he approached *Mariah*'s ladder to concentrate on the present needs of a war that was going badly.

The *Victoria* and *Mariah* sailed at dusk with additional lookouts posted to watch for unmarked sinkings in the harbor. Japanese bombers were attacking more frequently against little resistance and littering the harbor with half sunken wrecks after each new attack. Andy had heard that British fighter planes were all but gone, leaving the anti-aircraft guns and ground troops as the only defenses left. *How long can they keep up the pretense before the public realizes the worst has happened?* he wondered. Admiral Edwards said another convoy would be leaving in a day or two crammed with as many refugees as the small crafts could hold. Andy feared the voyage would encounter unprecedented dangers from an enemy that knew only triumph.

The small group of misshapen war ships arrived at the specified coordinates after sailing in the darkness of a moonless overcast night just before sunrise. "Our target is directly to the east, sir," Brian reported.

"We're to begin firing at 0450 hours on the specified coordinates along a five mile strip. We then give covering fire at these coordinates," Andy indicated on the chart. "Just beyond the beach when the troops are landing."

"Yes sir. The gunners have the coordinates and are ready when you give the word," Mason reported.

"One minute to go," Andy said, looking at his watch before keying the ship's microphone. "This is the captain speaking," reverberated throughout the ship. "I know you have given the best you can in the past. Keep your minds on the task at hand. Remember, the Army and Marines are counting on us to hit the targets...commence firing."

The *Mariah* trembled when her guns fired in unison, sending the first shells streaking toward the shore that did not hit the ground before the next rounds were loaded and ready to fire. The *Victoria* joined *Mariah*'s guns, sending a deafening explosion of thundering anger toward the last known Japanese lines along the sleeping coastline. At the halfway mark a large fireball soared skyward followed by the sound of violent explosions when a shell found its mark.

The *Victoria* and *Mariah* reversed course at the end of the specified stretch of land to make a second sweep. Shells streaked beyond the narrow beach perimeter in advance of the British landings. The remaining shallow draft gunboats out of Singapore began the run toward shore to land the Army and Marine troops while the exploding shells continued to pummel the shoreline. The earth shook from the fusillade until the last of the able bodied men disappeared into the jungle.

"That sure doesn't look like a company," Brian commented, and then formally reported, "Sir, we're at the final coordinates."

"Very well," Andy said, thumbing the mike. "This is the captain speaking, secure from firing."

The crew could only see occasional pinpricks of light from *Mariah*'s decks after the Army made landfall. The steady staccato of heavy automatic gunfire mingled with the heavier blasts from portable grenade launchers began to diminish as the fight moved further into the jungle's dense interior. All too soon there were only a few faint cries out of the depths of the jungle that brought a cold chill to those who considered what the sounds could mean to the human soul. The once peaceful coastline had become a blackened terrain of desolate landscape punctuated with the twisted bodies of dead British soldiers, lying in the arms of their dead enemy's eternal embrace.

The Japanese brought another bombing run during the late night hours over Singapore when the *Mariah* returned from her most recent sortie and brought her guns to bear. Sometimes there was a momentary victory when a plane was shot down. The euphoria died soon enough when another plane arrived to bomb the city, leaving behind the dead and wounded and more burning rubble.

The British government's infrastructure began to unravel at an alarming pace as Singapore's citizens cavorted in the streets in a frenzy of defiance toward an ever-increasing threat by the advancing Japanese Army. Theaters and nightclubs were filled to capacity, while soldiers fought and died defending the antiquated existence being hysterically clung to by a population in denial of the looming disaster facing them.

The following morning the enemy was forty miles from the city, and the troops landed the day before had not been heard from for the past three hours.

CHAPTER 43

The refugees from Helen's Landing watched unchallenged enemy planes fly over their thin daylight cover in ever increasing numbers. An enemy patrol boat traversed the narrow waterways one tense night, where God's hand reached out at the time of creation to mold the ancient volcanic rock, before His breath cooled the disputed isles peaking above the foliage covered refuge where the *Angelica* hid.

"We're just south of Singapore and should be able to get there tonight," Dr. Jamison said after he and Wesley had reviewed the chart. "We can hug the shoreline once we're in the Singapore Strait right into the harbor."

"Yes, I believe you're right," Wesley agreed before a sudden shout from Ernie brought him and Dr. Jamison to the deck. "What is it?" Wesley asked as his heart thumped inside his chest.

"Sir, in the distance, a ship sailing south to northeast."

Wesley focused his glasses on the distant horizon and saw what looked like a fairly good-sized ship bearing the flag of the *Rising Sun.* He handed Dr. Jamison the binoculars and looked around at the makeshift camouflage covering the boat, hoping their deception blended with the landscape enough to not be noticed.

"Martin, what is it?" Helen asked from the companionway.

"A Japanese destroyer it looks like."

"Will it interfere with us reaching Singapore tonight?"

"We'll have to wait and see," Dr. Jamison cautiously replied.

"I see. We'll need to find fresh water if we can't get to Singapore before long." Helen's manner was matter-of-fact, but her eyes gave away the heavy disappointment this turn of events brought.

"Maybe I could see more from the rise near those palms," Wesley suggested. "I'll see if I can spot any fresh water streams or ponds."

"Let's wait a bit, just to be sure our friend doesn't return," Dr. Jamison cautioned.

Wesley waited another hour before leaving the *Angelica,* realizing their best chance was to know what might be on the opposite side of their hiding place before moving on when nothing more appeared over the horizon. He carefully brought the binoculars up from a lying position at the top of the small islet's highest point. He quickly swept the sea in all directions and found it empty before looking the small island over more closely and spotted what appeared to be a fresh-water spring a short distance from where he stood. Wesley watched the empty sea another forty-five minutes before he carefully made his way down the small hill to investigate the potential water supply.

"I thought you were never coming back," Sally said in relief when Wesley returned.

"What did you find?" Dr. Jamison asked.

"I didn't see our friend," Wesley quickly reassured him. "I did find water. We can resupply I think just before dusk. A friend in the RAF once told me a pilot isn't likely to see anyone on foot then because darkness rises from the ground."

Ernie volunteered to sit on the rise of land and watch the sea until dusk came. "If you see anything make your way down so as not to be spotted," Wesley instructed.

"I'll be watchin' meself, sir," Ernie reassured him.

"We haven't seen anything since our initial sighting. We have to assume that destroyer is between us and Singapore," Wesley said, as everyone gathered around to listen when darkness descended.

"Yes, I agree," Dr. Jamison concurred. "We need to move on before we're spotted or that destroyer returns at a leisurely pace to look around more carefully. We can follow the islands all the way to Singkep," he indicated, tracing an imaginary route on the chart. "We might find some of our own around there."

"We'll need to conserve fuel, or find some before too much longer. I figure we have enough for about 300 miles at best," Wesley cautioned.

"There's a settlement at Sebangka. We might still find fuel there," Dr. Jamison said. "For now, all we can do is move on."

"I agree, sir," Wesley said, as he looked at the others around him.

Helen stood on the small deck facing Singapore when the *Angelica* reached open seas. She said a quick prayer for those still in Malaya and the *Mariah* before going below to help prepare tea and sandwiches for the night watch.

She hoped that Andy and his crew would soon be leaving the area before the *Mariah* was too severely damaged to continue the fight.

“Commander Burns, Admiral Edwards will see you now,” Sub-lieutenant Gaines summoned.

“Thank you, Mr. Gaines.”

“Sir, how is the *Mariah* fairing? I mean…is she holding up all right under the current emergency?”

“She has a few scars, but we've been fortunate to hold off any major damage.”

Opening the door, Gaines saluted. “He'll be right with you, sir.”

“Take care of yourself, Lieutenant,” Andy responded, returning the salute.

Eric Edwards laid a large stack of files and scribbled notes on his desk when Andy entered the office. “Commander, have a seat,” he said, acknowledging Andy's salute. “I only have a few minutes, so I'll get right to the point. The Japanese Army is about forty miles to the north. British command has ordered a mile wide strip evacuated on Singapore's north shore to build defenses. It might buy some time. It won't hold them as some believe. A convoy is leaving tomorrow night, one of the last larger ones most likely. The *Mariah* will be one of the ships escorting them to Jakarta.”

“You mean everyone will just be left here that didn't get away before?” Andy asked in disbelief.

“Many will, I'm afraid. There just isn't time to organize a full evacuation. The Army can't hold the Japanese in Malaya,” Eric Edwards bluntly stated. “Some believe they won't cross the Jahore Strait. As a sailor, you know at low tide it only has about four feet of water and is narrow enough that a bridge spans it. It's not like the English Channel between England and France, where a large body of water stopped the opposing German Army from invading.

“What about the Army?” Andy asked, still stunned by the Japanese Army's swift passage through Malaya. “Surely, we'll try to lift them off the beaches.”

Eric Edwards found he was unable to look directly at his inquisitor momentarily. The Navy had always been looked upon as the Army's refuge when battles went wrong, but this time it was different. The only sound in the small office came from beyond the door.

“I see,” Andy softly said, lowering his eyes, as a sense of shame washed over him during the uncomfortable silence.

“Commander, some things are out of our hands, as you well know. We can't always do what we want. I'm just thankful the decision was made by someone other than me.” Admiral Edwards looked away for a moment in distant thought before returning to the present pressing demands being placed on Army and Navy forces that were unprepared to meet the overwhelming circumstances they faced. "As to your ship, you'll be transporting some of the injured along with hospital staff to look after them," he continued in his normal brisk manner.

"Will you be leaving also, sir?"

"Not at this time. We plan to lay on one, maybe two, more convoys. I expect the Admiralty will be sailing with them. Lot to do here yet," Admiral Edwards succinctly replied. "That about covers it, Commander. Gaines will send over your orders later today."

"Yes sir. Admiral, good luck to you, sir," Andy said at the dismissal, before standing at attention and saluting his commanding admiral, perhaps for the last time.

"And to you, Commander," Admiral Edwards acknowledged while returning the salute and then, unprecedentedly, shook Andy's hand.

"Number One, we leave for Jakarta tomorrow night. We'll be doing escort duty for a civilian convoy," Andy informed his first officer immediately upon returning to the *Mariah.*

"Will we be coming back, sir?" Mason asked, a little surprised by the sudden orders.

"I don't believe so. My guess is we'll be sent on to Australia. From there, it could be anywhere."

"I'll see we're fully supplied. We've replaced some of our ammunition and food stores already," Mason reported, but sensed there was something more. "Sir, what else did the Admiral say?"

"Shows, does it? I'm not surprised," Andy said with some feeling. "It's believed the Army won't keep the Japanese out of Singapore, not that it comes as any surprise at this stage."

"We've thought that for some time now. I'm just surprised it's happening so quickly. How will they get the Army away?"

"I've been informed at this point it is thought to be impossible to remove them from the area," Andy answered, allowing his anger and dismay at the impossible situation to show.

"You mean they'll just leave the Army here?" Mason softly asked, giving a low whistle. "But...why? Surely we could rescue some of the forces."

"No time, and no defenses for those who would have to take them off the beaches most likely. The Japanese Navy would blockade the escape routes while their air force bombed the ships and evacuation points. At Dunkirk we had the RAF and the Channel. Here..." Andy shook his head while once again the sense of shame and discomfort washed over him at deserting the Army defenders in their hour of greatest need.

"Our orders will come over shortly," Andy noted in his commander's voice.

"We'll be taking on some wounded from the hospital along with staff to care for them. Let Doc know and have him see me about it when he comes back. That's all for now, Number One, carry on."

"Yes, sir," Mason briskly responded, knowing for now the discussion about Singapore was closed.

A continuous line of ambulances threaded their way through a circuitous route, avoiding the worst of the destruction from the previous night's bombing, shortly after sunrise. The exercise to move the evacuating wounded was repeated well into the afternoon, as the injured were distributed among the escorts along with as many staff as possible. The use of a hospital ship was dismissed when Japanese planes indiscriminately went after any ship leaving Singapore. The fortunate few holding the much sought after prize of space aboard a ship leaving Singapore faced even greater dangers than they had as yet experienced.

Andy was conferring with Dr. Patterson when Mason came to the bridge. "Sir, Harris reports the last of the wounded are aboard. We've placed the accompanying medical staff in the dispensary, and the wardroom is being used to accommodate the overflow."

"Very well. Dr. Patterson and I were just discussing the situation," Andy said.

Darkness was falling when the first evacuees were sent to the menagerie of requisitioned ships with the allotted single suitcase in their hand. Another air raid came about half way through the boarding process. It concentrated on the harbor area and interrupted the steady line of refugees pressing forward while sailors automatically answered the call to battle stations.

A steady drizzle began to fall, adding to the misery of those left behind that watched through the carefully guarded fence. Some watched a loved one until they were out of sight in the knowledge it would be the last time to look on their face and see love reflected back by the troubled eyes returning the gaze. Others watched in resentment that they were denied the escape because their place in this broken society prevented it.

Andy wondered how soon panic would set in on those peering with desperate eyes through the barrier that separated them from access to the ships preparing to leave the area. Many civilians had believed Eastern Command's assurances that Singapore would not fall. Now they would pay the price for that short sightedness. *How many would have left in the beginning? Did Helen's Landing wait too long, or is the* Angelica *out there somewhere carrying them to safety?* Andy resolutely turned away from the scene and tucked the concerns he carried aside to attend to *Mariah*'s sailing needs.

CHAPTER 44

Mariah's crew watched in silence while one ship after another let go her lines and sailed past the sentinel waiting to guard them against the enemy's merciless attacks. An eerie glow reflected off the oily harbor water and ships' hulls through the gauze like curtain of smoke as the ragged entourage began its dangerous journey that carried the fortunate few to be granted passage. Rain began when the gates of heaven suddenly opened to release the angels' mournful tears when St. Peter recorded the shameful chapter into *The Book of Life*.

Andy stood on *Mariah*'s bridge and watched the familiar landmarks pass in silence as Singapore's once proud harbor began to fade and slip away behind the dark mourning shroud of defeat. He wondered where his mother and Dr. Jamison might be. Was Sally with them? Or when he might see his boyhood home or Singapore again.

"Lookouts at stations, ship secure from leaving harbor," Mason reported.

"Very well," Andy acknowledged, turning his thoughts away from the scene. "Mr. Jones, where might there be a likely place the enemy could find a sheltered harbor to lay in waiting?"

"There's several, sir, but I would consider Singkep the most likely. The island has a bay to the north and one to the south where ships could anchor and wait in comfort, unless they're somewhere around Bangka."

"There's oil in southern Sumatra, and Bangka is just across the strait here," Andy noted, pointing to a position further south on the chart.

"The Japanese did say they would take raw materials wherever they were found in the Southeast Asian Basin before hostilities broke out here," Brian commented.

"Yes, well, we'll have to see," Andy concluded.

"Planes off the starboard bow," a lookout shouted the following afternoon.

"All hands man your battle stations," sounded throughout the ship. The men dropped their half eaten food and hurried to their stations with the familiar ball of fear forming in the pit of their stomach. *Is this the day I get it?* reverberated in their minds while their hands did the all too familiar task of making the guns ready to fire.

"Planes off the port quarter," another lookout shouted.

Andy raised his glasses to follow the two separate attacks. One contained six planes diving toward the small ships in pairs to the starboard with their guns throwing up geysers of water before spattering cannon fire across the defenseless decks. The second formation had four planes that appeared to be heading toward the lead ships. A maritime barge about a thousand yards away was raked the length of the ship, as their small 3-inch gun defiantly defended her against an ever more powerful enemy. The last pair of enemy planes used the barge as a shield to bring an attack against the defending destroyer until *Mariah*'s guns fired in unison at Andy's order. The Zeros roared over her deck in a destructive pass and started into a climb. One faltered and fell away when *Mariah*'s return fire found a vital spot. Cheers were heard from the barge even as another attacker dove toward her when the enemy plane plunged into the sea.

"Let's get these casings cleared away," Davis ordered. "They'll be back."

"Yes, sir. Clear these away. Bring fresh ammunition," Parker barked, passing the order on.

"Sir, no casualties. Ship at battle readiness," Mason reported.

"Very well. We'll stay at battle stations until we know if they're coming back right away," Andy ordered.

Again the lookout shouted, "Planes off the port bow," when another group of enemy planes came at the convoy firing their guns to strafe the helpless ships before dropping bombs. One smaller boat stationed at the middle of the convoy for better protection was viciously attacked and sank inside ten minutes.

"Sir," Midshipman Barnes called out, "they've hit the barge." Andy looked through his glasses to see smoke billowing across the deck as she slowed before her engine coughed and then quit, setting her adrift. Fire hoses were quickly being unrolled as the small crew fought to save their ship. A Japanese pilot saw the window of opportunity to sink the British interlopers and dove his Zero toward the defenseless barge with its guns rapidly firing. *Mariah* opened fire with a hail-storm of bullets and shrapnel against the Japanese plane when it pulled out of its destructive dive over the open water between the two ships.

The intense gunfire sent it away with smoke belching from the engine when it disappeared over the horizon.

"Come along side," Andy ordered. "We'll see what we can do."

"Sir, no casualties," Mason reported when he walked onto the bridge.

"Good. We're going to see what we can do for them," Andy indicated, conning the *Mariah* closer to the barge. "Maybe we can save it."

"I'll go down on the deck and see what's needed," Mason offered.

"Report back whether they're able to maneuver," Andy ordered.

"Yes, sir."

"Get those fire hoses over here," Parker yelled out. "Dowse that fire before the fuel tanks go."

"Mr. Parker, what is the situation?" Mason asked.

"We're gettin' the fire under control. Looks like it hit just behind the bridge, sir."

"Ahoy there, what is your condition?" Mason called through the loud haler.

To his surprise a well-bred voice calmly answered the urgent inquiry. "Not the best at the moment. However, my engineer believes we can restart the engine shortly. Thanks awfully for dropping by."

Mason looked at Tim for a moment with raised eyebrows and shook his head. "These Singapore people are something else," he commented, before raising the haler again. "Do you need any help to get underway?"

"Now the fire is out, we can try the engine. We could use some bandages though," the well-bred voice replied.

"Send someone for Dr. Patterson to see what they need," Mason ordered.

"You, Hansen, get the doc for the first officer. Be quick about it," Parker gruffly ordered.

With a sudden rumble, the engine on the barge started, followed by a muffled cheer from inside the hull. Dr. Patterson sent Harris in the whaler to assess their medical needs while the two ships got underway again. The day passed with the men at their battle stations anticipating another attack, but none came.

The crew kept a vigil near the radio room door waiting to hear what was happening to the world they had left behind. "This is Radio Singapore," they heard on the five o'clock report. "Today the Japanese Army felt the full wrath of British ire, when Singapore's massive guns fired across the Johore Strait onto the Malayan Peninsula and directly into enemy lines. Japanese planes counter attacked with little success against these well-protected defenses in an effort to subdue this formidable resistance to the invasion of our sovereign soil. Since the 9:00 p.m. curfew has been imposed on the city, civilian casualties caused by the lawless Japanese air attacks are decreasing. Singapore will resist the enemy invasion at every point," the announcer firmly concluded.

"If the guns from Singapore were used, they can't be more than ten or fifteen miles from the Johore Strait," Dr. Patterson commented after a few minutes of uncomfortable contemplation.

"This may be the last convoy out of Singapore," Davis quietly remarked.

"And we have to reach the Java Sea before there's a margin of safety," Dr. Patterson grimly pointed out.

The small ships hugged the islands as closely as they dared without grounding when dawn came again to give some cover against discovery by the enemy. The *Mariah* was making her turn to put a small outcropping of land between her and the open sea, when a lookout posted in the crow's nest with powerful binoculars shouted a warning. "Enemy destroyer off the starboard bow."

Rapidly crossing the bridge, Andy raised his glasses but could see nothing except a small bit of land and the sea. "Number One, check with the man in the crow's nest. Find out if that lookout is sure about what he saw."

"Yes sir," Mason acknowledged.

"You're sure it was a Japanese destroyer going south?" Mason asked when he reached the crow's nest.

"Yes, sir, same direction we be 'eading. It was movin' pretty fast."

"Sir," Mason reported, "it was definitely a destroyer going south at a rate of speed. The lookout lost him over the horizon when we swung around the island."

"He was alone, no other ships with him?" Andy closely questioned.

"None that were reported."

"We'll be passing on the western side of Singkep, so it shouldn't spot us," Andy contemplated aloud. "However, we cross open water to reach the Bangka Strait. We could run into the enemy destroyer and any other ships that might be with her if she swings west into the normal shipping lanes."

Many of the small ships being used were little more than those that carried passengers between the islands and not intended for the open seas they would soon face. The risk factor was high enough without having enemy fire rained down on them. They wouldn't stand a chance from a small 3-incher, let alone the firepower of a destroyer, or worse, a possible battle group. The very thought brought a vice-like grip at the pit of Andy's stomach.

"Mr. Barnes, signal the *Victoria* about the sighting. Tell her we will investigate," Andy ordered. "Make sure it's in code."

"Yes sir," Roger croaked in acknowledgment as his mouth went dry at the orders given. He raised the lamp and began sending the message. His mind was racing, wondering if there would be more than a destroyer out there while Commander Burns and Lieutenant Roden quietly conferred and looked at the chart. Roger had served in battle with them, yet their calm demeanor while they made preparations to face combat with a powerful enemy still awed him. *Will I ever be like them?* he wondered.

"Sir," Brian said, "we mapped the islands to the southeast of Bangka the last time we came through here. If the Japanese are looking for oil in Sumatra, they could use them for cover and come through the Gaspar Strait. It's not far from there."

"Which would mean our convoy could run head-long into an invasion force," Mason uneasily forecasted.

"It would be a massacre," Brian grimly agreed.

"We should intercept them if we come around here, and then head toward Bangka," Andy said, tracing a finger over the chart. "If they are planning to attack from the direction you indicated, I suspect the destroyer has been sent ahead to investigate before their main force is committed."

"A scout; just like we did a few days ago," Mason concluded.

"Precisely," Andy stated. "Bring us to fifteen knots until we pass out of the convoy's sight, and then increase to twenty-five. Tell the *Victoria* our intentions, in code." With question in his eyes, Mason started to turn to give the orders. "This way any civilians who know Morse won't become alarmed and cause panic to spread," Andy said, in answer to the unasked question.

"Yes, sir," Mason crisply responded, before confidently stepping to the center of the bridge to give the necessary orders.

"I'll speak to the men once we're under way, explain what we need and why. They deserve that much at least," Andy said to the bridge in general as the *Mariah* increased her speed.

Mariah quickly moved away from the slow moving convoy and once over the horizon increased her speed to twenty-five knots. She turned to the east to inspect Singkep's large southern inlet with no further results. Andy ordered *Mariah*'s bow to turn south again and cross the open span of water between Singkep and Bangka, intending to pass through the Bangka Strait, the same route the convoy would take, in search of the illusive enemy. Andy told the crew what they were looking for and why after *Mariah* turned into the busy international shipping lane. He said he knew they would give their best and more when called on, as they had always done. He concluded by stating he was proud to be serving with them.

When Andy replaced the microphone, there was a distant "hip-hip" followed by a resounding "hooray" from the crew in response.

"The crew is behind you, sir...one hundred percent," Mason quietly said afterwards.

Looking around the bridge, Andy saw every man give a solemn nod before returning to the demands of his duties. Returning his gaze to Mason, Andy gripped the rail to steady himself at the overwhelming emotion the crew's simple response had brought. "Every captain deserves the best from a crew, but few have received the honor just given me today. I'll carry this day with me to my grave."

A cry from the crow's nest, "Ship dead ahead," brought them back to the present.

"It must be just over our horizon from here," Andy noted, narrowing his eyes. "Bring us to general quarters."

"Sir," Mason responded, before sounding the alarm.

"Have those trays set and ready, Harris, and be prepared to take on casualties," Dr. Patterson ordered.

"We'll be ready, sir," Harris calmly answered.

Dr. Patterson turned his attention momentarily to the evacuating medical personnel traveling aboard the *Mariah.* "We'll set up a triage here and surgery through there. Be careful not to interfere with the crew. Our lives depend on their swift response to orders in an ocean battle." His thoughts drifted back momentarily to Captain Edmon and the time he had interfered, and how Troy Edmon had handled it. The lesson was ingrained forever because of Edmon's command ability. "Ladies, I want the female nurses to remain with our patients in the wardroom. The ship will be making sharp turns. Try to keep them calm."

The "closed up" responses quickly came from every station, indicating battle readiness.

"We'll come in at speed, give me all you can, Mr. Thompson," Andy ordered through the voice pipe to his engine room. "As soon as we're in range, all guns will be brought to bear."

"Aye sir, she's a fine lady and knows her duty. She won't play up none." Thompson affectionately patted the side of the hull and spoke to the ship in his thick East End accent. "You 'eard me give Commander Burns our word, girl, we'll be wantin' none a yer tricks."

"I see it!" Roger exclaimed, "ten degrees off to starboard. It looks like a small mine sweeper or some kind of patrol boat, not a destroyer. They look to be lowering a boat."

"Ten degrees starboard, bring all guns to bear. We'll come down her port side, and then swing around to her starboard. Mr. Jones, keep a constant flow of depths coming. I don't want to run aground and become a sitting target," Andy ordered.

"Yes sir. According to our chart, we have depth close in up to a thousand yards. Then it starts to shallow out, except for this large bay here." Brian briefly remembered his joke about not wanting to get out and push when the area was charted. It wasn't a joke anymore. As Brian completed his calculations and looked down again at the chart, the command for increased speed came followed by the command to commence firing.

CHAPTER 45

The small group of refugees agreed they had no choice but to sail through the closely-knit islands south of Singapore to reach Bangka. The *Angelica* would then follow the Bangka Strait, hugging Bangka Island for cover until it spilled into the Java Sea and make her way to the British held port at Jakarta.

"We can't make more than about five or six knots," Dr. Jamison commented, after taking a final look at the chart.

"From what you, Ernie and George have told me that means about six or seven miles in an hour. And it's between fifty and sixty miles to reach Bangka," Wesley interjected.

"Once we reach Bangka, we can follow the strait close to shore and duck out of sight when we need to."

"At least we found enough fuel to take us to Bangka," Wesley said. "I hope the old fellow who sold it to us doesn't come to any harm from the Japanese."

"Mm, yes. I suspect our British currency will be a deterrent."

"Martin, when do we leave?" Helen asked, coming onto the deck.

"In about ten minutes. Is everyone ready?"

"Yes, we're quite ready. Ernie wants to do, in his words, *a turn at watch.* He said he feels up to it and would rather face open water on deck."

"He can do two hours, but then he has to rest."

"Are you sure, Martin?" Helen asked, with concern creeping into her voice.

"I'll certainly welcome an experienced set of eyes until we're well under way. And two hours should be about his limit."

"Very well, I'll tell him."

Martin Jamison met Wesley's eyes after Helen turned away to deliver the message. "Once we're in the Bangka Strait, we'll monitor the wireless closely. But I don't want to alarm the others about our concerns if we can help it."

"I agree, sir."

"If Jakarta isn't safe, it will mean trying to squeeze through the Sunda Strait between Sumatra and Java and setting our sites on Australia."

"Or, we could try for Surabaya or Bali," Wesley indicated, tracing a finger along the map.

"We'll see what the next few days bring. First let's get to Bangka."

Wesley went below to speak with Arthur after the last vestiges of land dropped over the horizon. He knew Arthur was too ill to help or take command, but he felt it necessary to keep him aware of the situation in the hope it would give Arthur the will to survive. "We've started toward Bangka and should be there by sunrise I figure. Dr. Jamison said we can follow the Bangka Strait then and stay close to shore, maybe make a little faster progress."

"That sounds good, sir," Arthur weakly acknowledged. "I should be up and around in a day or two and can give you a hand."

Patting Arthur's shoulder, Wesley rose and spoke briefly with Peter. "What does it look like for him? I mean, will he ever be his old self again?"

"He's a long way from recovery. The extent of injury and the consequential surgery, the conditions, everything has contributed to slowing his progress," Peter frankly noted. "It will take at least six months in a proper hospital and nursing home after, maybe a bit longer. Even then, he might not make a full recovery."

"I see. What about Captain Jergen?" Wesley asked, briefly glancing at the ashen figure lying in the bunk.

"He's only regained partial consciousness," Peter succinctly answered, studying David's still body and wishing he could give a better prognosis. "He's still very weak. By rights he should be under constant hospital care with no distractions. I can't say what way it will go. He's endured more than most would survive up to now. All we can do is wait." He shook his head and met Wesley's eyes after a thought provoking look at the wane figure lying on the bunk. *Will death's hand reach out and claim this one?* he wondered.

The *Angelica* road the gradual swells with her engine running in a rhythmic pulse as her small screw sent the refugees closer to their intended destination with each revolution. Ernie watched the ocean's gradual swells rise and fall and then lifted his eyes to the horizon to search the darkness for a first hint that an enemy was approaching. A tell tale bow wave or chink of light, something that looked more solid than the shimmer of water and darkness that would tell him danger was close by, just as he had learned aboard the *Mariah* and those before her. He wondered if his mates were still afloat, or on the bottom like so many others he had seen come and go. A flash in the distance focused Ernie's attention to the here and now. Watching intently, he saw it again for an instant, then another, moving north by east. He brought the glasses up to be sure, and again he saw the chink of light. "Ship off the starboard bow," he hollered, turning toward the others.

Hearing Ernie's cry, Wesley quickly joined him. "Where is it?"

Ernie caught the light again and pointed, "There, sir, fine off the bow. See it?"

"The flash?"

"Aye, sir, 'hat be it. Commander Burns would be fierce mad 'bout it."

"I don't understand."

"Dead bolt on a port hole, sir, not screwed down proper," Ernie explained. "Commander Burns always went on 'bout it. Now I know why."

"Do you think they've seen us?" Wesley asked.

"Don't look like it. The admiral slowed right down. We ain't makin' no wake or bow wave, and we're low in ta water.

"How long?" Wesley bluntly asked.

"Commander Burns once said ta wait till tay be over your 'orizon, and 'hen give it a little longer if'n ya got it," Ernie answered, keeping an eye to the receding sliver of light in the distance.

Running his fingers through his hair, Wesley gave a slight nod of understanding to the lesson imparted by this man of simple words, yet filled with knowledge about their situation by generations of Navy experience and training. "Admiral, you heard, sir?" Wesley asked.

"I heard. Andy would know about this. Right now I'm glad one of his ratings is here." Dr. Jamison peered at the faint sliver of light before turning the *Angelica* slightly, hoping to be far enough away to not be discovered. "Do you still see it?"

"It's gettin' fainter, sir, just 'bout out a range. So far 'e ain't paid no notice to us. Must be goin' someplace special like. I mean, not just lookin' 'bout," Ernie reasoned.

"Yes, I expect you're right. Let me know when you can't see it any more," Dr. Jamison calmly ordered.

"Aye, sir."

"This means it will be full daylight when we get to Bangka," Dr. Jamison said, giving Wesley a pointed look.

"I know. Where's the closest place we can hide out until night comes once we get there?" Wesley asked.

"We'll have to look for an inlet of some kind as soon as we see any land," Dr. Jamison quietly answered. "Right now I'm steering by the compass. Bangka's big enough we can't miss it."

"The light's gone now, sir," Ernie reported about ten minutes later.

"Very well," Dr. Jamison responded, trying to sound confident. "We'll give it another twenty minutes then come up to seven knots instead of the original five. It might buy us a little time."

"Aye sir," Ernie replied as he had to others before who had commanded him throughout the years.

Daylight saw the *Angelica* continuing south at six knots after Wesley checked the fuel consumption and became concerned about the rate it was disappearing. The only sounds came from the drone of the engine and the sea slapping the sides of the boat, as it was pushed aside at their passage. No small bits of land could be seen on the horizon to give her refuges reassurance. The darkness had shielded them not only from the Japanese, but also to the realization they were totally alone in an alien environment.

Knowing the small arms they had would be no help to them, the men on watch all strained to be the first to sight land. The small band of refugees felt a sigh of relief when Bangka began to rise out of the sea. The first challenge of the open ocean would soon be behind them. An hour later the *Angelica* was entering a small inlet, when a plane flew over a few miles to the east.

"Get those nets spread quickly," Wesley ordered, even as the engine was being shut down and the anchor dropped. "Get the ropes on those trees over there. It's coming back," he warned, as the sound of the airplane's engine increased when it banked and started toward them.

"Do you think they saw us?" Helen asked when the plane moved out of sight.

"I'm not sure," Wesley replied. "They'll either send someone to investigate if they're unsure, or figure it's not important enough to bother."

"Let us hope for the latter," Helen said.

The sea and sky were empty the rest of the morning and into the early afternoon. It appeared the war had been left behind at Singkep and the remaining journey would be easier, giving everyone aboard a sense that the worst was over. One man was always on watch, even though there really wasn't anything to see and struggled to keep alert against the gentle slap of water against the boat that made his eyelids heavy. At first he thought it was a dream when he saw a hazy image in the distance. He shook himself to fend off the desire to sleep and looked more intently at the distant sun soaked horizon. Careful to not disturb his companions, he stood and walked to the front of the boat and lifted his binoculars to look more closely. What he saw sent a chill down his spine before he spun around to warn the others.

"Ship approaching," shattered the afternoon quiet, arousing his companions and startling those below at the sudden threat of danger approaching the peaceful sanctuary where they hid.

Wesley ran onto the deck with his heart in his throat. "Where?" was the only word he spoke.

"There, sir. I can just see it off to the east, almost over the horizon." the Army gunner indicated, pointing out to the sea.

Wesley waited to see if the small ship image would move away as it took on more distinguishable features, but it was definitely coming toward them. His mind racing, he tried to decide their best recourse while he returned below deck. It was too late to move on.

"What should we do, Wes?" Sally asked, wide-eyed at the sudden danger coming toward them.

"The only chance is to take everyone to cover on shore and make it look like the boat was abandoned some time ago," Wesley surmised.

"We don't have time to clear everything out to do that," Dr. Jamison said.

"Then we have to make a stand here, sir. There is no other way," Wesley stated matter-of-factly.

"Sir," Arthur urgently said. "My duffel, get my duffel you brought for me." His eyes shown bright with fever, but Arthur's manner indicated it was something important.

"Private, bring the lieutenant his duffel," Wesley ordered. "What is it, Arthur?"

Fumbling with the ties and mumbling disgust at his weakness, Arthur opened the bag. Instead of the usual personal belongings, he pulled out a grenade launcher and a supply of ammunition. "If the ship's not too big, we can do a lot of damage."

"You crazy bugger," Wesley said with a slow grin spreading across his face. "We might just do it."

"Looks to be slowin' some, sir," Ernie said, watching the approaching ship through binoculars from his vantage point on the cabin roof when Wesley came onto the upper deck.

"Keep an eye on them. Tell me what they're up to. We're going to set up some defenses over on that strip of land that juts out. What kind of boat do you think it is anyway?"

"Looks to be a patrol boat a-some kind, 'bout half the size a-our river boats, 'cept it's a deeper draft. Don't look near as long though. Jap for sure, saw the flag."

"Yeah, I figured it would be," Wesley grimly acknowledged.

"Looks like they're turnin' toward us now," Ernie reported.

"We'll see about that," Wesley said, setting his jaw.

Corporal Moore and Wesley set up the grenade launcher and what heavy machine guns they had to best cover the approach to the hidden bay where the *Angelica* awaited her fate. "Wish I had a few of those Navy mines right now," Private Jenkins remarked. The Army gunners knelt behind the two STENS they had brought to wait for the enemy to come into range.

"If that's a patrol boat, I don't want to see a battleship," Corporal Moore commented, as it approached.

"They're going to lower a boat, get ready," Wesley ordered, watching the activity closely.

"Ship at the northwest," Ernie cried from *Angelica*'s deck.

Wesley turned and saw an even bigger ship heading toward them. *So,* he despairingly thought, *this is where it will end. I'm sorry, Sally. I didn't protect you at Helen's Landing, and I failed you here as well. I didn't protect all of you,* he thought, *the twisting and turning and holding onto hope, all to end here.*

Wesley watched the other ship speeding toward them, as if it couldn't wait to send the final blow that would destroy the *Angelica* and all aboard her. He saw the flash as her guns sent the first salvo rocketing toward them, and then watched in amazement when the shot straddled the Japanese patrol boat. Wesley heard Ernie shouting something behind him and turned for a moment to see if the *Angelica* had been hit.

Ernie was on his feet running up and down the small deck and shouting. "Get 'em boys, get 'em. I knew I'd see ya again, I knew it. Sweet saints a h'eaven, it's ta *Mariah.* She's come ta get us," he cried out with tears streaming down his cheeks unheeded.

Wesley focused his glasses on the mast of the approaching ship and saw the British flag flapping in the breeze, as her guns fired again on the enemy ship that had come to destroy them. A sudden, brilliant, eye-searing flash soared toward the heavens in the distance, when the Japanese ship approached the horizon, followed by an intense ear splitting explosion that left a dark smudge across the ocean. Then there was nothing. *Angelica*'s crew was unable to comprehend at first the sudden deliverance from the lopsided battle that was never fought. An explosion near the *Mariah* a few moments after the patrol boat was destroyed caused the refugees to look up from their place of cover. A Japanese destroyer came into view with smoke and flame trailing from her guns, when another series of shots soared toward the *Mariah* in angry retribution for their lost comrades.

"Heaven have mercy," John softly gasped as he watched the two ships speeding toward each-other with their guns firing in rapid succession. He knew by instinct only one of the dueling ships would sail away from the battle he was about to witness. The winner would determine the fate of all those aboard the *Angelica. What will the gods of war decide?* he briefly wondered before turning his attention to the battle and another salvo striking the *Mariah* in a chilling blow.

CHAPTER 46

"Up 100, fire," Davis hollered over the din of explosive gunfire. "Reload, fire," he ordered again, watching the shot straddle the smaller ship.

Mariah's gunners had the enemy ship in their sites and were pressing the attack with all the firepower the ship could muster. The Japanese patrol boat turned eastward, trying to escape the more powerful British guns that were pursuing her like a cat stalking its prey. Andy knew it had to be destroyed to give the convoy a chance to pass through the area. Their radio was the danger. He watched *Mariah*'s shots straddle the Japanese ship again. Two more hits exploded on her aft deck, igniting a searing fireball. Burning cinders belched from her smoke stack onto the remaining deck, before she rolled onto her port side and gracelessly sank beneath the ocean's swell, leaving an eerie silence on the sea's glassy surface.

Mariah's crew, stunned by the sudden end to the engagement, sought an enemy that no longer existed, until an explosion near her stern brought them back to the presence of danger still lurking on the sea. "Destroyer to the northeast," Roger yelled.

Running across the bridge, Andy brought his glasses up to see the illusive Japanese destroyer charging toward them, and another enemy salvo soaring toward *Mariah*'s hull. "Turn fifty degrees to starboard," he ordered.

"Turning fifty degrees to starboard," the quartermaster calmly responded as the *Mariah* turned before the enemy volleys could penetrate her hull.

"Bring the starboard guns to bear, fire at will," Andy ordered, bringing the *Mariah* around to face the pursuing enemy.

Another salvo straddled the *Mariah,* causing splinters to fly onto the decks and pepper the hull with indiscriminate destruction to men and machinery. "Reload, up thirty, fire," Anderson yelled while his gun crew worked at a fevered pitch to send return fire before the enemy destroyer could inflict a fatal blow. *Mariah*'s heart and soul were dedicated to bringing retribution for the terrible price already elicited from this unmerciful foe and fought with a vengeance. But her soul was not enough. The enemy was raining the hell fire and brimstone that priests and prophets spoke about since before the time of Christ, and the *Mariah* had to find another way to turn the fortunes of war.

"Can you see anything, Martin?" Helen asked.

"Not much I'm afraid. Ernie, are you sure about what ship it is?" Dr. Jamison asked, while the others gathered on the small deck held a collective breath waiting for the answer. "You're sure it's the *Mariah* and not some other ship that looks like her."

"Aye, sir, it's her right 'nough," Ernie affirmed. "She still bears the scar from the bomb she took. She's a fighter though now. Don't be sellin' 'er short none. I know it looks a bit black, but she'll come through this trouble," he assured while his eyes never left the dueling ships.

"Oh, Martin, there's so much smoke!" Helen exclaimed, clutching his sleeve.

"All guns, fire," Andy ordered, while he twisted and turned the ship, using every skill and trick he had learned, in the attempt to escape the enemy's relentless pursuit. Twenty minutes time had seen six men killed outright, one not five feet from him who dropped where he stood, and several others wounded. Damage reports filtered in as shells came close and splinters found vital spots. A runner came from aft to report the guns were jammed by a direct hit. "Mr. Roden's tryin' ta clear 'em, sir. 'E said one as was out a it fer good. Maybe 'e can get tother ones workin'. Mr. Parker come ta 'elp 'im."

"Very well, keep me informed," Andy calmly ordered.

"Can we get it cleared do you think?" Mason asked as he and Tim Parker quickly examined the damage.

"This one I think. Bert, help me get this here cover off." Tim had kept Bert with him since his friend and mate, Ernie, was left at Helen's Landing and the town had then fallen to the enemy, leaving Bert at a loss. "We got it cleared here sir," Tim reported.

Mason and Bert began reassembling the cleared gun, while Tim moved on to the next. Another hailstorm of splinters showered the *Mariah,* falling like rain. A piercing high-pitched scream was heard from close by, when a female nurse who had slipped unseen to the main deck that said she wanted 'to see what a battle at sea is really like' was speared with one of the flying darts.

"Mr. Thompson," Andy said into the voice pipe. "I want you to give me all the smoke you can make. I'll be wanting every bit of speed she can generate when I give the order to turn; even if we red line."

"Sir, if she red lines it could seize the engines," Thompson cautioned.

"If we don't risk it, we could lose more than the engines," Andy simply answered.

"Yes, sir, she'll not fail you," Thompson assured him, knowing Commander Burns wouldn't risk it if the situation weren't desperate.

Andy turned the ship, pulling away from the enemy destroyer with clouds of black smoke engulfing her. The cease-fire sounded when the smoke obscured the gunners' aim. *They've done for us again,* the crew thought in despair.

"First Officer reporting, sir," Mason said.

"Number One, we'll soon be turning back into our own smoke screen. They're firing blind hoping to hit something vital," Andy explained when another shell exploded close by. "Mr. Jones is keeping track of their position, using the shell's trajectory as a reference. When we come out of our smoke screen, I want every gun to fire on the coordinates he indicates. I intend to use the torpedoes when we are in range."

"Yes, sir," Mason acknowledged. "That's why you ordered a cease fire. They won't know we've turned."

"It's our best chance; maybe our only chance," Andy responded mater-of-factly.

"I'll inform the gun crews. And sir, good luck to you," Mason said before leaving the bridge.

"Raise our battle ensign, Mr. Barnes," Andy ordered.

"Yes, sir," Roger replied in a strong voice as the infectious nature of desperate battle enveloped him. The crew watched the enormous battle flag rise above them and felt a swelling of pride to be fighting under it.

"Keep him still, that's better. Poor bugger won't be doin' any dancin' for a while," Harris said. "Help me get him below." Harris and Dr. Patterson had been hard at it since the enemy destroyer fired the first shot, in what seemed like several hours ago. Harris' eyes lingered a brief moment when the battle ensign was raised before going below with the latest casualty.

Dr. Patterson was bending over the operating table, deep inside a man's chest, as the *Mariah* made the sudden turns that rocked most off their balance. "Clamp, sponge, suction there, that's it. Here it is," he said, gently drawing the small deadly bit of shrapnel away from the heart. "Let's get this cleaned up now," he ordered. His only concern was the patient beneath his scalpel.

The *Mariah* turned back toward the enemy ship that was still firing into the smoke screen at Andy's order, "bring her around," to the quartermaster. "Mr. Thompson, give me everything she has," he ordered into the voice pipe before going to the torpedo-aiming device. Andy noticed the torpedoes had been replaced when he returned from the meeting about the convoy with Admiral Edwards. The supply officer in Singapore said no more torpedoes were available and there was nothing he could do about it. Andy didn't ask where they had come from, knowing sometimes it was best not to when things just appeared out of nowhere.

"You understand what Commander Burns wants now?" Mason asked. "If it comes prematurely, our position is given away and the chance of surprise lost."

"Yes sir, we'll fire when given the word," Anderson firmly acknowledged, with Davis and the others nodding their understanding in turn.

"Carry on then," Mason ordered. "Mr. Parker, things are ready aft?"

"Yes sir. The two on the outside are cleared and ready. The other will need a repair dock.

"Very well. We'll use what we have. Be ready on the 20-mm. It could be a close battle," Mason cautioned.

"Yes sir, we'll be ready," Tim confidently replied.

"Sir," Mason said returning to the bridge. "Guns are ready and awaiting your orders. The middle 4.7-incher aft is out of commission. The gunners have been given the last coordinates."

"Very well, take your station," Andy ordered. "It won't be long now.

"Aye, sir," Mason crisply responded.

"Look," Jane called out, pointing toward the sea.

"It's her, she's come back," Ernie exclaimed. "Commander Burns is going to fight to the end."

"Martin?" Helen faintly questioned, turning fearful sad eyes toward him.

"Hang on Helen, Andy will bring them through this," he reassured her in the hope God would hear his plea, all the time knowing he was asking that another mother's son be taken instead.

The refugees aboard the *Angelica* watched the *Mariah* emerge from behind the veil of black sooty smoke like an avenging dragon with her enormous battle flag unfurling. The thick curtain parted to reveal her intention to take the battle to the enemy in full force. *Mariah*'s guns spat flame in unison at the Japanese destroyer, causing the water to explode in towering geysers around her. A second salvo followed the first, with an explosion on one of the enemy's lower decks. The Japanese ship, taken off guard, turned and headed in the direction where the *Angelica* lay in hiding with her retreating guns trying in vain to return the unexpected British gunfire.

"Ernie, where do you need to hit to do the most damage?" Wesley asked.

"Bridge first, 'en most anyplace," Ernie answered without hesitation.

"Corporal Moore, let's get back to our launcher," Wesley ordered. "If they come close enough, we'll try to throw a few grenades at them."

"Yes sir," Moore acknowledged, cracking a smile.

"They're still coming our way," Wesley said. "Get ready; we want to be careful to get a good shot and not hit the *Mariah* in the process."

"Not to worry, sir, we'll hit the target," Moore assured him with more confidence than he had known for some time.

Wesley and Corporal Moore waited until the Japanese ship was in front of them for the closest range and fired a grenade that exploded just beneath the bridge, showering shrapnel into the gunners stationed there. They fired again after a slight adjustment and reached the target four more times before it was beyond the launcher's range.

"It seems to be turning funny," Moore said. "Like no one's steering it."

"Maybe we threw them off some," Wesley replied. "They're moving back out to sea it looks like. Heaven have mercy! Did you see that?"

"Fire, reload, fire," Davis hollered. "Clear these shells, quick there men, reload, fire." Davis had the range and didn't intend to lose the advantage knowing how quickly things could go against them. The sudden onslaught of gunfire coming toward the enemy ship from Bangka caught the *Mariah*'s crew by surprise before the battle moved out to sea again.

"We'll fire torpedoes at 1,000 yards," Andy calmly said. He felt no emotion while he aligned the sights in preparation to fire on the enemy destroyer, as a separate part of his mind made a mental note to investigate where the gunfire had come from on Bangka. "Ready, fire one...fire two...fire three...fire four."

Four torpedoes leapt from their tubes at sixty-second intervals and sped toward the enemy ship as she twisted in a last futile attempt to evade the destructive power traveling just beneath the surface on a collision course. The first exploded near the bow, just below the water line. Two and three struck to each side of the center in the next two minutes. But, number four, which hit three minutes after the first blow began pouring water into the pierced hull, exploded near the stern. The ship began to sparkle with a hundred minute twinkling lights, when fuses lying alongside heavy explosives began to ignite. A sudden white-hot explosion sent a smoke stack over 100 feet into the air when an underwater mine fell into the boiler. The concussion from the blast shook the *Mariah*, nearly a quarter mile away, while men struggled for their balance to fire the guns once more. The sound of tearing metal and escaping steam from the enemy ship's scream at death filled the air. The Japanese destroyer was broken in half by the massive explosion that filled the sky with clouds of black smoke and tongues of angry orange flame lapping the twisted steel that moments before had been a functioning bridge and solid deck. All that could be seen when the smoke finally cleared was the point of her bow before it slipped beneath the water's surface. *Mariah*'s crew watched in awe at the massive destruction they had just witnessed, too stunned to speak.

"They must have been carrying mines or heavy explosives to have it go up like that," Brian haltingly said in hushed tones.

"Both ships were probably intending to mine the Bangka Strait," Andy surmised.

"Boat approaching from Bangka," Roger hollered out.

Andy lifted his glasses to see the *Angelica* coming out of a small bay and recognized Dr. Jamison when it came closer with his mother and Sally standing beside him on the small deck. Lowering the glasses, Andy waited a moment until he was sure his voice would not crack. "Secure from battle stations, post extra look-outs, slow to five knots," the orders coming by rote from the discipline of training and experience passed on by others who had gone before him.

"I think we should go now before anything else happens," Wesley said when he and Corporal Moore were back aboard the *Angelica.* "We can follow the *Mariah* as far as they think we can keep up and continue on to Java."

"I agree, let's get underway," Dr. Jamison concurred.

Hastily removing the camouflage and raising her anchor, the *Angelica* came out of the small bay and made directly toward the *Mariah.* The small ship managed to come along side, and Dr. Jamison went on board the *Mariah.*

"Sir, it sure is good to see you," Andy said. "How many are with you?"

"The remaining hospital and Navy staff, Helen, and six patients we weren't able to evacuate, two from the *Mariah.* Wesley Vilmont with what's left of his unit and the harbor anti-aircraft gunners from Helen's Landing are also with us. We've been on the run ever since we were cut off from evacuating to Singapore. Wesley and Corporal Moore fired grenades at the Japanese destroyer. We thought it was all over when that first ship came. Wesley and Moore set up what defenses we had, and then you came along and saved the day."

"That's amazing," Mason interjected. "Sir, secured from battle stations."

"Casualties?" Andy flatly asked.

"Ten dead, sir, one a female nurse, seventeen wounded. The middle 4.7-inch gun aft is out of commission, a direct hit. Several splinter holes, none below the waterline though. The fire aft is out and the area secured," Mason reported.

"Admiral, what is your condition? Can the *Angelica* still maneuver?" Andy asked.

"Oh yes, she can maneuver fine. We need some medical supplies, and food stores are running low. We might need more fuel if we go as far as Java."

"Number One, send some supplies over to them and have Parker and Thompson look them over. I'll have Dr. Patterson send whatever else you need, sir," Andy said.

"Ask Quentin to come over as well when he's finished here. I need his opinion about one of our more severe cases."

"Martin, you old reprobate, I knew you'd come through somehow," Dr. Patterson greeted his friend with twinkling eyes.

"Good to see you also, Quentin," Dr. Jamison politely responded.

"What's this about a case?" Dr. Patterson asked, recognizing the signs of strain *Angelica*'s survivors had been under.

"Captain Jergen, he was severely wounded when the aid station near Kalang was abandoned. John and I operated a second time our first night out: peritonitis. He's only regained partial consciousness since then."

"You operated here?"

"It was that or see him die for certain."

"I see," Dr. Patterson softly said as he bent over to examine the patient. "Martin, I think we should move him to the dispensary on the *Mariah*. We can monitor him more closely, and we have more facilities available to meet his needs."

Andy left the bridge after *Mariah*'s crew had secured from general quarters and went to the *Angelica*. The sea was empty now, and the convoy out of Singapore would have time to reach the Bangka Strait in safety.

"Andy," Sally whispered in a choked voice. "I didn't know if I would ever see you again."

"I can't believe you're real," he softly responded, reaching out to touch the fading bruise on Sally's cheek.

"I killed a man. I wouldn't be here except for that," Sally haltingly told him, as tears filled her eyes and began to spill down her face. Seeing the haunted pain behind the unexpected statement, Andy put his arms around her as the tears turned to racking sobs, saying nothing. "I'm sorry, you have enough on your plate without me carrying on so," she haltingly whispered, trying to compose herself.

"I love you," Andy said, looking down at her tear stained face. "That's all that matters. After Malaya was overrun and the devastation since, I vowed I would tell you that if by some miracle I should see you again."

"Andy," Sally began in a broken voice, "I've loved you for so long—ever since you first called me Nurse Sally."

Andy returned to the bridge and ordered a course set to intercept the convoy. He felt renewed and could still feel the touch of Sally's lips when they kissed before returning to the demands of his duties. *Mariah*'s crew soon brought the *Angelica* to her top speed of eight knots, leaving the small-secluded bay where the refugees from Helen's Landing witnessed the desperate sea borne battle to its peaceful obscurity.

The *Mariah* and *Angelica* intercepted the ragged line of refugee ships that showed new battle scars and missing boats near the entrance into the Bangka Strait. Amazingly, the inter-island steam powered paddle-wheel boat was still keeping pace with the group, along with the battle scared barge that *Mariah*'s crew assisted the first day out.

CHAPTER 47

"Sir, signal picked up out of Singapore," the radio messenger reported.

"Read it aloud," Andy instructed.

"Yes, sir. *Ubin Island occupied. STOP. Japanese invasion at Singapore's western coast. End.* It's dated today, February 7, 1942, sir."

"So, it's happened. Thank you that will be all. Keep me informed if there are any further communications."

"Yes, sir."

"Sir, is there anything about the other convoy?" Mason asked after hearing the message.

"We'll have to wait and see if we receive any more signals. Once they sail, they'll maintain radio silence."

The convoy's journey ended at Jakarta on Monday afternoon. Some who had escaped this far were left to wait in uncertainty to be told what would become of them now. Meanwhile, the wounded were taken off the escort vessels to a hospital ship waiting for them in Jakarta with orders to sail to Darwin.

John boarded the *Mariah* to see his friend from the Kalang outpost before he was transferred to the waiting hospital ship. "David, you had me plenty worried."

"I told you I'd see you again when we left the aid station," David Jergen softly responded. "Guess the short straw was the lucky one after all." Dr. Jamison had said David's will to live and the *Hand of God* brought him out of the worrisome coma the day before.

"I'll see you in Darwin, Arthur," Wesley said. "I expect the Army will move us there before we're reassigned. By then you should be on the mend."

"Yes sir, I'll be ready when we're reorganized," Arthur weakly acknowledged.

"Take care, Lieutenant," Wesley smiled, shaking Arthur's hand. He did not believe Arthur Nance would be returning to the front lines again. The damage his body had endured was already taking a toll on the young energetic man, who was only young now in years.

Wesley sought out what he could find of the Army command to report in and, more importantly, to send a message home that he and Sally were safely out of Malaya. The overwhelmed Army major at the hastily established reception center had told him to take charge of and see to the needs of the soldiers with him until they were reassigned to new units. He returned to the waterfront after finding nothing suitable to lodge the men, deeming the *Angelica* to be their best recourse.

"Mrs. Burns, I'm afraid you're stuck with us for now. There simply is no place to house anyone," Wesley said.

"That's fine, Wesley. I feel better with all of you here anyway. After being alone as we were and now this mass of people, I feel a need for Sally, Jane, and I to have some male protection. The others are staying too."

"We'll try not to be a nuisance."

"You shan't be. John's coming back," Helen noticed, pointing toward the dock. "He seems in a bit of a hurry."

"Hello all, I've come to say good-bye. The hospital ship needs another doctor, and I volunteered to go," John said in somewhat of a rush.

"We'll all miss you, but I know you want to do your part," Helen said.

"Yes, I feel a need to do what I can to fight back. Is Peter here?"

"I think he's down in the cabin," Wesley answered, extending his hand. "Good luck to you, my friend."

Smiling, John shook Wesley's hand before he went below to find Peter. They had been together from the beginning of it all, and John wanted to tell Peter his plans before someone else informed him. "Peter, I've come to tell you good-bye. I'm sailing with the hospital ship this evening."

"You're leaving? But, I mean, how did you come to be assigned there?" Peter asked feeling a little overwhelmed.

"They needed another doctor, and I said I wanted to go. Dr. Jamison made the arrangements. I'll be at Darwin waiting for you when you arrive," John told him.

Peter knew the fighting in Malaya was more personal for John and hoped that his friend would find a way to peace within himself after the horrible destruction and loss of life he had witnessed at the small Malayan outpost. Maybe this was the first step in that journey. "I never thought of us not serving together. I guess I figured we would go on as we always have. So much has changed since we signed up that first day of the war in London. Jane and I will be in Darwin soon I should think. You can tell us where the best places to eat are located when we get there," Peter said, trying to be cheerful and giving John an embrace of friendship before shaking his hand and wondering when he would see his friend again.

The news about John's departure had quickly spread to those remaining aboard the *Angelica.* Everyone was waiting when he and Peter emerged onto the deck to say good-bye.

"Keep yourself safe," Jane said as she kissed his cheek and hugged him.

"Be careful, you promised to be a friend my whole life," Sally said before kissing him good-bye. The others all shook his hand and patted his shoulder as John made his way toward the dock.

"The best to you, sir," Ernie said, raising his hand in a salute. "It's been a right pleasure servin' wit you."

John returned the salute, responding to the honor that this regular Navy rating had shown him. "And with you, my friend." John turned and waved once more from shore before quickly disappearing into the crowds at the waterfront.

News came on Wednesday the Japanese were demanding that Singapore surrender. Later in the day those aboard the *Angelica* heard an announcement was made in Japan that the British Commander and Chief in Singapore had surrendered. "But, no announcement has been made here," Helen objected.

"Today is February 11, the celebration of Kigensetsu, the anniversary of the founding of Japan," Tom Linn noted. "They would want a major announcement for such a day, even if it was not true, or," hesitating a moment, he ventured, "premature."

"Sir," the messenger said, "signal from Singapore. You asked to be kept informed."

"Thank you," Andy acknowledged as he took the sheet and read through it.

"What is it?" Dr. Patterson asked.

"The final fall is coming," Andy told him. "They're at Tanglin, two miles from the city itself. There's a code in here from Admiral Edwards. He told me about it just before we sailed. The last convoy is leaving tonight, along with the rest of the Admiralty in Singapore.

"What about the Army, everyone else?"

"No more British ships will be sailing out of Singapore," Andy flatly stated.

"I see. It seems we are sinking to new lows," Dr. Patterson grimly noted.

Friday morning it was decided to send those boats that were sea worthy, along with their refugees, on to Australia to let the authorities there deal with the problem. The enemy was still moving south, but the expanse of water that separated Australia from the smaller islands gave people the sense of security the British felt when water stood between them and an aggressor.

"We sail in company tonight," Dr. Jamison said to Wesley and Peter. Wesley and the men still under his command were given hastily typed orders to continue on to Australia aboard the *Angelica* to be reassigned due to the shortage of transport ships and Command's uncertainty of what to do with the group of soldiers out of Malaya. "We'll have a few more walking wounded who weren't sent on the hospital ship," Dr. Jamison continued. "At least navigation shouldn't be a problem. We'll be with several others and have an escort to do the worrying for us this time."

"Everyone we're 'spose to 'ave is boarded, sir," Ernie crisply reported when he came to the tiny bridge area. Dr. Jamison had given him the job of seeing to the few walking wounded who would join them for the journey. He knew Ernie would not serve aboard a war ship again but felt compelled to give this brave rating a sense of belonging in Naval tradition.

The convoy left Jakarta and followed Java's coastline to the Lombok Strait east of Bali. Once through it, they turned their collective bows southeast and sailed toward Australia. A signal was intercepted on Saturday that Japanese paratroopers had been dropped near Pelembang, Sumatra, where rich oil refineries were located. This newest Japanese offensive made the Bangka Strait, a major shipping lane between Singapore and the Java Sea, even more dangerous for the British still trying to escape Singapore.

"The convoy out of Singapore will have a difficult voyage," Mason commented, after hearing the latest update.

"They may have to scatter and only sail at night. That is if they get clear of Singapore and through the first islands," Andy said.

Everyone listened on Sunday to the final broadcast from Singapore by British radio. "Singapore will live on," they heard at the end of the nine o'clock newscast. At 10:00 p.m., February 15, 1942, General Sir Robert Percival surrendered to General Tomoyuki Yamashita, and all communication to the outside world abruptly ended.

"History will condemn us for this day," Dr. Patterson commented when the announcement was made.

"You're probably right, Doc," Andy agreed. "We have a great deal to answer for after today."

Helen bowed her head in silent prayer for those who were left behind and then went to the wheel where Dr. Jamison sat in silence and placed a hand on his shoulder. "Martin, you told me not so long ago we would return one day. We will, Martin, and we'll rebuild what was lost even better than before."

Squeezing her hand, Martin Jamison nodded, "That we will, Helen; that we will."

The arrival at Darwin brought a sense of release and renewal to those aboard the *Angelica.* "Peter, we're here," Jane happily smiled. "I knew our child would be born in safety and that we would have a new beginning."

"Yes, darling, a new beginning for us all," Peter softly agreed, smiling at Jane's upturned face. "I believe we'll go back one day though when this is behind us. I want our child to know what a special place it was, what we left behind, and what we will rebuild when we return."

Peter and Jane stood hand-in-hand on the deck of the *Angelica* watching the lowering sun's resplendent golden rays wash across the vast harbor in uninterrupted magnificence. A sense of peace came over them as they watched the night overtake the day in the knowledge that one day they would return to the home where it had all begun, while watching the sun settle beneath the sea.

EPILOGUE

Mariah's anchor came to rest in Darwin's busy harbor, where softly shaded moonlight reflected off her battered decks and silhouetted the graceful lines of her hull. Her engines were silent while she slumbered, allowing her wounds to heal, before man called on her again to do his bidding.